Season's Flame

Season's Flame

Second Chance 5

Mary E Hanks

www.maryehanks.com

Suzanne D. Williams Cover Design:

www.feelgoodromance.com

Cover photo: PeopleImages @ istockphoto.com

Author photo: Ron Quinn

Visit Mary's website and sign up for her newsletter at

www.maryehanks.com

You can write Mary at

maryhanks@maryehanks.com.

For Jason

I'm looking forward to many more adventures with you.

I love you forever!

For Traci

Thank you for being a part of our family.

Here's to lots of fun Christmases and birthday dinners for many years to come.

Restore me, and I will return, because you are the Lord my God. ~Jeremiah 31:18

One

Max

"As most of you know, today is my last day pastoring at Darby Community Church." Maxwell Prescott gripped the side edges of the wooden pulpit, swallowing back an unwelcome tug of emotion. He'd already given his last sermon, one he agonized and prayed over. All that remained were his final words to the congregation he loved and served for twenty years. He would not break down or give in to the emotions tugging on him. Nor would he reveal to anyone how hard this day was for him.

His gaze traversed the first six rows of empty pews before he met the sympathetic—or apathetic—expressions of the fifteen parishioners who showed up for his last Sunday service. Jupe and Lila Johnson, retirees, leaned against each other as if holding each other up. Clint Ebbs and Lee Thomas, church council members who'd pushed for his termination, scowled. Derek Clark, a man opposed to pretty much every decision Max ever made, was noticeably absent. However, Derek's unwed, twenty-one-year-old pregnant daughter, Jayme, sat in the back row, snapping her gum and tapping her smartphone.

Texting her father about how bored she was, no doubt. Season sat in the pew closest to the door, her head bowed. Was she praying for him? For them? Mrs. Iris and a few others yawned.

He'd better get this business over with. "Attendance has been down. The loan payment is several months past due. The council has elected to, um"—he swallowed hard—"to sell the church property and disband our small congregation." Max didn't agree with their decisions, but he went along with the trio's advice for the independent church. Better to be good witnesses in the community than to ignore unpaid bills. Too late for bake sales or car washes to bail them out. But still, couldn't good yet come of this situation without him leaving the city he loved?

God, what is Your will in this mess? He already asked that question a dozen times. So far, he couldn't see a good reason for the church closing. Nor did he have any sense of direction for his future. Would he ever pastor again? The few resumes he sent out didn't elicit any replies.

Avoiding Clint's and Lee's gazes, he thought of the parsonage where his two sons, both in college now, grew up. The place he and Season spent twenty of their twenty-two years of marriage. Good times, mostly. Yesterday, they cleaned the house, and hauled furniture and a lifetime of collected stuff to Goodwill and the storage unit they rented. The rest went into the RV—their new home—his dad left them when he died last year.

And this fellowship, started in Darby, Montana, sixty-five years ago, was ending today. He carried precious memories of friendships he made during his twenty-year tenure. He glanced at Jayme Clark again, wishing he could have done more to help her, even if her father, Derek, disliked Max. "I want you to know, Season and I love each of you."

"We love you, Pastor!" Ninety-year-old Gladys Iris

grinned with what he knew to be dentures. Due to her being partially deaf, he doubted she'd heard the part about him resigning.

No one else said a word.

Wooden pews creaked.

Did anyone else agree with Gladys? Or were they relieved he was leaving? Perhaps they simply wished he'd finish talking so they could head to Annabelle's. Sunday's all-you-can-eat fish-and-chips drew in a big crowd.

But what had happened to his beloved church? A year ago it was a thriving congregation. With new converts. Young people growing in the Lord. Lives being changed. Last Easter two hundred squeezed into the pews to hear the annual cantata, some regulars coming from as far away as Florence, a fifty-minute drive. Then, as if a hurricane plundered the church grounds, everything changed. People became disgruntled. Individuals and families decided God wanted them to attend elsewhere. At the Living Faith Center outside of Hamilton, fifteen miles north, most likely.

He'd heard plenty about charismatic Pastor Paul. How his inspiring sermons included positive quotes and humorous anecdotes. No mention of troubles or sorrows. No guilt about sin.

If only that were true in this life. What of sickness and death? And how could a pastor not preach against sin? That topic was key to the Salvation message. Jesus died to forgive people's sins. Max was all for grace and love, but what about consequences?

"The culture is changing," Clint Ebbs, whose family had been farmers in the small community for several generations, had warned. "Pastor, you have to go easy on congregants these days or you'll run everybody off."

Did everyone think he was to blame for the empty pews?

Had his sermons become as dry as Lee Thomas said they were during a heated board meeting after Max questioned the man's financial report? Was he a "law" pastor instead of a "grace" man like Derek accused? Standing at the pulpit, Max's temples throbbed, and his throat went dry.

Season was right. Why was he putting himself through this ordeal? She advised him to cancel the service. Maybe he should have listened to her.

Jupe Johnson raised his hand. "I have something to say." He slowly stood, clutching the pew in front of him. "I want to thank Pastor Max and Season for their time here in the Bitterroot Valley, for their faithfulness, and wish them Godspeed."

Max appreciated the man's show of support, however he knew Jupe tended to ramble and get off subject. Ten seconds later, the old-timer was telling a story about a kid who'd let a frog loose in a service several decades ago.

Max glanced at his wife and noticed how her short, multi-toned blond hair seemed to glow in the light coming through the back window. He wished things were better between them. But hadn't he grouched at her before they left for church this morning? He'd have to apologize to her later.

As Jupe continued his tale, Max's thoughts wandered to earlier when he set his empty coffee cup in the RV's sink. Distracted with trying to figure out what he should say during his final sermon, he barely heard his wife glide up next to him in her stocking feet. "Do you have to resign publicly? Can't you cancel the service, and be done with the whole morbid affair?"

Morbid? Offended by her word choice, he glared at her. "I won't run, if that's what you mean. I care about the people too much." The old dig that she hadn't wanted to be a pastor's wife when he asked her to marry him twisted something tight in his gut. Strange that would still bother him all these years later.

Was she glad he was washed up as a pastor? He still hoped to find a pastorate elsewhere. But after the mess he'd been through closing the church, he deserved a break. He needed time to figure out what went wrong before he stepped into a pulpit again.

For a moment he came back to the present. What was Jupe saying? Something about the stream at the back of the church property, and how his kids had played there with toy boats. Max should probably intervene, but a picture of Season giving him a flirtatious smile, this morning, caused him to zone out again.

For just a moment, she'd brushed her fingertips over his shirt sleeve. "We could slip away and take the RV to the Oregon Coast. Disappear into our love shack." She winked like she used to do when they were first married. Back when he couldn't resist her charms. Before he'd become the serious pastor he was today.

He cleared the burning in his throat, like shoving away his regrets. His tie seemed too tight, so he tugged it a quarter of an inch looser. Had he been the perfect husband? No. Another regret.

Her words about "slipping away" were the same ones she'd whispered in his ear during other difficult spots they'd been in during their years in the parsonage. Of course, she assumed the joke might make him laugh. Not today. The church's impending demise gnawed at his insides too much.

She ran her palm over his chest. "I'll take time off from work to be alone with you, husband."

Husband. Her pet name for him. *My sweet,* he would have answered a year ago.

Still, their gazes snagged and danced to a tune they hadn't explored in what felt like years. As if seeing her for the first time back in college, his mouth went dry. His lungs heated up.

How long had it been since he let everything go and kissed her, loved her like a man starving for his wife?

But he had a sermon to prepare. He needed to pray. To ponder his disappointments. Yet, he couldn't break free of her tantalizing effect on him. She toyed with a button on his shirt. Unbuttoned it. Re-buttoned it. Intrigued, he pulled her closer—though it was Sunday morning, his most sacred time of the week. For just a moment, he'd set aside his personal rule about avoiding distractions before preaching. Today felt different. He needed her.

He longed to make up with her for every indifference and cold shoulder he'd given her in the last six months. To laugh and flirt and love her like the husband she wanted him to be.

Until reality flopped on his chest like a plunger hitting the toilet. Today was his D-day. In less than two hours, he'd be finished at Darby Community Church. It had taken all his energy the past couple of weeks to face the demise of his ministry. He couldn't escape to some vacation paradise. He wasn't free. Would he ever be free? "After twenty years of pastoring, don't you think I'd want to leave with dignity?"

"*Dignity?*"

He flinched. "Yes, and my wife should be standing by me. Not encouraging me to fail more." He regretted his words as soon as he said them. Hadn't she stood by him all these years?

"I was hardly doing that."

"No?" Then how could she think he'd slink away without ending things properly? Didn't she fathom how he felt about the parishioners? How he'd prayed with them during their worst crises. Performed marriage ceremonies and funerals. Loved them like family. Goodnight. What else could he have done? How much more grace could he have offered?

Max returned to the present as Jupe sat down and Mrs. Iris clapped for the storyteller. He took a full breath, then exhaled before addressing the group. "I've pastored here for two decades. Our time together has been filled with many joys. I'm thankful to have walked this journey with you. As friends, if you ever need someone to talk to or have a prayer request, don't hesitate to call. Season and I will be staying in town until we decide what we're going to do next. God bless you all."

Silence. Nothing but silence.

Season glanced up at him then. Her lips offered him a tentative smile. Her encouragement, even from a distance, filled him with something good. Like air or food he couldn't live without. But then, her words from earlier bounced over the raw plains of his spirit. *Let's get away from this whole morbid affair.*

He couldn't. How could he walk away from the burden on his heart? Winter was nearly upon them. Temperatures had already dipped into single digits. Who would make sure the Johnsons' pipes didn't freeze? Who would ensure that Gladys Iris had food in her fridge when she couldn't leave her house? What of Jayme Clark and her unborn child? Would the community reach out to the single mom?

"May the Lord bless and keep you." He concluded the service with the simple benediction.

The small group filed out of the church.

Brief handshakes.

Averted glances.

And twenty years of ministry were finished. What would he and Season do now? Other than the few elderly folks who might still need him, how would he fill his days until he found another position?

Two

Season

As much as she loved her job as a librarian's assistant, lately Season found herself checking the clock more often and wishing her shift at the Darby Community Library would end. Staying focused at work was becoming tougher as problems at home escalated—if their icy co-existence in the RV, located in a low-rent mobile park near the edge of town, could be called "home." She and Max had never learned healthy conflict management. If she got upset, he typically zoned out. Or he'd respond by saying something that sounded a bit too pious, like she shouldn't have had those feelings in the first place. Which translated in her mind to he didn't care. Or that he was a better Christian, since he'd been a pastor and all.

Inwardly, she groaned.

For weeks now, she'd come home from work to find him sprawled out on the couch in sweatpants and a sloppy t-shirt, as if he'd been watching infomercials and TV reruns all day. Not showering or shaving. Not job-hunting. Then giving her the silent treatment as if she'd done something awful. So what? She encouraged him to escape with her to the coast on his last day of pastoring. Was that such a crime? She was trying to lighten the mood. For all the good it did.

Five o'clock finally arrived. She tapped the computer screen to submit her hours, told the manager goodbye, then grabbed her purse and black peacoat. Hopefully, Bess hadn't noticed her dismal concentration. Her boss seemed to sense when her employees were going through personal struggles without asking embarrassing questions, which was nice. Still, Season hated the predicament Max had put her in. How did other women argue with their husbands yet continue their jobs as if nothing were wrong? She couldn't. Her current angst had her plotting an extended road trip to Boise, Idaho, three-hundred-plus miles away, where her sons attended college. Anywhere would do as long as she was far from her husband.

With tension taut around her neck, she feared she'd reach the end of her tether and snap at a patron one of these days. If that happened, or if she made a brainless mistake, would Bess fire her? Might be best. If she lost her job, maybe then Max would wake up and be concerned about finding work himself.

Oh, he told her he browsed for jobs online. Probably with one eye closed and the other aimed at the TV. That's what they fought about this morning. His lazy carcass draped over the sofa from morning till night. Sure, jobs were scarce in Darby, Montana, population 740 proud citizens, in winter. But there were plenty of commutable cities nearby where he could apply. Hamilton, Stevensville, or Missoula, an hour away. And couldn't he clean up after himself? She was sick of coming home from work to find dishes and empty junk food packages littering every surface.

He'd crossed his arms and given her a dull look that said she was being too emotional. Did she need vitamins or something?

Yeah, something.

Their relationship was in trouble. If he couldn't see that, he was living in La-La Land. And her fury at him wasn't just because he left dirty dishes and clothes everywhere without picking up after himself, or because he was depressed and wallowing in an after-pastoring postmortem funk. It had everything to do with the way he treated her for the last six months to a year. As if she didn't exist. As if church business were his whole life. And her thoughts and feelings were a nuisance to him. She might not have wanted to be a pastor's wife twenty-two years ago. But in the interim, she became the best version of one she could. If he couldn't recognize that, well, then, he was blind.

She knew what she did next could affect the rest of their lives. Especially if she followed her impulse to pack up and move further south by herself. Not that she wanted to do that. But after having her life examined under a microscope by other Christians and the church council, then putting up with Max's weird behavior for too long, she needed some space. Or a drastic change.

That's why, when she heard of a possible solution earlier today, her heart had raced with anticipation. The idea might work. Might not. If it failed, at least she could appease herself and know she'd done everything possible to salvage their marriage. Then could she leave him with a clear conscience?

What of the vows you made? She swallowed down her inner argument. She'd honestly tried to make things work with Max. Had stood by him through all the grief of him losing his pastorate. Had endured his grumpy sullenness with as much compassion as she could muster. And what did he do?

She hardly recognized Max as the same man she married. He was aloof and rude, and seemed miserable. That's why she needed something extreme to wake him up and to revitalize their marriage, even if it was a last-ditch effort.

This morning, after Season had entered the security code to the library's front doors, Janice, the children's librarian, mentioned receiving a text about a marriage conference happening next weekend near Blanchard, Idaho. She shared how she and her husband attended a retreat there last summer, and their marriage had been radically transformed. Sounded amazing.

The nearly three-hundred-mile drive north might be problematic mid-winter. Pricey too. With no guarantees for success. Still, wasn't it better for her to try something and fail than to do a big fat nothing?

During lunch, she browsed Hart's Camp's website for information. The marriage conference looked interesting. *Hearts healed. Lives changed. Marriages restored.* Sounded like a miracle. According to the home page, this was their first winter retreat with a theme on rekindling marital romance. *Romance?* She scoffed. Romance was dead for her and Max—thanks to the icy force field emanating from him.

Would the effects of his rejection burn in her heart forever? Along with the unkindness and mean words of several people in the congregation whom she'd previously considered friends? Her sons' absence felt like a rejection too, though she knew that wasn't true. They grew up. Life moved on. She was just lonely without them. And isolated since the closure of the church, and Max's withdrawal from her. Tears flooded her eyes. She blinked fast. *I'm not going to cry.* It wouldn't do for him to see her eyes red-rimmed when she got home, and then for him to think she was being emotional. Again.

She slipped into one of the public computer stations the library offered, then signed in with her name and card number. She tapped the URL for the camp's website and pulled up the online questionnaire she noticed earlier.

How could she convince Max to go? His cooperation was doubtful. What if she signed them up, then confessed later? Might be risky. And might make it more difficult for him to refuse.

Lord?

Without waiting for heavenly guidance, she typed their names and personal information into the response section. What could it hurt?

HOW MANY YEARS HAVE YOU BEEN MARRIED?

Twenty-two.

Two years dating before that.

Dating? How long had it been since she and Max went anywhere romantic? He took her to a live theater event maybe a year ago. Several times since they moved into the trailer, she tried coaxing him to go on a date night. He refused, then resumed his TV marathon. Seemed *M*A*S*H* reruns were the only thing he lived for these days.

HAVE YOU EVER ATTENDED A MARRIAGE RETREAT?

No.

Pity they'd never taken the time.

HOW DID YOU FIND OUT ABOUT HART'S CAMP?

From a friend.

Janice said she and her husband returned from last summer's conference crazy in love. Instead of divorcing, they were heading to Hawaii for a second honeymoon for Valentine's Day next month. Was it possible Max's and her marriage could be resuscitated at such a retreat? If so, shouldn't she do everything in her power to get them there? One last gigantic effort. Cost shouldn't matter. Who cared about the long wintry drive?

She toggled back to the home page and observed the smiling faces of couples at the top of the screen. She read one of the testimonials.

"Hank and I were at our wits' end. We could barely stand to look at each other."

Sounded familiar.

"After hearing Ty and Winter share about their divorce and remarriage"—the review continued—"God spoke to our hearts. We wept and talked to each other for hours, confessing our struggles."

Confessing? There were things she'd rather not talk about with Max. Like how many times she entertained thoughts of leaving him. How, in her imagination, her bags were already packed. How her heart was turning as cold toward him as his seemed to be toward her.

Recently, she spent two weekends with her mom in Idaho Falls. A couple more getaways in a motel near the boys' campus in Boise. While she was on the southern tip of Idaho, why not check out one-bedroom rentals—just in case? Would she have to mention that to him also? Although, Max might not even care. He didn't seem concerned about anything—other than himself—since the church gave him the boot.

With that grudge settling deeper in her heart, she clicked on the form and reread the question.

HOW WOULD YOU DESCRIBE YOUR MARRIAGE?

Pathetic. Desperate. All life sucked out.

Twenty-two years ago they promised never to threaten the other with divorce. And she hadn't, out loud. But inside? Hardly a day passed that she didn't contemplate the possibility.

Both sets of her grandparents divorced. The same with most of her aunts and uncles. Her brother was on his third marriage by age forty. But she'd been so certain she and Max would stay together until one of them died—like her parents had until Dad's heart attack. Now, she wasn't so sure.

Not that everything wrong between them was Max's fault. The empty-nest had affected her worse than she ever would have imagined. Since Logan, then Benny, born one year apart, graduated and left home, she ached for what their family used to be. Who she used to be as a mom with teenagers in the house. It seemed she was in a perpetual search for something she couldn't find. If not for her job, she would have gone crazy with loneliness. Or madness, since Max was home doing nothing, now, other than watching his programs.

She answered a few more detailed questions, then hesitated only a second before tapping in credit card information. Signing them up for the retreat was a serious leap of faith. Blind faith, maybe? Regardless, it was time for action, and then some intense prayer.

A monumental task lay before her—telling Max what she'd done.

Dear Lord, help?

Three

Season

For three nights in a row, Season convinced herself not to tell Max about the conference, yet. He was too grumpy. She should wait for the perfect opportunity. Maybe he'd be in a better mood the next day. Problem was, she knew what he'd say—she should have asked him first. Which was true if he were his old self. This guy, she had to tiptoe around and second guess.

She'd moved forward with plans, even though she hadn't talked to him. She cleared a week's leave from the library. Had the oil changed in the Forrester. Tires checked. Bought a pretty nightgown—in case Max encountered some sort of miraculous turnaround. Not that she'd hold her breath.

With three days left until the retreat, she had to tell him tonight.

His favorite foods might help. How about ice cream? And he enjoyed mystery novels. Maybe she'd pick out a couple from the best seller's shelf at the library. After work, she drove straight to Su Young's, a takeout restaurant on the south side of Hamilton, and bought sweet and sour chicken—something

Max loved. She made a stop at a mini-mart on the way back and grabbed extra-dark chocolate ice cream.

All the way home, she prayed. *God, You know Max and I are struggling. Please prepare his heart for this marriage retreat, because if he says no, I can't imagine staying. I know leaving him is wrong, but ...?*

She gulped down guilt and focused on what she needed to say tonight. *Max, the funniest thing happened at work. You remember Janice?*

When she arrived at the trailer she no longer dubbed their "love shack," Max barely glanced at her. She poured iced tea into fancy glasses and set out the cartons of Chinese food. "Dinner's ready."

"Takeout? What's the occasion?" His gaze pinged with hers, then targeted the television again. By his sweaty body odor, he hadn't showered again. Still wore the ratty t-shirt he wore to bed last night, and his navy sweatpants. How many days had he worn those?

She resisted the urge to plug her nose. No use being snide. "I just picked up your favorite foods." She kissed his whiskered cheek, offering mild affection she hadn't initiated in weeks.

He didn't turn in to her caress.

"Why?"

"Can't a wife get her husband something delicious because she ... loves him?" Even though they argued before she left for work that morning? Even though she was uncertain whether she did, in fact, love him?

His vision stayed locked on the TV.

Lord? How can I reach him?

A knot twisted beneath her ribs. A throb ticked at her temple.

In the past, Max rarely watched TV. Said it was a waste of time and intelligence. Hadn't he preached about Hollywood dumbing down society? There had been the rare occasion he joined her and the boys to watch an old movie like *Old Yeller, Davy Crockett,* or *It's a Wonderful Life.* Otherwise he pretty much avoided it. Was he making up for decades of TV abstinence?

"Come over to the table. Doesn't it smell great?" She hoped they could talk without the noise of the television.

"Mind if I eat over here?" He nodded toward the screen.

Yes, she minded. But if she snapped at him, her plans for a peaceful talk would be ruined. Seeing his zombie-like gaze aimed at a shopping channel, she wondered where her considerate, pastoral-minded husband had gone. Could he need something way beyond a week in the woods at a marriage conference to help him? What if he was clinically depressed? She certainly wasn't qualified to diagnose him.

"Hungry?" The aroma from their dinner hit her churning stomach and made her swallow hard.

"Eh." He shrugged.

By the cereal encrusted bowls and plastic containers stacked on the TV tray, he'd eaten plenty throughout the day. She'd noticed a significant rise in their grocery bill. And an increase in his waistline.

She dropped onto the bench hoping he'd change his mind and sit opposite her at the table.

He shuffled over, glancing back at the screen. Could he be any less interested? He piled rice and sauce on his plate, then returned to the sofa. "You should see the pans they sell on this channel."

Like she cared.

"Copper. Miracle working pans. Really amazing. Eggs slide off the surface like melting ice."

While that was the most interest he'd shown in anything in a long time, his prattle annoyed her. Couldn't he sit at the table across from his wife and have one real conversation? How else could she tell him about the conference?

Though her appetite had vanished, she dished up food on her plate.

"Stovetop to oven to table to dishwasher." He stuffed food in his mouth and chewed. "Scratch-resistant. Pretty fantastic. I'm sure you'd love it."

Yeah, yeah, yeah. He could have been the salesman. At least then he'd have a job.

She said a silent prayer for patience.

He aimed the remote at the television. The volume increased. A different infomercial salesman blared across the screen, bragging about the latest toolset every human on the planet should own.

"Turn it down, will you?" So much for things going as she hoped. "I thought we could talk for a few minutes."

He messed with the remote, but the sound didn't reduce.

She stuffed rice in her mouth to keep derogatory words at bay.

He leaned closer to the screen as if his next breath depended on the announcer's words. Did it matter whether five hundred people had already called to order that toolset?

Then something churned in her mind. Was it possible he was addicted to a shopping channel? In the absence of ministerial duties and busyness, did he have a compulsion to order stuff? Had he been binge buying? If so, where was his stash? In their storage unit? She could just imagine him buying a dozen ugly pottery Cheshire cats with glassy eyes. *Look at the collection I bought for you, honey!* Was their savings gone? What if he maxed out their credit card?

Whoa. She took a deep breath, hoping she didn't need a paper bag to breathe into. She'd just let her mind run on crazy there for a minute. Max had been acting strange lately, but he didn't have a compulsive nature. He'd never been a spending fiend. Had acted frugal with church-related purchases, as well as their own.

She slowly chewed a bite of chicken, calming herself. How could she entice her husband to the retreat? The red nightie pranced through her thoughts. *Forget that.* She left the price tag attached for a reason.

The salesman's southern drawl coming from the TV irritated her. "We've only got a limited number of toolsets for y'all."

I bet.

"Call the number on the bottom of the screen and get yours now for the unbelievable price of three payments of fourteen ninety-nine each. Can y'all imagine such a low price?"

She groaned. Who would be hoodwinked into buying that junk? Couldn't the audience hear the guy's phony diction? He probably wasn't even from the south.

Max braced his elbows against his knees and leaned his chin against his fists, fully engaged with the advertiser. A gray pallor shadowed his face. Was he ill?

Some of her anger melted. The anxious lump beneath her breastbone softened. She'd loved him for so long, even if she hadn't felt loving toward him lately. He'd been through a difficult spot with *that* church firing him.

So had she.

Did Max realize how hard it had been for her, as a pastor's wife, to make close friends in the congregation? To ever fit in? She always felt people were judging her to a higher standard, and she wanted to be accepted for herself, faults and all. Then she'd met Liza, a recently divorced, single mom of three who seemed to need a friend as desperately as she did. For several years, they were close, talking on the phone, meeting for coffee once or twice a week, and enjoying occasional shopping trips to Missoula. But then, Liza, her only friend, left the church to go to Living Faith Center. Their friendship dwindled. And that's when Season stopped caring much about Darby Community Church. That's when she started thinking of it as *that* church.

Considering Max's present discouragement, and his inability to find a job or a new task he enjoyed, she couldn't fault him too much for wanting whatever small comfort the salesman offered. Buying tools or pans wouldn't break them. Might cheer him up. Make him more agreeable? Hmm.

She grabbed her plate and, nudging a pile of his dirty clothes out of her path with her shoe, dropped onto the couch next to him. "You're drooling over those tools, aren't you?"

"Huh?" He tossed her a glance, as if surprised by her nearness.

"Why don't you go ahead and buy them?"

His eyes lit up. "You mean it?"

It wasn't like he had to ask her permission for small purchases.

"Why not?" She shrugged.

If he were hiding a garage full of junk would he look so unabashedly happy now?

"Would be handy." He swayed a forkful of vegetables toward the pullout in the living room section of the RV. "I've never seen a tool like that. Could fix up this old trailer. Might get a few more years out of it."

"Great. So order it."

"Wow. Thanks." He patted her hand. Not affectionately, but maybe with gratitude? He set his plate on the tray and grabbed his cell phone.

He stared at the TV, mouthing the numbers out loud as he tapped the cell's screen. His face was animated like a kid's while he talked to the operator. He asked her—Season assumed

26

it was a woman by the way his voice softened—how her day was going. And for those few minutes, he sounded like his old pastoral self.

The change in him brought tears to her eyes. Made her hesitate to bring up what could be a controversial subject. She closed her eyes and silently prayed for wisdom.

After the call ended, he leaned back with a contented sigh. Which made her think he did have an addiction. But they'd have to deal with that later.

She cleared her throat. Now or never. "Max, I need to talk with you about something important." She grabbed the remote and shut off the TV.

"Hey!" He glared at her.

"Sorry." Not really. She stuffed the remote between her outer thigh and the sofa's arm, out of his reach. "I know we haven't seen eye to eye lately."

He crossed his arms. Apparently, his joy had already vanished.

"I know you're going through a rough time since you aren't pastoring a church. I'm sorry for your pain."

"It's not like you ever wanted to be a pastor's wife." His eyes glinted.

What? He begrudged her that comment from twenty-some years ago?

"You and I both know I was immature when I said that." For twenty years, she'd tried to be a good pastor's wife. Hadn't she done a million things to make life easier on the man she loved? "You were the pastor. We were married. So I *was* the pastor's wife. I loved being your wife—before you went off the deep end, anyway." She muttered the last part.

"Deep end?" He acted like he didn't know what she was talking about. Then he thrust out his palm. "The remote? We're finished."

Was there a double meaning hidden in his words?

"No, we're not done talking." She clenched her palms together. "It's important that you listen to me with an open mind."

"So that's why we had takeout." He stared at his almost empty plate. "I'm surprised you didn't throw in ice cream."

He knew her well.

"Actually, I did." Her cheeks heated up. "Dark chocolate."

His eyes sparkled, then immediately clouded. "Shoot. Might as well get it over with."

How to begin? "Here's the thing … would you consider attending a marriage conference with me?" Too desperate-sounding? Maybe she should have talked about how nice it would be to take a scenic drive.

"Marriage conference?" His mouth dropped open. "Why?"

"Because our marriage needs help." Desperately.

"We're fine."

"We're not fine!" She nearly yelled. Deep breath. "There's a marriage retreat near Blanchard, Idaho, in a few days." She held out her hands to keep him from interrupting. "I'd like us to go together. A friend at work recommended it. Please, Max? We need this."

"I don't need some conference speaker explaining marriage to me." His hand jerked outward, crashing into the TV tray. Silverware clattered to the floor.

Along with her hopes for reconciliation.

"I've counseled enough couples to know what those seminars are all about."

"So what?" She fought back tears. "Our marriage is falling apart."

"I'm not going." His face darkened like a cloud going from gray to charcoal. "Just because I've been a little downcast—"

"A little?"

"Doesn't mean I need some confess-all counseling."

"What are you talking about?" Was he worried about confessing something to her? She felt a ping of guilt over things she'd rather not discuss with him either. But she stuffed them down. "This isn't just about you, Maxwell Prescott. It's about us—and the way you're flushing our marriage down the toilet!" Her breathing came in heaves.

His lips compressed. Arms crossed, he glared—his high and mighty stubborn look—and she knew he wouldn't budge. So she might as well let him have it. "You make me so mad. You're a grumpy, self-centered, lazy, pigheaded man. Why can't you cooperate and go to the marriage retreat with me? Why can't you choose us for once?"

He smirked, which irritated her and fueled her sense of injustice.

"You lost your church. So what?" She should probably stop there. "You're a man in his prime. Stop sitting around like your life is over. Make something good happen. Start another church. Get another degree. Look for a job at the hospital, a chaplaincy or something. Or go into teaching. Or find an engineering firm you'd like to work for. You've been stuck in the trailer for two months. Haven't k-kissed me." Her voice broke. "Don't act like you love me. Do you even want to be married?"

"Sure." His voice lacked conviction. "Look, I'm not trying to treat you badly." His husky confession made her think he might be serious. "It's just, everything has gone wrong. Like the world has collapsed on me, and I don't know what to do, how to live."

The boyish hurt in his tone dug at her.

"That's why we need this conference, Max. It might help us find our way back to each other. Please? Before we lose everything."

"I've already lost everything."

Pain arced through her chest. His "everything" was the church, right? Not her? For a heartbeat, she couldn't breathe. But she still had to try to convince him to go to the retreat. She'd deal with the heartache later. They needed help climbing out of their rut. "You haven't lost everything. I'm here—your wife. Please, go to the retreat with me."

He stood and dusted crumbs off his sweatshirt. They stared at each other. His dark eyes held her gaze. Then he glanced away. "No."

"No?" She leaped to her feet. "I already paid for our registration!" Her trump card.

"You wasted your money, then, because I'm not going."

"Fine." The firestorm erupted in her chest. "Stay here. Rot in your dad's old RV. I'm going to the retreat—with or without you!"

"Go then."

"I will." She couldn't stand to look at him another second. Thrusting her arms into her winter coat, she stomped down the outside steps, then slammed the door as hard as possible. The trailer shook. If she were a swearing woman, a blue streak would permeate the air.

Max probably doubted her gumption to attend the couples' retreat alone. *Think again, buddy.*

Only one question remained—when the dust settled, would she come back to this den of disappointment or head for Boise?

Four

Max

The call came so late Max thought it might be a prank. He glanced at the cell phone's screen. Jayme Clark? Why would the young pregnant woman be calling him at one o'clock in the morning? She wasn't near her due date. Was something wrong with the baby?

"Hello?" He muffled his voice so Season wouldn't hear him from the other room. He'd been skimming channels for news before he headed for bed, but she'd been asleep for hours.

"P-pastor?" Jayme's voice broke like something might be terribly wrong.

"Yes." He sat up straighter.

"I need to talk with you." Sniffles and a hiccup emphasized her broken emotions.

Someone needed him. Something powerful filled his chest. "Okay. Do you want to talk now over the phone?"

"No, it's too late." She cleared her throat. "Dad will get suspicious. Maybe we could meet in the morning?"

"Sure. That would be fine." Did he answer too quickly? She'd been a bit flirtatious as a teenager, and more so since she'd become a young woman. Something he generally ignored, but Season couldn't seem to do. Good thing his wife wasn't the jealous type. Still, he bet she wouldn't like him meeting alone with this woman.

"Could you meet me somewhere?"

He swallowed back reasons why he shouldn't. "I could. Best if it's in a public place." She might think it was silly that he added that. But when he counseled women, he always left his office door wide open, or met in public places. Better to be above reproach.

"I love Annabelle's. How about meeting me for breakfast?" Her voice trilled as if she hadn't been crying at all.

Huh. Was she faking a crisis? Why would she do that? It was late. Probably nothing more than her relief in knowing that he'd meet her.

"I can do that." The local diner would be active with customers in the morning. Hopefully, the town's chief gossips— elderly sisters Willa and Martha Clayton—wouldn't be present. "Say nine?"

"Sure. Thanks, Max."

Max. No longer *Pastor Max.* He felt that loss twist in his gut.

"No problem."

"See you then." Had her voice softened?

"Yeah, sure." Max clicked off the connection. What did she want? Money? That was a laugh. He had none. And her banker father was one of the wealthiest men in the valley. Advice, perhaps? What could he offer anyone in his state of discouragement? Still, that she needed him for wisdom or direction gave him a spark of enthusiasm he hadn't felt in a dozen Sundays.

"Who was it?" Season called in a thick voice from the bedroom. She hadn't spoken to him much since their argument about the marriage conference a couple of nights ago.

That she'd signed him up for the retreat without asking still churned in his gut like sour green apples about to be rejected. Why would she think he'd want to attend a marriage conference? "A parishioner needs help, that's all." He probably shouldn't mention Jayme's name.

"I thought it might be one of the boys."

"It wasn't." Logan or Benny would have asked for their mother anyway. Which bothered him. When had he lost influence with his own sons? They used to come by his office after school and the three of them would laugh and talk—just guys' stuff. When had that stopped? Seemed kids didn't want to be seen with their folks much once they hit thirteen or so. Kind of hard for parents to adjust. But he'd thrown himself into more work at the church. Did they begrudge his being in the ministry? That's all they'd ever known, so probably not.

Season didn't say anything else, must have fallen back asleep. *Good.* Gave him time to think. Jayme's father, Derek Clark—Max's previous council member and worst critic—could probably be a tyrant toward an unwed pregnant daughter. Jayme most likely needed a sympathetic ear to listen. Max prided himself on being a good listener who maintained an unbiased view. Two of his strengths. He sat a little taller. Maybe he'd try to clean up and put on a tie tomorrow. Couldn't hurt.

After Season left for work the next day, he cranked up the old '85 Chevy truck. It rumbled down to Annabelle's, then died. Worthless piece of junk. After his dad's passing eight months ago, Max decided to keep the relic in hopes of using it to haul the travel trailer. The way the engine barked and barely started, it was destined for the wrecking yard. Would the gas guzzler get him through winter? He couldn't afford a new rig. Hopefully, he'd find a job. Wishful thinking? Or maybe his luck was about to change.

Before exiting the truck, he glanced in the rearview mirror to straighten his navy tie. He ran his fingers through his hair—which needed a cut—then skimmed the back of his hand over his smooth chin. After not shaving in weeks, then almost scraping off his whiskers this morning, his skin burned. He'd let things go for too long. Before Season left for work, she commented on him getting around and putting on real clothes. Her words spiked his irritation. Almost made him want to throw off his sport coat and toss on a sweatshirt just to spite her. Which didn't make sense. Why was he so defiant toward her? Maybe because she kept nagging him.

Fill out some applications. Get a job. Clean up after yourself. Take a shower. Was she his mother, or what?

Who cared—other than her—whether he showered every day? After twenty years of abiding by every rule and every-one's expectations, he didn't feel like adhering to anyone's regulations—including hers! Especially hers! Most afternoons he hiked over to Gladys Iris's to help with chores. She didn't care what he was wearing. If he stopped by a few houses on the way back to shoot the breeze with old-timers or work on some of their projects, none of them cared either.

And he'd filled out a few online applications. Still hadn't heard back from any of them. Not many employment oppor-tunities available this time of year, especially in the small town of Darby. Maybe he'd start looking in Hamilton next week while Season was away.

Today, he felt better dressing up a little. Breathing in the winter air, he strode into the local cafe and paused just inside the doorway, looking for Jayme.

The 1950's style restaurant, with Johnny Cash's "I Walk the Line" blaring over the radio, bustled with activity. Every red vinyl booth along the outer wall overflowed with customers. Waitresses buzzed around small tables in the center of the room with coffee carafes in hand, refilling mugs. Eager eaters lined the long breakfast bar. The scents of sausage and huckleberry syrup and coffee hung in the air like a delicious fog.

Glancing to his right, he found Jayme seated at the corner booth. Her scarlet fingernails tapped her smartphone. She paused and sipped from an off-white mug, no doubt leaving a red stain from her overdone lipstick. He never could understand why women coated their mouths with the crimson stuff. He was glad Season had a more natural look when it came to makeup.

Jayme glanced up, met his gaze, and smiled.

He felt awkward as if she'd caught him staring. He strode to her booth. "Hello."

"Max! I'm so glad to see you."

Season wasn't going to like this. He debated telling Jayme he had somewhere else to go and that he couldn't stay. But then he wouldn't find out what she needed. So he stood awkwardly by the table, not sitting down, and not leaving.

Strange she didn't appear distressed. By the looks of her colorful makeup, sparkling fingernails, and flowing black-and-gold outfit—either a long blouse or a short dress over leggings—she could be a cover model for a vogue pregnancy magazine.

Max drew his gaze back to her kohl-lined eyes, expecting sadness. She didn't look the least bit unhappy. No red-rimmed eyelids. Bubbly smile. A good night's sleep? Or a con?

What was he doing here?

"Have a seat, Max." Jayme's slim hand bearing several rings motioned him to sit down. "Come on and order something with me."

What would Derek Clark think of Max meeting his daughter like this? What would Season say? Now hold on. He was a pastor. Correction—*had* been. He couldn't turn off compassion because three men said his time card expired. Had God dismissed his calling? Max still cared about people. Wanted to help where he could. Yet, something cautioned him to beware.

The Lord? Or his guilty conscience over how he'd been acting toward Season?

He'd anticipated breakfast ever since he woke up. Annabelle's coffee was the best in the city, if not the state. Only he wished Jayme didn't look so glitzy. And him dressing up for their meeting didn't help matters. He noticed a couple of people at nearby booths staring at him. He nodded and wondered what the locals might think.

Jayme was a twenty-one-year-old unwed mother in need of kindness. That was all, right? Hadn't she called him crying on the phone last night? Even if she was all smiles today. Everyone had two sides—the outer persona people let others see, and the one they kept hidden. What might Jayme be hiding?

"Need a place to sit, Pastor?" Sandy Duncan, a redheaded waitress who'd been in Annabelle's employ for two decades or so dashed by him, then poured coffee into Jayme's cup. She wrinkled an eyebrow at him. "A spot just opened up at the counter."

"I'll, uh, sit here." He nodded toward the bench across from Jayme.

"With her?" Sandy's head pulsed in the young woman's direction. "Does your wife know?"

Small-town talk. Max shook his head. Season rarely knew where he went or who he saw in a day. She trusted him. Or did—what had she said?—before he went off the deep end.

"Your funeral." Sandy did a one-eighty, topping off coffee cups on her way back to the kitchen.

Max inwardly groaned, then dropped onto the red vinyl

seat across from Jayme and placed his clasped hands on the table between them. "Good morning."

"Took you long enough." The pads of Jayme's fingers caressed the back of his left hand, skimming across his gold wedding band. Her laughter trilled like a sugar-inebriated bird.

He pulled his hands away and settled them on his lap. Was this the desperate woman who called him last night? Was she experiencing third-trimester mood swings or something? Better get to the point. Maybe he wouldn't order a meal. Coffee. Talk. Then skedaddle to Iris's. "So you're having some kind of problem?"

"I'll say." Sandy dropped a mug on the table, then filled it three-fourths full. "Creamer's there." She nodded toward a bamboo basket filled with individual french vanilla and half-and-half creamers.

"Thanks, Sandy." Max smiled at the waitress but seeing her wary glance aimed at Jayme he repeated himself a little louder. A few whispers from other tables reached him. What fodder for gossip was he giving them by meeting with a young woman like this? He wanted to slouch lower in the seat. Or disappear.

Sandy harrumphed and scurried from the table.

"What's with her?" Jayme scowled. She leaned toward him, her dark gaze pinning him to his seat. She winked. "I'm glad you're here, Max. You always understand me." She slid a menu to his side of the table. "Hungry?"

Double innuendo? And why had his thoughts jumped to that assumption?

The toe of her boot skimmed up his shin. Accidental? Not likely by the sound of her girlish chuckle.

He leaned both his legs as far as he could to the left. If he moved any closer to the window, his gray sport coat would leave smudges in the steamy glass.

Jayme's face turned rosy. Was she embarrassed? Or acting coy?

Five steps to the door, that's all it would take. Ten seconds and he'd be out of here faster than Superman on his best day. Joseph sprinted from Pharaoh's wife, leaving his multicolored coat behind. Max could do the same. He and his wife might not be getting along, but he didn't want people thinking he was after some tawdry side relationship. So far, he hadn't ruined his reputation—even though his church had closed. This morning's "meeting" could mean the end of more than what he'd already lost.

At Jayme's desperate phone call last night, he'd been thrilled one person in the world still needed him. *Pathetic.* Is that what his life had become? Rushing here or there to experience one more high of being wanted? His suppressed moan hurt. He tugged open a creamer and poured it into his coffee. Might need two. He peeled off another lid. "What did you need to talk with me about?" Better get this conversation going and leave ASAP.

"Can't you guess?" Her red lips parted, revealing perfectly straight white teeth that he remembered had been in braces a few years ago. "Why, Max, I need *you.*"

The empty creamer package dropped to the table. His jaw fell nearly as far.

Sisters Willa and Martha Clayton chose that second to shuffle into Annabelle's. Their gazes thudded with his, then Jayme's, then his again. Judgment oozed from their identical blue-gray irises.

Max shook his head to deny anything untoward was happening—other than that boot-skimming thing. But they hadn't been in here to see that.

He stood and nodded. "Miss Willa. Miss Martha. Nice to see you." He plastered a smile on his mouth. "How are you two?"

The elderly sisters pursed their lips in a matching pose and harrumphed. Noses high, they marched away from Max and Jayme, toward the back of the restaurant—where he doubted there was even a place for them to sit.

It seemed a perfect opportunity for him to pay the check and leave. But he hadn't yet heard what Jayme needed to talk with him about, so he dropped back onto the bench.

"I hate people like that." Jayme tapped her nails on the table. "Think they're so much better than me. Like they've never done anything they regret."

"They don't mean to be harsh." He was used to defending people, but in truth, Willa's and Martha's pious attitudes riled him. They'd attended his church for twenty years. Hadn't they learned anything about living a Christ-like example in dealing with others?

"Sure they do. They're mean old bats!" She ran her index finger around the rim of her mug. "I'm shocked to hear you defend them after what they say about you."

So he was the topic of their gossip-mongering? Shouldn't surprise him. Still, he drowned his reaction with a long swig of coffee.

The sisters had glared at Jayme as if she were a hussy, and he a cavorting playboy. Like he'd stoop so low as to cheat on his wife with a woman young enough to be his daughter, in public? Now, did the biggest gossips in Darby have tales to spread about him and Jayme? Ugh. Should he march to the back of the restaurant and give those two a piece of his mind? He was a man of God, for goodness' sake. And here sat a woman who obviously made a mistake in getting pregnant out of wedlock, but one who chose life for her child. For that, they should be proud. Jayme was courageous, in his book— although he didn't want to prolong this meeting another second.

When her boot's edge skimmed his shin again, he froze. Not an accident that time. "Don't do that again." He hoped his voice sounded gruff enough.

"Sorry." Her grin denied the apology. "You're cute when you get all, I don't know, indignant." She swished her black hair, which made her look more like the adolescent she'd been a few years ago.

He needed to end this so-far useless conversation. But he still hadn't discovered why she'd phoned in the first place. "Why did you call me last night?"

"Well—"

Sandy scurried to their table, pencil and notepad in hand. "Ready to order?"

"Just coffee for me." Max held up his mug.

Jayme ordered the sampler and a giant cinnamon roll. Guess she planned to stay for a while.

Sandy put her pencil behind her ear and hustled away—not before squinting warnings at the two of them. Was she thinking the worst of him too? She'd always been an ally of sorts. Never darkened his church door, but she maintained a camaraderie he appreciated.

He cleared his throat. "What did you need to talk with me about? I have other matters to attend to." Like getting out of here and taking off this wretched tie. He'd never hated wearing ties before. Must be the two months of casual attire. Not to mention the knot of guilt growing wider in his throat with each second he sat across from Jayme. He loosened his neck binding the best he could.

"You won't like what I have to say." She took a long drink from her mug. Then grinned cheekily.

"You need money?"

She guffawed. "You're too cute."

Hardly. Who else had heard her exclamation? "Then what?"

She toyed with the rings on her fingers. "Daddy's demanding to know who the baby's father is." A silly grin—one at odds with what she'd just said—made her red lips look crooked.

"You mean he doesn't know?"

"I kept it from him." She shrugged. "He doesn't like the type of men I date."

Neither did Max. But it wasn't his place to judge. His job was to be kind and show grace. "Will the father be involved in the baby's upbringing?"

She snorted. "Nope. But I had to tell Daddy something to get him off my case." She leaned forward. "So I made up a story."

Great. What sorry bloke would get the rap for leaving Derek Clark's daughter with child? "You should tell your dad the truth. He loves you. Does the baby's father know you're expecting his child?"

"No, he's long gone." She shuddered. The first glimpse of a serious strain since he sat down. "And you know how Daddy gets."

He did.

She rested her hand on her belly that resembled a small basketball. "He threatened to throw me out. Disinherit me. Thanks to my 'condition.' So I lied." She wiped her finger beneath her eye as if swiping away a tear that didn't exist.

What game was she playing? Why would she lie to her dad about her baby's father? Derek Clark was a lot of things—rude, argumentative, self-righteous—but Max doubted he'd do his daughter harm.

"You want me to talk with him?" Perish the thought. He'd argued with Derek plenty of times before, and none of those arguments were of such a personal nature.

"No. In fact, I think you should keep your distance." She worried her lower lip.

"Why?" A warning went off in his brain. His throat went dry.

"Because"—the flirty smile was back—"I had to tell him something, Max. I didn't think you'd mind. You of all people would want to protect me." Her voice grew strangely loud.

Or had the volume in the restaurant decreased?

She ran her index finger down the back of his hand again. Her touch was light and—

He jerked his hand away. A premonition scaled his shoulders. Something evil? "What exactly did you tell him?"

"Only that we had a wild affair. That *you* are … you know … the baby's father." She winked at him.

"What?" Max lunged to his feet, nearly knocking over his coffee. "How could you perpetrate such a lie?" This was terrible. Unbelievable. Had his heart stopped beating? "I can't believe—"

His hands gesticulated outward just as Sandy sidled up to the table with Jayme's platter, striking the tray. Eggs and sausages sailed through the air, splattering on the wood floor amidst busted plate shards.

Max stared into Sandy's shocked eyes that had to mirror his own. When she dropped down to pick up broken stoneware, Max didn't know what else to do other than help. On his knees, trembling with rage, he scooped up eggs with his fingers and begged God to make this nightmare disappear. Couldn't he go back to being a pastor people admired? A good citizen of Darby? Would anyone believe the heinous untruth Jayme had concocted? Did her dad believe her? If so, would he come after Max?

The chime above the door jingled, and he jerked, suddenly jumpy. A couple he didn't recognize entered the diner.

"Tsk-tsk," a female voice behind him muttered. Willa Clayton stood peering down at him like a cranky teacher, her wrinkled face puckered with more frown lines than he'd ever seen on a human. "Well, well, Pastor, wallowing in the mud? Reminds me of the prodigal son and the pigs, hmm? Oh, how the mighty have fallen."

Indeed. But he didn't answer. Just kept picking up slimy eggs and sausages from the floor.

Willa's booted feet shuffled back the way she'd come.

When he stood, Jayme was gone.

He dropped onto the bench and moaned. Things had gone from bad to terrible. He rested his forehead against his clenched fists. How could God have allowed so many trials to land on his head? He hadn't had time to catch his breath before the odious clock of doom struck again.

He took two twenties out of his wallet and plopped them on the table. Hopefully, that would cover Jayme's food, their coffees, a tip, and the broken plate.

He stood but didn't dare meet any customers' gazes for fear they knew the shame that wasn't even his.

What if someone reached Season at the library and told her what just transpired before he could call and do damage control? Things had been so rough between them. At first, he'd wanted to protect her from all the fallout from the church going under. But then, the whole mess sucked him down like an anchor in a troubled sea. Now, this?

His wife was leaving for the retreat in the morning. If he told her what Jayme had accused him of, would she even believe him?

Five

Season

Season figured she was either courageous or an idiot. From morning until evening, she'd been driving through the worst whiteout, blizzard conditions she'd ever seen, en route from Darby, Montana, to Blanchard, Idaho. She'd clutched the steering wheel tightly for so many hours her curled fingers felt permanently sculpted in place.

A travel mug refilled with coffee as often as possible, and the heat blowing near her feet, kept her from freezing. And her anger toward Max made her blood boil, which warmed her core and kept her mind alert. In her imagination, he sat right here in the passenger seat where she could yell at him all she wanted. How dare he refuse to join her—especially after breaking the news to her that Jayme was spreading hideous rumors about him and her!

Last night, she'd wanted to rail at him, but mostly she packed her stuff and stayed in their room, stewing. Now, after listening to all the dreary weather announcements—storm warnings, more like—on the radio, she'd gladly take the opportunity to get a few things off her chest. "Stubborn man.

Icicle heart. Time for everyone else in the world but me!" she shouted toward the other seat. As long as angst ran through her veins, she might as well keep the car moving forward through snow and ice.

In the last town, she'd seen an archaic motel with a vacancy sign. Totally uninviting, but maybe she should have gotten a room. Slept off her anger and fatigue. But she was trying to get to the campground in time for registration.

So her foot applied steady but slight pressure to the gas pedal, and she continued hurling accusations at Max. *Egotistical. Arrogant sloth. Miserable midlife man!* And now, rumors were spreading around town about him and Derek Clark's daughter like a contagious disease? Oh, she wanted to scream at him some more.

Before she'd left the RV this morning, he had the nerve to mock her ability to drive in winter weather. He wanted to stay safe and warm in his daddy's trailer? Let him. She had real stuff to do. Life-changing possibilities, with or without him.

She took another long drink of coffee. Then doubts assailed her. Whoever heard of a wife attending a marriage conference without her husband? She'd be the only woman without one. They might turn her away. Laugh. Ridicule her. Had she come all this way for nothing?

Max was to blame. He was the one not valuing their marriage. He was choosing to do what he wanted—sitting around the RV watching TV—instead of choosing to be with her. Well, maybe he'd run out of propane and freeze. He deserved to be miserable. Cold. And lonely.

Like her.

Her teeth chattered. She stared at the white flakes blasting against her windshield, wishing this journey of Arctic pro- portions would come to an end. How much farther? Her eyes ached. She could use a fresh cup of coffee. A warm bed.

The turnoff for Hart's Camp finally appeared beyond the snowfall. She wanted to hop out of the car and do a snow dance. But according to the GPS, there was a little way more to go. She slowly maneuvered the two-mile stretch of tree-lined back roads. Snow continued falling with nearly blinding conditions. After several S-turns, glowing lights pierced the darkness. Was that a lodge? Hart's Camp? *Yes. Thank You, Lord, for getting me here safely.* She brought the Forrester to a stop in the middle of what was probably a gravel road beneath all the snowpack. Despite the tumultuous weather and the way her hands shook from gripping the wheel, this haven in the middle of a cotton candy forest looked amazing—like a winter fairyland.

Her boys would love this. Max would have loved it when he was younger—when he had vitality for life. Boy, that was a long time ago. The present Max would hate the seclusion. Cell service probably didn't exist here.

Along the base of the mountain to her left, a dozen log cabins nestled like chicks under hens within the frosted woods. Smoke curled from every chimney. Was one of those cabins prepared for her and Max? To her right, a snow-peppered sign displayed enough letters to make out the words, "Hart's Camp—Changing lives one heart at a time."

Changing lives. A shiver raced across her shoulders and up her neck. She needed Max here to experience this with her. For their marriage to be restored, it would take both of them. What good would it do to be here alone? She'd been so certain a few days ago, but maybe she should forget about staying here and drive back to that motel. Max need never know. She could binge on marital self-help books. Return with a head full of knowledge. Talk about the chicken's way out. After yelling at him that she was coming to this camp with or without him, wasn't she obligated to follow through? Not to mention, she was exhausted and starving.

And Max could still have a change of heart and join her tomorrow. Slim chance considering he hadn't kissed her goodbye, and since he'd still have to deal with the lies. And they were lies, right? Was it possible for her to hate the man she loved? She sucked in a needy breath, then let the air release slowly.

Maybe she'd hide out in her cabin during couples' talks and avoid hearing about the "perfect" relationship. Yet wasn't that the reason she came all this way? To receive encouragement for her marriage?

Was she brave enough to do this alone?

A fist rapped hard against the window.

She jumped, then clutched her window scraper to use as a weapon. With her other hand, she wiped the steam off the glass.

A younger man with snow covering his hat and shoulders lifted his gloved hand in greeting. He held the wooden handle of a shovel in the other hand. His wide smile made her feel silly for gripping the plastic scraper like a dagger. Little good it would do anyway. She dropped it to her lap.

She lowered the window an inch. Snow swirled inside. "Yes?" The freezing wind brushed her cheeks, clumping snow-flakes to her mascara. She blinked them away.

"Everything all right?" Dark hair escaped the man's black knitted hat. "Car trouble?"

"No. I was contemplating staying ... or leaving." Why was she telling him this? Who was he?

"Here for the conference?" There was that enigmatic smile again. He leaned down as if expecting to find someone in the passenger seat.

"Just me." She fought off tears. No crying in front of strangers. "I'm having second thoughts, that's all."

"Is your husband joining you later?" Again the glance toward the other seat.

She lowered the window to half-mast. More flakes blew in on the frigid wind. "I wish that were the case. Are all men as stubborn?"

"As—?" One of his eyebrows rose

"As my husband."

His robust laughter filled the car. "Can't say. I'm sure I was the worst before God changed my life."

She doubted that. "Who are you?"

"Oh, sorry." He removed his glove and extended his hand through the window.

She lowered the glass a little more.

His fingers were surprisingly warm, probably from shoveling snow. "I'm Josh Hart. Camp proprietor. Musician. Snow-removal guy. And I wear a few other hats. Come down to the lodge and meet my wife, Summer. Grab some coffee. See how you feel after you meet the gang."

Coffee sounded divine. Her eyes were barely staying open. "The gang?"

"Workers. Attendees. You have to meet Aunt Em. She makes the best cookies on this side of the mountains. You'll love her." He nodded toward a log cabin barely noticeable on the white-covered hill. "I think she's up there watching. I bet she's been praying for you."

"Really?" She leaned forward and peered through the foggy window. The shadow of someone in the log cabin moved. A light flickered in the background. A fireplace? "Your aunt?"

"Yep. She's pretty fabulous." He chuckled. "She loved me through my rough years."

Season's mom had prayed for her all her life. She'd like to meet this woman whose nephew held such admiration for her. "It was stupid of me to come here by myself." This wasn't some hotel she could drop by for the evening. This was a marriage retreat that involved husbands and wives. Not half the duo.

"You're married, right?"

She nodded.

"Then you are welcome here." Josh swayed his left gloved hand toward the tall log structure ahead. "We have a great cook, Maggie, who's made a fabulous opening night dinner of lasagna and garlic bread."

"Lasagna?" Her all-time favorite. She could almost smell the garlic.

"It'll be magnificent." He must have seen her interest. He grinned and gestured for her to drive forward. Then he trudged down the road as if expecting her to follow.

What would it hurt to eat and warm up? She put the engine in gear and followed him slowly. She'd be relieved to climb out of the driver's seat.

Josh scooped up clods of snow from the edge of the road and tossed piles into the ditch as he walked. He seemed nice. Proprietor *and* musician? Would he give a concert? She imagined herself sitting cozily in the lodge, sipping coffee, gobbling lasagna, listening to—? What genre? Inspirational? Country? Staying here became more appealing with each crunch of her tires across the packed snow.

She'd like to meet "Aunt Em." The house on the right hill glowed through the snowfall—a beacon in the storm. Smoke rose from the chimney, reminding her of her grandmother's farmhouse when she was a girl. A warm feeling of nostalgia enveloped her.

Okay. Maybe this camp was exactly what she needed. Seclusion. Beauty. Time to think. Make some new friends, perhaps?

If only Max were here, everything would be perfect. Or at least hopeful. Marriage retreats like this were last-ditch efforts.

What did it say about their relationship that she was here alone, and he couldn't be bothered to come?

* * * *

Season enjoyed second helpings of turkey burger lasagna. Had anything ever tasted so cheesy and rich? The peppermint mocha so divine? No doubt, she'd regret drinking two mugs of the brew this late in the day, especially after all the coffee she drank on her drive. She begged the cook for the rhubarb custard pie recipe. Now she sat contentedly sipping herbal tea and chatting with two couples at her table. So far no one had made her feel bad for being here alone.

The man next to her, who introduced himself as Gar Bevere and his wife, Autumn, from the Seattle area, asked about her husband. When she told them the truth that he refused to attend, Gar and his wife smiled and nodded as if that made sense to them. Which notched up her curiosity. Why did such a cute couple, ones who held hands and met each other's gazes as if basking in romance, need this kind of marriage retreat?

However, the second couple at her table bickered constantly. They might need separate cabins to survive the week.

"I'm Missy, longsuffering wife of Fred." She rocked her thumb toward a heavyset man shoveling food into his mouth at an alarming rate. Was he even chewing?

"You think I'm thrilled to be here? Twice!" Fred guzzled down half his soda. "Without my fifth-wheel!"

RVers? They might have something in common. "Hard to pull a trailer in this weather, huh?"

"You bet your baby blues." Missy cackled. "Fred doesn't like to stay anywhere other than in his RV. Can you picture us in such a tiny space out here in the freezing cold?" She smirked. "No, thank you, very much."

Season swallowed a gulp of tea to hide a snicker.

Fred groaned. "Mattresses in those log cabins are miniature-sized for kiddies. How do they expect me to get a good night's sleep?" He stuffed lasagna into his mouth.

Missy lifted her fork. "Who cares when the food is this great?" She stabbed a rhubarb chunk. "Too bad our first time here didn't stick, huh, Fred?"

He shoved away from the table. "I'm getting some more."

"Stress makes him hungry." Missy shrugged. "He put on thirty pounds last year." She stood and followed him to the dessert counter.

Season met Autumn's glance, then forced herself to look away before being tempted to comment on Missy and Fred's contrary relationship. Of course, if Max were here, an outsider could sum up *their* problems easily too. The great wall separating them would be obvious.

When she arrived, Josh had introduced his wife and explained Season's situation to her. They were both so nice and said they'd pray for her and Max. Summer led her to the dining area where she was directed to fill out paperwork, warm herself by the fireplace, and drink all the coffee and tea she wanted.

According to Josh, the glistening walls of the lodge were local pine, cut from the property by his ancestors decades ago. Soft lighting intensified their sheen. The high ceilings served as a pleasant respite from the travel trailer lifestyle. She hadn't been shown to her room yet. But if it compared to the wonderful hosts, the attractive lodge, and the unbelievable food, she was in for a treat—despite what Fred said about the mattresses. If only Max—

Stop! He chose not to be here. He made his decision. She would not spend her week feeling regrets. She'd listen with an open mind. Learn healthy stuff about marriage. And best of all, she'd enjoy herself. In the registration packet, she saw the itinerary included sledding, painting, and theater. She'd always wanted to learn how to paint. This could be her chance!

Gar stood and rubbed his flat stomach. "I can't resist Maggie's apple pie. Anyone else?"

"No thanks." Too stuffed.

"None for me." Autumn set down her fork.

Before he moved from the table, Gar ran his finger down his wife's cheek. Their gazes met and held as if they were alone, about to kiss. He leaned in and whispered something in her ear.

Season gulped. Glanced away. Too private to watch, yet she was intrigued by the couple's tender exchange. Why were these lovebirds here?

Autumn giggled as her husband walked away, then sighed. "He likes to quote Shakespeare to me."

"Ahhh. A romantic." Max would never think of such a gesture. "A husband who quotes poetry and gazes into your eyes? You are one lucky girl!"

"I know." The thirty-something woman laughed, then fanned her rosy cheeks with her hand.

"So, what do you do?"

"I'm a high school English and, more recently, drama teacher." Autumn sipped her water. "Probably directing another show soon."

"Sounds fun. How did you hear about this conference?" Hopefully, she wasn't being too snoopy.

"Actually, Gar met Ty Williams, one of the main speakers, while he was working at Ty's mechanic shop in Coeur d'Alene last fall." Autumn shrugged. "Ty suggested we attend this week at Hart's Camp since we got back together only a few months ago." Her voice lowered. "We were separated. But God changed things. He changed *us*."

"Wow! Do you mind if I ask how things have been since

you got back together? Sorry if that's too nosy." What if she and Max split up? Would she enjoy her life in Boise too much without him? Would he follow her? No, his heart was still tied to Darby. And every time she thought about him saying he'd lost everything, something heavy and foreboding clenched in her stomach.

Autumn seemed to be thinking. "We're 100 percent better than before we split. Still working through some things. On the cool side, we're adopting an eight-year-old boy—Jimmy." Her face glowed. "He's a darling mischief-maker. But he keeps us laughing."

"How wonderful!" Talk of children always made Season long for a phone visit with Benny and Logan. "I have two college-aged sons whom I miss terribly. They're only a year apart. Freshman and sophomore at Boise State." She relaxed into the conversation. "I know what you mean about laughter. I miss that so much." Just thinking of her sons brought tears to her eyes. How could she ever resolve that emptiness?

Autumn scooted her chair a little closer to Season's. "I couldn't have my own kids, so adopting is a huge thing for us."

And here Season had been prying. "I'm so sorry."

"Thank you." Autumn's gaze lowered to the table as if she were holding a moment of silence or collecting her thoughts. Then a smile brightened her face. "But Gar and I have rediscovered such a deep love for each other, the Lord, and the people He's put in our lives—like a young woman who's staying with us and is expecting a baby any day—that I couldn't be happier."

Questions stirred within her. How did Autumn and Gar reconcile? How could a couple go from not loving each other, being separated, to falling so deeply in love they leaned into each other, smiled, and touched every time they were close? If she could find such magic, she'd spend every penny on it. But love took two willing hearts. She didn't know if one even existed in her and Max's relationship.

"Did you say you're a pastor's wife?" Autumn pointed at the name card on the table.

Season shrugged off her unease. "My husband was a pastor. I was his wife." Her typical response. She remembered Max's accusation about her not wanting to be a pastor's wife. Had she given him cause to think that in recent years? It seemed he carried a grudge, despite his admonition for parishioners to be forgiving.

There had been parts of sharing in her husband's ministry she didn't enjoy—like his continual absences, people calling at all hours, and sometimes the brutal gossip. But there'd been things she enjoyed too. Like when Max invited her to go on hospital rounds in Hamilton. She always felt connected with people waiting for family members in surgery or ER. She related to their fears and concerns, especially when children were involved. Usually, Max went into the sick person's room to pray, while she bought coffee and gift cards for moms and dads or grandparents waiting in the lobby.

She'd been proud of Max when he was behind the pulpit preaching. And she enjoyed standing by his side at the door of the sanctuary afterward, greeting people. She may not have loved all aspects of the ministry, but they had been a good team, she and Max. If only he could have seen that.

Autumn nodded like she understood. "I picked up my husband's responsibilities at the school after he left. But I wondered why people thought I should replicate his gifts and talents. I'm me. Sure, I'm a better person with my husband in my life. But still, this is who I am."

"I get that." Season felt the old ache.

"Where is your husband's church?"

"*Was* in Darby." No need to go into details, but honesty

prevailed. "He was forced to resign. He's struggling with that. *We're* struggling as a couple." What a relief to tell someone.

Autumn held such compassion in her gaze. "Tough on any marriage." Tears filled her eyes, and she patted Season's hand.

Salty water flooded her own eyes, dripping down her cheeks. For once, she didn't care. "Yes." Some of her apprehension about being here alone eased.

Autumn toyed with a watermark on the table. "Sometimes the other person changes, almost sours, before your eyes. It's hard to know what to do. How to pray."

"I know." Season felt a kinship with this new friend and wanted to talk more.

Missy dropped onto her chair, her hand holding a dessert plate piled high with pie, ice cream, and cookies. "What secrets are you girls sharing?"

Season shrugged, then wiped the back of her hand discreetly beneath her eyes.

"Ask me anything. I'm a wealth of knowledge about marriage." Missy chuckled. "I've been to five of these conferences around the Northwest. Not that they did any good." She slurped her coffee and shook her head.

Autumn wiped her napkin over her mouth. Was she hiding a grin?

Season leaned toward her. "Continue later?"

"Definitely. I'll tell you my story, sometime, if you're interested."

"I'd like that." Seeing a shadow cross Autumn's eyes, Season wondered about her pain. Autumn had said she and her husband were still working on some things. The journey of restoration took time and intentional effort, didn't it? Hadn't she read something like that on the Hart's Camp website?

Missy shuffled her chair closer to Autumn's. "I'll tell you what, Fred is about to drive me nuts!"

Fred groaned as he dropped into his chair. By the disgruntled look on his face, he'd overheard. However, Missy didn't seem the least bit embarrassed.

Gar returned to the table, and the conversation changed to the weather and the anticipated sledding expedition the following day. Fred and Missy said no one would catch them sledding like a couple of teenagers. To Season, a winter outing sounded delightful.

She gazed around the room full of married couples and wondered about their stories. They'd all come to this retreat for a reason. Some might be in desperate need like she was. Others, such as Autumn and Gar, seemed to just want to hold hands and be close—a dream come true.

What had happened to her and Max's love? Death by pastoral termination? Was there any way to rekindle what they'd lost?

Six

Max

Max stuffed the bottom five inches of his jeans into his boots, then zipped his coat up to his neck. A north wind had been blowing all day. Several times the travel trailer shuddered so hard he thought it might rock off the jacks.

This morning, Season had driven to the retreat without saying goodbye. Was she still angry about him not going with her? Or was she, now, more upset about what he'd told her Jayme accused him of? Revealing that bomb the night before she left might not have been his smartest move. But ever since those moments in the diner when his world flipped off its axis, his gut had been churning. He'd been tempted to let his wife go to the conference without knowing the gossip swirling around Darby, probably all the way to Hamilton and beyond. But taking that route had seemed cowardly. And unfair to her.

Confessing about the lie had been one of the hardest things he'd ever done. Second to leaving the church. Season took the news stoically. Didn't rant. But her mouth was clenched so tightly he could hardly see her lips. Then her eyes filled with tears, which he hated. He tried downplaying the accusation, focusing on its ridiculous nature. And she didn't seem to doubt him. Yet her silence, her leaving so early this morning without a proper goodbye, spoke volumes about how she felt.

In the last two hours, he'd sent her a couple of texts and left a voice message. So far, she hadn't returned any of his attempts to check on her. What was she thinking driving in such wretched weather? She should have stayed home. Or he should have gone with her to ensure her safety. But nothing about the conference had appealed to him. Still didn't.

Benny called earlier to check on his mom, much to Max's chagrin. He hated breaking the news to his son that she'd made the trip north on her own. Disbelief, then accusation, bled into Benny's tone before he ended the call. It seemed Max was batting zero no matter which way he turned. There wasn't anything he could do now other than go out and check on some elderly folks who might need his assistance in the storm. Season obviously didn't.

But he hated the thought of her driving under the influence of rage. What if she had a wreck? Or car trouble? No. Nothing bad was going to happen. She'd attend the conference for a day, see how outrageous it was for her to be there alone, and then come home. Maybe then they could talk about more than Jayme's lies. Maybe face what had happened over the last six months. It was probably time he owned up to his share of mistakes.

He grabbed a knit cap out of the overhead compartment near the door, then yanked it down over his ears. Needing a task, his plan was to hustle over to Mrs. Iris's and make sure her house was warm enough. He'd already called the Johnsons to double-check their pump house situation. Jupe said all was well. However, things might change if the temperature dropped below zero like it often did in January.

He prayed that it didn't happen. The RV's furnace had been running almost non-stop already.

He opened the trailer door, and the wind knocked him off the steps. *Whoa.* Good thing he landed on his feet. After slamming the door, he pulled his cap down over his forehead. This wind was crazy! Too bad the truck was unreliable. He'd trot the mile to Gladys's on foot—despite the windchill—then hightail it home and spend the evening watching *Perry Mason.* He'd keep his cell phone on high volume to hear his wife's call if she tried contacting him. Maybe he'd text her a few more times. Would she even have cell service at the campground?

Frigid air skimmed his cheeks, snatching his breath away. Barely able to see two feet in front of him due to heavy snowfall, he trudged forward, his boots crunching over the frozen ground. Ice formed on his whiskers and made his mouth stiff. His nose froze. Thoughts of warmth and comfort tempted him to turn around and head back to the trailer. But Gladys depended on him. He really should check on her.

A clump of snow dropped from the trees overhead, just missing him. He leaned into the windy onslaught of snowflakes. His boots shuffled through neighborhoods where someone should have shoveled the sidewalks by now. He knew a few senior citizens lived in those houses. Maybe they could use his help. Adrenaline charged through his veins. He liked feeling needed. Was there anything wrong with that? How could Season expect him to walk away from what he'd done for the last twenty years? He still wanted to be in ministry. Still ached to feel like he was doing something meaningful with his life. So he shoveled snow, hauled groceries, mended fences, and walked dogs. He didn't like that the weight of breadwinning fell on her right now, but it wouldn't always be the case.

He'd worked as an engineering draftsman during college. Although, he hadn't thought much about that skill during his years of pastoring. Would anyone hire him in that field after such a long absence? Maybe he'd check the online job sites again. If he were employed by the time Season returned, she'd be thrilled. And he'd feel more like the provider he wanted to be.

He kicked a clump of snow, thinking of Season's determination to go to the marriage retreat without him, even though the roads were nearly impassable. She had to be one of the most independent women he knew. And an excellent driver. Still, he worried. Accidents happened. What if she lay in a hospital bed somewhere, hurt? Or worse? A chill chased up his spine. His heartbeat hammered in his ears. He forced his numb feet to tromp faster en route to Mrs. Iris's. Once there, he'd check his cell. Surely nothing else bad would happen. His heart couldn't take it. Season was probably making a point by not contacting him, letting him know she was angry. He'd keep trying to contact her, but he didn't want to interrupt her concentration when she was driving, either. He could barely see the sidewalk in front of him, how was she able to see the road?

In his mind's eye, he pictured her before she left—a purple knit cap pulled down beneath her eyebrows, standing by the door with her suitcase in hand, glaring fire darts at him. "You are a stubborn man, Maxwell Prescott!"

Yep, she got that right.

He hadn't realized such weaknesses in his psyche before. Since his career crashed and burned, he wanted things his way more than ever. He needed to have control in his life—even if it meant how many hours he watched TV, or whether he attended a marriage conference, or which jobs he applied for. Was that so horrible? Couldn't stubbornness be a good thing? The fact he was tenacious about helping people was honorable. That he had compassion toward Jayme had seemed honest and right, although that had gone horribly wrong. He'd tried to be a good pastor—no matter the cost to him or his family. Which Season and his sons probably judged a bad thing. But didn't God create him with a stubborn streak? He tilted his face to the gray heavens, a question on his tongue.

Just then, a pile of snow from a tree limb overhead plopped down onto his face.

"Ow." Icy shards burned his skin. He swiped his glove over his cheeks, which only made the pain worse. Blaming God for his shortcomings might not have been wise. Max rushed out from under the trees and kept to the side of the road. Some days it didn't pay to leave the trailer.

When he finally reached Gladys's 1960's single-level dwelling, everything looked dark inside. Was the power off? Nah, street lights were on. She must be napping. He grabbed the shovel leaning against the back porch he'd used many times, then went to work clearing steps and walkways. Good thing he'd braved the storm. If Gladys had walked out onto the icy steps, she might have fallen.

He scraped the shovel against the broken sidewalk and heaved mounds of snow into a pile. His hands ached from the bitter cold, but he kept working.

Wouldn't Season be surprised to find out how many doors he knocked on this winter, asking if folks needed help with shoveling or hauling groceries? He never accepted payment for his services either. She didn't need to know about the food he purchased for his needier stops. Or how small kindnesses appeased his gnawing regrets.

Better that than railing at God. Or hurling a sledgehammer through the trailer's windows. His dad really should have hauled that thing to the dump years back. It needed more money in remodeling than it was worth. Still, for now, it was home. He should be grateful for a roof over their heads.

He shoveled the path toward Gladys's back door. The light

over the porch was either off or burned out. He'd have to check into that after he had a chance to look at his incoming texts and messages.

He shoveled the sidewalk in front of her house. *Scoop. Throw.* If only he could shovel away heartache as easily. If he could go back one year and do everything differently, he would. Like fire Derek and Lee from the council. Seemed they'd been troublemakers for years.

He scraped off the porch steps, glad the wind had died down a little. Maybe this was his true purpose. Serving where he could. When he finished here, he'd stop by a couple of houses on the way home.

He returned the shovel to its designated spot, then rapped three loud knocks on Gladys's door. Due to her hearing loss, they had a system. He'd knock three times. Repeat. If she didn't answer by the third round, he'd grab the key from under the pet rock one of her great-grandkids painted and open the door.

After knocking the right amount of times, he scrounged under the rock. He'd done this before, but he always felt weird entering her home uninvited. "Gladys?" he called into the kitchen. "Mrs. Iris? This is Pastor, um, Max Prescott."

"With only three payments of nineteen ninety-five, you'll be the proud owner of this classic dome clock." Max recognized the salesman's voice booming in the living room. *He'd* wanted one of those clocks.

"Anybody home?" Why was it so cold? Had the furnace gone out?

He removed his boots and left them on the rubber mat just inside the door. Mrs. Iris didn't like snow tracked onto her floors. He shuffled across the kitchen linoleum in his wool socks, then rounded the corner ready to say something cheerful or witty. Instead, he found Gladys slumped over in her recliner, her head tipped to her left, mouth open wide, afghan cuddled to her chin, sleeping so soundly she wasn't snoring. *Wait.* Was she asleep? Or—? "Mrs. Iris?" He rushed to her side. "Gladys?" He shook her hand. Cold to the touch. *Oh, no.* He pressed his fingers against the vein on her wrist. No pulse. Her neck? The same. *Oh, God, no.* "Don't call her home just yet."

Too late. It seemed she'd departed this world, maybe hours ago. Had her frail heart given out?

He yanked his cell phone from his pocket and punched in 911.

"This is Max Prescott. I entered Gladys Iris's home at 3501 Tenth Street, and she's unresponsive. Elderly. Appears to be ... dead." He blew out a tired breath. This wasn't the first time he'd seen a lifeless body. But he hated finding someone who passed from this world to the next, alone. He should have been here. Might have, if not for his turmoil earlier in the day. "What should I do?"

"Mr. Prescott, I'm dispatching an emergency team right now. Remain where you are and hold the line, please."

"I will."

Gladys, you were a classy lady. I'm going to miss you.

"Is the door unlocked?"

"Yes, ma'am."

"Paramedics should arrive in approximately four minutes."

"Thank you." Fortunately, Darby had its own ambulance service.

He turned off the TV, then paced the narrow space between the kitchen and living room, thinking of the kindly woman he'd enjoyed visiting over the years.

The wail of the ambulance alerted him four minutes had passed. Keeping the line open, he walked into the living room and rested his hand on Gladys's shoulder, praying for her one more time just in case a breath of life could be found.

If she'd gone home to be with Jesus, she wouldn't want to come back. Her husband, Peter, was in Heaven. A daughter too, if he remembered correctly. He sighed with regret and resignation.

Glancing around the open space, he noticed tidy stacks of papers and magazines on the dinner table that he'd seen a hundred times before. Gladys said her table was her office, and she'd explained the piles. Magazines. Correspondence. Outgoing. Recyclable. She had been a secretary in her early years, and it seemed the organizational habit stuck.

Above the stacks, a large portrait of her and her husband spanned the wall. A decade ago, Max prayed with Gladys's husband on his deathbed, then conducted his funeral. Who in town other than him would mourn Gladys's life? She did have a brother. Barkley? Barton? Something like that. Several grandchildren lived on the East Coast.

The siren's wail grew insistent. Max flung open the door. Two young men dressed in matching navy EMT uniforms rushed into the house with serious faces, their bags ready.

Max pointed to the living room. "I think she's gone. She took heart medicine."

The first man strode into the other room. The second guy nodded once before following him.

Max told the operator the paramedics arrived, ended the call, then dropped onto the chair at the table where Gladys used to serve him tea and fresh-out-of-the-oven oatmeal cookies. He'd miss her friendship, hospitality, and her ability to accept others as they were—including him. He glanced at the papers and magazines. An envelope lay askew on the outgoing pile. He leaned closer. *Pastor Max.* Addressed to him? How kind of her to still consider him a minister.

What was in the envelope? A prayer request? Sermon idea? Was it possible she knew she was dying and hadn't confided in him? That hurt. He would have insisted someone stay with her, if he knew. Maybe that's why she didn't tell him. Didn't want to be a burden. He would have gladly spent those last hours with her, hearing her stories, singing, or praying—whatever she wanted.

With a sigh that burned upward from his lungs, he grabbed the business envelope and stared at his name written in Gladys's broken script. He pictured her grandmotherly face.

Voices reached him from the other room. One of the paramedics talked on his cell phone, apparently giving directions to the coroner.

Gladys really was gone.

He ran his index finger down the backside of the envelope and pulled out the single piece of notebook paper.

Dear Pastor.

Would anyone call him that again?

You're a good man.

He sighed.

A loving pastor.

If so, why did all those people leave his church? Would his wife have gone to a marriage conference without him if he were so loving?

A faithful son. (I think of you as my son in his absence.)

That's right—Gladys's son died in Vietnam. Man, this felt strange reading her words when she'd left this life such a short time ago.

I have something on my heart to say to you.

He gulped.

Please accept these words with all the love they're given. I care so much for you and your wife.

His wife?

"Is there anyone we should call?" The man who seemed in charge of the emergency stood under the archway between the living room and kitchen holding his hat. "Family members? Friends? I'm Mike, by the way."

Max lowered the letter. "She has a brother. I can't recall his name. Check her cell phone for a man's name beginning with B."

"Looks like she's been gone for several hours." Mike ran his hand over his buzz-cut hair, then positioned his hat on his head again. "The coroner will be here any minute."

Max nodded. "She was alone in this world. Other than me and a few church people who stopped by occasionally. Grandkids live a long way away."

"You can go now." Mike swayed his hand toward the door. "You're a neighbor, right?"

"Friend. Was ... her pastor."

"Oh, I didn't recognize you in the dim lighting." The younger guy rocked his thumb at himself. "Rich Palmer. Remember me? I used to attend youth group. Mom made me go." He grinned like he'd told a joke.

Max's face felt too broken to smile. Rich didn't look familiar. But ten years had probably passed. He remembered his mother, Violet Palmer. Always wore paisley dresses. "Attending services anywhere?" The same question he'd asked people a thousand times. It was hard to shed his pastoral concern.

"At Living Faith Center."

"Oh, sure." Along with the other members of Max's former congregation. "Your mom?"

"She's fine. Had a bout with cancer last fall." Rich shrugged. "Now that she's feeling better, she attends with me and my brood."

"I'm glad her health is improving."

"Thanks."

The paramedics returned to the living room. Max remained

at the table. He lifted the piece of notebook paper to the light to finish Gladys's letter.

I don't know what went wrong at our church.

That made two of them.

You and I never talked about the church closing. Why was that?

Because he enjoyed knowing one person who treated him as if he weren't a failure. He could be himself with her. Like how he felt as a kid hanging out with his grandmother.

I'm going to be blunt. I sense something is wrong between you and Season. You don't reveal much about yourself, do you? I'm sorry for not having this conversation in person. But I fear I don't have much time left.

So she had known her time was short. He emptied his lungs on a long sigh as that confirmation settled in.

I was married to Peter for sixty years. I know about marital troubles that weigh on your mind. But here's my two cents of advice.

He was tempted to stuff the letter in his pocket. Read it later. Next year, maybe. But knowing these were Gladys's last words to him compelled him to keep reading.

Max, my friend, whatever you must do to make things right with your wife, do that. Be humble. Confess wrongs. Apologize. Your life will be sweeter with her in it. Alone can seem like forever. I know.

Alone. He already hated that feeling. He'd closed himself off. Protected himself. Season too, he'd thought. He knew he let her down. But couldn't she see he needed time to muddle through the sludge? Then he'd face life again, hopefully, with her at his side. Of course, if he explained that instead of hiding in his moodiness, she might have been more understanding. If he were the kind of man who could expose his heart, share his deepest heartaches, everything might not hurt so badly either. But like father, like son. His dad had been the brooding type. Not that Max wanted to be like him. Heaven forbid. And he dearly hoped he hadn't passed on that trait to his sons.

He folded the single sheet and tucked it inside the envelope.

Gladys would never need her sidewalks cleared again. Wouldn't need him delivering soup or toilet paper. Emptiness spread through every sinew.

Whatever you must do to make things right, do that.

Like him telling Season he loved her? Like him going to that wretched conference? Even if he wanted to, how could he get there? Driving his beater truck was out of the question. Renting a vehicle cost too much right now.

When the coroner arrived, Max placed Mrs. Iris's letter in his jacket pocket, pulled on his gloves, and left the house that held such fond memories.

Had he still been pastor of Darby Community Church, he would have prepared a lovely memorial. Who would do the honors in his place? Probably someone her brother chose.

There was nothing he could do now, other than go and help someone else with snow removal. Physical work might ease the guilt Gladys's letter stirred up and appease the worry he felt over not being able to reach his wife.

He checked his cell. No calls or texts from her. He tapped a quick note asking Season to call him, then he went back out into the storm.

Seven

Season

"Edelweiss" playing on her cell awakened her. Strange, considering she'd had intermittent cell coverage ever since she reached Hart's Camp. She stretched in the lower bunk and debated answering. Last night, Josh told them not to expect reliable cell service or Wi-Fi at the campground. He encouraged everyone to turn off their mobile devices, so married couples could focus on each other, but she didn't want to shut down her phone, in case of an emergency. She tapped the screen to see who was calling.

Husband.

She groaned. Was she ready to talk to him?

She glanced through the cabin window and noticed a crystal blue sky. Quite the contrast to yesterday's storm. And a perfect day for sledding. She grinned in anticipation of the outdoor event.

"Edelweiss" played again.

She probably shouldn't ignore him. She slid her finger over the surface to answer. "Yes, Max?"

"I see you're safe." He spoke in a tight voice.

"I am." She snuggled the comforter up to her neck in the twin bed, wishing she banked the fire last night. It took a lot of wood to keep a cabin built for eight campers warm. Summer had apologized to the couples about not having full-sized beds. During the summer months, their cabins accommodated groups of eight campers each. But for the marriage retreat, she said couples could push two bunk beds together to form a bigger bed if they wanted.

"I wish you were here with me." The words popped out before she censored them. At least if Max were here, he'd keep the woodstove going. However, she doubted she'd use the double-bed setup, even then.

Dead silence.

"I asked you to call." Why was he so grumpy?

She was the one who drove nearly three-hundred miles, alone, through a horrible storm. The one whose husband was accused of having an illegitimate child with a former parishioner. In fact, she had reasons to be burning mad.

"Don't you think I'd want to know you arrived safely?"

"Sure. And I think you should have come with me." And that he shouldn't have been hanging out with Jayme in the first place.

"Maybe you should have stayed here." His words ignited her anger.

Or I could be on my way to Boise to see the boys. No way would she let him make her feel guilty for not staying home and watching their lives deteriorate. For not wanting to be at the library where people might stare at her with pitiful glances and whispers about Jayme and her baby. At least she was doing something positive for herself. She took a deep breath. "Last night I was busy meeting people and registering. The cell service is bad here, especially with the inclement weather." Her voice softened. "We had a cool prayer time, asking God to transform our lives and marriages. Stuff like that." Did he even care? "Everyone else had their spouse with them." With his silence, her frustration rose again. Did he only call to appease his conscience? She might as well end his misery. "Thanks for calling, Max."

Silence.

"Max?"

"Gladys Iris died last night."

"What? Oh, no." She choked over the sudden dryness in her throat. "I'm so sorry." The woman had been one of her favorites in Darby. She'd never acted judgmental or unkind to anyone that Season knew of. On many occasions, Mrs. Iris hugged her and wished her well. "She was one of the best."

"I know."

"I'm sorry you had to face that alone." She waited, thinking he might say he wished she were there with him. After twenty-two years of marriage, wouldn't he want his wife by his side?

"I just called to check on you—since you didn't call me."

Why would I call when you only make me feel worse? She almost answered with the bitter retort. Instead, she bit the inside of her cheek to keep quiet.

"Have fun this week. You deserve it." His kinder words surprised her.

"Thanks." It sounded like he didn't have any intention of joining her. "Max—" No use begging. "I'm praying for you."

"Thank you."

She couldn't let the conversation go without adding something else. "I still think we need this conference. Both of us, together." A truth pinged in her heart—she wanted something more for their marriage. But what kind of hold-on-tight fight would it take? And did she have the courage to hang on after all they'd been through?

"*You* have the car." His pointed words irked her.

"And *you* have the truck." Yet she knew his truck had problems. "You could rent a car."

"Probably not."

Hopes dashed. "Thanks for calling."

"What are you doing today?" Thinking the call was finished, she almost didn't hear him.

"Sledding, if you can believe it." She masked her enthusiasm. No use gloating over anticipated fun while he mourned the loss of his parishioner. "Something about becoming childlike. Letting go. Silly at my age, right?" If only he'd disagree and say something about her still being youthful, even though she was in her mid-forties. How many years had it been since he called her beautiful? "You only live once, right?" Too glib given his circumstances? "I'd have more fun with you here, *husband*." She held her breath a moment. She'd taken an emotional risk in calling him that. Would the nickname bring back good memories in him?

He snorted as if he couldn't fathom them having fun together ever again.

Why did she hold on to false hope that romance was still possible between them? When did he stop feeling attracted to her? She still maintained a thin waist, had decent skin, wore makeup and nice clothes. The last time she looked in the mirror she hadn't grown hairy warts. She sighed.

"I'm also going to learn how to paint." Last night, she'd been undecided between attending Summer's class on acrylic painting for beginners, or Gar and Autumn's theater ministry group. Today, she couldn't imagine passing up an art class.

"Sounds like a full week. I'd better let you get to it."

"Max, I wish—"

"I know." He ended the call.

She held the phone to her forehead. Was there anything she could do to reach him? He probably thought her attending this conference alone was foolhardy. And maybe it was. But what of their marriage vows? Shouldn't figuring out how to fix their relationship take priority in their lives? Maybe he was the one acting the fool, not her.

However, it did little good to sit here begrudging his attitude and wishing for things that couldn't be. Today was a new day with exciting things to do—like sledding and painting. After saying a quick prayer for inner healing, she muted her cell. Max probably wouldn't call again anyway. She hopped out of bed and grabbed her extra-warm clothes before heading to the lodge for more of that fabulous coffee.

* * * *

Her first time down the slope on the four-foot toboggan, Season sat in front of Autumn, squealing and laughing most of the way. But near the bottom of the incline, they suddenly veered left and, out of control, crash-landed into a giant cedar tree. The impact jarred them harshly and sent Season tumbling into the snowbank, face first. For a moment, she gasped in nothingness. Suffocating seemed a possibility until her survival instincts kicked in, and she shoved her hands against the snow. Her gloved hands sank a foot before she reached something solid enough to give her leverage. She made her way to a standing position, coughing and spitting. She sucked in a deep breath, grateful for air, and that nothing felt broken.

Next to her, Autumn leaned over coughing, her hands on her knees.

"You okay?" Season wiped snow from her face as best she could with wet mittens.

Autumn groaned, then nodded.

Season dusted snowflakes off her shoulders and arms. "That was unreal. And scary."

"I know what you mean."

She met Autumn's gaze, and in the next second, they were

laughing and somehow crying too, then laughing some more. Would their teardrops form icicles? She scrubbed her mitten across her face. "Crashing into the tree could have been really dangerous."

"I know."

Season grabbed her knitted cap that had fallen and hit it against her snow pants. "But I guess we accomplished our homework in becoming childlike."

"I think so. You all right?"

"Yes." She laughed, although her face burned as if she exfoliated with sandpaper. "Was I leaning the wrong direction?"

"I have no idea. Sorry about that." Autumn shrugged. "I couldn't control the beast."

"Let's try it again!"

"Are you kidding?" Autumn's jaw dropped.

"I had fun. Why not go again?" She nodded toward the peak of the snow-covered trail they'd descended in a blur. "If we were kids, we wouldn't stop because of a minor disaster." She'd been a spunky child, willing to try all sorts of things— including toboggan racing with her brother Todd on Peets Hill, which was fondly referred to as "Hospital Hill"—a popular sledding site in Bozeman. Anything her brother could do, she could too.

"You're right, but"—the Seattleite rubbed her right hip— "I'm going to feel that crash for a few days." Her eyes squinted toward the slope like she was pondering her willingness to take another risk. "Okay. You're on. You steer this time."

"All right!" Season grabbed the towrope and dragged the sled up the snowy incline. Her thigh muscles tightened as she tromped the mountainside. Her breath made steamy puffs in the crisp air. Her lungs hurt. But she was determined to make it to the top. She was stronger than this mountain. Tougher than wimping out after a crash. She'd sled down this hill however many times it took to make it to the bottom without a collision. Right then, the slope became symbolic of every hardship and difficulty she experienced in the last year—including her problems with Max—and she'd conquer all or die trying!

She'd forgotten how exhilarating it felt to zoom down a slope at such high speeds. The wind whipping her cheeks. To let herself go and not worry about what others thought of her.

Why hadn't she and Max ever gone sledding together? Or played together? What would their lives have been like if they'd had more fun as a couple? What if the next time Max saw her, he could see that she was different, more relaxed? Maybe they could have some great adventures together. Would he be open to that kind of change?

She picked up her knees a little higher as she frolicked along and sang a ditty about climbing up "snowy" mountain instead of "sunshine" mountain like she used to sing with the children in Sunday school.

Autumn laughed at her. But then she made up her own lyrics. "Turn your back on crashing. Get down the hill alive—!"

They both chortled and came up with other renditions.

"Look out!"

A sled barreled toward them.

"Yikes!" Season leaped into a mound of snow on the left side, yanking the sled with her.

"*Soooooooorrrrry!*" Josh lifted a gloved hand as he zipped past with a young girl—maybe four or five?—seated in front of him, cackling.

"Go, Daddy, go!" The girl's laughter trilled in the air.

Season lifted her hand, but the duo were already too far down the hill to notice. "Daddy?"

"That's his and Summer's daughter, Shua. He calls her 'Shua Day.' So sweet." A tender expression crossed Autumn's face. A yearning for motherhood?

"She's so cute." Season imagined Logan at that age. He'd ridden with his dad on a sled like that, both laughing and having fun, too. Where had the years gone?

Autumn stood from the pile of snow where she landed. "Jimmy would love this."

"My sons would be wild about snowboarding. I think I told you, they're college-aged." She made her way out of the deep snow. Her nose and ears felt frozen. Her side ached. It would be tempting to turn back. *No way.* She dragged the sled into the center of the hill and faced the peak. "I am going to beat you, mountain—and enjoy doing so!"

Autumn reached her and they trudged up the path in silence.

Then Season thought of something. "Shouldn't you be sledding with your husband?" She would wish that for her and Max if he were here and willing.

"I'd like to be with him." Autumn nudged her arm and chuckled. "He's preparing for his theater group." Her eyebrows rocked. "We'll try the hill later by ourselves."

Season was glad to know she wasn't intruding on their couple time. "He's a playwright?" That interested her since someone at the library had recently asked for help formatting a script.

"Wants to be." Autumn shrugged. "He used to teach drama but got fired. Now he's working in an athletic shop. I'm sure he'll write and direct again someday."

"You're into theater too?"

"Not as much as he is. But I enjoy it."

Season slipped on an icy section but caught herself from falling. "What about the girl at your house who's expecting? Are you related?"

"No. We're helping Sarah. We don't know how long she'll stay with us. But I can't wait to hold her baby. We know she's having a girl—Cassie Lynn. And I'm going to be Auntie

Autumn." A smile stretched across her face. "When school's over, we plan to sell our house. Maybe move to Montana."

"How exciting! We could be neighbors." Although, Montana was a wide state. And she didn't know how much longer she and Max would be in Darby. Strange, how even though she was angry with him, she wished he were here to experience this retreat with her.

"I'd like that." Autumn scooped up a handful of snow and pressed it in her hands. "I'm looking forward to tonight's seminar. I hear Ty and Winter are fabulous speakers."

"Me too. But I feel weird being here without my husband." She was glad she could express herself to this new friend who seemed to glow with some indefinable joy.

"Don't worry. No one is judging you." She tossed the snowball toward a clump of trees. "I think God has you here for a reason."

"Thanks. That's encouraging to hear."

At the top of the hill, she plopped down on the back of the sled ready to steer. Once Autumn sat in front, Season used her hands to shove off the packed snow. "Here we go!" Flakes flew in her face as the toboggan raced downhill. She peered through the splatters of snow and ice flying up, attempting to keep them centered on the incline. They passed another couple heading uphill as the sled skimmed downward like frosting slipping off a cake. All thoughts of Max or marital woes fled as she squealed and laughed.

Autumn cheered when they came to a natural stop at the bottom—without crashing. "That was amazing!"

"Woohoo! Let's go again."

"No," Autumn protested. "Let's go eat some fudge instead."

"Fudge? Where?"

"I forgot to tell you. I brought a container of double-layered fudge to share."

"Fudge and coffee? What could be better?" She grabbed hold of the towline and headed in the direction of the lodge. She could sled again another time.

A snowball hit Season's back. "What?" She whirled around and caught one in the cheek.

"Oops. Sorry. I was aiming for your shoulder!" Autumn cackled, but she was already forming another snowball.

"Now you did it." Season scooped up snow and made a half dozen snowballs. She flung them all rapid-fire at the other woman. But her shot was terrible. Autumn dodged every one of them, then returned an onslaught of ice bombs. Season leaped out of the way, but she still took a couple of hits. "Truce. I give."

Laughing, the two of them made their way to the lodge following the scent of fresh coffee. Season couldn't wait to try the fudge. She felt lighter than she had in—well, forever, it seemed.

Josh was right. Letting go, becoming childlike, was more freeing than anything else.

Eight

Season

When Season sat at her assigned table spread with art supplies during the afternoon session in the loft, she stared at the blank canvas with an equally empty feeling inside. Summer had encouraged them to paint with freedom and to not worry about the outcome. Then she suggested they might want to paint something symbolic of their marriages, since they were at a marriage conference. That's what had Season stumped. In the first place, she didn't know how to paint. Secondly, what could she possibly create that would represent her and Max's relationship? Black clouds over their RV? A bonfire burning up hopes and dreams? A bleeding broken heart? She shuddered.

She'd never boasted of natural artistic gifting. In high school art class, she had envied other students' talents and moaned over her inadequacies. And in recent years, the crafty ease of coworkers made her jealous.

But needing to put some sort of color on the canvas, she dabbed her brush into black and white acrylics and mixed them on her palette. Then swirling the dark gray slathered brush in a circular motion across the flat surface, she tried to replicate clouds. The result was more like a series of Hula Hoops with repeated blotches in their centers.

She leaned her forehead into her palm and moaned. Then realizing she probably just smeared gray paint over her skin, she wiped her clean-up cloth over the spot.

This was supposed to be relaxing? Freeing? Her shoulders were bunched tight. A throb pulsed in her neck. Her jaws were clenched. *Ugh.*

And why was she paired with Suzanne, a woman who had to be an award-winning artist at her table? "Snowflakes?" The lady aimed her brush at Season's speckled canvas.

"Not really." She glanced at the other woman's rendition of rose petals floating in a bowl of milk. "Nice work." She cleared her throat. "I was attempting clouds."

"Ahhh." Suzanne nodded, then continued painting, her eyes squinting at her canvas.

That's it? How about a little advice? Like what should she do next? Season swished her brush through a glob of blue. Maybe a stroke of color here? And there? *Oops.* Not the right choice.

She heard Summer offering praise about someone's painting at the next table. But Season didn't want the class leader commenting on her futile attempts. She flung a messy cloth over the canvas.

"What have we here?" Summer sounded too chipper.

"Nothing." Season groaned. "I think I'm giving up."

"Oh, please, don't do that." Her tone held no censure. "Remember to relax. It doesn't matter what the picture looks like. Think of it as play. Fun. Therapeutic."

Fun? *Hardly.*

"May I look?" Summer picked up the paint-splattered rag without waiting for an answer. Her eyes brightened. "It's a great start." She patted Season's shoulder. "Why don't you keep trying?"

"You mean, you can tell what it is?"

"That doesn't matter."

A polite way to say she couldn't tell?

"This is about expressing yourself." Summer gesticulated as she talked. "It's like dancing in the wind, your body free to move. Let your paintbrush do what it wants. No right or wrong. No rules. Just enjoyment."

For the record, Season liked rules. Color in the lines. Cook at such and such a degree. Drive the speed limit. She pointed at her neighbor's canvas where highlights made the rose petals almost sparkle. "*That's* right. I know what her painting represents." She jabbed her index finger at her own. "*This* is wrong."

"Not wrong." Again, with a gentle smile. "What were you hoping to recreate?"

"Storm clouds."

Summer nodded. "I can see that now. Why did you choose clouds?"

"Symbolism, I suppose." She shrugged. "I hoped they would be easy."

"And?"

"Clouds are harder to paint than I imagined." Kind of like marriage was harder than she'd thought it would be.

Summer gave her a sidearm hug. "Clouds do have a story to tell." She walked on to the next set of painters.

With a sigh, Season glanced at the table behind hers. One woman painted polka-dots. A man outlined a simplistic car—almost cartoonish—in black. At the next table, Missy splattered purple and white splotches all over her canvas as if she were spreading confetti. By the grin on her face, she was enjoying herself. No one criticized anyone. Season picked up the one-inch wide brush and cleaned it meticulously. How about starting over? A do-over? Was that symbolic too? As in, her starting over with Max? She gulped. Did she want that to happen?

She plunged the paintbrush bristles in white, then more aggressively than before, she streaked it back and forth, covering over all the previous shapes. She needed a clean surface again. If only marriage reconciliation were as easy as swishing paint across a canvas.

* * * *

At the evening session, Josh stood in front of the group of twenty couples and Season with a grave expression replacing his usual grin. "I'm sorry to have to tell you, Winter and Ty have been detained."

Groans followed his announcement.

Disappointment rustled through her too. She had had a fabulous day of sledding and visiting with Autumn. And her painting improved when Suzanne, the artsy woman next to her, gave her a couple of pointers for adding realism. But tonight, she was ready for some serious how-to-fix-a-broken-marriage wisdom. Some of the couples here—like Autumn and Gar, or Summer and Josh—had found love with each other again. But what were the chances she and Max could do the same when he wasn't present? She didn't think it was possible unless both partners were willing to give it a try.

And what was he doing now? Attempting to calm down the gossipmongers from spreading Jayme's lie? Or hiding out, watching television in the RV?

Josh continued his explanation by telling how Winter and Ty were involved in a legal matter in Bend, Oregon. Something about a woman in jail, and how they needed to see her before heading north. They'd reach Hart's Camp the following day, God willing. Not a terrible wait. Still, Season felt impatient to get on with the meat of the conference.

She thought of Summer's words from this morning. What had she meant when she said her marriage had been trans-formed by the love of God? Season remembered when she first pulled into the camp and asked Josh if all men were as stubborn as Max. What had he answered? Something about him being the worst before God radically changed him. The two of them must have come a long way to seem as happy as they did now.

She and Max had served God since their teen years. They both believed in prayer. Both were trusting God to see them through the difficult days. Yet, given their constant disagreements, could they have missed something?

The young musician took up his guitar. *Oh good.* She'd been anticipating hearing him sing and play. When he led the group in worship songs, she joined in and sang all the lyrics she knew. She appreciated the leader's tender spirit as he closed his eyes, strummed his guitar strings, and sang to the Lord. His songs were like whispered prayers. The tears on his cheeks made her think he truly believed in the words he was singing. *I surrender all to You. Make me new again—so I can live free.*

Free. That idea kept popping up in songs and lectures and activities. She'd never thought about her service to God and her love for Him having anything to do with being free. As a pastor's wife, there'd been many rules and expectations. *Be a good leader, support Max, listen to congregants, show up to everything, never speak unkindly, raise kids who weren't rebellious and never caused embarrassment.* She tried her best to live circumspectly. Even when she felt sick or emotionally unwell, she stiffened her spine and pasted on a smile. She made a deliberate effort to be polite at church and in public. She'd stood by her husband through all the garbage. Respected his church council—to their faces, anyway. Kept hurts and grudges to herself. Didn't complain around the boys. She rarely shared her true feelings, even with Max. Yet something ugly had been simmering in her, she couldn't deny it. Anger, for sure. But something else she didn't want to identify, because to do so would name the blackest sin she may have allowed into her heart.

Tightness pinched her neck. Her stomach clenched. Freedom sounded more appealing by the second.

When the singing ended, Gar's acting troupe strode to the front of the lodge and lined up, a few at each side. Gar and Autumn and three other couples held scripts, making her think of a radio broadcast in the '30s.

The lights dimmed. Autumn walked to the middle of the impromptu stage. "*Marriage Disaster* by Gar Bevere."

A marriage disaster sounded familiar.

Season's sledding buddy strode off stage.

A man and a woman she hadn't met walked toward each other, one from the left, the other from the right. The darkness, the lack of sound, their cold gazes aimed away from each other, set a somber tone. Slowly they crossed the platform, then passed each other without speaking.

"Marriage disaster," a voice sounding like Gar's said from the right side.

Another couple—Randal and Bev, who Season met during the coffee and fudge break—walked center stage, both with a brown mug extended in their hands. They grimaced at each other, almost snarling. Tense music played from a speaker. Other actors hurried to Randal and Bev with empty cups out-stretched in their hands. Suddenly, the couple's expressions transformed. They giggled and chatted with everyone while pouring water into all the other cups. The actors left the stage, leaving the couple alone. Randal extended his cup toward Bev, one eyebrow arched in question. She tipped over her cup and shook it—empty. He did the same. Then they walked away in opposite directions.

The room went dark.

"Marriage disaster."

The words hit her like a mallet against a gong. For years, Max gave most of his time and effort to his congregation. She and the boys lived without him around a lot. Oh, they hadn't been completely neglected. But hadn't he expected her to be understanding of his limited hours? Loyal even? And she had been for such a long time. But like the skit, hers and Max's cups were bare and dry now. They had nothing left for each other.

A chill settled in her chest as she watched a few more skits, all pertaining to unavailability in marriage. The ache in her heart grew.

After the dramas, Josh spoke for about ten minutes. He said he wasn't much of a speaker, but she would argue against that. He seemed a natural as he strummed the guitar softly while he shared. She found herself tearing up when he talked about how he felt after he'd returned to Hart's Camp following a five-year absence. How he'd come home to make amends with his uncle and aunt, only to find Summer Day living and working here. How he'd been drawn to her like a flower to sunshine. And when he'd met Shua? His heart had melted into a puddle of regret for the years he'd missed.

Tears flooded her eyes. *No crying in front of anyone.* Maybe she had a mint or a piece of gum. She searched her purse for anything to distract her.

The most poignant moment came when Josh sang a love song dedicated to Summer. Hearing the lyrics he wrote about the woman who knew his heart, the one who made him a "better man," Season doubted there was a dry eye in the place. She brushed her own waterworks away.

After the final "amen," she grabbed her coat and hurried out the door to be alone and contemplate everything she'd heard. Trudging through the fresh layer of snow to her cabin, a giant knot of suppressed emotion built in her chest. She ached from the weight of it. If she was this troubled after one evening session, what would the rest of the week be like?

Nine

Max

A sudden pounding at the door awakened Max from a sound sleep. A nightmare? He pried his eyelids open. Looked around, listened. Still dark. Silent. He scrubbed his hand over his face. Closed his eyes.

The pounding came again like thunder.

Who in the world was at his door at—he grabbed his cell phone off the built-in end table—five in the morning?

The next series of knocks rattled the walls.

"Okay, okay. I'm coming." He leaped to his feet, not pausing to grab socks or slippers. Realizing he was only in boxers, he searched for his sweatpants.

Hard rapping vibrated the windows. Someone sure was impatient.

"Just a sec!" He stomped to the door and swung it open. "Yeah, what do you—"

Clint Ebbs, his ex-council member, scrambled into the trailer and slammed the door faster than he would have imagined the late-sixties guy could move. He leaned a trembling hand against the wall as if to support himself.

"Clint?"

Several hard gasps later, the man clutched his chest. Was he having a heart attack?

"What's wrong?" Max shouted. Should he call 911?

Clint peered around the room as if expecting something to leap out at him. He grabbed Max's upper arms, his fingers shaking around Max's biceps. "Two thugs in black cl-lothes." Clint's teeth chattered. "After you next. I h-had to warn you b-before I left town."

"What?" Max's heartbeat ramped up a notch. "What do you mean?" He peeled apart two blinds over the sink and stared into the inky darkness.

He flicked on the light. Then shut it off. Best if whoever was out there didn't see their shadows. Clint had already made enough noise to wake up the whole trailer court. And Max shouted too. By the stove's overhead light, he got a better look at the older man. Black eye. Sallow cheeks. Dried blood and a torn gash near his lip.

"Goodness, what happened to you? Who did this?" While Clint Ebbs could state his opinions in a decidedly rude manner, Max knew him to be a non-violent fellow. "Should we call the police?"

"No." Clint moaned and buckled over, gripping his stomach. "They said if I did, they'd come after me again."

Max clutched his elbows, stopping him from collapsing. He helped Clint to the dining booth, where the man dissolved onto the cushioned bench as if he couldn't stand another second.

"Need water? Aspirin?" What else should Max do to help his former parishioner who'd shunned his aid in the past?

Clint grimaced. "I can't pay. No matter what they say. I don't got that kind of money." He grabbed Max's sweatshirt sleeve. "I'd help if I could."

Max knew Clint and Eloise lived meagerly in an old farmhouse between Darby and Hamilton that had been in Clint's family for a century. "What's going on?" Was he in financial trouble? "Is Eloise okay?" Concern for Clint's wife—who had a kinder disposition than her husband—filled him. "Where is she now? You didn't leave her on the farm alone, did you?" Whoever had hurt him could come back.

"I dropped her off at her sister's place." Clint wiped his hand over his face.

"Good. Now, who exactly can't you pay? And why would they come after me?" Max resisted the urge to peer through the window again.

Clint pressed his lips together. Then he broke into a sob. "I can't b-believe this happened."

This was all too weird. Other than patting the man's shoulder and waiting for him to explain, what could Max do? Maybe Clint could use a drink of water. Max opened the miniature fridge. He grabbed a plastic bottle, twisted off the lid, and handed Clint the container. "Drink this." He found a Kleenex box in the bathroom and stuffed several tissues in the other man's hand.

Clint sniffled and wiped his nose, then drank from the water bottle. "We're in big trouble, Pastor."

Pastor? The former council member who'd helped Max get fired was calling him Pastor?

"Worse trouble than ever, I wager." He covered his face with his hands. "The four of us on the church council are doomed. Dead, if they have their way."

Dead? Someone was coming after Clint, Derek, Lee, and Max? Was Clint crazy? Had he crashed his four-wheeler, and maybe was hallucinating? Or could he be serious? Max swallowed hard. He'd argued with his share of council members, but no one had ever physically harmed him because of it. Good thing Season wasn't here. "What do you mean 'dead?' And what does this have to do with me? I don't work at Darby Community anymore."

"The Barrister brothers don't know that." His wide gaze darted left and right. His shoulders hunched forward, and he looked like a shriveled up old man. "They could be outside listening right now."

"You mean the Mob from up north?" Max had heard rumors about ruffians and money laundering. But he never took the stories seriously. After all, this was Darby.

"And their henchmen." Clint nodded.

The whole thing sounded ridiculous. Yet, of all three of the other guys on the church council, Clint had been the most straightforward, even wise some of the time. Tremors ran a marathon through Max's spine. Were bad guys waiting to beat him up as they'd done to Clint? If so, why?

The older man's hands shook so violently the plastic container missed his lips on his next slurp. Water splattered against his skin and dripped down his chin. He scrubbed the back of his hand across what had to be a very sore mouth.

"Tell me who did this." Max slid into the other side of the booth and faced Clint, taking in his gaunt features. The two of them had never gotten along well. Yet seeing him broken down and bruised tugged on Max's compassion.

Did I lock the door? That thought made him jump up and rush to secure the lock. Although, if someone wanted in badly enough, all they had to do was break the narrow window to the side of the doorframe. Where was that bat he used to have when the boys were home? Probably at Goodwill with their other stuff. He returned to the table, wondering if he should call the police despite Clint's reticence. First, he'd get information. "From the beginning, what happened?"

"Lee." Clint mumbled.

"Lee beat you up?" The most upstanding member of Darby Community Church pummeling Clint Ebbs?

"No, but he caused the mess." Clint coughed. "His son has troubles."

Max was aware of Lincoln's leukemia treatments, followed by drug abuse and rehab. But what did that have to do with criminal activity?

"Lee did something bad." Clint grabbed more tissue from the box on the table and wiped blood from beneath his nose. "Went off the deep end. Money problems. Business failure. His son's terrible health. Then stealing."

"Stealing?"

Clint groaned. "I used to consider that man my friend. No more. He turned his back on us. Used being church treasurer to pad his pockets."

"What? No way." Lee was a trusted businessman in the community and in the church.

"Watching a kid die can make you do crazy things." Clint's eyes got buggy again.

"Sure, but—" Max tossed up his hands. When would Clint get to the point?

"I heard rumors about you too."

The change in topic confused Max.

Clint's eyes squinted. Judge and jury right there.

"About?"

"Do I have to spell it out?"

Jayme. "You heard about that, huh? Well, it's not true." Max's voice rose.

"Figured not. But Derek will be blazing mad. Got coffee?" Clint changed topics faster than the weather in spring. He wagged his thumb toward the kitchenette.

"How about you explain first?" Max wanted the story now.

"Coffee will w-warm me up." His teeth chattered. "S-so cold." Was he going into shock?

"Okay, fine." In two steps Max was at the sink making coffee in his bare feet. The cold penetrating the floor made him wish for his wool socks.

"You actually live in this shoebox?"

"Yep." At least they owned it. He flipped the heat switch farther right. The furnace rumbled.

"Where's the wife?" Clint peered around the room as if she might materialize any second.

Max poured water in the coffeepot. "Away." No need to explain.

"Huh." The guy's beady expression said a lot. Despite his miserable condition, he was itching for information about the pastor's life.

But Max wasn't a pastor now. His problems and trials were his own business. Not speculation for his uptight ex-councilman.

He put two scoops of coffee in the top portion of the machine, flipped the On switch, then went in search of a blanket. Locating a throw, he spread it over the man's shoulders. He opened the small freezer and grabbed a bag of frozen veggies. He handed it to Clint, then he dropped onto his side of the booth. "Now for the love of Pete, will you tell me everything?"

Clint clutched the bag to his upper cheek. "You and I have our differences."

"That's the truth." Max didn't soften his response.

"Here's something we can agree on—Lee threw us under the bus." Clint glared. "He's worse than a rattler."

"What did he do?" Max leaned forward, his elbows braced against the table.

Clint glanced up at the ceiling. Tears filled his eyes. From pain? Or sorrow over whatever Lee had done? Other than the purplish bruising, his face appeared pasty green.

"You okay? I could drive you to the ER in your truck."

"I'll be fine after coffee. Been years since I got my jaw clobbered." He ran his hand over his whiskered chin and winced.

It was hard to see the older man in pain, tough geezer that he was. But back to the topic. "Are you implying Lee stole from the church?" Lee had been treasurer because of his honesty and integrity.

The skin beneath Clint's eyes creased into a deep scowl. "Remember Lincoln had cancer last year? Radiation, chemo, complications? Almost died. Spent extra time in the hospital. Then rehab."

"I remember." That had to have cost a bundle. "But Lee stealing from the congregation?"

"A fellow will do almost anything to take care of his kid. He said we'd do the same." Clint shook his head. "That the church would have to understand. C-coffee ready?"

"Well, I don't understand!" Max shoved away from the table. "Cream?"

"Black." Clint snorted. "Real men take it black."

"Oh, right." How many times had Max heard him mockingly say that? He poured a double splash of french vanilla creamer into his own cup—pretty much out of spite. He was a *real* man with or without creamer.

He plunked the hot cup of coffee down in front of Clint. The man set the frozen bag on the table. Then his trembling fingers circled the mug like a lock.

Dropping onto his side of the booth again, Max sipped his own brew and waited. "So—?"

"So Lee borrowed money from a loan shark last fall to pacify the bill collectors hounding him over the medical debts." Clint seemed to shrivel into his flannel shirt. "Enter the Barristers."

"Bad idea. And—?"

"Thugs came after him to collect. Threatened to do him and his wife harm." Clint's Adam's apple bobbed. "So he sticky-fingered church funds to pay off part of his debt."

"And you went along with this?" Max slammed his hand against the table. Then he tensed, worried the sound might have been heard outside. "How could he do this?" He lowered his voice. "How could you?"

"Me? Now you're talking crazy. I just found out." He rocked his thumb toward his black eye. "I called Lee after my early morning visitors left. Said he planned to pay back every penny."

Sure he did. A conversation when Max disagreed with Lee's presentation of bank figures came to mind. "So that's why Lee's numbers were off." He couldn't believe it. "He said I was a reprobate when it came to finances. That I was too blind to be a pastor or lead effectively."

"Things didn't add up for a reason." Clint took a long swallow of coffee.

"It wasn't my fault." Relief and pain dueled inside him, setting his nerves on edge. Not that his being absolved changed anything. Wasn't he in worse trouble now? Yet he felt a sense of satisfaction. There'd been underhanded scheming in the church's downfall. The rotting stench wasn't all his doing.

"Maybe not *that* part." Clint threw one of his piercing glares.

Max wouldn't go down that road. "This thing reeks of illegal activity." He stood quickly. "Let's go talk to Lee. Make him confess to both of us. We'll get the police involved."

"Can't." Clint's sober gaze deadpanned with Max's. "He's already gone. And I told you what those brutes said."

"Where is he?"

"Emptied their house. Left in the night." Clint shrugged. "Gone to Canada, I figure."

Max dropped back into his seat. "And the thugs?"

"Demanding repayment—from us."

"Why us?" Had his voice squealed like a girl's?

Clint leaned in, squinted his eyes. "Lee gave them some lame excuse about the church not coughing up what it owed him—mainly you, me, and Derek."

"Lies."

"I know. But they'll be coming after you."

Acid burned up his ribs. What could he do? Hitch up the trailer and flee to Season? The two of them could make a run for southern states incognito. And the boys? Would the bad guys come after them too? How was he going to get out of this mess?

"What now?" He wouldn't run. But he wasn't going to stay in his trailer, a sitting duck, waiting for gang members—or whoever they were—to come after him.

"They threatened to take my farm. Do Eloise harm." Clint linked his fingers together. "We're hightailing it out of town."

"No, Clint, we've got to stick together and fight this thing." Max had to think of something. "We can't let Lee get away with stealing."

"He already did." The farmer's mouth puckered like he was chewing on the inside of his cheek. "Never thought I'd lose everything because of the church."

"Not because of the church. Because of Lee."

Clint pulled a battered envelope from his coat pocket, slid it across the table. "To make matters worse, according to this bank letter, the church council—including you—are responsible for all the church's debts until the unincorporated building sells. We're six months behind."

"I thought four."

"Lee's doing." The older man's eyes narrowed. "Your name's listed first."

Max grabbed the letter. He adjusted the paper to read it better in the dim light.

Due to the six-month delinquency on the Darby Community Church loan, and per the loan agreement, the following trustees are responsible for the entirety of the delinquency: Maxwell Prescott, Derek Clark, Clint Ebbs, Lee Thomas. All monies borrowed, including legal fees, must be paid in full. The trustees will be held accountable for all unpaid debt.

All? That could ruin him and Clint. Derek had money. But now, he'd hate Max for not only reportedly fathering his grandchild, but for allowing loan sharks and the bank to come after him.

Clint was right about Max's name being at the top of the list. "You were supposed to take my name off this official document when you fired me."

"Lee's task." His graying eyebrows drew together. "What now, Pastor?" That time his use of the term sounded derogatory.

"As you know, I am no longer the pastor of Darby Community Church." For the first time, Max was relieved. Let the bank come after the rest of them. He was ready to abandon the RV, rent a car, and go find his wife. She'd been talking about them pulling up stakes and moving to Boise. Maybe now was a perfect time.

Clint's nose protruded farther across the small table. "Fact is"—he shuffled on the bench—"seems you're more responsible."

Max nearly dropped his cup. Hot coffee sloshed onto his sweatpants. "How do you figure?"

Clint scraped his thumb against his scruffy chin. "What's that verse? Something about those who teach being *more* accountable."

"That's taking Scripture out of context."

A shadow crossed his eyes. "I'm sorry it came to this. But I need your help. So does Lee."

"Lee can go to prison." Max emptied his mug.

"Guess there's a verse or two about still showing him love."

Max didn't want to think about that right now. "I'll go talk to the loan officer. See if anything can be done."

Clint pressed his hands against the table, shoved himself to a standing position, and moaned. "You hear about Gladys Iris?"

"I did." He didn't want to talk about that, either. "I found her. I visited her every day, same as usual."

"Huh." Clint stared at something on the wall with a puzzled expression, then he shuffled to the door.

Max hadn't planned to confess he was the one to find Gladys. That he'd continued visiting her. Some might think he hadn't relinquished his post, after all. *Guess they'd be right.*

"Stay safe." Clint exited, then slammed the door.

Safe. That sounded appealing. Max locked the door, for all the good it would do.

But if the church building didn't sell soon, especially now with this loan shark business, Max and Season could be in for a time of testing unlike anything they'd experienced. How would their marriage, with its crumbling erosion, hold up then?

He grabbed a towel off a cabinet door where he'd left it hanging yesterday and headed for the shower. Looked like he'd have to do two things he never planned to do again—talk to the bank and face Derek Clark.

Ten

Winter

The interrogation room with its cement block walls smelled of Pine-Sol and body odor. The first to cover the second, no doubt. Winter stared curiously into the three-foot by five-foot mirror along one wall. A one-way mirror? Was someone watching her from behind that glass? She shuddered. No, that only happened in TV shows, right?

She imagined herself seated on the other side of the table being questioned by a detective. *Where were you on the night of October twenty-second? Do you have an alibi? A motive?*

Thankfully, she wasn't the guilty party here.

She turned her chair slightly and faced the metal door, opposite the mirror, steeling herself. Any moment, her former friend turned nemesis would walk in. The person who'd kidnapped her, slapped her, battered her confidence, and then asked for leniency in court while she sat watching, would sit across the table from her. How would she feel then?

Tension raced up her spine. She swallowed down her nervousness. *Everything will be okay*. But the reassurance fell short. Randi would have abducted her from the building that night if Ty hadn't overpowered her. She'd seemed bent on destruction, her scheme filled with evil. Would Winter be alive if her husband hadn't intervened?

Oh, Ty, I'm sorry for causing more trouble between us.

Randi's lawyers had blamed that night's debacle on drug use after a plea for temporary insanity was denied. Winter agreed with the attorney's assessment, even though the court psychologist did not. When she'd seen Randi's wild gaze at the Bend church where she was holding a women's conference last fall, she thought her old friend must be mentally unstable. Or on drugs. Either way, she never wanted to experience such a traumatic occurrence again.

Now, she was about to face Randi alone to try to make peace, and to ask her about the stolen journal—without Ty's protection. Her arms were shaking as if she were feverish. She had to forcefully relax her jaw. After all, Randi had been charged with assault and battery, theft, and kidnapping. Her fingernails left an inch-long scar on Winter's cheek, one she'd wear for the rest of her life. Since then, she'd been asking for God's help in forgiving the woman who caused so much trouble and pain. She was supposed to love her enemy, right? This meeting was part of the process. It was time for her to move on, to forget, if possible. But seeing Randi again, and talking to her, would be difficult.

When her previous assistant petitioned the court for early release on good behavior—*hard to believe*—Winter and Ty traveled to Bend, Oregon, to make a statement and watch the proceedings. Winter wasn't convinced prison was the best solution for Randi, but she didn't believe the woman should be free to continue with any wrongdoing, either. A rehabilitation center might have been a better fit, although that hadn't worked for her in the past.

Ty didn't want her facing Randi unaccompanied. But she

held her ground and insisted she had to follow her heart. She'd be okay. God was watching over her. When she asked the lawyer to arrange for her to see Randi by herself, Ty had acquiesced. However, she could tell he wasn't pleased.

Married one year this second time around, they'd had their share of conflicts—including problems over this tense reunion. In the end, she won. Or lost, depending on the outcome.

If Ty had insisted on being present, she knew Randi would have refused to meet her. For whatever reason, she was angry at Winter, but Randi was outright vengeful toward Ty.

Two months ago, Winter sat through the trial broken-hearted over all that had happened—and regretting some of her own past mistakes too. When she'd run into Ty over a year ago, she should have told the team about their previous marriage right off. Maybe then, some of the troubles with Randi could have been averted. But she'd wanted to give Ty a chance to prove himself to her, and the team. For both to see if God might have a plan for their lives together. And she'd known Neil, her co-leader for Passion's Prayer, would have sent him packing if he found out their mechanic used to be her ex-husband. A sticky situation, for sure.

Thankfully, God forgave her secret-keeping. His mercy covered her. Now, she needed to extend that grace to others, namely Randi. She wanted to be able to tell her she forgave her. Or at least, that she was trying. Nightmares of the attack still afflicted her. A part of her brain seemed to be wrestling with the darkness she experienced. But even with that struggle, she'd petitioned the judge for kindness toward Randi, despite Ty's objection. However, the State took it out of her hands. The legal system shared the same view as her husband—Randi deserved prison time.

"It's okay with me if she spends the rest of her life in the slammer!" Ty's words gnawed at her. Surely, he didn't mean it.

Even if Randi deserved the law's judgment, she couldn't wish it on her. And Winter longed to be rid of the arrow of rage. Free from bitterness and resentment.

She'd speak with her former assistant this once. Try to reach her and get some answers. Too bad she couldn't do that and honor her husband's wishes, too.

This morning, Ty reminded her Randi not only injured them but harmed their good friend, Deborah. Thinking of their musician friend who'd suffered serious bruising to her side and kidney—who still struggled with emotional trauma—made Winter ache inside. She whispered a prayer that Deborah would find healing during the worship conference they'd sent her to in Seattle. The younger woman had been in seclusion for weeks, hadn't played the piano or sang. Surely a time of refreshing in the presence of the Lord would help.

For the last three months following their attack, Winter and Ty had taken a sabbatical from speaking engagements. Neil covered for them in a few conferences. The rest were canceled. Even now, her co-leader was back in Spokane at their home office making calls and planning their upcoming year's schedule.

Winter and Ty had spent a lot of time praying and talking about their future. They were still receiving requests for marriage conferences around the country. It seemed God would continue using their reconciliation story for His glory. If they could just get past this quarrel about her meeting Randi. Last night they were expected at Hart's Camp—their first time speaking since their leave of absence—and they'd missed it. How frustrating!

Hopefully, her discussion with Randi would be worth it. Or had she just stirred up more conflict?

Ty knew all the details of today's arrangements, yet he maintained his disapproval. How would they be able to speak at the marriage retreat with this hanging over them?

She smoothed her index finger down her cheek. Touched the scar. Nothing could be done about that—other than plastic surgery. To her, it was a battle scar. One that would always remind her of the night she came close to dying. And how her husband risked everything to rescue her.

Doors leading into the building clanged. A few seconds later, the interrogation room door opened.

Winter's heart thumped to a powerful beat.

Randi, arms cuffed in front of her, was propelled into the room by an armed guard. Her ankle chains clanked. She wore an orange jumpsuit. Greasy hair and no makeup made her look sickly. A curled lip and squinty eyes dominated her features. Hate? Only her shadowed irises betrayed any fear the woman might know.

"Oh, Randi." Winter didn't conceal her pity. Part of her wanted to lunge forward and wrap her arms around the skeleton of a woman she used to call her best friend. She didn't move. Protocol and the rules of safety kept her glued to her seat.

The officer scraped back the metal chair on the other side of the table. Randi dropped into the seat. The man fastened her handcuffs to a metal hook on the table. Her chains rattled. Her gaze never wavered from Winter's.

"I'll be right outside." The man's gruff tone and his dark brown eyes glinted a strong warning.

"Thank you." Winter nodded once. *It's going to be okay.* She gulped, trying to believe her attempt at comfort.

A barely heard "whoosh" of the door's closing, then they were alone.

Randi nodded toward the mirror. "Who's back there?"

"No one." As far as she knew. Ty had returned to the motel.

As she stared into the gaunt eyes of the woman who kidnapped her, anxiety pulsed up her neck. Why did she push for this meet-and-greet? Why didn't she heed her husband's words of caution?

"Ty better not be back there." Randi yanked her chains and lunged forward.

Winter scooted her chair back. "He's not."

"You made a terrible mistake picking him." She jerked her head toward the mirror, the whites of her eyes widening.

Winter swallowed down her fear. "Let's not talk about Ty. You and I have things to discuss." She was glad Randi's hands were cuffed. Otherwise, how fast could the other woman grab her before Winter had time to yell for the guard?

"You heard it all in the trial. Now the inquiry." She smirked. "Don't know why you showed up today."

"I tried to get them to go easy on you."

"Sure you did." Randi scoffed. "I bet you and Mr. Mechanic were happy as clams I got sent back to the pen."

"I'm not happy about it." Tears flooded Winter's eyes. Regret gnawed at her. It was so hard seeing her old friend like this, not knowing how to reach her. "I wish things could be different. That we were still friends. I don't know why you did what you did—"

"Not going to either." The cuffs on Randi's arms rattled. "Too bad these are so confining." She yanked hard against the links binding her to the table. "Let me out of here!" A rabid craziness gleamed in her eyes.

The guard thrust open the door. "What's going on?"

Fire and ice sprinted through Winter's veins. Her survival instinct made her want to flee out the door. But she couldn't waste this moment. "Please stay. I want us to talk."

"I'm done in here!" Randi pulled against the chains, shuffled the legs of her chair back and forth.

"Wait. Please?" Winter implored the officer. "A few more minutes?"

Randi sighed as if bored senseless. "Oh, all right. Two minutes."

The guard backed out the door but glared like he distrusted both of them.

Winter knew that Randi would eventually have to own up to her mistakes. That nothing Winter had done caused her to vengefully attack her and her team. Still, she wanted to try to bridge the chasm between them. "I'm sorry for however I failed you or hurt you in the past."

The prisoner's laughter came harshly. "You think if you say sorry, I'll say sorry?" She jerked forward, her nose straining toward the midpoint above the table. "I'm not one speck sorry." Randi spit out each word, saliva landing on the table an inch from Winter's hands.

She pulled back. Resentment frothed in her chest. Maybe she'd skip pleasantries. "Where's my journal?" Ty had been right. Randi could still do her harm, even locked up in chains.

"Can't stand having something taken away from you, can you?" Randi's face contorted into a creepy grin.

"I want it back." She felt a surge of bravery. "It was private. *My* words. Containing personal information about Ty and me. You were wrong to take what didn't belong to you."

Randi snorted. "It's not private anymore."

She should yell for the guard. End this fool's errand for information and reconciliation. What did she think? That Randi would be contrite? Obviously, that wasn't happening. But she had to push for answers, even though their two minutes were probably over. "What do you mean? Did you read it?"

"You bet." The mocking laugh again. "Soon everyone else will read it too."

Everyone? "Who has it now?"

Randi shrugged. "Before long, your dirty little secrets will be Internet fodder. Poor Winter. Everyone will feel bad for you. Just like I intended."

"What are you talking about? I want my journal back!"

"Too bad." Randi's dark eyes grew almost golden. "I have an orchestrated plan in place. I was your perfect assistant, and you cast me out on the street. This"—she swayed her head as if talking about her chains or her situation—"is a mere delay. But not for long!"

She still had a plan for what? To harm Winter's team? Or her, personally? "Why are you doing this? To get back at me for marrying Ty?" Was she still hoping to bring down their ministry, like Ty and Neil thought? "What does it matter now?"

"It matters more than you know." Randi leaned over and wiped her nose against her knuckles. She glanced up from that low place near the table, reminding Winter of Sméagol in *Lord of the Rings*.

She inwardly shuddered over the sinister comparison.

"You were my friend." Randi's glare was so intense her eyes almost crossed. "Until *he* came along. Liar, embezzler, and adulterer." Her voice rose with each indictment.

"Was. Not is." She'd forgiven Ty. What he'd done was wrong, but it was in the past. "I love him. He's my husband. Those crimes had nothing to do with you. If anyone should be outraged, it's me. Not you."

"It was my job to protect you. You fired me for doing what you hired me to do—guard you against men like him." She squirmed restlessly in her chair. "You lied. Humiliated me. Stabbed me in the back. Some Christian you are."

An ache grew deeper in Winter's chest. "I never meant to hurt you. Please—" Their time was up. "If you won't tell me about the journal, what of that night? How could you hurt me like that? And Deborah?"

Randi yanked against the handcuffs and growled. "I didn't hurt either of you bad enough to cause permanent damage."

"No?" Winter turned her face and pointed her index finger at her scar. "What about this?"

"An accident."

Hardly. "What of Deborah trying to talk to you for weeks after the attack? You turned away from the one person in the world who still believed in you."

Tears? If so, she quickly blinked them away. "Deborah's naïve."

Winter remembered those same words Randi hurled at Deborah that night in Bend. "You did hurt her, you know."

"She'll recover."

"She will." God was working in her friend's life, she had no doubt. "What of you? Will you ever find peace again?"

Randi flinched. "Peace is overrated."

"We all need peace. Hope. Forgiveness." Winter had to force out the next words. "I need you to know"—she paused— "I forgive you. I've struggled. But I forgive you for what you did that night in October. Not just for your sake. For mine. And Ty's."

Randi's jaw dropped.

"He's a good man." Winter kept her gaze on the prisoner. "Yes, he made some bad choices in our younger years." She pointed at herself. "So did I. And when we went to Coeur d'Alene, I should have explained about him. I should have told my team everything. I regret not doing that." She took a big breath. "I'm sorry for the awkward position it put you in. And the hurt my choices caused."

"I don't believe you. You'll say anything to get the journal back." Her sneer made crease lines around her eyes and nose.

"I do want it back. But I needed to say the words too." Something else came to mind. "I don't know why you hate Ty so much."

Randi's face turned crimson. "What a waste of time. I'm done here. Guard!"

Winter stood.

The metal door opened, and the big man walked in.

"Get me out of here!" The chains rattled as Randi jerked them back and forth.

Winter walked to the door, and the guard let her exit. She stood in the doorway a moment. "Goodbye, Randi." She could barely contain the sorrow rolling up in her chest. She'd opposed Ty for this chance. Yet nothing had been accomplished but stirring up old wounds.

"You'll thank me later," Randi spoke quietly.

She glanced back. "For what?"

"You'll see." Maybe Randi was delusional, even though she'd been off narcotics for three months.

Winter stepped from the room, eager to find her husband and ask for his forgiveness. She'd been certain seeing Randi was the answer. She'd been so wrong.

* * * *

Ty stared eagle-eyed through the one-way window—dark on his side, brightly lit in the interrogation room—with adrenaline pumping through his body. Randi was restrained, but he was on high alert. He couldn't believe Winter expected him to return to the motel. As if he'd let her face this thing alone? Not in a million years.

He wouldn't interfere, either, unless something went south. Then nothing would stop him from protecting his wife. He hadn't lied to her about returning to the motel, however, he knew she'd be upset with him for not telling her the whole truth. But wasn't he supposed to protect her? Wasn't that his God-given responsibility?

He'd run out of ways to argue his case with her. She'd been adamant if he showed up, Randi wouldn't meet her. A good reason for him to stay close as far as he was concerned. But she'd defended her plan to retrieve her journal and try to reach some sort of reconciliation between her and her previous assistant. He wanted her to stay clear of the woman. The journal wasn't worth the trouble. Tired of the argument, he'd let her think he gave in. Then he asked the lawyer for access to this room. Winter need never know—unless Randi tried something stupid. Although he hated keeping secrets from his wife.

Movement in the next room captured his attention. When Randi shook her handcuffs and lunged toward Winter, he nearly lost it. Blood boiled through his veins as the playback of the last time he faced this woman splashed across the screen in his brain. He clenched his fists. Groaned. Waited to see what would happen next. Yesterday, Winter accused him of holding a grudge. He denied it. But his current hyperventilating confirmed the truth. He was probably carrying a grudge. Or worse.

Wait. Why was Winter apologizing? Randi was the one who owed her, and the team, an apology. His wife looked pale. Sickly? Had she finally realized this meeting was a waste of time? That she'd caused a rift between them for this? Sounded like Randi didn't plan on telling her anything about the journal, either.

Still alert, he watched his wife, then the demon in the orange jumpsuit, then Sas again, barely taking time to blink. He could see that Winter felt bad for Randi. He remembered how she'd wanted the court system to go easy on her. He believed in mercy too. But right and wrong? He was a black-and-white sort of guy. He committed his share of wrongs in the past and paid for them. It was Randi's turn.

Are you her judge?

Bile crept up his throat at the words whispered in his spirit.

No, if he were her judge, he'd sentence her to ten or fifteen years. Ought to be enough time to give him and Winter space to grow their family and carry out their ministry. But not very loving or forgiving, he admitted.

He focused on what Randi was saying. She still hated him? So what! He could have dealt with her venomous nature if she stayed clear of Winter and Passion's Prayer. And who was Randi to say Winter shouldn't have married him? They were happy most of the time. Their relationship had been idyllic—except for the problems Randi caused. *Spiteful woman.*

Anger over the woman's actions ignited in him way too easily.

You must forgive her, whispered through his thoughts.

He knew that's what his wife was trying to do. He swallowed down the dryness in his throat.

Forgiving had been so much harder this time. For months, he'd wrestled with overcoming his antagonism toward Randi. Now, not only had he not been forgiving, he'd broken his wife's trust by spying on her. If nothing happened in the next room, he'd hustle back to their hotel and finish packing. And keep to himself how he'd spent the last few minutes.

He listened in again. Winter sticking up for him pleased him. He appreciated her loyalty and love in the face of Randi's mean-spirited answers. Something melted in his chest. He loved his wife so much. Didn't want to disappoint her. But he'd felt justified in listening in on this conversation. Would she understand that?

They were expected at Hart's Camp this evening—a solid seven-hour drive from Bend. He remembered the last time they'd been at odds with each other during a marriage retreat and how he'd pulled her out of the service to apologize. He didn't want that happening again.

Winter exited the room, and Ty was relieved the meeting ended without a dangerous situation developing. The guard unfastened the prisoner from the table, then handcuffed her hands again. Randi whirled around and stared straight into Ty's eyes, even though he knew she couldn't see him. She spat at the glass. Right at him!

So she knew he was there? He watched her warily. When the guard led her out the door, he released the breath he'd been holding. It was over.

Now, he had quite a few hours of driving to work through his remaining irritation, and to ask God, again, to forgive him for his grudge toward Randi Simmons.

Eleven

Max

Max adjusted his tie and cleared his throat as he faced Rhonda Dennett, the blond, thirtyish loan officer. "Neither the church board nor I can repay the full mortgage. It's simply not possible." With what he hoped was a sincere expression, he stared at the woman dressed in a bulky red sweater unbuttoned over a black dress. She'd been courteous, although she seemed suspicious of his account about being fired by the other three. "I'm not the pastor anymore."

One eyebrow quirked. Rhonda leaned forward, her slim arms crossed over the desk. "Yet your name appears at the top of the list of those responsible for repayment, Mr. Prescott."

"S-so it does." He choked on his own saliva. "But if the building sells, this is all a moot point, right?"

"Possibly. The delinquent payments are due today."

"T-today?" What was with the adolescent crack in his voice? "We need more time. The property may sell soon. Couldn't the bank give us an extension?"

"So you do take responsibility?"

"No, I'm not the pastor." How could he make her see

things from his perspective? "I realize I signed the loan papers with the other three trustees five years ago, but they fired me two months ago. My name should have been removed from the record."

"That's not how it works. Do you remember reading and signing the loan agreement?" Her eyes squinted at him, reminding him of a judge presiding over a court.

"I read it at the time." He'd known trustees of an unincorporated church could be held liable for repayment in the case of foreclosure. But they were honestly trying to sell the building. And he'd thought his name had been removed from the liability. When he'd signed the documents, he certainly hadn't expected to be fired *and* held accountable for the loan. That Darby Community Church was unincorporated had always bothered him. He, Clint, Derek, and Lee had gone around and around about the possibility of incorporating. But Lee and Derek held to Jonah Trebor's, the previous pastor's, opinion that an unincorporated church was the more biblical way. *Give to Caesar what is Caesar's.* And that Christ was the head of the church, not the state. But Max had simply preferred legal protection from just such an issue as the one he faced now.

"Seems you and your friends will have to dig a little deeper." Rhonda tapped her keyboard. The printer along the opposite wall made a humming sound.

Friends? That was laughable.

"Ma'am, I'm not trying to shirk my duty. How much farther can we dig when the well is already dry?" He'd understood the risks at the time, but now he wished he'd never taken out the loan. However, they'd needed funding to remodel the front entrance of the building for wheelchair access. The church was built prior to 1992 and didn't fall under ADA requirements, but he'd felt strongly about adding the new ramp and entry.

Plus, they incurred windstorm damage to the roof that same year. That had to be fixed. Old plumbing in the archaic bathrooms required a complete remodel, so they threw in those expenses. And while they'd been doing all the other things, why not include new carpeting throughout the building? As usual, everything cost more than planned. Back then they were running close to two hundred in attendance, which meant more funds in the offering basket.

Rhonda stood and retrieved papers from the copier. "You might want to look at these." She passed him the stack, then returned to her seat.

He glanced over the loan pages, which reminded him of easier times gone by. He noticed the signatures of the other trustees. Derek Clark. Clint Ebbs. Lee Thomas. Men who used to be his friends, but who now seemed his adversaries. A tightness clogged his throat.

What could he do to pay his share? Sell his truck? The RV? What a laugh. Probably wasn't worth the cost to haul it away. And what about the loan sharks that came after Clint, thanks to Lee's debts and irresponsible financial decisions? If thugs paid Max a visit on some bogus claim, he had nothing to cough up as a means of protection.

Should he load up the truck and make his getaway? Turn his back on Darby and leave the other three men holding the bag? Clint didn't deserve that. Derek might. Lee did. But according to Clint, Lee had already vanished. And with his truck, Max doubted he could get more than fifty miles, if that, before the jalopy broke down.

What would he counsel someone else in his shoes? Run? Or stay and trust God? *Face it like a man,* he imagined his father saying. What kind of man had he been lately? He didn't want to contemplate the answer right now.

What of God's plan in this mess? And what about all the

times Max preached on good coming out of bad situations? Was that still possible? Verses flashed through his mind.

Beauty instead of ashes.

God works for the good of those who love Him.

I know the plans I have for you ... plans to prosper you and not to harm you.

Give thanks in all circumstances.

He certainly hadn't been thankful lately.

What if more disappointing stuff happened? His stomach tightened. Well, he was done sitting around doing nothing. He wasn't giving up his faith because he was going through a little fire. He made promises to God. And to Season and his sons.

But he needed to focus on the present situation. "Would it be possible to have an extension?" He tried to maintain a professional tone. "I need to talk with the other men."

"I'm sorry." The loan officer ruffled her blond hair with her fingers and smiled—like her words weren't cutting out his heart. "We already extended 'more time' twice."

"You did?" News to him.

"I spoke with Lee Thomas, the treasurer, on two separate occasions. He asked for, and was granted, more time on the loan." She tapped the desk with her pen. "We feel we've been more than generous. Time is up."

Stomach acids rolled up into his throat.

"In the future, you should incorporate your church so board members are protected. Whose idea was it not to do that anyway?" She grinned like it was a joke.

Lee and Derek may not have chosen that route in the first place, but they'd approved of it. "I didn't start this organization. I had no choice in the matter. My name was added to the roster twenty years ago."

"Unfortunate."

What else could he say? "May I speak with a manager?"

This woman seemed young to be deciding the fate of four
families.

"I am the branch manager." She did the hair shuffling thing
again. "I thought I mentioned that when I introduced myself."

The familiar sense of failure rushed through him. He used
to feel like he had the Midas touch. Like he was favored in the
community. In his life. Where had things gone so wrong?

"The building and properties, formerly known as Darby
Community Church, are set for auction February 1st." In his
mind's eye, the judge's gavel fell. "You and your associates will
be responsible for the amount we are unable to secure."

"So soon?" A heavy weight pressed against his chest, nearly
suffocating him. Was this how a heart attack felt?

She tapped the document on the desk. "The trustees of
Darby Community Church are fiscally and mutually responsible
for the ensuing balance following the auction. If the amount
isn't paid in full, legal action will be taken."

Legal action, as in sued? His breath came short. The room
spun. He bent his head over his knees. *Breathe. Need air.* Panic
attack?

"Are you all right, Mr. Prescott?"

Five more deep breaths.

*God, help. Don't let me die. I need to make things right with Season.
Help me out of this.*

"Do you need an ambulance?" The woman's voice sounded
high above his head.

Had he fallen? He pried his eyes open. Swirling walls sped
past his line of sight.

"Shall I call 911?"

He winced, realizing he'd landed hard on his knee. "No."
Eyes shut again, he breathed deeply. "I'm okay." Or would be
if he could leave without vomiting all over her red shoes.

She linked her hand under his elbow. "May I help?"

He doubted she could assist him to a standing position. But he could see she was trying to lend a hand. He shoved against the chair he'd left, wobbling slightly. As soon as he was steadier on his legs, he pulled away from Rhonda and shuffled toward the door. "I'll be in touch about the loan."

"I do wish you well, Mr. Prescott." Her voice softened. "I'm just doing my job."

He lifted his hand. That was about all he could do. Somehow, he made it outside without a catastrophe. Keeping his gaze on the chunks of snow peppering the sidewalk, he walked to his truck with feet that seemed to weigh twenty pounds each. He climbed onto the seat. He turned the key seven times before the engine engaged. *Great.* If the bank repossessed his worldly goods, they were welcome to this piece of junk.

He stared at the green car parked in front of him. The vehicle contorted before his eyes. Maybe he shouldn't drive quite yet. Could be he was hungry. He hadn't eaten all day. Sick of TV dinners, the thought of Annabelle's specials tempted him. He had a few dollars left in his wallet.

Maybe he should walk. The air would do him good. He turned off the engine then rammed his arm against the door that usually stuck and swung his feet to the sidewalk. As he trudged along Main Street toward the restaurant, his brain fog cleared. He remembered Clint's warning that thugs were coming after him. Had he made a bad decision in walking? He checked over his shoulder. Anyone following him?

Someone could jump out at him from any shadowed space—shop entrances, corners of buildings, behind cars. He'd have to be careful. Watch his step. He forced himself to walk faster.

He should have left town while he had the chance. In his experience, pastors who'd been removed from their pulpits usually left the city they served. But he'd convinced himself folks needed him. Not anymore. Gladys was gone. Jupe and Lila, the elderly parishioners he usually worried about, hadn't called on him all winter. Season drove for hours in record snowfall and did fine on her own. He thought he could help Jayme. Look where that got him.

When he reached Annabelle's, he sighed with relief. But as soon as he entered the bustling cafe, he knew he'd made a mistake in coming here. Chatter stopped. Gazes clashed with his.

Maybe he wasn't hungry, after all.

"Sit wherever you like." Sandy rocked her thumb toward an empty booth by the window.

The scent of french fries and burgers kept him from doing a 180. He covered the distance to the nearest vacant table in five steps.

Sandy followed with her coffee carafe and lifted it in question.

"Yes, please."

After pouring the coffee, she rushed to the next booth. He'd always liked Sandy's friendly, outgoing manner. She'd been on Annabelle's payroll for as long as he'd been stopping by for lunch.

He dumped creamer into the off-white mug, then took a long sip without stirring the liquid.

Glancing up, he met the hardened gaze of Harold Smith, a utilities worker and past member of his church, a few booths down. Max nodded once. The greeting wasn't returned.

Willa and Martha sat on the opposite side of the cafe, staring at him. If gazes could singe skin, he'd be on fire. They whispered to the couple at the next table, then all four gaped at him. Because of Jayme? Or had news of the forthcoming auction reached the small hub? Their judgmental glares made the hairs stand up on the back of his neck.

He should have avoided Annabelle's altogether.

Sandy scooted up to his table and topped off his coffee. She leaned closer. "Don't mind those old gossips."

Nice that someone understood.

"What will you have today?" She pulled a stubby pencil from behind her ear.

He'd been planning on a pile of eggs and hash browns. "Got any pie?" He could use some comfort food.

"Annabelle makes a tasty meatloaf." She was tempting him.

He licked his upper lip at the thought of home-cooked food. Maybe he was a little hungry. "I could go for some meatloaf."

"How about a piece of apple pie à la mode to go along with that—on the house?" Sandy's smile widened her dimples. "I might take my lunch break with you. Maybe throw a little gas on the fire?" She winked and nodded toward Willa and Martha.

"Uh, sure." He could use the friendship.

"Be right back."

What could it hurt? He'd have a chat with someone who'd never darkened his church doors, enjoy a nice meal, then head back to solitary confinement in his RV.

"Good to see you, Pastor." Marsha Dickins, a previous friend of Gladys's, shuffled to his table, her cane keeping time on the uneven wooden floorboards. She patted a wrinkled hand against his shoulder. "Thank you for caring so much for Gladys. I was sad to hear about her passing."

"Me too." He met the woman's almost silvery gaze and saw no condemnation. "Have you heard when the funeral will take place?"

"Day after tomorrow, noon." She shook her white hair. "Her brother attends Living Faith Center. So Pastor Paul will be officiating."

Something heavy thudded in his chest. "Okay. Thanks."

She leaned closer to his ear. "I'm sure *your* words would have been kindlier spoken."

The knot in his gut evaporated. "Thank you."

She patted his shoulder again before moving to the exit.

He wished he could have officiated Gladys's funeral service at his own church. But since he'd handed in his keys, and was picturing the "For Sale" sign near the entrance of the church parking lot, he knew that was impossible. By now, the building was probably cold and musty. Was anyone taking care of it? He'd have to ask Clint. It wouldn't matter much longer since it would go up for auction soon.

He sipped his coffee and pictured Season sledding like a kid. Her cheeks pink, her blue eyes shining, and her beautiful smile huge—like when they were young and did fun things together. He missed her. And hated imagining what his future would be like without her. If she were here, she'd link her fingers with his and sense what he was feeling. She'd always been good at understanding him. Yet, how many times in recent days had he accused her of doing the exact opposite? Of *not* getting him? Of *not* being the ideal pastor's wife? What a judgmental cad he'd been. He hadn't seen her best qualities. How she'd stood by him when things were tough. How she smiled and winked at him and made life easier for him and the boys. The best thing that ever happened to him—after his salvation—was marrying her.

Season, I'm so sorry.

After this financial disaster was resolved, he'd make everything right with her somehow. If they were turned out of their home, poor as dogs, and living with relatives, the person he most wanted to be with on this planet was her.

It really was true. You didn't know what you had until it was gone. Not that Season had left him for good. But she could. Then where would he be? Had he ruined everything beautiful between them in his quest to become—what? A successful pastor? He scoffed at the notion.

Sandy set a steaming plate of meatloaf and mashed potatoes swimming in garlic butter on the table in front of him. She dropped another plate with a hamburger and fries across from him, then plopped down on the other bench.

He bowed his head and said a silent prayer of thanks for the food.

"You can do that out loud. I don't mind." Sandy scooped up her thick burger and took a wide-mouthed bite, then chewed. "Here's my plan, I think we should bust a gut right about now." She appeared to swallow, then she guffawed like he'd said something hilarious.

"Why are you laughing?" Life had become too painful for laughter. He hadn't thought anything was genuinely funny in months.

Without explaining, she bellowed out another "hardy har."

Ignoring her eccentric behavior, he dumped ketchup on his meatloaf. He took a big bite, then sighed. First real food in days.

Sandy nudged his elbow, nearly landing his forkful of food in his lap. "Come on. Laugh! It's good for you. Medicinal, they say." She cackled like a hyena, drawing strange looks from some of the customers. She bobbed her head toward the older sisters. Then laughed again.

Martha and Willa stared wide-eyed at them.

"Then I said"—Sandy brandished the ketchup bottle in the air—"dump it out, or I will! Bwahahaha!"

Max appreciated Sandy's efforts at comedy, and her trying to make him look like he still had a friend in town. So he chuckled a little. Ending with a cough.

"Can't you do better than that?" She rolled her eyes like a glowering teenager.

Now that was funny. Real laughter manufactured itself. Humor was a gift when it had gone missing for too long.

"Well, at least, that's something." She bit into her giant burger with gusto.

He glanced at his previous parishioners to see their reaction.

Willa's and Martha's heads leaned in close, their mouths opened and closed like goldfish. They cranked out their cell phones—odd they were so technologically advanced—and talked rapidly into the instruments.

Gossips. Meddlers. Rumor spreaders.

All of Darby would know the ex-pastor was laughing—flirtatiously?—with the waitress by day's end. He should have gone back to the RV and avoided the public.

"Why'd you do that?" He stuffed green beans in his mouth. Not his favorite vegetable. But he liked the bacon bits cooked in it.

Sandy doused a french fry in sauce. "I'm sick of hearing those two cat-eyed gals spreading their tales."

"About me?" He should let it go. "What have they been saying?"

"This one hates that one. Love triangles. Who's stabbing who in the back. Who's the *father* of someone's baby?" Her eyes glistened.

So she'd heard about that.

"Thought I'd make their lies a little more fascinating."

"Lies?"

She scrubbed her napkin over her mouth and chin. "How you cheated parishioners."

"What?" He'd been determined not to let Jayme's rumor get to him. But malicious lies about him cheating church members? His meatloaf turned over in his belly.

"How you brought your congregation to its knees."

Who would say such a thing—other than Lee or Derek?

She guzzled a long drink of water. "Scammed everyone."

He could barely breathe. "That's not true."

"Of course not." She stuffed a fry in her mouth. "You and the missus living high on the hog these days?"

He snorted. "We live in an RV park."

"Mmhmm." Looked like she was staring at Martha and Willa, a deep frown on her forehead. Suddenly her eyes danced. "Follow my lead, Pastor." She reached over and grabbed his hand. Winked. "Oh, Max"—she blew him kisses—"I just *looooove* you."

He yanked his hand free of hers. Now she'd gone too far. She cackled uproariously.

Willa and Martha stood to their feet, gaping.

Oh, no. Oh, no.

Martha clomped over to their table in her thick Dr. Scholl's. "I'm surprised at you, a married man!"

"Pastor." Willa tipped up her nose and scurried toward the glass front door.

Max considered running after them, confessing it was all a setup. He pinched his nose, shook his head. "I wish you hadn't done that."

"But it was funny. Didn't you see their faces?" She scrunched up her nose and gawked at him, imitating them.

He almost snickered. Instead, he stabbed a large chunk of meatloaf and stuffed it in his mouth. No use letting good food go to waste, although he might have to chew a few antacids when he got home.

Another couple rushed past their booth throwing glares. Apparently, more customers than Willa and Martha had seen Sandy's fake overtures. The waitress was only trying to help. But how could helpfulness turn out so ... unhelpful?

He'd better skip pie.

Sandy scooped up their plates and scrambled back to the kitchen. Her lunch break must be finished.

After he paid his bill, he hightailed it back to his truck. He ignored the impulse to check over his shoulder. Should he call Martha and Willa and explain what Sandy had been trying to do? How much gossip had they already spread? Did they consider him a playboy in sheep's clothing? A cheat? How quickly would they tarnish his name? But, apparently, his name was already stained in this town.

How much worse might things get before he was good and ready to leave Darby?

Twelve

Season

As Season hiked toward the lodge for the afternoon session, her boots crunched in the freshly fallen snow. She breathed deeply, noticing how light and clean the air smelled here at the base of Mount Spokane—much different than in town. She remembered seeing the ski runs in the distance lit up at night, which brought to mind the last time she'd skied on Lost Trail Powder Mountain, near Darby, fifteen years ago. She imagined herself standing at the snowcapped peak, ski poles in her hands and goggles on, her heart in her throat as she faced the steep slope. Just like the other times she'd skied, she had to decide between playing it safe and really going for it. Kind of like turning points in her life, when she had to choose between trying something new or staying in her comfort zone. Like in their marriage. Like her coming to Hart's Camp alone.

And ever since this morning's session, Summer's words from her lecture had been churning in Season's mind. "I want you to remember the day you and your husband met. Think about how you felt when you gazed into each other's eyes."

Did Season even want to recall how she felt when she met Max? Wouldn't that just stir up more anguish?

Summer had grinned like she was picturing the first time she met Josh. "When he smiled did your knees go weak? Was he the handsome guy playing his guitar like Garth Brooks?" She laughed. "Oh, no, that was me when Josh was on stage at a high school dance."

Giggles had erupted from the ladies in attendance.

Now, as Season continued hiking downhill through the snow, despite her decision not to reminisce, her thoughts drifted back to a wintry day much like this one, when she and Max met in the cafeteria at Montana State University. Charming and witty, and maybe showing off a little for her, he'd made her laugh over something awful they were served for lunch. *Soupy slurpy sloppy joes?* Or some such nonsense. He was the proverbial tall, dark, and handsome guy, with a dash of shyness. If she remembered right, his hand had skimmed hers as they both reached for sugar for their coffees. On contact, tremors raced through her veins. That spark of attraction made her want to get to know Max Prescott better. And when he smiled, oh boy, she was lost. Especially when his dark, brown-sugar eyes shimmered like candy. She still loved his smile. When he smiled at her. When had he stopped doing that?

It seemed something in their marriage had been wrong for a long time. What? Maybe Max struggled with inner conflict or a tragedy he kept secret from her. Could there be someone else? Jayme? Ugh. Not her. But what if he'd been tempted by someone? She held her breath, searching for another woman's name. But none came.

She and Max used to laugh and share so many secrets. Walk. Talk. Hold hands and kiss. But that was before rules and schedules and *that* church took over Max's life.

What had Summer said? "For this exercise, try not to focus

on the bad stuff between you and your spouse." From her spot behind the makeshift pulpit, she smiled at the twenty or so women attending the morning session like she understood their dilemma. "I know that's hard. But please try."

Missy rolled her eyes. "She should hear what I put up with. Fred's like a sore tooth. Can't ignore him. I would if I could."

Sometimes when Missy grumbled about her husband, Season chuckled over the humorous things she said. Today, intense pain burned up her chest at the thought of her and Max's marital failings, and she felt truly sorry for the other woman's struggles.

Listening to the relationship-themed lectures was more challenging than Season had imagined. Max was the one who walked away from the closeness they shared. He ignored her most of the time. Was indifferent toward her. He needed to hear all this marriage talk. Of course, it took two of them to create the muddle they were in. And it would surely take both of them, and God, to fix it—if it wasn't already too late. But for any of that to take place, he needed to be here.

What if Max didn't want to mend their relationship? Or he'd already given up? Maybe he wanted out. Would he look into getting a divorce while she was away? The thought crushed the fragile wings of hope she'd been trying to nurture that their marriage might survive their current crisis. She'd considered separating from him plenty of times over the last year. Told herself she wanted out. But what if he took the first step toward divorce? Left her without a choice?

Stop panicking. If Max chose a separation, she'd have to deal with that. Right now, she was supposed to be focusing on her own inner healing.

She paused near the edge of the clearing and stared up the hillside to where she'd gone sledding yesterday, yearning for another lighthearted experience like that. Suddenly, a snow-muffled thudding of footsteps came from behind her. Branches snapped. A snort? She whirled around.

Ooh. A giant moose stopped twenty feet away. Its shiny nose nuzzled a clump of dry grass protruding through a mound of snow at the base of a tree. Season froze. Was the animal dangerous? This wasn't a character like *Bullwinkle*. This was a massive hungry beast. Its large teeth yanked at the weeds, tearing and chomping. When the creature snorted, a puff of steamy air rose above him. Suddenly, he stilled. Did he smell her? He sniffed loudly. A long strip of grass dangled from his mouth. Muscles flexed. Big brown eyes darted left and right. His gaze met hers. She gasped. He let out a loud snort then bolted away, giant legs plowing up the snowy hillside.

She released the breath locked in her mouth. *Wow.* Wait until she told Max. He would have loved seeing a wild animal like that. Then she realized what she just thought—that she wanted to tell Max something. That she still longed to share experiences with him. Hadn't she always wished for a deeper closeness between them that invited talking about everything? She sighed, and it hurt.

She walked the rest of the way to the lodge in sober contemplation. As she rounded the corner, the wooden door creaked open. Missy stepped out and dumped the contents of her coffee cup over the railing, without noticing Season. A groan rumbled from her. Was she tired? Or sad?

"Hey, Missy." Season hated to intrude on her solitude, but the next session was about to begin.

Missy's eyes widened. "Oh, hi, Season. I didn't see you." She waved her mug. "Cold coffee's disgusting."

"I agree. Ready for more marriage discussions?"

"Not on your life. Ty and Winter better get here soon, or Fred's leaving. Said we paid good money to hear them. Not the others. Blah, blah, blah." Missy flapped her fingers and thumb like a duck's bill.

"They're probably on their way." Not that she knew for sure. She only hoped to alleviate Missy's distress, especially since she related to the woman having frustrations with her husband.

"Fred needs help, God love him. He respects Ty. Things have been—" She mimed an explosion. Then suddenly, she broke into sobbing. Tears streamed in rivulets, smearing her mascara and blush down her face.

"Oh, Missy." Season rushed up the steps and wrapped her arms around the woman's bulk. "It'll be okay."

Missy's outburst coaxed the tears Season had been fighting all day. Salty liquid trickled down her own cheeks. Good thing Max wasn't here to see all this emotion.

"S-sorry." Missy scrubbed her knuckles beneath her eyes. "Didn't mean to unload my burden on you. But it's been right here"—she thudded her palm against her chest—"since yesterday."

"We both needed this." Season wasn't the crying type, but something within her heart had been breaking. So many problems and hurts and disappointments were piled up within her like a stack of blocks ready to topple over. This struggle she was experiencing was Max's fault.

"It's all Fred's f-fault!" Missy hiccupped.

The nearly identical words twisted a knot beneath Season's ribs. She rehearsed the line in her mind about it taking both to make their mess. But wasn't it more Max's fault than hers?

"He doesn't notice that I'm a real person with hurts and wounds." Missy sniffled and wiped at her face. "He just sees his own selfish pride."

Like Max. "Men."

"I'm sick of the lot of them."

"Me too."

She wasn't sure which of them started laughing first. In the next second, they were both snickering. Which transformed into gales of laughter intermixed with tears.

The door opened, and Autumn stepped onto the porch. "There you two are." She rubbed her hands over the arms of her sweater. "Chilly out here." She must have noticed their red-rimmed eyes. "Sorry to interrupt."

"It's o-okay. I was having a glorious breakdown." Missy sobbed again. "S-Season was being u-understanding. Listening to my griping." Then she wailed.

Autumn wrapped her arms around Missy. "I'm so sorry, sweetie."

Season draped her arms around both women's shoulders, crying and praying for strength and healing for all of them. This was the first time she'd ever felt like this around other women. Like she could let go of her barriers and weep if she needed to, unashamed of her brokenness and imperfections. And who cared whether mascara was streaking down her face at a camp in the woods? Not having to bury her feelings felt amazing. Freeing. She was glad these women understood.

Several moments passed.

Missy dislodged from the hug, wiping her eyes and clearing her throat. "If Fred saw me now, he'd be upset."

"Why?" Season searched her pocket for a tissue.

"He thought I was emotional before." Her grin widened the flushed spots on her cheeks. "Sisters, he ain't seen nothing yet."

"God has something good planned." Autumn patted Season's shoulder too. "For all of us."

"I hope so." For years, she'd schooled herself not to let anyone watch her break down. Oh, she sniffled over sappy movies. Even her sons did that. But as a pastor's wife, she'd tried so hard to be strong. A pillar Max could be proud of. Had he ever noticed? Or did he only see her weaknesses? Better change the subject or the waterworks would start again. "I saw a moose over there." She pointed toward the woods.

"And I missed it?" Missy wiped her sleeve beneath her nose.

"Just before you came outside. He was this big." Season extended her arms as far as she could horizontally, then vertically. "Magnificent creature. Larger than a horse."

"Oh, wow."

"Let's get started, ladies." Summer's voice reached them from inside the door that was slightly ajar.

"Better do as we're told." Missy marched into the log hewn building as if she hadn't just been bawling like a baby.

The trio sat at what had become *their* table. Autumn grabbed coffee and vanilla creamer for all of them. She added a dollop of whipped cream. And she set a plate of fudge on the table. Now that was comfort food!

Season wrapped her hands around her mug and sighed when the warmth permeated her skin. She indulged in two pieces of dark chocolate fudge. She'd have to ask Autumn for her recipe later.

Feeling vulnerable, yet enjoying the sense of relief after crying, she listened intently as Summer shared her story of how Josh left her, five-and-a-half years ago, to follow his musical dream. She told of the struggle she'd had, of the years she carried immense anger toward him. *Who wouldn't?* How she kept her pregnancy a secret from him. Then years later, after his life had been redeemed by the Lord, he returned to make amends with his aunt and uncle. And the prodigal found the wife he'd abandoned in charge of the family's camp.

All those years, she hadn't divorced him because she knew she had to find him and introduce him to their daughter, Shua Day, first. When he volunteered to help her restore the camp, and after attending a marriage conference like this one—where she'd wrestled with forgiving him for his wrongdoings—their love had been rekindled. Eventually, they renewed their vows, and Shua's dream for a daddy came true.

"Now for your assignment!" Summer cheered like the retreat was all fun and games.

The ladies groaned.

"Is she kidding?" Missy grumbled. "This isn't school."

Season held in her disgruntled feelings. If the homework had to do with her having a heart-to-heart with Max, she'd opt out.

Summer laughed. "If it's any consolation, Josh and I are doing this task alongside you and your husband."

Except for me. My husband isn't here.

Season's phone buzzed in her pocket. Should she step outside and take the call? No, she needed to pay attention to Summer's instructions, even if she hadn't decided whether she'd participate.

The young woman held up a green, quart-sized, wide-mouthed canning jar with a single unlit candle inside. At the top, a wire handle had been secured around the rim's gold band. "For the next couple of days, you and your husband will take care of a lantern just like this. You'll light the candle, and do everything in your power to keep it lit. You'll carry it wherever you go around camp—except for sledding, riding a four-wheeler, or anywhere that would be considered dangerous to bring a flame. Josh is also explaining the project to the men upstairs."

Missy waved her hand. "I don't get it."

"You will." Summer picked up a lighter and clicked it several times. When a flame shot out, she tipped the jar and lit the candle. "This flame represents Josh's and my love for each other. Our attempts to keep it going is an object lesson of us doing everything we can to keep the flame of our love kindled and on fire."

"And if it goes out?" Missy almost growled. "'Cause I'm pretty sure mine already has."

Mine too. Season crossed her arms.

"Just like in our marriages, we have to work to keep the flame vibrant." Summer strolled near their table displaying the homemade lantern with its wick burning. "Imagine how the wind might snuff out my candle as I'm walking up the trail. What might remove the light of your marital love?"

Voices called out answers.

"Adultery."

"Alcohol."

"Drugs."

"Falling out of love."

"A grouchy spouse." Missy's voice rose.

A man whose ministry means more to him than his wife. But Season didn't say the words out loud. Sometimes a marriage grew cold without the glaring sins of adultery, unfaithfulness, drug or alcohol addiction. Instead, the flame slowly withered and died. Like hers and Max's.

Moisture filled her eyes.

Summer held up a disposable lighter. "This fire starter is the only product you may use to relight your candle." She walked to the table at the right of the lodge, and removed a cloth, revealing a table full of identical lanterns.

"Ahhh." Exclamations of interest skittered about the room.

"When you're in your cabins, please keep the Mason jar on the table by the window." She lifted a twelve-inch square hot-pad. "We've left a heat-protective mat there for that purpose."

"What if the candle goes out in the night?" Missy sounded exasperated.

"In the morning, head down to the lodge and light it again." Summer set her jar on the small table that served as a pulpit. "Just like in our marriage, we don't want the flame to go out. But if it does, we're going to stop everything and do whatever is necessary to bring it back to life."

Whatever is necessary? Wasn't Season showing up at this camp a drastic enough step to mend her relationship with Max? And yet he'd remained unwilling to budge, even though their dying marriage needed a jumpstart. A love defibrillator?

"Can you imagine who the fire starter represents?" Summer waved the lighter.

Missy leaned near Season. "Fred's not going to like this. I'll be stuck babysitting the fire myself."

So would Season.

"Jesus is the light of the world." Summer clicked the lighter, emitting a burst of fire. "When you light your candle, it's a picture of Him, the mender of hearts, healing your relationship. Giving both of you new life and purpose."

"And if it goes out again and again?" Missy thrust out her hands. "I'll be tromping down to the lodge twenty times a day."

"As many times as it takes." Summer smiled without seeming annoyed by Missy's questions. "Let's pray together."

All the other women had their husbands to help them keep watch over their symbolic flame. When, and if, Season lit a candle, could it represent something other than marital bliss? Because renewal in their marriage seemed a slim possibility.

Her phone buzzed again.

A voicemail? One of the boys? Maybe she should listen.

As the women gathered around the table picking out lanterns, Season hurried to the exit and stepped onto the porch. She tapped in her retrieval code for messages, then listened.

"Mrs. Prescott? This is Martha Clayton."

Martha Clayton? Not Benny or Logan. Even hearing from

Max would have been preferable to Darby's chief gossip and talebearer.

"You'll be surprised to hear from me, but I felt it was my duty to call." In the recorded message, Martha drew in a raspy breath like an asthmatic. "Something downright sinful is going on with your husband." She coughed.

Going on—as in with another woman? Like Season would believe anything Martha said.

Max had told her the Clayton sisters were present at Annabelle's the day Jayme told him the lie. Had Martha heard something else?

"I thought his wife should know the truth." Her tone was saccharine sweet. "Brace yourself, dear. Your husband is seeing someone."

Someone, as in Jayme? She almost deleted the message. But she ought to listen to the end.

"Two someones, actually."

What? She groaned. Then deleted the woman's words. Considering Martha was the one spreading tales, she refused to accept any of it as fact.

But hadn't she even questioned whether Max might have been tempted by a woman other than Jayme? However, him playing the field in her absence seemed far-fetched. Perhaps Martha had been indulging in too much Irish coffee again. Or her imagination was running wild.

Autumn stepped onto the porch carrying her lantern. "Everything okay?"

Season stuffed her cell phone in her back pocket. "I just got a slanderous voicemail about Max. Not that I believe a word."

"So, this person isn't a reliable source?"

"Definitely not." Season laughed. "Picture the most gossiping human you know."

"I have a troublemaker in mind." Autumn nudged her arm. "No worries then. Whatever she told you is probably false or half-truths. Trust God. And talk to Max."

"You're right." She sighed. What good would worrying do when she was so far away?

"Are you going to grab a lantern?" Autumn nodded toward her Mason jar resting on the handrail. The wind blew, and she shielded the jar's opening with her hand. "I think this is going to be a challenge."

"I don't see how tending a candle representing romance will help without my husband here."

"Eh, give it a try. What could it hurt?"

That's exactly what she was afraid of—how much it might hurt. Aching over the symbolism. Questioning their missing romance. Wishing things were different. Could she and Max ever change? Most of the couples at the retreat were in their thirties. Not mid-forties and married two decades like her and Max.

Autumn picked up her jar. "Someday, we can laugh over our experiences—and mishaps." She faked dropping the jar.

Season supposed she could give it a try, if for no other reason than to share in the assignment with Autumn and Missy. She went inside and made a beeline for the lantern table. One candle remained. Hers and Max's symbol of romance? She groaned.

How many times in the coming days would she have to be reminded of their lack of love?

Thirteen

Ty

Their conversation on the drive from Bend, Oregon, to Coeur d'Alene, Idaho, lacked their usual traveling banter. Ty wondered if his wife was mulling over her meeting with Randi, or if she were distracted preparing for the conference. His own contemplations kept him quiet.

Back at the hotel, she'd apologized profusely for not listening to him about Randi. Her sincerity and remorse made him want to share his side of the story. But rushed for time, they grabbed their overnight bags, checked out, and hit the road.

Six hours later, he was still praying for Randi, pondering his attitude, and debating if he should tell Winter that he observed their discussion. He took a long swallow of sweet tea he picked up at a gas station, thinking about their marital pledge to be honest about everything this second time around.

"Are you ready to speak tonight?" She touched his arm resting on the console between them.

He let their fingers link loosely. "Not really. You want to take the lead?"

"Sure. You've been driving all day."

He removed his hand from under hers. Felt her gaze. He still needed to work out the angst in his system before he could speak in front of a group about being honest and humble in marriage. Not that he was perfect, by any means, but he wanted to have a sincere spirit before his wife, and God.

"You've been quiet today. You okay?"

He swallowed. "Just thinking." He'd felt justified in choosing to watch her conversation with Randi, but he knew his wife well enough to know she'd be unhappy with him when she found out. If he pulled over to explain, they'd arrive at the camp late. Besides, he didn't want to interfere with her preparation for the retreat. She needed her focus. They could talk another time. Maybe tomorrow. Or next month. He groaned again.

"What is it?"

"Nothing." Not exactly the truth. He'd been stewing most of the day. At the next wide place in the road, north of Rathdrum, Idaho, he pulled over. "I need a break. Just a short walk." He shoved open the door, jumped out, and strode to the end of the pullout, breathing in the winter air. He stopped near a bank of snow and gazed at the mist-covered hills, praying for peace.

"What's wrong, Ty?" Her voice so close startled him.

Tell her your heart, whispered through him.

He recognized those words from other times when he needed to talk to his wife. Still, he inwardly wrestled for a few more minutes until he came to a decision. Even if it made them late, sharing his heart with her would help him feel better. Both of them, hopefully. Taking her hand, he met her gaze. "I need to tell you something."

"Okay."

He led her back to their vehicle. As soon as he sat down in the driver's seat, he started the engine and got the heater running.

"Ty, what is it?"

He smoothed his hands over the steering wheel. No time for small talk. "Weren't you curious why I didn't ask you more about your meeting today?"

"Not really. I didn't want to discuss it. Why?" She rested her hand on his arm.

"I was there."

"What do you mean? Where?" Her eyebrows dipped in a frown.

"Did you notice the mirror in the interrogation room?"

"How do you know about that?" Her hand withdrew from his arm.

"I got permission to watch you and Randi." He closed his eyes for a moment. "I felt it was right for me to be near in case anything happened. But I heard everything."

"You said you were going back to the motel." Her glare was probably meant to make him squirm. Instead, ire raced up his spine.

"No. You told me to go back." He hadn't meant that as an accusation, but he was pretty sure it sounded like one. "I couldn't go back to the motel room and wait. Not after what happened last time."

"The guard was there. I wasn't in any danger." Her voice rose.

"That's not how I saw it." He remembered Randi rattling the chains. Her hateful grimaces. Her spitting at the window. If she'd had half a second to do something illegal, she would have.

"I told her you weren't back there." Her eyes darkened. "I trusted you."

And he'd disappointed her, he could see that.

She leaned against the headrest and closed her eyes.

Would she struggle with speaking this evening, now that they'd had this disagreement? Maybe he should have kept the whole thing to himself. But, as husband and wife, they needed to share openly with each other. He'd told her the truth. What else could he say?

"Look"—he took a breath—"I've been arguing with myself for hours over whether or not to tell you. I'm sorry if what I did hurt you." His turn to lay his hand over her arm. "But I had to be there." And he couldn't apologize for that. "Randi's done all the harm to us that she's going to get away with."

She let out a long sigh. Would she be able to get over this breach of trust?

He had one other thing to tell her. "You were right. I still do have negative feelings toward Randi. I keep praying. But when she rattled her chains at you, I was ready to do whatever was necessary to stop her."

She opened her eyes and met his gaze. "I admit, I was scared." She shrugged. "In hindsight, I do like that you were close. Looking out for me." Her tone softened. "I caused friction between us by meeting Randi alone. I'm sorry about that."

Relief surged through him. He pulled her into his arms the best he could between the two seats. "It's over now."

"You're wrong. Based on what Randi said, it isn't over."

"Whatever threat she's holding over us, we'll face it together." He held her slightly away from him. "It's late. We should probably get going."

"Could we pray first?"

"Absolutely."

They clasped hands and prayed for their marriage, the upcoming conference, and for Randi.

As Ty drove the remainder of the miles to Hart's Camp, one thing still bothered him. How might Randi's plan affect them and their future ministry? He'd said it wouldn't be a problem, but that was for Winter's sake. Inside, he stewed about what might be coming next.

Fourteen

Max

Standing beneath the gazebo roof in the snow-covered park, Max rehashed the cryptic text he'd received from Derek. *Meet me. Community gazebo. Five p.m.*

What did Jayme's father want now? To express his outrage over his daughter's pregnancy and Max's supposed involvement? Or to criticize Max for the loan debacle?

Nervously, he waited at the specified location not far from the library, hands in his pockets, his boots stomping to stay warm. Derek was ten minutes late. Not like the banker at all. The man ran a tight business. Expected perfection. Didn't tolerate tardiness. Was he trying to make Max anxious? Hoping he suffered in the freezing temps? Might not show up at all?

Five more minutes. That's all he'd wait.

A second later, out of the corner of his eye, he watched in horror as a black-gloved hand reached around his neck. Max lunged forward. Tried to break away from the ominous grip. Was this the thug who beat up Clint?

"Hey! Leave me alone."

The guy's arm wrapped tighter around his neck, squeezing

him in a choke-hold like he'd never experienced before. He caught a glimpse of shiny black men's shoes and black slacks. Where had the guy come from? Was he after money?

"Let g-go!" Max yelled, but the leather glove muffled his words.

With his other hand, the assailant yanked Max's arms behind his back.

"W-what's going on? Why are you doing this?" He struggled to see the guy who wore a ski mask. "What do you w-want?" His words came out stuttered due to the hand over his mouth.

Better to fight off an attacker, right? Max wrenched his arms, threw his elbows, kicked his booted foot backward. Made contact a couple of times. He wouldn't go down without resistance.

Except for the hold on his neck grew tighter, making his breathing ragged. Buildings blurred. Was this how he'd die? At the hands of a mugger? Without making things right with his wife? *God, help me.*

While the attacker held onto Max, a figure dressed in a black trench coat and a fedora filled Max's view. Derek? When had he arrived? His hands were stuffed in his pockets. A mocking smirk covered his lips. Why wasn't he helping Max?

"Let him go." The voice of authority?

The arm around his neck loosened.

Thank You, God. As if in a distance, Max heard himself gasping for air. He wanted to pull away, but his wrists were still pinned behind his back. "What's going on?" He forced himself to stand taller and face his ex-councilman.

"My daughter said you had an affair with her." Derek's squinting eyes made his irises look metallic. He stepped closer, almost nose to nose with Max. Derek's breath smelled of garlic and alcohol. "That true?"

"No. She's lying." Max coughed.

Derek's chin jutted forward. His eyes gleamed.

Faster than he thought possible, the ruffian spun him around and punched him hard in the gut. Max buckled forward, gasping. The guy whirled him around to face the red-faced father again.

He could barely breathe let alone speak. "What ... she says happened ... didn't." He shook his head to clear his thoughts.

"I never liked you." Derek's already gravelly voice deepened. "You're a spineless, deadbeat pastor who should have been something else—a mortician, trash man, or the shoe cleaner at the bowling alley."

Painful words that struck Max's spirit as intensely as the brute's fist had done to his stomach. He'd tried so hard to be a good pastor.

"I never thought you'd stoop so low as to violate—"

"Nothing happened"—he gulped in a breath—"between me and your daughter." How could he convince the elitist control freak? "I didn't ... do anything wrong."

"Why did she tell me you did?" He spit near Max's boots.

For the first time since he'd become a minister, he wanted to pummel someone in the face. The arm at his neck stopped him.

"Why would she lie? Because you're a—" The creep in black jabbed him in the ribs. Max sucked in a breath. "Because she's pregnant and afraid of you. Go figure." His sarcasm won him another ram in the ribs.

"Rumor is Jayme isn't the only one." Derek stroked his chin. "So you're having a fling with a waitress now?"

"So you're hiring thugs now?"

Derek gestured for the brute to get lost. The stocky man let go of Max and ran toward the parking lot. "Personal bodyguard. Security."

Like that made this altercation legal. Max needed to sit down. He dropped onto a bench.

Derek turned away as if the meeting were finished. "There will be a paternity test."

A non-threat. "Fine. But why don't you ask Jayme?"

"I did."

Just then, acid rolled up Max's throat, most likely from the punch in the gut. He lurched over the railing and lost his lunch. He moaned.

Derek turned back toward Max. "It's time for you to leave Darby—for your own good."

"Right." Like any of this was for Max's good. He leaned his elbows against his knees, his fists against his forehead. And yet, as miserable as he was, he still felt the need to offer an olive branch. "If, uh, you and Jayme need a mediator, I might be able to help."

The banker guffawed. "You're the last person I'd ask to help my family." He strode from the gazebo like a king descending his throne. "I'm serious about the test."

"Whatever." Max never wanted to see Derek Clark again. But there was the matter of the church foreclosure and their joint names on the deed.

Moaning as he hobbled to his truck, Max crawled inside. Fortunately, the engine started on the first turn, and somehow the truck got him to the RV. There, he dropped onto the couch and fell asleep

Several hours later, his cell buzzing awaked him.

Unknown number flashed across the screen. He debated answering it. But it could be someone in need. "Hello?"

"Leave town or we'll make things worse for you."

"What? Who is this?"

Silence.

"Hello?"

Nothing.

He threw the phone on the TV tray.

The cell buzzed again. Mumbling, he answered.

"Don't call the cops or you'll be sorry."

"Tell me who this is."

An evil laugh. "We know where your wife works." Then silence.

They were coming after Season? Now, they'd gone too far. With one hand gripping his stomach, he scrounged through closets and cupboards in search of a weapon. Shoes? Books? A cast-iron pan?

His stomach and ribs hurt, so he climbed into bed. Better to sleep it off. In the morning he'd call Season. Tell her to avoid Darby. Maybe she should drive to Boise after the conference.

They knew where she worked? What did the guy mean by that?

What did Max ever do to get on the bad side of so many people?

Fifteen

Season

As she ate the juicy hamburger served with Maggie's home-made rolls for dinner, Season rehashed Martha's voicemail. Max wasn't in a good place emotionally, but him crossing the line the older woman had insinuated? Not likely. She might not like him very much right now, but she trusted him. Odd as that seemed.

Still, doubt whispered in her ear. What if he had done the unthinkable?

She groaned. Time to think about something else. Like her jar lantern. A few times walking to or from her cabin, she'd coaxed it along as if the flame had ears. "Don't burn out on me." "A little way and we'll be inside." "Come on, you can do it!"

Humorously, she'd overheard similar comments on the trails made by some of the couples to their candles.

However, by their dour expressions, Missy and Fred didn't find any pleasure in their keep-the-flame-going assignment.

Missy set her lantern on the table with a clunk. "Stupid thing went out three times."

"Oh, no." Season tried to be sympathetic. "Was it the wind?"

"That, and once, Fred blew it out on purpose." She scowled at him.

His shoulders lifted and fell. "Gave her something to do while I tried to listen to the news on my phone. Terrible service here."

Missy harrumphed. "I had to walk all the way to the lodge to light it with the 'special' lighter." She made air quotes. "Don't see why we can't use any old match."

"If you did, who would know?" Fred stuffed the rest of his burger in his mouth. He seemed to be enjoying the food despite whatever else made him grumpy about Hart's Camp.

"We'd be living a lie, you big oaf!" Missy shuffled her chair away from his.

Summer stopped at their table. "Good news! I just got a text from Winter. They're almost here."

"Great." Season was eager to hear what the duo had to share tonight.

"Good thing. Me and Fred were about to leave." Missy rocked her thumb at the lantern. "This might push me over the edge."

"I'm sorry, Missy." Summer patted her arm. "Anything I can do?"

"Got another cabin I could move into?"

The camp proprietor shook her head. "Our accessible cabins are filled. The others are too far up the mountain."

Missy's eyes widened. "Can I move in with Season?"

"Oh, well, I, uh, I don't know." Season didn't like not having her husband present. But listening to Missy complain about Fred 24/7? No thanks.

"Your hubby isn't here. Hate for you to be all sad and lonely." Missy made a pouty face like she was being empathetic, but Season figured she was mostly thinking of herself. "What do you say, friend?"

"Wouldn't it be better if you and Fred stayed together and worked things out?" God bless Summer for saying so.

"I told you what would happen if you got another cabin." Fred waved his forkful of potato salad.

"Yeah, yeah. You'd head home." She thrust out her arms. "See if I care." She leaned over the lantern, her gaze on Fred, and blew out their candle.

"Missy." Summer gasped.

Fred stuffed more food in his mouth.

Missy's face reddened. When she leaned forward as if she might blow out Season's flame too, Season yanked the lantern toward herself. The small fire flickered.

"Don't do that. Keep going. That's it," Season coaxed her staggering flame.

"Who are you talking to?" Missy glared.

Season felt heat skitter up her cheeks. "To my candle. Silly, huh?"

"I'll say."

"I do the same thing." Autumn laughed.

"That's the truth." Gar put his arm over his wife's shoulder. "In fact, I walked into the cabin and found her singing to the flame. 'Oh, my darling. Oh, my darling.'"

"Oh, you!" Autumn smacked his shoulder playfully. "Don't tell them that."

Everyone laughed—other than Fred and Missy, whose scowls deepened.

"People talk to their plants." Autumn shrugged. "Why not a candle?"

Gar kissed her cheek. "Why not?"

After his display of affection, Missy seemed more agitated. She shoved away from the table and stomped to the large coffeepot, which had to be big enough to hold a hundred cups, grumbling about "those romantics."

Autumn pushed her chair back as if to follow her.

Summer laid her hand on her arm. "Let me try." She hurried after Missy.

After Season finished eating and drank one more cup of coffee, she left the lodge and hiked up the trail through the woods. She clutched the lantern's handle in one hand and shielded the flame from the wind with the other. Every time she went outside, the elements proved a formidable force. Who would have imagined the difficulty in keeping a little blaze alive? She was thankful when she reached the cabin and could set the jar on the table near the window, safe again.

In preparation for the evening session, she changed out of her slacks and got into a black skirt with matching leggings. Then she sat on the bed to write some texts. She sent a note to Logan first. The message failed. She walked around the room, checking various locations for the best reception. One corner seemed to get a better signal, so she stood there. When the text went through, she quickly sent one to Benny.

Both boys seemed to be doing well in their college studies. However, Benny said he was struggling with a design concept in drafting class. When she mentioned he should call his dad, who'd taken similar courses in his younger days, he changed the subject. She finished her response, thinking it was a shame Benny didn't seem comfortable interacting with Max. While Max had spent time with the boys when they were young, in recent years as his church responsibilities expanded, he'd been away more. She was the one at home, fixing meals, playing board games, helping with homework, and hosting teenage get-togethers, and bonding more. Boy, did she miss those days.

She wondered how Max was doing tonight. Did he miss her? Maybe she should send him a text, just to check in.

How are you? Staying warm in the RV? I'm enjoying my time at Hart's Camp.

There was no response. Could be the intermittent snowfall messing up the service. Or Max didn't want to talk to her. Oh, well, at least she tried.

When it was time to make her way back to the lodge, the wind was calmer. What did Summer tell them this morning? "Each time you check the flame, think something positive about your husband."

Hm. What could Season think about Max?

Just then, snow fell off the tree overhead and plopped down in front of her. Before she could put her hand over the jar's opening, a clump of wetness landed on the candle, snuffing out the flame.

"Oh, no." She'd tried so hard to keep the wick lit.

At the lodge, she found several others relighting their candles.

"You too?" Autumn passed her the lighter.

"Unfortunately."

"I hoped to make it the whole week without losing the flame. Wishful thinking." Autumn shrugged. "Gives us more ideas to mull over about rekindling romance, huh?"

"Uh-huh." Not that she was interested in that subject right now. After several tries, she got the wick going, then she sat down next to Autumn at their table.

Josh led worship and played his guitar as accompaniment. Through most of the songs, he kept his eyes closed, truly worshiping, it seemed. Season felt warmed by the inspirational lyrics and time of focusing on the Lord.

During a round of "Father, I Adore You," the door opened and a couple, who were younger than Season, scurried inside, stomping their shoes and shaking off snowflakes. Winter and Ty. She remembered the day she signed up for the retreat and saw their pictures displayed on the camp website.

148

Ty waved at the group as he and Winter scurried to the front table and shed their coats.

Josh brought the song to an end. "Perfect timing, guys. Bad roads?"

"Oh, yeah." Ty walked to the front and shook hands with Josh. "Good to see you, bro."

"Same here." Josh nodded toward Winter. "Welcome."

"Thank you." The redhead with green eyes smiled at him, then waved at everyone.

A buzz of expectation filled the room. A few people hurried to the coffeepot for refills. Season was tempted to do the same. But if she wanted to sleep tonight, she'd better stick with water.

Josh removed the guitar strap from his shoulders. "How's everyone doing with their lanterns?"

A groan went up around the room. Some laughed.

Missy leaned toward Season. "I lit mine again." She pointed toward the center of the table where three lanterns rested. "Summer says I should try to work things out with Fred." Missy put her hand alongside her mouth as if telling a secret. "Your husband should be here too."

The comment stung. Hadn't she told herself the same thing plenty of times? What if she texted Max again and asked him to join her? Would he?

Josh introduced Winter and Ty, and a round of applause followed. Then the couple who'd walked in late strode to the lectern with their fingers linked. By the way their gazes met, the wink Ty sent his wife, and their obvious closeness, they must be happily married. But hadn't they been divorced? Season leaned her elbows against the table, her chin resting against her fists, and gave them her full attention.

Twenty minutes later, after Winter and Ty both spoke briefly about their divorce, what led up to it, and their mutual failings, Season sat in awe of them. They gave God glory for everything He'd done to bring them back together—and praised Him for some of the rough times they'd experienced since their second wedding. *Wow.* Season couldn't imagine sharing personal stuff like that about her and Max's marital journey.

Winter spoke about the flame of their love having been tested in recent events they'd be sharing about in the next few days. Tonight, they wanted couples to focus on each other. "Life is short. I know people say that all the time. But Ty and I had a brief marriage the first time around. Then we spent ten years apart. For the last year of being married again, we've been trying to make up for all the days and nights we experienced alone, without each other." She took his hand. "We're truly home with each other now. He has my heart. And I have his."

Oh, Max. I wish that were true of us.

"I want to hold his hand every chance I get." Winter laughed. "I want him to kiss me. Hold me in his arms."

Ty kissed her cheek as if to prove her point. She smiled at him.

"The honest truth is we've failed many times." She perused the group. "However, in every prideful moment or flawed experience, we've dusted ourselves off, and asked God and each other for forgiveness. All of you can know the beauty of your spouse's love, and forgiveness, too."

Season blinked back tears.

Winter took a step back as if yielding the podium to her husband.

"Our marriage isn't perfect, because 50 percent of this relationship is me." Ty pointed at himself and chuckled. "I'm imperfect. Guys, you with me?"

A few men raised their hands.

"Guilty!" Gar called out.

Autumn leaned against his shoulder. They were so cute.

But watching them, and after having listened to Winter and Ty, Season felt like a giant dam of emotion was on the verge of exploding within her. It would take all her willpower to delay it. Later, when she was tucked away in her cabin, alone, she could weep. Not now.

"Ladies"—Winter took the lead again—"tonight as you care for your lanterns, I want you to think about the man you married."

Ugh. Season wanted to avoid thinking about her and Max when they were young and in love.

"The handsome guy you share your cabin with is the same man you fell in love with and pledged your life to on your wedding day." She patted Ty's upper torso. "Sure, he might have put on a few pounds."

Several guys groaned.

Winter laughed. "Maybe he grew a mustache or he's balding. But in here"—she rested her palm over the middle of Ty's chest—"he's the same wonderful man you married." Her gaze locked onto her husband's. "Think about the guy who asked you to spend forever with him."

Ty's eyebrows rocked toward his wife's.

If only Max were as romantic with her as Ty was with Winter.

"He chose you. You chose him. Both of you are here as a celebration of your commitment to each other."

"Both" didn't apply to Season. Sure, she could recall the warm and passionate feelings she'd had around their wedding—all those vows of loving each other first and staying committed for the rest of their lives. Those promises seemed worse than distant memories now. They seemed … impossible. Knowing Max didn't want to be with her, wouldn't put their relationship first, nagged at her like a stomachache.

"Tomorrow, we'll talk about the man you wish he was."

The ladies snickered this time.

Gar groaned. "I'm in trouble."

"We all are." Fred frowned.

"And guys"—Ty draped his arm over Winter's shoulders—
"you took a vow to love, honor, and cherish your wife. Have
you been adoring her lately? In the morning, we'll talk about
how you can make your wife radiant. Look at that flame
shining on your table. Consider all it represents. Is your romance
well and alive?"

Silence filled the room.

Season knew the answer. The candle in her lantern was
burning just fine, but the flame of the Prescott's romance was
kaput. Zilch. Nada.

"We're going to have a great week reconnecting with the
women we love. Gents, you can be your wife's hero again. And
you may not think so right now, but it's time to win back her
affection. Work on your romancing." Ty turned Winter toward
him, whispered something in her ear, then gave her a thorough
kissing—right there in front of them all!

Chortles, whistles, and hand-clapping resounded.

When they broke apart, Winter's face was pink.

A few guys in the room followed Ty's example. A man at
the next table tipped his wife back and kissed her as if they'd
finished a dance. Autumn kissed Gar. He let out a whoop!

Season laughed at the romantic frivolity going on around
her. But if Max were here, he wouldn't kiss her like that. Not
considering how he felt about public displays of affection.

Besides, he wasn't here. And if he wouldn't attend, if he
didn't care enough to try, what hope did they have? Nothing
could fix this marriage if she were the only one who was
committed to it. That lonely place in her chest burned. All her
nagging him to come hadn't worked. What if she asked nicely?
What if he changed his mind and still came?

What if he didn't?

After the closing prayer, voices escalated around her. Maggie had left a bountiful array of snacks on the counter at the back of the room, but Season needed time alone to think and pray. *Please, God, mend my broken heart. Help me not to give up on my marriage. You can still do a miracle, right?* While everyone was distracted, she grabbed her coat and lantern and headed for the door, then slipped outside. Blinking back emotion almost too strong to corral, she reminded herself to keep the candle going and to not fall as she hiked up the trail.

A crackling noise in the woods made her think of the moose. What else might be out there? A cougar? Someone had mentioned they should be aware of wild animals in the forest, despite the winter weather. Now she was nearly jogging. She tried to keep her hand over her candle. "Please stay lit. Light my way home."

The flame sputtered but didn't go out. As she entered the cold cabin, she set the lantern on the table, then she turned up the thermostat. Forced air from the heater and a comforter on the bed would have to be enough to keep her warm tonight.

All the other couples would be returning to their cabins with their spouse. Even Missy, who wanted distance from her husband, was near him tonight.

But Season was alone.

Fully dressed, minus her boots, she crumpled into bed, buried herself under the blankets, and released the sobs that had been building all evening. After a while, she imagined herself curled up in God's arms, His love surrounding her. And she prayed for Max, for them to have a second chance to find healing and love in their relationship.

Sixteen

Max

Pounding at the door awoke Max out of a dead sleep. *Not again.* He groaned at the soreness in his ribs when he moved to check his cell phone. Four a.m.? Was it Clint? Derek? Or, heaven forbid, his henchman?

The second thumping sounded like a sledgehammer instead of knuckles rapping. Were the thugs at his door? His heart raced.

Should he call the police even though Clint told him not to? He clutched his cell. If he remained silent, would they think he wasn't home and leave?

"We know you're in there." A deep voice boomed from right outside the bedroom window.

Banging at both doors let him know he couldn't escape out either exit.

He sat up, wincing at the pain in his stomach where he'd taken that punch yesterday. He shoved his feet into slippers. He considered his options. One, call the police. Two, try to escape. Three, talk to the brutes and pray they didn't pummel him.

He held his cell phone in one hand and picked up a large wrench he'd brought in from the truck with the other hand. He couldn't imagine hitting anyone with it, but he wouldn't passively take violence either.

He trudged to the far end of the trailer. *God, I could use some help here.* He gripped the sixteen-inch wrench.

"Who is it?" He yelled toward the door.

A bat smashed through the small window at the side of the door.

He gasped and backed up until the couch stopped him. His hand shook so badly he could only try to punch in 9-1-1.

The second breaking of glass and a black glove reached in and unlocked the door. Two men wearing dark ski masks and black clothes charged into the living room.

Max had only gotten as far as 9-1. "What do you guys want?"

The taller guy snatched Max's cell phone out of his hand and hurled it at the back wall of the trailer.

"Hey!" Max's heart pounded like a jackhammer. He clutched the wrench but didn't swing. Probably a stupid idea to pit himself against these two. Time for plan number 3? "What are you after?" His voice came out high.

"What do you think?" The shorter thug—the same one who'd slugged Max yesterday?—punched the light switch by the door, breaking it into a dozen pieces. Max's teeth chattered.

The taller fellow towered over Max.

He begged God to save him. Bartered, even. If he got out alive, he'd make amends with Season. With his sons.

"Hand over the money you owe." The taller brute grabbed Max by the shirt and shoved him onto the couch.

"I don't have any money." He jumped up and held out his hands. "Look around. I live in a dumpy RV park."

The shorter one leaned in toward Max, his rank breath fouling the air. "Your buddy said you do."

Lee? "He's no buddy of mine. If Lee said I have cash, he lied." Max needed to reach the door and run. He swung his wrench, missed the goons, and struck the back window, busting the glass.

The tall guy grabbed the metal tool and jabbed it against Max's throat. "Your 'friend' borrowed cash from my boss. Said you'd pay up. So shell out now!" His voice boomed loud enough that Max's neighbor, Nellie, had surely heard. Would she call the police?

"I ... don't have ... money." He clenched his jaw, anticipating a punch.

The hit came solidly in his gut. "Uuuuuugh." He bent over, gripping his belly. He had a moment's impression of Stephen, in the Bible, being killed. Not that Max was a martyr. Just possibly dying. In horrible pain.

The tall guy's dark eyes gleamed through peepholes in his mask. "You have twenty-four hours. Deliver the funds and get out of town. Or else."

The shorter fellow raked his arm over the kitchen counter, knocking dirty dishes and silverware to the floor. Glassware exploded. Max jumped. The thug opened cupboards and scraped his arm over every surface. More stuff fell to the floor. He dumped out the drawers.

"Knock it off!" Max reached for a broken piece of pottery to throw at one of them. But the taller one grabbed him around the throat, stopping him. Breathing became a struggle as Max watched the criminal ransack the place.

The shorter one opened the fridge and threw out containers of food and liquids that splattered everywhere. Lids fell off. Chili beans ran down the wall. The pungent smell of vinegar permeated the small space. "Twenty-four hours. Or we'll be back." He drew a finger sharply across his neck, knife-like.

Something crashed against Max's skull. He moaned and slumped over.

Sometime later, he awoke, his body draped over the couch. His head throbbed. His torso hurt. Squinting at the room, he couldn't believe the chaos. Pans and clothes and food were piled across the floor. Did a tornado hit? Did the RV tip over? He shoved himself to a standing position. The room spun. He gripped his head and groaned. After touching the back of his head, his fingers came away bloody. Did someone hit him?

Where was his cell? If he could find it, he could call the police.

He grabbed an unopened water bottle off the floor. He barely had the energy to twist off the cap. Finally, he succeeded and guzzled the container dry.

Where did he leave his phone? He nudged piles of junk out of the way. Still dizzy, he grabbed the divider between sofa and dining booth, then held on to the table. Nearly collapsed. Lunging for the wall, he clutched a cabinet handle, then pushed himself into the bedroom. Landed on the mattress. *Umph.* He stretched out. Dozed. Then awoke suddenly.

What was he looking for? His cell?

He heard a beep like he just got a text. He stood and shoved socks and a tennis shoe out of the way. His phone was faceup on the floor. A series of cracks spanned the screen from corner to corner. Stepped on? Flung at the wall? He groaned, then he noticed he had a message. He tapped the screen. All the symbols were blurry, but the cell phone seemed to be working better than his brain.

He read the text from Season. Nice of her to check in.

He laid back down. Stuffed two pillows beneath his neck. He should reply. Why did his head hurt so badly? An image of a ski mask flashed through his mind, then was gone. He skimmed his thumb across the phone icon in the corner of the cracked screen and tapped Season's name. Her phone rang.

"Hello."

The sound of his wife's voice made him jerk awake. Had he fallen asleep again? "You're there. I miss you." He swallowed back emotions that felt close to the surface.

"Max? What's wrong? Are you stuffed up or something?"

"Uh-huh." He just needed—

"Max?"

He jerked awake. "Here." He tried to focus on the light emanating from the ceiling fixture. Radiant circles spread out like years marked on a tree stump.

"What's going on?" She sounded strange.

"Are you upset with me?" Although, he couldn't fathom why she would be angry with him. He was nice to her, most of the time, wasn't he?

A long pause.

"Maybe." She made some sniffing noises.

He'd deal with whatever was bothering her later. He was too fuzzy for deep conversations. He called to tell her something. What? "S-something happened." He groaned. "I think someone might have beat me up." He touched his head, then his stomach, and bit back a groan.

"What?" She sounded worried. That made his heart feel warm. "Someone beat you up? Who? Are you all right?"

"A guy in a ski mask." Or maybe he imagined that.

She gasped. "Have you been drinking?"

"What? No." He drifted off.

"Max!"

He awoke. "Y-you know me better than that."

"I thought I did. You sound drunk."

"Never drink on Sunday." He never drank, period. His father had been an alcoholic. Drank on Sunday. Monday too.

What was it Max didn't do on Sundays? He felt the back of his head. "Have a lump on the noggin."

"Someone actually hit you? Did you call the police? An ambulance?"

Did he? He couldn't find his phone. Oh, right, he was using it. "Nah. I'm tough." His head pulsed like his heart was in his cranium. He might puke.

"What can I do to help? Someone should be there with you. Shall I call Clint or Derek?"

"No!"

"Why not?"

"I don't know." Why did he have such a strong reaction to her suggestion? "Just don't call either of those guys."

"Okay, I won't call them. I could drive back there today."

"No!" Why didn't he want her here? The place was a disaster. A break-in? "I think it's safer where you are."

"Max, I don't like not being there with you." That made him smile. "You have to go to the doctor." He'd never liked it when she used her bossy voice with him. "Call 911. An ambulance will come and take you to the ER."

"Okie dokie." Better to agree than fight. He sank into the pillow. Closed his eyes.

"And call the police." Did she have to shout?

"K." He sat up. The room spun. "Gotta go." But he'd wanted to tell her something.

"Promise me you'll see a doctor."

"Uh-huh. Have to sleep first. Bad headache. Later, Sea-girl."

She made a sound. A gasp?

Had he ever called her Sea-girl before?

"Head for the emergency clinic. You hear me, Max?"

"Under and out." So tired. He ended the call. Laid down on the pillow again. Nice to hear her voice. *Sea-girl.*

Seventeen

Season

Ever since Max's call a half hour ago, Season had alternated between standing in the corner of the cabin where phone reception was the strongest, praying for him, and throwing her clothes in her suitcase. Her romantic feelings for him might be all mixed up, but after two decades of marriage, she was seriously concerned about his well-being.

Her cell vibrated, and she hoped it was Max. Instead, it was an emergency notice from Summer. *Heavy snowfall during the night. Morning session canceled. Josh will clear trails ASAP. County snow-removal services may not reach our road until tomorrow.*

Tomorrow? She was stuck at Hart's Camp? This couldn't be happening—not now. She needed to go to Max, even if he didn't want her there.

She tapped his name on the screen. Four rings later, his voicemail kicked in. "Call me when you get this, okay?" She left the message, then ended the call.

Even if she could hop in the car right now, in perfect road conditions it would take five hours to get to Darby. Now, it sounded like she was snowed in. Who could she get to check on Max this early? Clint? Or Nellie? Or should she just call 911 herself? First, she'd try getting ahold of their neighbor. Season searched her contact list, found the woman's number, and tapped the screen. "Come on, pick up."

Static. Then the phone went dead.

"No." She tried again.

"Hello?" Nellie's voice sounded cautious like she didn't have caller ID.

"Mrs. Brandt? This is Season Prescott, your neighbor." She rushed through the introduction. "I'm sorry to bother you, but I'm afraid something is wrong with Max. Could you walk over to our RV and check on him? Right now, please? I'd appreciate it."

"I thought you two had a doozy of a fight this morning." The morning news on the TV blared in the background.

"You did? When?"

"Real early." Nellie chuckled. "Four-fifteen."

"I'm sorry the noises awakened you. I wasn't home. And this really is an emergency."

"What's going on?"

Season didn't know the extent of what happened to Max. "Could you knock on our door, and if he doesn't answer, call 911? He seems to be injured."

"Max? You're s-sure?" Her voice went in and out with a bad connection. "Where are you?"

"I'm away." No time for details. How could she convince the woman who spent most of her day in her bathrobe to hurry? "That noise you heard may have been someone, perhaps a robber, beating up Max."

Nellie gasped. "I'll head right over and check. I promise."

"Thank you. And be careful." She started to hang up. "Nellie? Call me back as soon as you know something, okay?"

But the call had been disconnected. She'd try again in a few minutes.

Her boots scudded across the wooden planked floor as she grabbed a few more items and tossed them into her travel bag. If Max needed her, and it sounded like he did, she'd be ready to leave as soon as the road was cleared. Fortunately, Darby had a clinic, an extension of the hospital in Hamilton. If Max went there, she should hear something soon.

Lord, have mercy. Protect Max from—? She didn't even know how to finish that prayer.

Five more minutes passed. She redialed Nellie, without getting a response. Ten minutes later she tried again.

"H-hello?" Nellie sounded out of breath.

"How is he?" She skipped pleasantries.

"Not good. The ambulance came and got your husband. Took him to the ER in Hamilton." Nellie's voice wavered. "I-I'm so sorry for whatever happened to the poor man."

Why did they take him to the hospital, not the local clinic? Season swallowed hard. "Is he going to be okay?"

"EMTs said they couldn't tell me anything since I'm not family." She sounded offended.

"Poor Max." She felt terrible to be so far from him and unable to get to him quickly.

"Your place looks like a cyclone hit."

"What do you mean?"

"The cupboards were emptied." Nellie made a tsk-tsk sound. "Stuff all over the floor. Food, juice, clothes."

"Goodness." Maybe someone broke in. Wreaked havoc. Hurt Max.

"I saw broken windows too. Looked like a dump, I'm sorry to say." A knock sounded in the background. "I have to go. Police are here for my statement."

"Thank you, Nellie. Your help means a lot to me." She disconnected the call.

Max was injured. Their RV trashed? Had this been a random burglary? Or something else?

In a few minutes, she'd call the ER in Hamilton. When she knew something definite, she'd notify the boys. Although, waiting for the road to be cleared would be hard.

Twenty minutes later, she located the hospital's number.

"I'm sorry, Mrs. Prescott. No word on your husband yet." The receptionist sounded in a rush to end the call.

"Thank you."

She texted Max.

I'm so sorry for whatever happened to you. Call me when you can.

A troubling half hour passed as she made more phone calls and texts, and stared out the window at the fresh layer of snow that had fallen—what was it, eight to ten inches more? She groaned. Normally, she'd appreciate the beauty of the forest all white, and almost magical. Not now. Today, she wanted a clear trail and a means of getting away from camp as quickly as possible. How long would it take to get the trail and parking lot cleared, not to mention the two miles of back roads?

She paced and prayed, then she stood in the corner, hoping for better cell reception.

When her phone finally rang, and without looking at the screen, she answered it. "Max?"

"It's me." His voice sounded distant, but not as slurred as it had been earlier.

"I'm so relieved to hear from you." She clutched the cell phone to her ear.

The following silence was unnerving.

"Max?" Oh, no. They must have been disconnected. She located his recent call and swiped the screen. "Max?" she spoke as soon as he answered. "How are you?"

"My head aches like I fell off a building."

"What did the doctor say?"

"Concussion. Rest. Drink fluids."

"A concussion? I've been so worried. Mrs. Brandt told me you're in Hamilton." She cradled the cell phone with both hands, imagining how he must be feeling.

"That ambulance ride, plus my time in the ER, will cost us our yearly food budget."

"Don't worry about it."

A long pause. Had they been disconnected again?

"Max?"

"I'm here."

"Did someone actually break into our trailer?"

"I might have let them in. I don't know." He sighed. Or moaned. "Could we not talk about this right now?" A definite groan. "Truth is, I don't remember what happened."

"You don't? What's going on?"

"I just need to go home and rest." He cleared his throat. "Doc says it will come back to me eventually."

"Oh. You mean, you really don't remember?" If that were the case, she needed to be with him.

"Best not to force it, I guess."

"My bag is packed." She talked fast so he wouldn't tell her not to come back. "Normally, I could have been there in five hours, but thanks to last night's storm, the roads are impassable. I'll leave as soon as—"

"No, I'd rather you stayed there."

"Why?" Didn't he want her to try to be with him? Maybe he didn't like the idea of her taking care of him. Or her coming home.

"Actually, I'm glad you're a long way from the trailer and Darby." He sounded gruff.

"Because of the break-in?"

"Or whatever happened." At least, that response negated her idea that he didn't want her there because of their personal problems.

What if he'd been seriously hurt, or died? Praise God that didn't happen. "Are you sure you don't want me to come home? I'm concerned about you."

"I'm serious. Stay where you are."

"But—"

"I need to rest, that's all. And I want to know you're safe."

"Safe? Max, I wish you could tell me what they wanted."

"Money, no doubt."

She scoffed. "They should've broken into a better neighborhood. Not an RV in a trailer court."

"Never know, Seas, maybe they're deranged."

Seas? Sea-girl? What was with him calling her nicknames? Was it the concussion?

Should she do what he said, and stay here? Or should she show him she wanted things to work out between them by driving home as soon as the roads were cleared? There was another option. "I wish you were here at the camp with me." Away from danger. Closer to her. She held her breath a couple of seconds, wondering if he'd even consider her suggestion.

"Me too."

The air burst out of her mouth. "Really?" That he might want to be with her too made her pulse rate hike. Even though something awful had happened to Max, and it looked like the storm would keep her cabin bound, perhaps God was answering her prayers about bringing them back together.

"Of course, I'd rather be with you. You're my wife." His gently spoken words tugged on her heart.

"Oh Max, come to me, then." She felt her heart softening toward him a little more. Was that because of her worry over his injuries? Or because of all the reconciliation talk she'd heard in the last couple of days?

He chuckled in a husky way she used to love. "I can't drive, doctor's orders."

A thought came to her. "Why don't you fly into Spokane later today? Flights will be going through by then. And hopefully, the road here will be cleared. You could ride the bus to Missoula and catch a flight. We have a little money left in savings." She waited. "Please, Max?"

A sigh. "Okay."

Okay? Thank you, God!

"I'll try ... tomorrow. I'm going to crash for the rest of the day."

Not today. Still. "I'll look forward to seeing you. Be safe, Max."

"I'd better get some sleep before I fall over. Seas?"

She already liked him calling her that.

"Yes?"

"Thank you for being concerned about me. And for calling Nellie. I, uh, know we need to talk." A pause. "I'll let you know about the flight." The phone went dead.

He knew they needed to talk about what? A separation? Was that still a possibility? Maybe he needed to talk with her about Jayme. Had the gossip wheel churned out more lies about her and Max? Or had the break-in really shaken him up?

Eighteen

Season

After the next day's morning session, where Winter had shared more on the flame's symbolism, Season laid down to take a nap. Her sleepless nights were catching up with her, and she just wanted to close her eyes. Earlier when she called to check on Max, he didn't know his flight plans yet. So as she dozed off, she held onto her cell phone to not miss his call or text. Two hours later, she woke up suddenly and discovered she'd slept right through "Edelweiss" and missed his call. With a groan, she accessed the message.

"I booked a late flight." Max's voice sounded stronger. "I caught a ride with Joe Benson's delivery truck to Missoula. The estimated arrival in Spokane is six p.m. Flight 496. See you then." No softly spoken "Seas" this time.

She sighed, and rested her cheek against the pillow again, appreciating the warmth of the homemade quilt. It was two o'clock now. If Max was arriving at six, she'd leave camp at four to get to the airport on time. That gave her two hours to wait and pray and contemplate. Fortunately, Josh cleared the trails yesterday afternoon, and the county opened the road out of Hart's Camp this morning.

Whenever Season thought about Max calling her *Sea-girl* and *Seas,* her spirit felt lighter. Maybe something good might still be happening between them. Even now, she envisioned him stepping off the jet with a bandage wrapped around his head, and her running to him like a heroine in a romantic movie. He would tell her how sorry he was for his mistakes. Kiss her passionately. Whisper sweet reassurances in her ear. But then she groaned. In real life, Max would never do those things.

Her cell phone vibrated, alerting her to a text. It seemed the reception was working better this afternoon, which must mean clear skies. Although, she'd heard Josh say another storm was in the forecast.

Summer, here. Aunt Em wants to know if you'll come over for tea. She'd like to meet you.

Although Season was still worried about Max, chatting with Josh's aunt sounded like a perfect way to pass the next hour.

I could do that.

Awesome!

She should mention something about Max.

Max will be joining me this evening.

That's fantastic! I look forward to meeting him.

After pulling on her boots and putting on her peacoat, Season grabbed her lantern and trekked down the trail to the main lodge. She crossed the bridge over the creek to the other side of the road, thankful for Josh's snow removal efforts, then hiked up the slope to the log cabin on the opposite hillside. Didn't Summer say she lived farther into the trees? She even said something about an altercation with a cougar last fall. Yikes! She was a brave woman.

When Season knocked on the front entry of the cabin, a spry elderly woman opened the door. Her hair was gorgeous, like the gray sky over an ocean. Her twinkling eyes sparkled with a youthfulness that belied her years. "Hello, my dear. You must be Season Prescott."

"Guilty."

"Come in, and welcome. I'm Em Hart." She gave her a quick hug, then swayed her hand toward the living room behind her. "You can set the candle on the coffee table."

"Thank you, Mrs. Hart." Season entered the room with glistening log walls, then set down her lantern, thankful it hadn't blown out.

"Call me Em." She removed a crocheted item off the couch. "Have a seat. Tea?"

"Yes, thank you." Season sat down where Em cleared the cushions.

The older woman scurried into the kitchen.

"Your house is beautiful," Season called after her.

"Thank you." Josh's aunt returned to the doorway. "Simple, but homey, I hope." Then she moved out of sight again.

The woodstove crackled with a hot fire. The aroma in the room hinted at a mix of burning wood and—chocolate chip cookies?

A few minutes later, Em returned with a platter bearing two china cups filled with tea, and a plate of chocolate chip cookies.

"Mmmm. Looks delicious."

"I love to make cookies." She chuckled as she sat down and took her own cup in her hands. "Our worker, Hank, who's more a brother than a laborer, carries on about my baked goods. Butters me up for more, that's what. He's away for the winter, visiting relatives in the Midwest and taking a well-deserved break."

Season took a bite. "I can see why he loves these."

"I'm glad you like them. Have you met our Shua?" Her eyes lit up more, if that were possible.

"I saw her on the sledding hill with Josh." A picture came

to mind of father and daughter laughing and speeding down the slope.

"She and Joshua come over for daily visits and eat my desserts." Her eyes twinkled. "I love spending time with my family."

"Me too. I have two sons." Season sipped the tea. "I miss them."

"I couldn't bear children, but I couldn't love Joshua any more than I do if he had been my own." She patted her chest. "Shua is my dream-come-true granddaughter."

"That's so sweet." She remembered Josh's comments about his aunt the day she pulled into Hart's Camp. "Your nephew loves and admires you so much."

The older woman grinned. "That boy was a rascal. But I loved him, regardless." Her eyebrows raised. "Sometimes we've got to love our rascals right back into our arms. Sometimes, right into the Kingdom."

Was Max the "rascal" in Season's life? Although, she doubted he'd appreciate being called by that term.

"Have anyone in your life who fits that description?" Em set down her teacup, a guileless look on her face, but Season suspected she knew the answer. Em picked up what looked to be a baby bootie in progress. Her crochet needle worked over the pink yarn.

Season nibbled her cookie. "I do know someone who fits that description."

Em eyed her over the needlework. "Feel like talking? If not, that's okay."

Did she want to tell a stranger, albeit a kindly one, her deepest thoughts?

Em chuckled. "I confess, I asked Josh and Summer to tell me about the couples attending the conference. Who I should pray for and such."

"That's nice of you."

"I stay inside during the winter months." She nodded in the direction of the lodge. "But my heart is in that building. Every time they're in session, I'm praying for husbands to love their wives. For wives to fall in love with their spouses again. For people who don't know Jesus to come to Him. For God's grace to saturate the place." Her eyes moistened. "God's love can change the hardest of hearts."

Her words flowed into Season like sunshine over a wilted flower. "I've believed in Jesus since I was a child. And I pray for my sons every day." Maybe she should have prayed for Max more.

"That's wonderful." Em nodded. "Ever gone through a season of doubt?"

More like a wilderness. "Lately, I have."

"We've all struggled in faith at one time or another." Her gaze met Season's. "Can't enjoy the mountain peak without the climb, right?"

"True."

The soft sound of Em rocking in her chair kept time with the old clock on the mantle. The fire in the woodstove crackled and popped. Season sipped her tea and relaxed into the soft couch cushions. For a while, neither of them spoke. Yet the silence was comfortable.

"I think you are a brave woman." Em laid her crocheting in her lap, then reached for her teacup and lifted it like a toast. "Here's to your strong will and determination."

"I'm not sure whether that's true."

"Coming to a marriage conference alone? My dear, that must have been the hardest of journeys." Em's face wrinkled with a hundred beautiful lines. "You wanted your marriage healed so much you were willing to do anything to see that happen."

Season swallowed hard. She had driven a long way in a terrible storm to get here. Was it because she wanted her marriage healed? Or to show Max that she was the one willing to try anything to make things work between them—while he sat at home doing nothing?

"God smiles at that kind of faith."

Did He smile at her, even though she'd been prideful, angry at Max, and determined to have her own way? She let out a long sigh.

Em rocked her chair slower. "I'm praying for you and your husband. That night when Joshua talked to you, I felt such an urgency to pray. I sank my knees on the floor by this old couch. Those cushions have been soaked with my tears many times during prayer."

So Josh had been right. Em was praying for her during the storm.

"I'd love to hear about your life back home." Em untangled some yarn.

In the cozy warmth of the log cabin, Season described the parsonage and church in Darby. She explained about the property's park-like grounds where her boys used to play. And she couldn't skip telling such a good listener about Logan and Benny—the joys of her life. She revealed some of her and Max's marital deterioration, and what she knew of Max's injury. Baring her heart to Josh's aunt, while she kept crocheting, her eyes only occasionally glancing up, was easier than Season would have thought possible.

"You've been under such a heavy load." Em's gaze focused on something outside the window. "I married a tough critter myself. Josh's Uncle Mac was a bitter man for years. A mile-wide canyon of hurt existed between the two men I loved most, him and Joshua. Still, I prayed and believed. What's that verse? 'This is the confidence we have in approaching God: that if we ask anything according to his will, he hears us.' Boy, did I hold onto that Scripture. And He heard me!"

"That's inspiring." It gave her more hope for her and Max.

Em's gaze grew pensive. "You have a wounded heart, don't you, my dear?" It was as if she could see right into Season's pain. Em dropped her yarn into a tapestry bag on the floor.

"I suppose I do." She half nodded, half shrugged.

"God has heard you crying out to Him." Em leaned forward and clutched her hand. "He will answer your prayers."

The woman's kindness was almost Season's undoing. When was the last time anyone spoke to her so lovingly and reassuringly? "Thank you, Em. Max is arriving today, even though he said he wouldn't. That has to be an answer to prayer."

"Praise the Lord!" Still holding Season's hand, Em prayed out loud. Her words to "Father God" were powerful. When the prayer ended, Season added, "Amen."

The door opened and nearly crashed against the wall. In ran Shua, snowflakes peppering her hat and coat, her arms wide. "*Gwammy!*" She charged into Em's outstretched arms and gave her a long hug.

"You're home, sweet pea." The older woman hugged the child to her and rocked her.

From outside, it sounded like a truck pulled out of the driveway.

Em turned Shua to face Season. "Shua, this is Mrs. Prescott. She lives in Montana."

Shua's blue eyes widened. "With all the *howsies?*"

Season laughed. "Yep, there are a lot of horses in Montana. But I don't own any." Her sons would have changed that fact when they were young if they could have.

"My *fwiend Lexi* gots two *howsies* at *hew* house." Shua looked at something else. "Cookies! *Gwammy*, can I have one?"

"Yes, you may. Then go change out of your school clothes."

Shua nabbed a cookie, then rushed down the hallway and disappeared into one of the rooms.

"She's in preschool. Lexi's mom drives them to and from their school in Newport." Em grinned. "Shua loves to tell us what she's learning."

"She's so cute." Season glanced out the window and saw that snow was falling heavier again. She picked up both cups and placed them on the tray, then she stood. "I should go. I need to drive to the airport and get Max, and it looks like we're in for some more bad weather. Thank you for sharing your heart and your home with me." Season embraced her almost as enthusiastically as Shua had.

"I'm praying"—Em patted her shoulder—"that God will heal your marriage."

She seemed so confident, making Season wonder how this prayer warrior's requests might get answered.

Nineteen

Max

For most of the four-hour flight time, including a stop-over in Seattle, Max's thoughts had been on his wife. He couldn't wait to see her. Talk to her. Hold her in his arms. What could he say, where could he begin, to make things right between them? Should he apologize, right off, for letting her leave without saying goodbye? Him and his foolish pride.

He kept rehashing how she'd begged him to go to the retreat, yet he refused, over and over. Now, here he was on his way to meet her—weary and a bit broken. But they'd soon be spending time alone in a cabin in the woods. Walking down a wintry trail through the forest—holding hands, he hoped. Attending marital seminars together. Would the lectures help them overcome the heartaches of the past months? Could Season forgive him for his negligence toward her, and his self-centered behavior for those months while his ministry collapsed? He'd never meant to hurt her. Hadn't intentionally meant to withdraw from their marriage. But he knew he had, on both counts.

They had a lot of reconnecting to do if they were going to

survive as a couple. And it started with him today. What could he do to bridge the gaping chasm between them?

He was ashamed to admit it, even to himself, but he hadn't prayed much since he'd lost his pastorate. He'd been drowning in discouragement for too long. Up to his neck in the quicksand of doubt. Maybe, now, was the time to start talking to God again. *Lord, could You help us save our marriage? Help me to be a better husband for Season. I know I messed up in so many ways.* He quoted a couple of his favorite verses, trying to get his heart in a better place to greet his wife.

As the plane landed and taxied down the runway in Spokane, his head throbbed from the pressure. All he wanted to do was lie down and forget the white world outside. How far did Season say the camp was from the airport? Were the roads cleared now? Would she expect him to attend something with her tonight?

Max let the other passengers vacate the aisle before he grabbed his carry-on and exited the jet. He followed the crowd through the deplaning corridor. Once he reached the airport lobby near the ticket counters, he scanned the area. He couldn't wait to see her, his wife of twenty-two years—his home, his haven.

There she stood with her winter coat draped over her arm, her short golden hair free of a hat, and her gaze searching the crowd. Their gazes met. She lifted her hand and smiled. His heart pounded. The name he'd called her yesterday skimmed across his mind. *Sea-girl.* He'd never called her cutesy names, but he might just try it again.

"Hey, Max," she said as he drew near.

She was so beautiful. Regret over how he'd acted toward her lately, him clamming up, zoning out in TV land, and not treating her like a beloved wife, raced up his chest. He didn't deserve her forgiveness, nor her grace, but he longed for it.

Bruised ribs aside, he wouldn't mind pulling her into his arms and begging her forgiveness right here—if only they weren't in a crowded airport.

He came to a stop about ten feet from her. Just stood there, drinking in her beauty. How had he gotten so lucky as to marry her?

"Max?" Her softly spoken word dug at a tender place in his chest.

Man, he'd missed her. No way would he stand there like a frozen statue. He released his carry-on and rushed toward her, not sure if she'd accept his embrace. Probably surprising her, he took her in his arms. "Mmmm, Sea-girl." He inhaled the familiar scent of apples and cloves and her. "You smell nice."

"Good to see you too." She leaned her cheek against his coat for a moment.

He liked standing close to her like this, holding her. If only they could be alone for a few minutes for a proper greeting.

He glanced at a TSA agent who watched them. But Max kept his arms around his wife. He couldn't believe he'd let a reservoir of heartache build between them.

She pulled away first. "How are you doing? How's your head?" She made a circle around him as if looking for his injuries.

"I'm okay." He shrugged, not wanting unnecessary attention.

They didn't kiss, but, boy, did he want to. What would she say if he leaned her back and gave her a real I-love-you-forever sort of kiss? She might have a heart attack. No, he'd better wait until some things were resolved between them. He just hoped his struggles hadn't killed every spark of life between them.

"Shall I get your bag?" She hurried back and grabbed the handle of his suitcase.

"I can do that." He wasn't helpless.

"Let me." Her smile seemed more like a warning. Stay back? Give her space?

Okay. He sighed. They had a lot of making up to do. He could see he'd have to take it slowly.

"Need anything?" She pointed toward the men's room. "It's about an hour and a half to Hart's Camp. Two, if road conditions worsen. I was hoping to make it back for part of the evening session." She cringed like that might be an unrealistic goal. Which was what he was thinking.

"About that." He touched a tender spot on his stomach. Then remembering he didn't want to make her anxious, he let his hand fall away.

"Max?"

"It's been a hard day, is all." Nothing some pain relief tablets for the soreness and swelling, and a night of sleep, wouldn't fix.

"A warm cabin awaits." She linked her arm with his as if to support his weight.

He didn't need her assistance, but he liked how she walked close to him, her head almost touching his shoulder. Outside, snow fell lightly in the dark. Hopefully, the roads were safe. Unless she'd be willing to do something else for tonight, like get a room so he could rest.

When he lowered himself into the passenger seat of their car, and she slid behind the steering wheel, he laid his palm over her hand, detaining her from starting the engine. "What would you say to us getting a motel room around here for the night?" His words thudded in the empty space. By her sharp look, he wondered if she thought he was asking for something else. "Just to sleep." Anything else would be unthinkable with the canyon of mistakes and hurts between them.

"I'd rather not miss any more of the seminar." She sighed. "Are you in a lot of pain?"

"Mostly, I'm desperate for sleep." He yawned. "Sorry to ask, but I'm exhausted."

She stared out the window as if contemplating his situation and the snowy weather.

Silence filled the car.

He woke up suddenly and realized he'd dozed. They were still in the airport parking lot. "Sorry. That keeps happening."

"You really are tired, aren't you?" Her tone was gentler now.

He nodded.

"We can stay in town for the night if that would make it easier on you." She nodded toward the windshield. "The snow's coming down pretty heavy now. Good thing your flight made it in."

"I'm thankful for that." He shuffled in his seat to see her better. "Sleeping at the Sea-Tac airport tonight wasn't on my wish list."

"I bet." She pulled out of the parking lot and switched on the radio. An announcer said something about a winter storm warning. Maybe staying in town was for the best. But by the resigned look on his wife's face, he wasn't so sure.

Season checked them in to a hotel in downtown Spokane that they probably couldn't afford. Good thing it was the off-season with cheaper rates. They rode in an elevator, and he made it to their room without tripping or falling asleep.

Hours later, he awoke in an unfamiliar, darkened space. A nightlight cast just enough glow that he could see a door. He barely remembered anything after arriving here. Seemed he stripped down to his boxers and t-shirt and crawled under the sheets. What time was it? He found his cell phone on the end table and tapped the broken screen. Light from the phone shot pain through his eyes. Six in the morning? So much for feeling better after sleeping. Where was Season?

He smoothed his hand over the covers until he touched her. She must have been lying as far from him as the bed allowed. Even in sleep, her back was rigid as if to keep her distance.

A sigh rumbled from deep inside him. He'd botched everything with her. He had been self-absorbed. Critical. Unloving. How could he hope to make amends? He closed his eyes and prayed for a few minutes.

He really needed to stand up. Every muscle hurt. However, staying in bed wasn't an option. He and Season had a marriage conference to attend. He wasn't an idiot. The fact that their marriage was in serious trouble was now as obvious as the throbbing in his skull.

As soon as he pushed off the bed, dizziness swamped him. Where was the bathroom? He needed a shower. A drink of water. And more pain relief. He clutched the bedspread, then edged around the foot of the bed, trying not to wake up his wife.

"Max? Do you need help?"

"I'm okay. Go back to sleep." But he hadn't released the blanket.

She jumped out of bed and hurried to him, scooting her bare shoulder under his arm. She was dressed in a dark camisole and leggings. He leaned into her. Nice how she fit against him, her skin warm. And she smelled good. Seemed his senses were working fine, despite his sluggish brain. Finally, they reached the bathroom.

She flipped on the light switch. "You all right?"

He squinted hard enough the light stopped blinding him. "Yeah, thanks." He grabbed the door frame. "I'm going to take a shower."

"You don't need any help with that, right?" She didn't meet his gaze as if embarrassed by the question.

He almost laughed. It had been a long while since either of them had been undressed in front of the other. "I'll be okay." He hoped. "Try to get back to sleep."

He closed the door. The longer he stood there, the steadier his footing became, and his equilibrium returned. In the shower, he stood beneath the hot stream until he felt more human. Clear thinking returned, except for that blank section on the timeline when he got hit in the head.

Needing his clothes, he wrapped a towel around his waist and opened the bathroom door. Season wore yesterday's dress, and she sat on the edge of the bed tapping her cell phone. He entered the dimly lit room in search of his bag.

"Is there a problem?" Hopefully, the people at the campground didn't mind that they hadn't returned last night.

"Not at all. I thought I'd let Summer know I won't make it to this morning's session either."

"You okay with that?"

"Sure. Whatever is best for you."

Best for him was getting some food in his stomach. "Would you mind if we ordered breakfast? I probably shouldn't take any medicine on an empty stomach."

"Actually, there's a complimentary breakfast." She stood, then slipped into her ankle boots.

He'd always liked seeing her in those and a dress. Had he ever told her so?

After zipping the sides of the boots, she grabbed her door fob. "I'll fix our plates and be right back." She finally looked at him. "You'll be okay while I'm gone?" She stared at him with such concern that her show of tenderness almost took his breath away.

"Sure. I feel better." Minus the headache. "Shower's a miracle worker."

"I'm glad to hear it." She closed the door.

With a sigh, he dug through his clothes until he found the shirt and underwear he wanted. He'd wear yesterday's jeans.

But the weightier matter settled on his shoulder like a two-hundred-pound barbell. How could he make things right with Season when tension thick as a cedar plank hovered between them? So much distrust. He remembered that day in the RV when she tried to coax him to run away to the Oregon Coast. If only he had! If they'd left Darby that day and stayed away, the thugs wouldn't have come after him, he wouldn't have heard Jayme's lie, and he wouldn't have such bad blood between him and Derek. Maybe God had wanted him to leave with his wife. Why hadn't Max asked Him about that? But then, he couldn't do anything about the past. The future? That was a different story.

What had Iris said in her letter? *Do whatever it takes to make things right.* What would it take for him to show his wife he really loved her? That he wanted them to get back together?

She returned with two plates of eggs, fruit, and toast. She buzzed into the room, set the food down, then rummaged around with the coffeepot near the sink, pretty much all without looking at him. His awareness of the chill in the room escalated, even as the fabulous aromas made his stomach gurgle. How long had it been since he'd eaten? Pretzels on the plane? He dove into the eggs like a starving man.

Season picked up her plate, then crossed the room to one of the two swivel chairs. She took the time to bow her head. Something he hadn't done.

He dropped into the other chair, and they ate in silence. He wished she'd say something. Or at least meet his gaze. He didn't know how to broach any personal topics. Maybe they needed a marriage conference more than he'd realized.

He ate the last half of his toast, mulling over his thoughts as definitively as he munched the bread. What if she'd already decided to leave him? How would he survive as a single, divorced ex-pastor? Ugh. Such thoughts were too painful.

"Ready for coffee?" She jumped up.

"Uh, I probably shouldn't have any today." He pushed off the chair, hiding his groan, and threw the paper products in the garbage by the end table. "Doc said I should avoid caffeine."

"I didn't think of that."

"That's okay. You go ahead."

"Maybe I will since it's made." She fixed her cup of coffee, then walked to the far side of the window. She pulled back the blinds and sipped her drink. Was she keeping a distance between them?

"What floor are we on?" He couldn't remember, but the snow-covered roofs below made him think they were on the tenth floor or higher. A bit of blue was showing in the sky, and the clouds didn't look as heavy and dark as they did yesterday.

"Twelfth. This would be a great view in the summer."

"Then let's come back in the summer."

She smiled but didn't agree. So much for him trying to lighten the mood.

"Are you rested enough to head north?" She glanced at him.

"I do feel better." He took a deep breath. "Would you mind if we talked for a few minutes first?" Somehow, he had to try to bridge the gap of communication.

She set her empty cup on the table. "Okay." She shrugged. "What do you want to talk about?"

"Some of the stuff that's happened this week, for starters."

"I'd like that." Her eyebrows drew together. "But if our discussion turns into a disagreement, what then? Will you still go to the camp with me? Or head back home?" Her gaze clouded like she thought he might do that.

Did she think he procrastinated about going to the camp

last night because he didn't want to attend the retreat? He moved to stand beside her near the window. "Look, I am going to the marriage conference with you, like I said, no matter what." Maybe she needed a stronger assurance. And he was feeling like pushing the boundaries of flirtation a little, even though he hadn't initiated any affection with her in a long time. Starting now, that was going to change. "What would you say if I sealed my promise with a kiss?" He stroked a strand of her hair back. "Would you believe me then?"

He leaned closer to her, and her sea-blue eyes widened. Not waiting for her answer, he met her lips with a butterfly-soft caress.

She broke away. "Max—" She shook her head, her eyes downcast.

While the kiss seemed to have made her uncomfortable, it made him hungry for more. Made him want to fix their problems faster so they could make up like a married couple. But it had taken six months to a year for them to get into this stage of awkwardness between them. As a previous pastor and, sometimes, a marriage counselor, he knew it would take time to unravel their problems. The kiss had been a start. "I promise I'll go to the retreat with you no matter how our talk turns out. But really, I just want to share some things with you."

She sighed and nodded.

He swayed his hand toward the chairs in front of the window. Such a strong desire to hold her and kiss her again came over him. But he refrained. Talk first. Go slowly. Convince her of his sincerity. If only she could see into his heart, she'd know how sorry he was for the way he'd neglected her. Should he tell her he was sorry about that right now? In his counseling sessions with other married couples, he'd always encouraged them to apologize and ask for forgiveness. Why hadn't he been more proactive in doing that in their relationship?

She dropped into the chair, her body stiff like he was about to tell her he was dying. Or that he'd had an affair. *Oh, man.* Did she think that? He pulled the other swivel chair closer to hers, gathering his thoughts.

He cleared his throat and wondered where to start. Diving right into their relationship troubles seemed overwhelming and possibly explosive. Maybe he could work up to that conversation over the next couple of days. The important thing was that they were getting used to each other again. Talking like a husband and wife.

She didn't know about Derek's bodyguard hitting him, maybe he could begin there. "I still can't remember who hit me in the head. But the day before yesterday, Derek set up a meeting to question me about Jayme. His security guy punched me."

"You're kidding!" She scooted to the edge of her chair, her eyes wide. "Derek hired a thug?"

"Yep. He's convinced Jayme's telling him the truth."

"Unbelievable. I'd like to tell him what I think of his ungodly behavior and his daughter's lying." Her eyes squinted like she was glaring at Derek in her imagination.

He almost chuckled over her vehemence. But the fact she was sticking up for him, and not believing Jayme, made him feel relieved.

A tender expression crossed her face. "Where did the guy hit you?"

"In the gut. Then jabbed my ribs." He shrugged. "No big deal."

"That is a big deal. I'm so sorry." She shook her head. "And here, we trusted that man."

He sighed, still trying not to bring attention to his soreness. "I told him Jayme lied. He didn't take that well."

"I can't believe Derek would stoop so low as to have someone attack you." She touched his knee, and at that moment, her hand on his leg felt like more than just a slight touch. It was as if she were telling him everything was going to be okay. That they would be okay as a couple.

"He's also demanding a paternity test."

"Oh, brother." Then she gasped. "Do you think Derek sent someone to the trailer to hurt you?"

"Could be." He laid his hand over hers. "Honestly, I can't remember. The police questioned me at the hospital. But there's a fog shrouding my memory from the time I went to sleep the night before the attack until I woke up on the couch in pain."

"I'm so sorry for all that happened to you." After a pause, her gaze became troubled. "I had a strange voicemail from Martha Clayton. She claims you're involved with two women." She pulled her hand from his. "Do you know why she might have that impression?"

"I have no idea." Then he remembered about Sandy. He sighed and briefly explained what happened at the restaurant when the waitress was putting on a show for the gossipers, and who observed. Season nodded and seemed to relax into the chair. One issue at a time, they were working through the past week, hopefully getting closer to some deeper topics between them.

She sat quietly for a minute. "Is that all you wanted to tell me?"

"For now." They had plenty to discuss, but his head hurt too much to dive into a turbulent discussion. "I'm sorry about this thing with Jayme. And Sandy."

She stood and dusted off her dark blue dress. "I warned you to be careful around Jayme."

"You did." He swallowed hard as he stood. Too bad he hadn't listened.

"She's a flirt. Blaming you for her situation serves a purpose only she knows. Look at the trouble it's caused already. And

Sandy? I don't know what she was thinking." She stepped in front of him, almost touching him, yet not. "But I know you, Max. You're honest. A man of integrity. You'd never have an affair while we were married. I'd stake my life on it."

She probably didn't want him touching her, but he opened his arms toward her anyway. She stepped forward and they exchanged a hug.

"Thank you for believing in me, Seas. Especially with how I, you know, how moody I've been."

She pulled back from his embrace. "Counting today, there are three days left of the retreat. If you're feeling well enough, I'd like us to sit together and listen to everything that's said with open hearts. Will you do that with me?" She slipped into her winter coat.

"I will." He grabbed his jacket. "But you should know, when we return to Darby, things may look bad for us." He hadn't explained their financial troubles. And who knew what lengths Derek would go to in avenging his daughter's honor?

"We could always escape to the coast." She winked, then picked up her purse.

That remark and the remembrance of times she'd said it before made him chuckle. "One of these days, I'm going to take you up on that offer." He grabbed his carry-on, double-checked the bathroom, then followed her out of the hotel room.

All the way down the elevator, he wondered what the days ahead might hold for the two of them.

Twenty

Season

Season dressed for the evening session in a corner of the cabin away from where Max had slept all afternoon. On the drive to Hart's Camp, they talked about the scenery for a few minutes before his head bobbed and he was snoring.

She spent the trip praying for Max, their marriage, Logan and Benny, and some of the people back in Darby. Especially Jayme. What would make a young woman like her lie about a pastor? Did getting him in trouble take the spotlight off her? Or did it have to do with her father, who seemed to be a meaner person than Season ever realized? She knew Max experienced difficulties getting along with him on the church council. What kind of trouble might the money mogul create for the one accused of fathering his grandchild illegitimately? And he believed Jayme's claim against Max enough to demand a paternity test? Too weird.

She wondered how the police investigation was progressing. Nellie had given her report. Max said he was questioned by an officer at the hospital, but he couldn't recall anything about the attack. Had they discovered any leads by now? And when the conference ended, would it be safe for them to return to the RV?

"Max?" She called gently, hoping he'd wake up without stress to his injuries. Would he feel up to walking down to the lodge tonight?

She cinched a black belt over her burgundy dress. As she stepped into her favorite low-rise boots, her thoughts went back to the hotel room, this morning, when Max promised to attend the conference with her. And his sweet kiss—she couldn't forget that. They had issues to overcome, but his affection stirred up a smidge of hope that romance between them might not be as dead as she thought. But how could they get over all the hurts in their marriage?

"How are you feeling?" She nudged his shoulder, being careful not to touch his head. "Think you can hike down to the lodge with me?"

He groaned and rolled onto his side. "For dinner?"

"We already ate. I carried our plates up here, remember?" Tentatively, she stroked her fingers over his hair.

He squinted. "Hi."

She withdrew her hand. "Hi, yourself. Feeling okay?"

"I smell pizza."

"Good. That's what we ate earlier."

He looked confused for a moment, then he shook his head.

She recalled the list of concussion symptoms she read about online. It seemed he had most of them—headache, fatigue, poor balance, confusion, sleepiness. When they got to the cabin, she'd let him crash. Apparently, he needed a lot of sleep. It was good to have him here, even if he wasn't fully recuperated or engaged with her.

"What do you think about walking down to the lodge for the retreat?" She'd already set their unlit lantern near the door.

Most likely, Ty or Winter would talk about reasons to keep the blaze going. Would Max be alert enough to fathom the symbolism?

"I'd go anywhere with a pretty lady like you." He winked like they were already more romantic with each other than they'd been in months. Hopefully, this sweeter side of Max was showing because he'd missed her, and not just because of the concussion.

Earlier, while he was sleeping, she'd checked the lump on the back of his head. It felt swollen and, most likely, painful. It made her wonder about pushing him to attend the evening session. Maybe they should both stay here and talk. Or would the fresh air do him good?

She wanted Max to be as inspired by the speakers' reconciliation story as she was. But if they stayed here, working through some of their problems, couldn't healing come to them as well? God could work anywhere. But she'd thought if she could just get her husband to this conference, everything would change. That their wounds would be healed just by being in the same room with other couples who'd come through their storms victoriously. Maybe the Lord had a different plan for her and Max. One that had more to do with their hearts reconnecting.

She passed him a water bottle.

"Thanks." He twisted off the lid and took a long drink.

"So, what do you say?"

"I'd like to take you dancing." Fuzzy thinking? Or was he trying to be romantic again?

She helped him into a sitting position, bunching a couple of pillows behind his back. If they stayed here, she could keep watch on his condition.

"I'd slow dance with you."

"Well, that's nice." She sat on the edge of the bed beside his waist.

He gave her a lopsided grin, his eyes pinching at the light as he guzzled from the bottle. "What's a fellow got to do to get a girl like you to notice him?"

Her heart skipped a beat. "What do you mean?"

"Did you know I like blonds?" He'd told her he liked her blond hair when they went on their first date.

She hid a grin. "You know what they say about blonds."

"Do you ... have more fun?" At least he remembered the saying.

Was he asking her if she had fun with him? Or in her life? "I had fun sledding a couple of days ago."

His face brightened. "I would go sledding with you. Can we do that right now?" Was this the concussive Max talking?

"It's too dark. But sometime, we can go sledding together."

"I'd like that." He took her hand and gazed into her eyes. Her heart stilled.

He sighed. "Didn't you say we were going somewhere?"

"To the marriage conference, if you're feeling well enough."

He waved his finger in the air like he had an epiphany. "That's what we're supposed to be doing." He climbed out of bed.

"Are you sure you're up to attending?"

"I made a promise to you." He stroked back a wisp of her hair. "I even sealed it with a kiss." He gazed at her lips so intently, she gulped. "Or maybe I was dreaming."

She chuckled but didn't offer him any clarification.

Later, after slowly descending the trail, her arm linked with his just in case he got lightheaded, and her other hand clutching the lantern handle, they arrived at the lodge. He tromped up the steps as if nothing were wrong with him.

"Feeling better?"

"The night air's therapeutic." He inhaled a deep breath.

"That's great." She was glad he didn't feel worse after being out in the cold.

They entered the main building, and several couples greeted Max.

"Welcome."

"Glad you made it."

"Sorry to hear about the concussion."

Max rolled his eyes toward her like she shouldn't have said anything.

Gar lingered by Max, talking ministry stuff.

"So, how are you?" Autumn gave Season a hug.

"Okay. Weird twenty-four hours though."

"Nice that your honey showed up. God's answering prayers." Autumn nodded toward Max. "What happened to him?"

"An interrupted burglary, it seems. Sketchy details. Someone in town is spreading rumors. Sullying his name."

Her friend leaned close. "I'll be praying."

"Thanks."

Josh played his guitar at the front of the lodge, and the worship song drew them to their seats.

At their table, Missy's gaze surveyed Max. "Well, well, well. Welcome to the misfits' club."

"If there is such a club, I belong." Max shook her hand.

"Nice looking man you brought with you, Season." Missy grinned. "One of your sons?" She had the audacity to wink at Max.

He laughed. Probably good for his ego.

"Missy, Fred, this is Max—my husband."

"Well, it's about time." Missy guffawed. "Thought you were a figment of her imagination."

Fred nudged her arm. "They're starting."

"Yeah, yeah, I'll be quiet."

Season enjoyed the music, having heard the same songs on her first night here. She glanced at Max a couple of times. He wore a pleasant expression as if he were taking everything in. Later, she found him yawning. Would he be able to stay awake?

Not much she could do about his fatigue, but she'd keep checking on him to see if he were over-taxed by the experience. At least, he was here. *Praise God.* Hopefully, they could learn useful ideas to help them repair their marriage.

Gar's group performed a skit about the Mason jar lanterns. As soon as he introduced the title "Candle Mishap," she realized that in her rush to get Max situated, she'd forgotten about lighting her candle. She'd have to take care of that when the seminar ended.

After they clapped and cheered for the actors, Winter walked to the lectern carrying her jar. The lights dimmed. Her face glowed in the candlelight.

"As Ty and I walked down here tonight, I asked him to set our lantern in the snow. He put branches beneath it as a temperature barrier, and then we strolled until we couldn't see the candle anymore." She carried the jar to the front of the lodge and set it on the floor. Then she jogged to the back of the room. "Like then, I can't see the lantern, but I can see the glowing light brightening the whole area, welcoming me." Her voice grew stronger as she returned to the lectern. "Like the flame, my husband is a light in my life, welcoming me to him. I hope I'm a light to him also."

"Definitely," Ty called from his table.

The house lights came up.

"When I lose my way, my husband's love leads me home. And should he ever get lost, I pray that my light will lead him back to me."

Beneath the table, Max's fingers linked with Season's. His touch surprised her. He held her hand, stroking her palm with his thumb as if talking to her, and she didn't pull away. Did he agree with what Winter said? Had Season been a light for him during a dark time?

Winter sat down, and Ty strode to the front. He told how he'd hit rock bottom several times in his life. "Bottomed out. Tanked. Scraped the bottom of the barrel. You get the picture." He shared his story about being in prison, using his experience as an analogy for the prisons people can make in their lives and in their marriages. Then he compared how, with God's help, couples could burst open prison doors and step into marriage and life as new men and women, ready to fall in love with their spouses all over again.

Season was so engrossed in the lecture, she barely noticed Max's relaxed fingers. What she became aware of, what she thought every person in the room might be hearing, was his snoring!

She nudged his shoulder.

His eyes blinked open. "Oh, uh, thanks." He sat up straighter. "Sorry."

He seemed embarrassed, so she shrugged. "It's okay. Ready to head back to the cabin?" At least, he'd been able to stay that long.

He cringed like he didn't want to make them leave, but then he nodded.

She helped him stand and wrapped her arm around his waist to help him walk to the back door.

Tomorrow, would he recall holding her hand during the lecture as if what was said had personal meaning? She hoped so. She'd enjoyed having her husband sitting beside her tonight. Not being alone at the marriage conference. But his getting better was more important than whatever she might wish he'd remember about the evening. If only she'd keep that foremost in her thoughts in the coming days, putting his needs before her own. She prayed it would be so as she helped Max back to their cabin.

Twenty-one

Max

Max woke up in the early morning light and gazed at the other bunks in the log cabin. Why was he sleeping on a twin-sized mattress of a bottom bunk? And what was Season doing on the other side of the room hunched over on the floor? He drew the blankets closer around his neck. "Seas?" Was that the right name? He leaned up on his elbow. "Uh, Season, you okay?"

She peered up at him. "I'm fine. Just praying."

"Oh." He laid back down. Closed his eyes. The reasons they were in this cabin sleeping in separate beds slowly came back to him. Jayme lied about him. Someone who worked for Derek attacked him. A ski-masked invader apparently knocked him out cold. He'd flown to Spokane. He was at the marriage retreat with his wife. But she was keeping her distance from him. "Where's the shower?"

"Facilities are down the trail." She stood up. "Need help?"

"No. I'll be all right." He pushed off the bed, then gave his head a chance to catch up. A hot shower would help. "Got any coffee?"

"There's some down at the lodge, but I thought you were avoiding caffeine." She rubbed her arms as if warding off the chill.

"Not today. I'm definitely having some." He was ready to start acting more human.

"I could get some while you're cleaning up."

"That would be great. Thanks." He pulled on the jogging pants he'd left on the floor. Brrrr. "Any heat in this place?"

She smiled. He was glad to see her looking happier than she had a few minutes ago.

"Be glad it's warmer now than a few hours ago."

"You've been awake for hours?"

"I couldn't sleep." She yawned. "Thought I'd go down to the lodge and light our candle since I wasn't able to last night. Then I came back and prayed." She swayed her hands toward one of those homemade lanterns the speakers talked about last night.

"You went all that way through the woods by yourself?" Who was she? He'd known his wife was independent, but where had this bravery come from?

"Remember, I was here a couple of days by myself. I'm used to it." She seemed pleased with her achievement. "Lighting the candle is a special part of the conference. I'd like us to talk about it too."

"Sure." What did the speaker—Winter?—say about the lantern? Something about coming home. Lighting the way. He remembered clasping Season's hand. Strolling up the trail together. He'd like more times to experience that kind of closeness with her.

He gathered clean clothes and donned his coat. "I'll be back." He left the cabin and hiked a ways before he realized he'd left his cell phone on the bed. Oh, well, he wasn't expecting any calls.

* * * *

Season prayed while she made beds and put yesterday's clothes in a pile. *Please move in Max's life. I really don't want to go back to Darby with things unsettled. We need You, Lord.* She ran her fingers through her hair, glad she wore a no-fuss hairdo. She sat down on Max's bed. *Please heal his head. And help him stay awake through the sessions today.*

His cell phone vibrated against the mattress. Strange, since cell service was so sporadic.

Usually, she didn't answer his phone, unless she could see it was one of the boys. Maybe she should check.

Jayme? Why was she calling him? More threats up her sleeve? Maybe Season should tell the younger woman just what she thought about her deception.

"Hello, Jayme. What do you want?" Not her politest tone.

Silence on the other end, but the phone showed the call hadn't dropped.

"Jayme?" She softened her tone. "This is Season. I know what you told my husband." She'd like to call the police and report that lie. But what good would it do? Lying wasn't against the law, though it was against the Commandments. "How may I help you?"

"I need to speak to Max." Was that a fake sniff? "Is he there?"

"No." Answering the call was probably unwise. But now that she did, she might as well express herself. "Jayme, I don't want you calling my husband again. What you accused him of was wrong. A terrible lie. You should be ashamed of yourself." Maybe that was too harsh, but still.

"I-I know." Jayme broke down sobbing. "I am so ashamed."

What? "If you know you slandered him and spread rumors, then why are you crying? I'm Max's wife, and you accused him of—"

"I know wh-what I told everyone."

Everyone? *Oh great.*

"It was a lie. And I'm so so-o-o-r-r-ry." More crying.

"Perhaps, you should call back later. We could do a conference call with Max." Especially if she was willing to admit her wrongs. Could she put a retraction in the *Bitterroot Star*? Did she change her story so her father wouldn't threaten Max again?

"You both have always been nice to me." Jayme's voice shook as if she shuddered. "I don't know what I was thinking."

That made two of them.

"I'm so mad at him, I'm not going to keep quiet a second longer." Her voice rose.

"Who, Max?"

"My f-father." Jayme hiccupped. "He made me spread the story about Pastor Max."

"What?" Her father did this? "Let me get this straight. Derek knew of your plan to set up Max? To blame him for immoral behavior that would ruin his character?"

"My plan?" The young woman barked out a laugh. "His idea, not mine. Said he'd disinherit me if I didn't follow his wishes. I'm single, having a baby. I need my dad's financial support. So I did what he told me." She sniffled. "I'm sorry I asked Max to meet me that day."

Why would Derek sabotage Max? Season's stomach gurgled with agitation, or possibly hunger. "I still don't understand why your dad would cause Max such trouble."

"You know my dad." Jayme groaned. "He'll do anything to grow his portfolio."

This was about money? Derek needed more cash like the ocean needed water. "How does demeaning a pastor increase his funds?"

"I shouldn't say."

"But you called."

"To apologize." Jayme's voice rose. "That's all. Goodbye."

"Jayme, wait." Season's pulse raced. "Did you know Max was seriously injured?"

"What do you mean? Is he okay?"

"He has a concussion and doesn't remember the attack." Maybe Season shouldn't have told her that since she didn't trust Jayme. "The doctor expects him to make a full recovery. Do you think your father could have been involved?"

Jayme gasped. "Dad's obsessive, not violent. I've got to go."

Silence.

"Jayme? Hello?"

No response.

Season tossed the cell on her bunk, then paced the room, pausing to stare out the window at the falling snow. Max should be returning any minute. She dropped into a wooden chair. After that phone call, she needed to pray again.

A short time later, the door opened, and Max entered, stomping his feet. His hair was wet, meaning he'd made it down to the facilities and back on his own. He must be feeling better.

His eyes lit up. "Coffee?"

"Oh, no, I forgot." She jumped up. "Jayme called, and I got distracted."

"Jayme?" He dropped dirty clothes and his bag at the end of his bed. "What did she want?"

"To apologize."

"That's good news."

"Not really." Season crossed her arms. "Derek put her up to the lie in the first place."

"That doesn't make sense."

"I know. She says he drummed up the story for financial gain."

"The man buys a new truck every year. I drive a rig that I don't even know will start." His fingers smoothed over his wet hair, wincing when he touched the back of his skull. "Derek accused me of fathering the child and had me trounced by one of his bodyguards. Why would he cause the mess?"

"I don't know." She thought of him meeting Jayme at Annabelle's. How the younger woman accused him of intimacies, and people in the community—including Season's coworkers, past congregants, and friends, like Liza—may have heard and believed the lie. In the past, she wouldn't have been bothered by Max meeting someone at the restaurant that had become a hub to the small city. But now, after all that had happened, a knife twisted in her stomach. She needed to think. She shoved her arms into her coat. "It's almost time for the morning session." She scooped up the lantern. "We can grab coffee and a pastry at the lodge when we get there, okay?"

A grimace crossed his face. Was he in too much pain to walk down the trail again?

"What is it?"

"I think I should stay and make a few phone calls." He nodded toward the cell on the bed. "Follow up on that one."

"Max, you should avoid talking with Jayme alone. At least, wait until I'm in the room." She stepped closer to the door. "Are you coming with me?"

He swallowed hard. "I have other calls to make also."

So this wasn't about him feeling ill? He was backing out of attending the conference? "What about your promise?" She thought about the "sealed with a kiss" part, but she didn't mention it. Since he could get down to the showers on his own, and asked for coffee, she'd hoped he was improved. Or maybe he was, but he still didn't want to attend the seminar with her. Had he come all this way to stay in the cabin like he'd holed up in the RV?

"I will go with you, later, to the evening session, okay?" He probably needed more rest.

"Okay, fine. Take it easy and get better." She set the lantern back on the hot pad. "Watch that candle, will you? Don't let it go out."

"Sure."

She walked outside, shut the cabin door, and took a deep breath. She shouldn't be surprised by his reluctance, given he hadn't wanted to come here in the first place. Yet, she was disappointed. She wanted things to improve between them so badly, and this felt like a setback.

As she tromped down the trail, she tried to pray instead of complaining. At least, Max was here. They had some nice interactions. Things were getting better slowly, right?

But a couple of things bothered her about their conversation back at the cabin. Did he plan to call Jayme despite her objection? And what were the other phone calls about?

Twenty-two

Season

As soon as Season entered the lodge, Summer hugged her. "I was so excited to see your husband with you last night." She clapped her hands. "Isn't God great?"

"Yes." Max being at the camp was an answer to prayer. If only God would answer her other prayers about her husband.

Summer glanced toward the door. "Where is he?"

What could she say? That his calls were more important? That someone in his old congregation accused him of fathering a love child? "He has phone calls to make. He'll be here tonight."

Summer patted her shoulder. "You okay?"

"Trying."

"Em wanted me to tell you she's praying for both of you."

"Thank her for me, will you?"

"Definitely." Summer moved on to greet other ladies.

After grabbing a cup of coffee and a muffin, Season sat down and glanced at the handout on the table. "Complain about Your Spouse Day!" The bold title, displayed in red, made her chuckle. Here she'd been trying not to complain about Max this morning.

"Where's your mister?" Missy pointed at the empty chair next to Season. "You two fighting?"

"More like, he's playing hooky. And I'm exasperated."

Missy rocked her thumb between her and Fred's empty chair. "Us too. Never been so bad." She scooted her chair closer. "Last night he mentioned d-i-v-o-r-c-e. I can't even say the word."

"I'm sorry." Season patted Missy's shoulder. "If there's anything I can do, let me know."

"Got room in your cabin?"

"Max is there now." Season offered what she hoped was an empathetic smile. "If you need a shoulder to cry on, we could get coffee later and talk."

"Thanks."

Season nibbled on a blueberry from her muffin and wondered about Autumn's empty chair. It was strange for Season and Missy to be the only ones at their table.

"Good morning, ladies." Winter waved from behind the makeshift pulpit. "Autumn and Gar wanted me to tell you they received a middle-of-the-night call to hurry home. Their houseguest, Sarah, went into labor, so they took off for the West Coast to take care of their son, and to meet the new baby."

Cheers went up around the room.

Season was happy for Autumn, but she also felt a twinge of sadness. Now she wouldn't get to hear her reconciliation story or go sledding with her again. She hoped they'd stay in contact.

Missy's eyes widened. "You know Autumn can't have her own kids, right?"

Season nodded.

"Nice they get to have a baby in the house." She seemed sincere. "Nothing like littles to put the shine back in your eyes."

"True." Although, Season hadn't had "littles" in her life in a long time, other than Sunday school kids she'd taught and the children who visited at the library.

"This morning we're going to complain about our husbands!" Winter chuckled. "Good thing they're upstairs."

"My favorite topic." Missy clapped her hands.

Hmm. Season wondered if this was a good idea. Once she got started complaining, it might be hard to stop.

"Recently, I chatted with a gal who had an extensive list of grievances against her hubby." Winter ticked off the points on her fingers. "He was inattentive. Yacked with his buddies too much. Spent their money. Watched excessive TV. Drank. Yelled. Ignored the kids. Listened to his mother when he should have been paying attention to her. Get the picture?"

Season could write plenty about Max too. Starting with the fact he wasn't upstairs attending the men's session right now.

"Every word out of the woman's mouth was negative toward the man she'd vowed to love." Winter grabbed a chair and stepped up on the seat. She flicked her wrist and unrolled a long cream-colored scroll that almost reached the floor. "I decided to write a list of my own. Here's my record of the flaws and habits I dislike about Ty." Her laughter lightened the mood in the room. "Does this surprise any of you?"

A few women nodded.

Season wouldn't have imagined a loving wife having so many grievances about her husband.

"As much as I love him, Ty has flaws that I would change if I could." She stepped down from the chair, dragging her scroll with her. "Ever felt that way?"

Missy leaned forward. "I could make a list twice that long."

Season could too. But were they supposed to be focused on their husband's shortcomings? Thinking of Max back at the cabin, injured and in pain, she didn't feel like dwelling on his faults.

"I won't take time for you to write a list right now, but how about if you mentally make some bullet points? I'm sure you've thought of five or ten offenses already." Winter appeared to be waiting.

"This is easy." Missy nodded and winked.

Though she didn't plan to ponder them, a few of Max's bad habits ran through Season's mind. His stubbornness. Neglect. His need for honor from the church to the detriment of his relationship with her. No romance.

Then his tender kiss flashed through her mind. Ummm. Was her heart pounding faster? Probably because she was so love starved.

"How did mentally writing that kind of list make you feel?" Winter asked.

Confused.

The leader dangled her scroll in the air. "It's easy to point out someone's faults. But blame casting is like a mud fight. It's hard to hurl mud at someone without getting your hands filthy."

Blame casting? Is that what she'd been doing?

Winter set the scroll on the pulpit, then grabbed her Bible. "What do you think about this verse in First Corinthians thirteen? 'Love keeps no record of wrongs?'" Her eyes widened. "What about the list I just made about my husband?" She placed the book beside the scroll, then pointed at her temples. "What about the inventory I have in here? When you argue, do the points on your list pop out as accusations against the man you love?"

Bingo.

"'Love is kind.' 'Does not envy.' 'Never fails.' *Never fails?*" Season and Max's love had certainly failed.

"Here's what I'm going to do." The speaker gripped her scroll in both hands and tore the whole thing in half, from top to bottom.

Missy gasped.

Winter turned the papers sideways and tore them again and again until she held a pile of ragged-edged fragments on her palm. "I never want Ty's and my love to fail, so I choose to destroy this list."

"Not fair." Missy harrumphed.

Season didn't comment, her own thoughts in turmoil.

"Ever considered the faults your husband might write about you?" Winter perused the group.

"Fred already told me," Missy whispered. "Called me lazy, a gossip, and a terrible cook."

Season didn't know what to say. Which flaws would Max pen about her? That she'd never wanted to be a pastor's wife? That she spoiled the boys—they'd argued about that a few times. Too emotional? Even though she tried to be strong for him.

"I'm not trying to make you feel guilty." Winter chuckled. "Goodness, I'm flawed. And honestly, Ty and I have worked through a lot of stuff. We don't have a perfect marriage."

While Season knew Ty and Winter had been divorced, she did have preconceived notions about some of the couples here. As if their marriages were easy. And, yes, perfect.

"But every day we work on our relationship." Winter walked around one of the tables. "Ty and I know how bad things can get. How fast we were signing divorce papers."

Missy clutched Season's hand.

"I hate to think of the disaster we were in." Winter drew in a shuddering breath. "If you find yourself in that struggle, take heart. God loves you right where you are. He feels your pain. He wants you to experience His peace and amazing love."

Unexpected tears dripped down Season's cheeks, so she let go of Missy's hand to wipe them away.

Winter sat down in the chair she'd stepped on earlier. "If I focus on Ty's faults, that's all I'll see in him. But if I ponder his loving qualities—his sweet spirit, the tender way he looks into my eyes and my heart turns to mush, how he kisses me and makes me think I'm his princess—then I'll see him as that man."

Something pinged in Season's heart. How had she been seeing Max?

As a self-centered fallen pastor? She groaned.

"At some point, we've got to acknowledge that every one of us is imperfect and broken. We are human. We all make mistakes."

A somber quietness filled the room and sank into Season's gut. She'd thought Max was the one who was lacking. Anyone could see he wasn't the man he used to be. What about her?

"Are you blaming your husband for something?" Winter stood.

Yes. But he was to blame.

"Even if he's the one at fault, you need to forgive him." Her voice went soft. "This week I almost allowed something to build a wall between Ty and me. He told you about us visiting someone in prison. But he omitted my part of the rift. I did something he felt strongly against. I demanded my way, even though I knew he was troubled by it." She paused. "Ever been there?"

Season thought of the times she'd harped at Max about finding a job. As if he had no intention of doing so. Called him a stubborn, lazy man. Disrespected him.

"But what about the bad-habits list?" Missy stuffed a cookie in her mouth and chomped.

Winter waved a piece of paper. "Let's all grab something to write on. Maybe the back of the handout? Then, I want you to make a list of your husband's finest qualities. Okay, everyone get started."

Whispers followed.

Missy broke her pencil in two.

Season groaned. What could she write about Max? She'd told Jayme he was honorable. So she wrote that. *Honorable.*

What else? He cared about people. Mrs. Iris, the Johnsons, Jayme, and past congregants.

Caring.

That made two positive qualities. Neither was personal. Or romantic.

At other tables, ladies' pens moved like they were motorized. As if the writers had endless ideas.

Missy's paper was blank.

Season's had two words. How many points were they supposed to conjure up?

Max's kiss hadn't been far from her thoughts all morning. She could write something about that. *Nice kisser.* She covered the words so Missy wouldn't see and laugh.

Thinking of his kisses reminded her of his beautiful brown eyes. How, when she and Max were younger, his gaze had spoken to her of love even across a crowded auditorium.

Loving eyes. There. She had four things.

Around her, women's pens still danced. The air felt stifling, the fireplace too hot.

"I've gotta get out of here." Missy stood with tears streaming down her cheeks.

"Me too." Season grabbed her coat and crammed her scrap of paper in her pocket. She met a few sympathetic gazes as she hurried to the door after Missy.

Outside, Missy linked arms with her, and Season felt a bond with the other woman. Two misfit wives who couldn't drum up enough positive affirmations about their husbands.

No one stopped them. Or asked any questions.

Twenty-three

Max

The phone call ended abruptly, frustrating Max. Clint Ebbs said he'd been harassed by ruffians a second time, and he didn't want to speak with Max again. And no, he wouldn't talk to the police. Clint and Eloise were headed for the East Coast, where they could disappear for a long while.

It seemed Max's ties to Darby and Hamilton were breaking, person by person. Probably for the best, yet it hurt.

He called the police station in Darby, but they hadn't discovered Max's assailant. They were patrolling the mobile home park for any suspicious activity and talking to other residents.

After the call ended, he laid back down on the pillow, stroked his chin, and closed his eyes. Staying here to make phone calls had pretty much been a waste of time. And probably caused Season more annoyance with him. When would he learn to think of her before trying to solve every other problem? Must be a casualty of two decades of ministry. At least, he hadn't attempted to contact Jayme.

He imagined himself gazing into his wife's amazing blue

eyes. Immediately followed by the pain he'd seen in those same orbs when he said he wanted to stay here instead of going to the morning session. Hadn't he traveled this far to be with her? But the first seminar of the day was split, guys and women, so he wouldn't have been with her, anyway. Plus, hadn't the doctor told him to rest?

Maybe he just didn't want anyone knowing how far he'd fallen. That he'd lost his pastorate. Was accused of immoral things. And was a lousy husband, apparently.

At last night's meeting, he could tell many of the couples were in a better place in their marriages than he and Season were. Some held hands. Others leaned into each other as if they couldn't get close enough. A few guys had their arm over their wife's shoulder. One husband may have kissed his wife. Now that was taking things a bit far in public. Made him think, though. Made him a tad jealous too. How long had it been since he and Season acted like they really loved each other?

Yet, when he'd been flat on his back in the ER at Hamilton, wasn't she the person he longed to see? To sit close to. And hold. Here he was being standoffish—again. What was wrong with him?

He sat up, letting his head adjust. He felt more improved. As each hour passed, he seemed to be getting better. He stood and shuffled across the room, wondering what he should do next. He could join the session in progress. Or wait until the next one.

He paced across the wooden floorboards, trying to recall the night of the attack. Why couldn't he remember? In his mind's eye, he pictured a ski mask. Or two? Maybe loud banging on the door? Oh, hey, did he just remember something else? One of those jerks was a short, stocky fellow dressed in black. Had he knocked stuff out of the cupboards? The sound of plates breaking resonated in his memory.

Suddenly, someone knocked on the cabin door.

Max ducked below the bunk's edge. Had the short guy followed him?

The knock came again.

"Hey, Max!" A male voice he didn't recognize yelled. "You in there? This is Josh Hart. Thought we could chat."

The song leader from last night? Feeling silly for cowering, he strode to the door and opened it.

The younger man waved in greeting. "Hello. I hope you don't mind my stopping by like this." He extended his hand, and Max shook it.

"Come in." He nodded toward the two wooden chairs on the opposite side of the room. "Not very comfortable, but they're the best seats in the house."

Josh guffawed. "I should replace those."

Max hadn't considered this guy owned the camp. "Uh, sorry. I didn't mean to speak poorly of your antiques."

"No worries. Uncle Mac made those a couple of decades ago." Josh stomped his boots on the doormat just inside the room. "Chilly out there today."

"No kidding. Nearly froze going to the showers."

Josh removed his thick jacket before he sat down. "I see your candle is still lit." He nodded toward the lantern.

"Seems to be a life or death issue if it goes out."

"As well it should be." Josh laughed heartily. "It represents your love life, you know."

How embarrassing that he hadn't realized. "Makes sense." Why didn't Season explain its significance? Or maybe she did, and he forgot. He lowered himself into the chair opposite his guest. "Isn't there a seminar you should be attending?"

"Yep." Josh chuckled. "You too."

"Yeah, I guess."

Josh shuffled in his seat like he was trying to get comfortable. "I met your wife the night she pulled into camp during the snowstorm." He shrugged. "Seems like a real nice lady."

"She is." Max knew he was blessed to call her his wife.

"Don't get me wrong, I'm not trying to snoop into your business." Josh chuckled like he was embarrassed. "All of us at this retreat are on a journey in our marriages. Everyone has struggled in one way or another." Josh raised his hand as if including himself in the count. "Sometimes we do well. Sometimes not so great, you know?"

"Sure." Not that he wanted to talk about it with a stranger.

"My aunt shared a little bit"—he held his thumb and index finger about an inch apart—"of your situation with me after her and Season's visit."

Max's chest spasmed. What did his wife tell everyone about him?

"Rest assured, Aunt Em's no gossip. She just wanted me to know enough to get my lazy carcass over here." Josh laughed again. "That, and the Holy Spirit's nudging, I think."

How could Max feel so uncomfortable, yet comforted? "Good to know He's looking out for me." Even when he hadn't been as faithful to Him in the last couple of months as he should have been.

"Exactly." Josh rubbed his palms over the knees of his jeans. "We have a great group here. Ty's available if you want to talk with him. And I'm here."

Max swallowed a dry lump in his throat. "Talk about what, exactly?" His defenses were on alert. Wasn't his concern that someone might prod him to "confess all" one of the reasons he hadn't wanted to attend this conference? Although, he'd thought it would happen in a group setting.

"Believe me, I know how it feels to be coerced into one of these retreats." Josh rocked his thumb at himself. "Aunt Em twisted my arm. Begged. Tricked me. For a time, I flat out refused. So I won't pressure you into talking or attending anything."

That was a relief.

"But, hey"—apparently his "no pressure" comment didn't exclude him from conversing—"we all want our marriages to be the best they can be, right?"

"I believe so." Maybe he could change the subject. "Beautiful place you've got here."

"Thanks. The camp's been in my family a few generations." Josh beamed with pride. "My daughter, Shua Day, hopes to run the place when she grows up. Already calls it *her* camp."

Out of habit, Max touched the back of his head. Still tender.

"Would you mind if I told you about my story?" The younger man clasped his hands together.

"Um, okay." What else could he say? He'd always thought of himself as a good listener.

"Last summer, when I refused to attend the marriage conference, Ty moseyed into my backyard, sat down like this, and shared his story. His tale sounded nearly as bad as mine." He chuckled. "Considering how well that turned out—I went to the conference, and God changed my heart, and Summer's too—I thought maybe I could share my journey with you."

Although Max might not appreciate Josh's sermonizing, he had all morning. "Sure, fine."

"Ever had a dream that seemed bigger than you?" The musician gesticulated as he spoke.

"I wanted to be a great pastor." Had he ever wanted anything more?

"Excellent aspiration."

He'd thought so. "Started out good. Ended badly." Like his marriage, but he still hoped to fix that.

"Sorry, that's rough." Josh shook his head and drew in a long breath like he was gathering his thoughts. "I dreamed of becoming a musician and traveling the country playing guitar."

"You played great last night. Enjoyed the singing too."

"Thanks." Josh leaned forward, elbows on his knees. "Meathead that I was, I gave up everything I had to pursue what I deemed the most important thing in the world." His eyes darkened. "I got drunk, had a horrific fight with my wife, stole my uncle's truck, and hit the road for an extended BBD."

"BBD?"

"Aunt Em calls it my Bigger Better Deal." He wiped his hand over his chin. "Anyway, I was stupid. Trotted down a potholed road of sin and selfishness. But"—his voice lightened— "fast-forward a few years, and God radically and miraculously turned my life around, redeemed me, and set me free from addictions. A few months later, I found myself heading back to Hart's Camp to try to make amends."

Max felt drawn into Josh's story. He used to enjoy sharing this kind of redemptive illustration in his sermons. His thoughts were leapfrogging ahead, guessing the outcome.

The guitarist described seeing his daughter for the first time, gazing into the eyes of the woman he'd failed and hurt— Max could relate—and then, finding peace in knowing God had been working in both of their lives the whole time. He said it took prayer and intentionality, but Summer came to a place of forgiving him. Then they fell in love again and renewed their vows.

"Sorry for going on and on. But maybe, I don't know, maybe there's something here you can relate to?" Josh sat back in his chair as if he had all day.

Josh had obviously hurt his wife. Hadn't Max done the same by taking Season for granted and ignoring her needs? She really did deserve better than him.

"You're a pastor, so you know this, but whatever you and Season have gone through, God's been right there with you." Josh's eyes moistened. "You might be discouraged or hurt, but He can mend your brokenness. If it's pride or sin"—his voice grew quiet—"God meets us right where we are and forgives and rebuilds us. Summer and I experienced a season when we needed His healing. But we had to get humble and honest with each other too."

A pause followed. Max hadn't asked for this talk. Would have refused, given different circumstances. But he could see, every word out of Josh's mouth had been kind and compassionate. He wasn't pointing fingers. Not demanding that Max fess up. Just sharing his experience. Max wondered if talking to someone about the disappointment and heartache he'd had might help his clarity. *How could I have neglected my wife? My sons? And in pursuit of what? A pastoral pat on the back?* He sighed as if exhaling every painful thought he'd ever had.

Josh sat quietly for a few minutes. "Is there anything I could pray with you about? Any needs you'd like to share? If not, no worries."

His opt-out ticket?

The room stood quiet.

So far Max hadn't confided in anyone. He'd dreaded revealing his own downfall as much as getting his wisdom teeth pulled. But after hearing how Josh opened up about the broken parts of his life, Max probably could tell a bit about his life. He sucked in a deep breath. "I, uh, I lost my pulpit. Got kicked out, actually." Basic facts anyone in Darby might know.

"That's rough." Josh stared at him, his gaze intent.

Maybe he should skim the surface of his story. Without emotion. As a pastor, he'd negotiated plenty of heartrending situations where he'd had to batten down his emotions. He could do that now. "You mentioned your 'potholed road.' I've

215

been down my own war zone of despair. Watched my church go from two hundred attendees down to fifteen. Was kicked out by my council. Mocked. Lied about. I've floundered. I found myself stuck in a depression I've never known before. I kept wondering why God let all that happen to me. But then, why do any of us have to go through the storms in our lives?" He paused. "As I degraded into my self-absorbed, victim mentality, Season and I grew further apart." His eyes suddenly flooded with water, and he blinked to keep tears from dripping down his face. He wouldn't break down. They were men, having a discussion, that's it. Still, he sniffed a couple of times.

Josh's eyes glistened like he might be near tears also.

Max stared at the floor. Then at the hand-hewn wood ceiling. "I felt so far from God. My calling. And from my wife." A wave of emotion hit him like a tidal wave. He gulped. He wouldn't cave. Not now.

The younger man still didn't speak, as if he were waiting for Max to finish.

"There's a financial hatchet about to fall on my head back in Darby. It has to do with the church property." His voice broke. "I haven't explained it all to Season." He swallowed. "I've taken her down a bumpy road too." He glanced out the window. "I wouldn't be surprised to hear she wants to leave m-me." A bark-like burst of air shot out of his mouth. Like he'd been holding his breath for a week. "I don't know what I'd do without her. I feel such an awful weight on me."

"I can see that. What's the heaviest thing troubling you?" Josh folded his hands. "I'd like to pray about that. By what you've said, you've gone through the valley. The fire. Climbed a treacherous mountain. But I'm guessing you aren't at victory yet, huh?"

"Not by a long shot." He sketched in the details about his bank dealings, the physical attacks he didn't fully remember,

216

and the rumor Jayme had circulated. He exhaled a sigh that felt dredged up from his toes.

"You didn't mention it, but do you want to make things right with Season?"

"More than anything." Where to begin evaded him. "Sometimes, it feels like we're not even married. And I don't know how, or when, that distance happened."

"Based on my reconciliation with Summer, I'd say the first thing you need to do is find that secret place with the Lord you may not have visited in a while. Spend time praying and laying all your struggles at His feet. Cry. Tell him the honest-to-goodness truth about your hurts. Doubts. Questions. Whatever. Trust that He's working in both of your lives."

Max had expected Josh to lecture him on how to fix his marriage. Instead, he'd shared his story, listened while Max talked, then recommended he draw closer to his Savior, which Max knew he needed desperately. Then Josh prayed with such humility and confidence, Max felt like crumbling to his knees.

God, I'm so sorry for my hardened heart. For the ways I didn't listen to You. For all the times I hurt and neglected my wife.

When the younger man implored heaven for God to wrap Max and Season in a covering of His love, sobs, that Max couldn't hold back if his life depended on it, rushed out of him. The burden on his chest felt suffocating. He had to let out the anguish and the bleakness of the last six months, or it felt like he'd die right there. "God, help me." He repeated the phrase over and over.

After a few minutes, Josh stood. "I'll leave you to spend time with the Lord. When you're done laying it on the line with Him, find your wife. Bare your heart to her. Tell her everything. Ty calls it having 'the talk.' Hurts like crazy. But once it's done—after you've been humble and honest, assured her of your love, and prayed together—your hearts will be melded together in a new and beautiful way." He threw on his coat and left.

Max stayed on his knees on the wooden floor, his face pressed into the curve of his arm which rested against the striped mattress of a bed they weren't using. "God, I've clung to bitterness and pain in my heart. Forgive me. I need Your love. I want You." Why had he thought he had to be so strong? Invincible as a pastor? Obscure with his feelings? Now, it felt as if his heart had broken open wide. He sensed God was hearing him. And loving him, still.

But how could he express himself to Season? Would she understand?

He glanced up at the candle glowing in the jar on the table and pondered the flame. A symbol of their romance, huh? Part of him wanted to jump up and find her. But first, he'd ask God for a miracle, because he was pretty sure he'd need one to truly convince his wife of his love.

Twenty-four

Season

By the time Season and Missy returned from getting coffee and lunch in Newport, eighteen miles away, they were almost late for their afternoon art class. Season had texted Max about her leaving the camp with Missy, but so far, he hadn't responded. With the questionable cell service, she didn't know if he received her note or not. Hopefully, he was okay. Probably sleeping again.

She stared at her unfinished painting, wondering what she could add to make it more realistic. At least the storm clouds spreading across the top third of the canvas were recognizable to her. Would anyone else be able to tell what they were?

Season glanced at Missy, who sat at the next table flicking paint over her canvas as if she were miserable, and wished she could have helped her more.

Over lunch, Missy confided that she'd been frustrated with Fred for years. According to her, he'd said one hurtful thing after another, and those offenses were piled so high, resolving their differences seemed impossible. Last summer, during the previous marriage conference they attended, she'd gone through the recommended steps to forgive him. He'd done the same, it seemed. But then, she said, he started the verbal attacks again, and she returned the favor. An endless cycle.

"What's going on with you and your hubby?" Missy had thumped the table in the cafe with her mug as if demanding an answer.

Season didn't want to dig up her wounds right then. She'd come here to support Missy. "I'm not sure where our relationship is going, but I have hope now."

"That's good." Missy sighed, then opened her purse and withdrew a photograph. "See this?" She tapped a photo of a sandy beach. "Someday, I'm going to live near the ocean. Fred says it's too windy near the coast. Storm warnings. Blah-blah-blah." She stared at the picture like it was cake and she could eat it. "My dream place. All the bad stuff between Fred and me will go away there."

"You think?" After twenty-two years of marriage, Season knew it wasn't that simple. If it were so easy to find marital bliss, she would have moved to the beach long ago.

"I'm sure of it. 'Cause if not—?" She shook her head. "Maybe he's right, divorce is in the cards."

"Let's keep praying. Something good may be just around the corner for you two."

"I sure hope so."

Now, focusing on her painting, Season dabbed her brush in burnt umber, then flicked the bristles across her palette to thin the paint. She stroked the brush lightly back and forth across the lower third of the canvas, adding layers to represent contours of dirt.

Suddenly her neck itched like a bug was crawling on her—perish the thought—or else someone was watching over her shoulder. Had Missy come over to talk? Was Summer observing her painting? She turned around, expecting to see a woman. Instead, Max stood there, grinning.

"Max? What are you doing here?"

"Hey." His cheeks were flushed. From the cold weather? Or was he feverish? With the way his eyes danced as if he had mischief in mind, she doubted he was ill, other than his injuries. In his hand, he cradled their lantern, and the candle was lit. Had the flame gone out and he hiked down to the lodge to relight it?

"Is something wrong?" She dropped her brush into the water can.

"No." He set the jar on the table. "I'm good. Really good, actually." He leaned in and kissed her cheek. She was shocked that he'd show her affection in front of other people. Was he trying to make up for not attending the morning session?

"I just wanted to come by and say, 'I love you.'" Surprise number two. Was that the concussion talking again?

She was about to comment on his upbeat mood when he smoothed the back of his index finger down her cheek. Now she was the one with foggy thinking. He stared at her lips like he was considering a redo of yesterday's kiss.

Wait a sec. Max didn't do PDAs, and she wasn't sure where they stood as a couple. Didn't they have a lot to discuss? Even though she'd allowed that one romantic interaction, she needed a heart-to-heart talk with him before anything else physical happened between them. Didn't he need that too? She picked up her paintbrush.

He blinked slowly as if realizing what he'd been about to do, and where they were. He nodded at her canvas. "That's really good. I'm impressed, Seas."

"Thanks." Did he like it? Or was he just saying that? "I almost gave up and threw it in the trash."

"I'm glad you didn't." His voice turned husky. Was he

picturing a dual meaning in her words, like maybe she'd thought of quitting on them too? "How long until the session is over?"

"A half hour."

"Think we could take a walk and talk, then?"

His request surprised her. "Sure, I'd like that."

"I'll come back after a while, sweetheart." He winked at her.

Sweetheart? Max winking at her? She hardly knew how to react.

"Yeah, uh, okay."

He strolled out of the room—whistling? It seemed as if he might be standing taller, his shoulders back. Maybe she should run after him and find out what was going on. Forget painting!

Then, wondering if she'd only imagined a difference in him, she glanced at the picture she was supposed to be focused on. She dipped her brush in burnt sienna, adding dabs of color to make pebbles in the scene.

The flame in the jar flickered. Its fluttering and snapping made her think it must be lapping up oxygen. Starved for air? Kind of like her, famished for romance and attention in her marriage. And yet, she hadn't gone along with that almost-kiss. She felt the old ache of hurts and frustration and sighed again.

What did her painting lack? Maybe it needed a focal point other than storm clouds. She picked out a smaller brush, then mixed white and green paint on her palette. Careful not to smudge any elements in the picture, she outlined the shape of a small jar, like the lantern, sitting on the dirt she'd painted earlier. She didn't know how to make it look real. And maybe no one else would be able to tell what it was. Still, she wanted to add more symbolism. After she filled in the shape of the jar with color, she snatched up a clean brush and painted a candle with a flame. She tapped blotches of yellow and white in an arc to represent light rays around the wick.

After putting in a few flowers and strands of grass, she sat back to admire her finished work. Not bad for a beginner. With a feeling of accomplishment, she cleaned her brushes and tidied her painting area.

At the end of the session, and after most of the participants had left the room, Max entered, bundled to his chin in wintry outdoor clothes. In his arms, he clutched a pile of outerwear—her snow pants, hat, mittens, and boots. It looked like he was prepared for more than a walk.

"What's going on?"

"Instead of taking a walk, how about if we go sledding on the hill?" He rocked his eyebrows.

"You're kidding, right? That hill can be brutal." Although her heart had turned over at his request—hadn't she imagined a romantic sledding date with him?—he was injured and in no condition for winter sports.

"Come on, please, I want us to do this." His deep brown eyes appealed to her.

"Max, it's dangerous. Remember your concussion?" What was he thinking? He was supposed to be resting.

"I haven't forgotten." His smile didn't diminish. "But let's make some memories, Seas. I'll be super careful. I'm feeling better, and I want to be with you." His voice softened. "Will you go sledding with me?" He held up her boots and grinned boyishly. "Let's make some memories."

He seemed more vibrant and alive today. Maybe his health had improved. But what if he hurt himself again? Despite her concern for him, she imagined the sledding hill and all the fun she had the other day. "You really want to go sledding with me?"

"I do." He picked up her hand and brushed his lips against her skin. Ticklish sensations skittered up her arm. "I'd like us to spend the afternoon having fun, talking, kissing."

"Kissing, huh?" A spark of flirtation sizzled between them.

"Mmhmm." He nodded slowly.

"But Max, you're seriously hurt. How about if we hike back to the cabin and talk?" That's what they needed to do, right?

"I promise I'll be careful." He dropped her outdoor apparel on the chair. "Please?"

"Max—"

"As long as we don't crash, I'll be fine." He squeezed her hand. "Don't worry."

How could she not be concerned for him? Should they take such a risk? She drew in a long breath, debating. "Okay"— although she might be sorry later—"as long as we're extremely careful."

"Yes!"

She picked up her snow pants and tugged them on over her jeans, wondering if she'd made the right choice. She shoved her feet into the boots and donned her hat. Why was Max staring at her as if he'd never seen her before? As if he were ... attracted to her? She gulped.

Since the candle shouldn't be lit in the art room when no one was present, she blew out the flame. "I'll return to you soon." Maybe in fifteen minutes, if she changed her mind before they reached the summit of the hill.

As soon as they exited the lodge, Max took her mittened hand in his. "Ready?"

"I can't believe you want to do this." When was the last time he'd initiated an outing? "Don't get me wrong, I'm glad. It's just—"

"I know." He turned to her quickly. "For months, I've been a self-centered grouch. Sound about right?" He winked as if taking his flaws in stride.

If she said yes, would he be offended? She remained silent.

They tromped along the cleared trail, him leading her in the direction of the sledding hill.

"And now"—he said as if the conversation had never stopped—"you can't believe I want to go sledding with the woman I love?" His eyes sparkled.

"Well—"

Suddenly, he wrapped his arms around her, right there in the middle of the three-foot-wide trail. Fortunately, no one was walking behind them. As she gazed up at him, a gulp of air caught in her throat. Why were his eyes gleaming? Was he thinking of kissing her again? Their thick winter coats were the only barrier between them, and her arms went around his back—more for balance than anything. But when she felt his heart hammering like a drum, she guessed hers might be racing as wildly.

Then, as quickly as it happened, he ended their embrace—without a kiss. *Good.* They had things to talk about first. But why did she feel bereft? Like she wished he'd gone for it and kissed her anyway.

He stared at her intently. "Seas, I realize I haven't treated you as the precious woman you are to me." He adjusted her hat, his fingers lingering an extra moment near her ears. "But we'll talk about that later, okay?" He smiled with such an endearing grin. "For now, I just want to be close to you. Spend time together. Have fun. So let's try out that sledding hill, huh?"

"Um, okay." She gazed into his chocolaty eyes she used to adore. She remembered the assignment from her first day at the conference, and how exhilarated she'd felt after sledding and being playful. Maybe that kind of freedom would help Max too.

At the base of the incline, he grabbed one of the toboggans standing vertically in a pile of snow and pulled it behind them with the towrope. They tromped up the sledding hill and he breathed in a deep cleansing breath. "So, I had a visit from Josh today."

A tree could have fallen in front of her and she wouldn't have been more surprised. "Oh?" Was that why he was acting unusual? What did they talk about?

"He said you had a visit with his aunt." His tone sounded conversational, not accusatory. Still, unease crept up her spine.

"I did." Had Em told Summer or Josh what she shared? She had confided personal information she'd rather Max not know.

"He seems like a nice guy. Compassionate." Max shrugged. "Concerned, even."

"He is. They all are. I'm sorry you didn't meet Autumn and Gar. They were great too." She swallowed hard. "I did share a little about us with Em. I hope you don't mind. She's a sweet grandmotherly sort of lady."

"That's good." He tugged on her hand. "I'm sure you needed someone to talk to."

"I did." Was that all? He didn't care that she'd told Em about their marriage? What of his discussion with Josh? Had the leader mentioned something about how a husband should treat his wife? Max had been acting chivalrously toward her this afternoon. "What did you guys talk about?"

He chuckled. Max laughing was like a birthday gift and a Christmas gift wrapped in one. "Guy stuff. Husbandly stuff."

A warmth spread over her. "Like?"

"How about if we talk about that later? And we will." He seemed to be breathing harder. Was the climb too much for him?

"Are you okay? Maybe we should take a break." Or they could head back.

"Nah, I'm all right."

She hoped him doing such strenuous activity wouldn't jeopardize his improved condition. They tromped in silence for a while. Then, nearing the final rise, he tugged on her hand and led her off the trail.

"Where are we going?" Her boots sank into drifts a foot deep, and she was reluctant to go off-trail any further.

"Right here is beautiful." Beneath a massive cedar tree, he turned her toward him, clasping both of her hands. He stood there, just gazing at her.

She gulped. "Max, what's going on?"

"Sea-girl"—his whispered word stirred a romantic flame that had been sputtering in her heart—"I just wanted to tell you how much I love you."

Oh, Max.

"That I've missed *us*."

"Me too." She'd missed this kind of them for years.

Almost in slow motion, as if giving her all the time she needed to pull away—which she didn't—he leaned in and brushed his cool lips against hers. So much for not indulging in romance before they had a discussion. His kiss deepened, filled with tenderness and longing she'd almost forgotten he possessed. Snowflakes fell over them from the tree above, landing on their noses and cheeks. They both pulled back at the same time and gazed up and chuckled.

Max was so different today. He seemed younger and carefree. Because of his talk with Josh? The concussion? Or had something else happened? She wanted to ask him about it, but she didn't want to spoil the unexpected time they were sharing. Still shaken from his kiss, she let him lead her back to their sled.

"Shall I steer? Or you?" His grin and eager expression made her think he wanted to take the lead, although he was being polite in asking her.

She remembered how much fun it had been the other day as she and Autumn flew down the hill. "You can be first. I'll do it next time." A thought hit her. "Unless traipsing up the slope twice is too much for you. If it is—"

"It won't be. Let's enjoy this. No worries, hmm?"

How could she ignore his head trauma? How could he? "Just be careful."

"I will. Man, look at those ski slopes on the mountain." He pointed toward the white peak in the distance. Was he trying to distract her from fretting about him?

"Mount Spokane."

"Maybe you and I should try skiing again." He was a handsome man, especially when his eyes glimmered with adventure, like now.

"I'd like that."

He took a deep breath as if it were his first taste of fresh mountain air. She'd known he would love the rugged beauty up here. They hadn't been to Lost Trail Powder Mountain south of Darby in years, but they used to ski there.

He lowered himself, somewhat gingerly, onto the sled. He held up the towrope, his feet straddling the sides of the toboggan. She felt reluctant about Max sledding down such a steep hill, but she dropped down in front of him, her heart in her throat.

Lord, keep him safe. I'm sorry if we're doing a stupid thing.

"Whatever you do, keep the sled in the center of the trail, okay?" She hoped she didn't sound too bossy. But, still. "I don't want to pull you out of a snowbank, or worse."

"Says the voice of experience." He nudged her arm.

She relaxed a smidge. "You're right. I had a face-down mishap the other day that could have ended badly."

"I'll do my best not to let that happen." His cold nose nuzzled her ear. "I have to keep my lady safe."

She liked the way he said, "my lady."

He shoved off from the snowpack more effortlessly than she could have, his hands working like ski poles. In seconds they were zipping down the slope.

"I don't think the doctor would approoooooove! Max!"

Down the hill they went. Snow specks flew up at them like sparks off a campfire.

Max yelled and laughed.

She joined him in cheering.

They were staying in the center of the trail, flying low. They'd almost made it to the bottom when suddenly the toboggan turned sharply, careening toward a tree.

"Max!"

He dug in his heels, ice spitting at them. Barely avoiding catastrophe, he veered them back toward the middle of the trail just in time. He had the strength she and Autumn lacked the other day. In moments, the toboggan came to a natural stop.

She exhaled with relief. "You saved us." She patted his legs with her mittened hands, thankful they hadn't crashed.

"That was fantastic!" Max chuckled. "Let's do it again."

"Are you sure? That was a close call."

"It was great." He winced, and then as if recovering, smiled.

"Max, are you okay?" How badly was he hurting? "Maybe you should rest."

"I'm good. I can rest later." He was the best judge of his limitations, right? Still, she worried.

They climbed off the sled. As soon as they were standing, he leaned toward her, or maybe it was her leaning in toward him? Either way, their lips met in a kiss that left her breathless.

"Ready to go again?" His whispered words vaguely penetrated her haze. Did he mean ready to climb the sledding hill? Or ready to love him as her husband again? Talk about dazed.

His arm wrapped around her shoulder, drawing her into his side as they hiked uphill. The feel of him holding her spread warmth through her. Made her lean into him a little more. His affection this afternoon was unlike anything she'd experienced in a decade. Goodness, he acted smitten. Like he was *in* love with her. She couldn't fathom such a mysterious change. Oh, she wanted to fall on her knees and thank God for it. But what if his romancing evaporated the second she laughed or sneezed or pulled away to tie her boot laces?

If this were a fantasy, could she please live in it forever? For her husband to act like he adored her and loved her like he did when he fell in love with her? Nothing could be as sweet. Or as terrifying, if it disappeared.

When she asked Max again how he felt, he said fine. His coloring looked normal, but she'd seen a couple of grimaces. One more downhill run, then she'd insist he take a break.

At the top of the slope, Max lined up the sled as if mapping out a perfect route for her. "Your turn." He handed her the rope and winked.

She lifted her booted foot to step into the sled, and suddenly she was whisked into his strong arms, almost unbalancing her. His plan all along? His eyes were intense pools of rich chocolate. She thought he might kiss her. Instead, he Eskimo-kissed her nose. And she relaxed into his arms, not wanting these last moments on the sledding hill to end.

The moment passed and he guided her onto the sled, then dropped down in front of her. Sitting behind his broad back, she realized seeing the trail ahead might be difficult for her. Maybe she'd scoot a little closer. With one arm strapped around his waist—for leverage, only—she gripped the towrope with the other hand and peered over his shoulder.

"Ready?" she called.

"Go for it."

Goodbye mountaintop experience. *And our first date.*

She let go of the rope and Max's waist long enough to shove her hands against the ice. Like oars in the sea, it took both of them shoving against the snow to get the sled moving this time.

A breath later, they were racing downhill, squealing and laughing as before. She grabbed hold of the rope and tried to glimpse the path over his shoulder. *Bump.* Uh-oh. Were they headed the wrong way? She couldn't see well at all. *Thud.* She dragged one hand against the snow, trying to turn. She dug in the heel of her boot. "Help me!"

Max jutted out his foot also, both scraping the ice. She tugged harder on the rope.

"Turn!" He yelled.

"I'm trying."

The crash came suddenly. She thudded into the pile of snow on her side with a groan. A chill cut through her body. Max landed next to her with a deep-sounding moan.

Oh, no. "Max! Are you okay?" Ignoring her own discomfort, she crawled to him on her knees and leaned over his still body. "Can you hear me?" Was he unconscious? "Max?"

"Ugh." His eyes remained closed.

"Thank God, you're alive."

"Barely." He mumbled something about lousy timing.

"This is why I didn't want you sledding." Her hands sank into the snow, bringing her closer to him. She felt his breath on her cheeks. "What can I do?"

"A kiss might help." He grinned impishly.

"What?"

He opened his eyes and winked at her.

"Max, you scared me." She groaned. "Is anything hurt?"

"Only my pride."

"What about your head?" She sat back on her heels, still feeling stressed.

"Ehhh." He pushed up from the snow, then gripped his stomach. "My head's okay."

"Did you hurt your stomach now?"

He shrugged. Was he being evasive? "Just hurts from before."

From when Derek's bodyguard hit him? With all her anxiety over his head injury, she'd forgotten the punches and jabs he took. She got under his arm and helped him stand. He seemed wobbly, so she stayed close to him.

"I'm sorry for crashing. I tried staying in the middle of the trail, but I couldn't. I can't believe that happened." She knew she was chattering.

"Hey, it's okay." He chuckled. "I'm just glad we got to do this."

She'd been glad too, until that moment when they crashed, and she heard his moan. Then fear and guilt had flooded her. She grabbed the towrope and dragged the toboggan as they descended the hill to where the other sleds were standing in the snow. "Let's get back to the cabin."

"I'm okay." He tugged on her hand and made her look at him. "I'll be fine, Seas."

"I'm glad you're not hurt worse." But she knew he wasn't "fine."

"How about if we get some coffee and fudge at the lodge, and prolong our outing? I've done enough lazing around to last a lifetime." His smile seemed genuine, not like he was hiding his pain. "I'd like this date to last longer."

So he'd thought of it as a date too?

Some of the tension over their accident eased. "Okay, we'll go get coffee. Then to bed with you." The phrase popped out before she could censor it. "Oh, I, uh—"

"I can't argue with that." His eyes sparkled.

"I didn't mean that as an"—invitation?—"oh, never mind." He just laughed.

Coffee, fudge, and spending more time with Max sounded perfect. But she wondered if he might be delaying their talk about the real issues that remained between them.

Twenty-five

Winter

Winter touched up her lipstick and glanced at Ty through the mirror on the cabin wall. He'd been quiet this afternoon. He sat by the window writing in his journal, and every now and then, he'd stare at something outside as if lost in thought. Was he worried? "How do you think the conference is going?"

"Nice to be back, doing what we feel God wants us to do." He shrugged. "Helping other couples. Encouraging folks." He jotted something down, then glanced out the window again.

After Randi had stolen Winter's notebook, they'd decided to write daily entries in their own journals, with the intent of eventually publishing a workbook for conference attendees. The project hadn't materialized as quickly as they'd hoped, but they were working on it. Sometimes, in the evenings, they shared what they wrote that day.

She tucked her lipstick tube in her purse, then stepped behind his chair, curious about what he might be working on. Massaging his shoulders for a moment, she glanced down and caught a few words: "I thought things were going fine until—"

He shut the book, leaned back, and made a purring sound as she rubbed his neck muscles. Why did he close the journal so abruptly? Did she distract him? Was he stopping her from seeing what he wrote? They had an open-book policy. Either of them could read each other's entries. However, he seemed tense. Maybe something was wrong. She kept kneading his neck muscles. "You okay?"

"Better, now." He sighed. "Thanks."

"Something bothering you?"

He stilled.

She stopped massaging his shoulders. "You closed your journal so fast I wondered what's going on." She didn't want him to feel cornered, but they were attempting to be honest about everything. "If you don't want to talk about it right now, that's fine."

Leaning forward, he sighed. "I've been pondering some things I'm not ready to share. I will eventually."

"Okay." Was he still bothered about her seeing Randi?

"It's nothing to worry about." He took her hand and drew her to the opposite chair. It creaked as she sat down and faced him. His eyes looked weary.

"Tired?"

"Yeah, I didn't sleep well last night." He ran his fingers through his hair. "I spent some hours praying and thinking. Then I jotted down a few thoughts."

"Did I say something that's troubling you?"

"It's not that." He groaned. "Actually, I think I've finally gotten the victory over my feelings about all we went through last fall."

"That's great." She patted his knee.

"Except for one thing." A frown line grew between his eyebrows.

That puzzled look reminded her of other times when he'd

been stressed about something. She waited while he seemed to be formulating his thoughts.

"At the strangest times, I find myself contemplating that night back in October. I get angry with how Randi hurt you and Deb." He stared at her, and she wondered if he were looking at the scar on her face. Her fingers touched the spot. "Then I think"—he continued—"what could I have done differently? What if I'd found the hiding place sooner? Bugs me still."

Determined not to be self-conscious about the mark on her cheek, she lowered her hand and ran her palm over the sleeve of his dress shirt. "I have moments like that too. Every time it comes to mind, I think we should release the past to God. We can't hold on to offenses if we want Him to use us."

"I know. That's why I've been praying for healing and peace for both of us."

She nodded toward the book in his lap. "Is journaling helpful?"

He chuckled like he was embarrassed. "I've mostly been rambling. And I sketched a cartoon." His gaze held steady with hers.

She wanted to know her husband's heart, and to understand what troubled him or what made him happy. But she also respected his need for introspection.

He picked up the leather-bound journal. "I'll show you, but promise not to laugh?"

"Ty, you don't have to share it right now. It's okay."

"I want to." He opened the book and showed her a sketch of an angel with oversized wings wielding a sword. On the ground, he'd drawn a creature—or a woman?—with its hands braced toward the heavenly being. Sheltered safely behind the angel was a small cluster of people, their names written in bold lettering. Neil, Deb, Winter, Ty—the members of Passion's Prayer.

"That's cool. The angel's protecting us, right?" The emotion he'd captured on the faces of the people amazed her. Big smiles. Sparkling eyes. Peace?

"In the middle of the night, I got to thinking. What if I'm more worried about the future than mad at what happened in the past? Fear. Anxiety. You know?" He closed the book, laid it down on the table, then took both of her hands in his. "I've wrestled with why God let us go through that." He took a deep breath. "But we got through it. We survived. I believe you and I, and our team, are stronger and more caring because of it."

His words excited her because she'd recently contemplated the same thing. "I agree. I've felt more honest and compassionate in the sessions, this time, than ever before. I'm thrilled for you to be free of discouragement too. Everyone goes through rough times, but He *is* with us." She leaned closer to him. "Ty, He was with me that night too."

"I know." Tears filled his eyes. She loved that he could be tender, yet strong. "He was with me too." He stood and drew her into his arms. "I'm believing for healing and resolution for my bad attitude and unforgiveness toward Randi."

"Me too."

His hand slid down her cheek. His thumb gently circling her dimple reminded her of other times when he'd caressed her like that. They gazed into each other's eyes before he kissed her. His passionate embrace made her want to stay in the sanctuary of his arms, and the privacy of this cabin, instead of heading down the hill to their next session.

A knock at the door drew them apart.

"Expecting someone?"

"No." She hurried to the door, still feeling the sweetness of her husband's arms around her. She heard him following her as she reached out to grab the doorknob.

When she opened the door, her co-leader for Passion's

Prayer stood on the front porch, his hand lifted as if to knock again. By the grimace on Neil's face, he wasn't here to bring good news. "Neil, hello. Why are you here?" Why had he driven over from their place in Spokane?

"What she meant was, welcome, and come in." Ty opened the door farther and embraced Neil. "Looks like you have something to tell us."

Winter waved him into the room. "Yes. Come in. Grab a chair by the window."

Neil crossed the room carrying a bulging manila envelope. He didn't say a word. That couldn't be a good sign.

Winter dropped onto one of the bunks they weren't using.

Ty sat in the last available chair. "So tell us what's going on."

She was thankful for him getting right to the point. They had forty-five minutes before they were expected at the lodge.

Neil ran his hand over his gray-and-black peppered hair. He'd been such a strength to her during the five years she traveled with the team before Ty joined them. What if he were here to tell them he was leaving their ministry? Inwardly she gasped, thinking of what that might mean to their team. Did he ever think about finding a wife again?

Neil tossed the envelope on the table. "I know what Randi was up to before she went to prison. And you're not going to like it."

At least he wasn't here to tell them he was leaving. "What is it?" Was this the "plan" Randi referred to in the interrogation room? Winter reached for Ty's hand. He met her gaze and nodded as if reminding her of what they'd discussed earlier. Everything was in God's hands. They were protected.

Neil tapped the envelope. "Mat Kaplan, VP of Design Tech Media says Randi sold him book and movie rights on a project based on the two of you."

"What?" She and Ty spoke at once.

"She can't do that!" But wasn't the notion that Randi might use Winter's journal to make some book deal exactly what she'd feared?

"The book is set to release next month." Neil gazed at her, then Ty. "The television movie is already in pre-production."

"Next month?" Ty moaned. "And a movie?"

"Why would anyone invest in a book, let alone a movie, based on Ty and me, or Passion's Prayer?"

"What topics does the book cover?" Ty let go of her hand.

"Your downfall, mainly." Neil glanced at him. "Winter's gullibility in your relationship. The failings of our ministry team."

With each point, her heart thudded louder in her ears. So Randi planned to broadcast their weakest moments to the world? How could her old friend have done this to her? To their team?

"How can we stop this?" Ty's words sounded expelled through gritted teeth.

"Stopping it might be out of the question." Neil shook his head as if resigned to the outcome.

But she wouldn't give up easily, and she knew Ty wouldn't either. "There's got to be something we can do. Randi said everyone on the Internet would know my story. Feel sorry for me. So this is what she meant? A book detailing our flaws. What can we do?"

"Mat sent a copy of the first three chapters. I printed them out for you to read." He passed her the 9x12 mustard-colored envelope.

They'd waited months to hear what Randi was concocting. Now that she knew, she wished the whole thing could disappear. She dropped the envelope on the bed, not even wanting to touch it.

For years, she'd looked up to Neil for ministry advice. Even now, they could talk over this dilemma for hours, studying it from every angle. But she needed to stand with Ty, also. Randi had attacked not only their ministry, but them as a couple. She remembered the angel in his drawing, sword raised to defend them. "How can we battle this, Neil?"

"By what I've read, it looks like Randi's plan may have been to harm both of you. And our group." He let out a long sigh. "But what if, in her own twisted way, she actually was trying to help us?"

"By hurting Winter and Deb?" Ty jumped up and paced across the small space like a caged tiger, his jaw clenched. "I don't believe it."

"Not that." Neil squinted at Ty. "The book? The movie? Remember when she was gung-ho about getting Winter's story told? How she wanted Passion's Prayer to go worldwide?"

"For her own selfish gain." Winter didn't want the story muddled.

"I know." Neil groaned. "But even if she meant this for evil, couldn't God still turn it into good? Beauty for ashes? Gladness instead of mourning? Isn't that what we share about in our conferences?"

"Yes, of course." Did this mean Neil thought they should go along with the project?

Ty stopped pacing. "What are you saying?"

Neil dug in his pocket and withdrew a folded scrap of paper. "Randi had someone text me this earlier." He passed Winter the paper. "I copied the words."

She unfurled the paper. *I'm sorry for what I've done. Tell Winter I never meant to hurt her. Randi.*

"She never meant to hurt me?" Some of the problems Randi caused her and Ty came to mind. The adversity she'd brought against their team could have been life-threatening. "Now she's sorry? What changed?" She passed the note to Ty.

He stared at the paper, then handed it back to her. "You believe her?" Thick doubt in his tone made his position clear.

"I'd like to." Neil sighed. "But I don't know."

Something didn't seem right about the note. "Randi was spitting mad the last time we spoke. Did she experience a change of heart?"

"Not this again." Ty moaned.

Neil's gaze zigzagged between them. "I called the prison. She's had a mental breakdown."

"What?" Winter groaned as she pictured Randi's hands chained behind her in the interrogation room. The wild glare. The hate oozing from her eyes. And something melted in her heart. She had to do whatever she could to reach Randi. No matter what she'd done.

"She was vomiting, so they were transporting her and another inmate to a hospital." Neil tapped his foot against the floor. "Might have been a ruse. En route, both women attempted an escape."

"Oh, no."

Ty muttered something indistinguishable.

"The police captured her, but she was injured. Any hope of a lesser sentence is gone." Neil's shoulders rose and fell. "If anything, she'll get more time."

At least Ty didn't say "good" this time.

Randi's decisions had been terrible and thoughtless. Winter didn't know what awful things she might have said about her and Ty, or Passion's Prayer, in those chapters in the envelope. Even still, compassion flooded her. How would God have her help Randi?

"A nurse sent the text from Randi's psych ward." Neil blinked quickly like he was fighting tears.

Winter stood and faced Ty, knowing he wouldn't like what she needed to say. "I have to go back to Bend and see her. I've got to do anything I can to reach out to her."

"You tried, and it didn't work." He shook his head. "We're not taking the risk again."

"Please, I want to help her. However many times it takes." She gazed into his eyes. "I love you, Ty. I respect you as my husband. But didn't Jesus say to forgive people, again and again, even if they do the same bad stuff to us a bunch of times?"

"Sure, but you're not going without—"

"You?" She wrapped her arms around his waist, pressed her cheek against his chest. When his arms encircled her, she sighed, thankful this wasn't going to cause another rift between them. "Will you go with me to see Randi? I won't go alone, I promise. But I must see her. To pray for her. She needs to know someone still cares. That I care. And that God loves her."

He blew out a long breath. "We'll pray about it, okay?"

"Okay. Thank you." When she faced Neil again, she stayed close to Ty's side. "What else?"

"Mat said he'd give us a few days to go over the legalities. If we want to fight their rights to the intellectual property, we'll need a lawyer." He stood. "DTM already put out capital, so Mat doesn't want us backing out. Says the storyline is an 'epic tale of love lost, resilience, and love found'—even with the inclusion of what we might perceive as negative publicity."

"You don't mean let them publish the book, do you?" Ty expressed her thoughts accurately, albeit with a harder edge.

"Wouldn't that hurt our ministry? And Ty and me?" She linked her fingers with her husband's.

"Consider this"—Neil drew in a breath like he anticipated their rebuttal—"God is using your story here, at Hart's Camp, the same way He has in churches and conferences all over the country. Couldn't He use this media resource too?"

"But what if Randi lied about us?" Winter had to ask.

"She did." Neil's somber gaze met hers.

"She did?"

Ty groaned and gripped her hand tighter.

Neil nodded toward the envelope. "Those chapters are filled with fallacies."

"Then why proceed?" Ty's voice rose.

Neil stepped behind the chair he'd vacated. "I'm sorry if this sounds harsh, but did Ty have an affair while you were married the first time?"

"Yes." Although, she hated answering.

Ty shuffled back and forth on his feet.

"Did we have trouble in our ministry when you kept his identity a secret?"

She knew Neil wasn't being mean, but she squirmed anyway. "Yes."

"Then some of the story is true. If our pride can take a beating, there's an amazing message of reconciliation and restoration in it that could touch millions."

"Millions?" She and Ty both whispered.

The room stood silent. Ty seemed to be pondering the situation as thoroughly as she was.

Could God use a thing that felt invasive and revealing and awful about their past to bring healing and restoration in marriages? Might even more couples be touched by her and Ty's road to redemption and love?

"What do you think?" She gazed into Ty's eyes that still looked vexed.

"I don't like her doing this without our approval and twisting the truth. But we should read the chapters and see for ourselves." He stared at the wall for a moment. "Neil, could you find out how the story ends? Is it redemptive?"

Their co-leader's eyes brightened. "Sure, I can do that."

"Because that's what's important, right?" Ty pulled her to him in a quick embrace. "We've made our share of mistakes. But ending well is what we want as a couple, and as a ministry."

"Yes, that's true." She nodded.

Neil turned toward the door. "I'll head back to Spokane. I'll let you know what I find out." He gave a small salute, then exited.

Winter followed him to the door. "Thank you for driving all this way, Neil!"

"You're welcome," he called, then disappeared down the forested trail.

When she closed the door, Ty was on his knees by the bunk, his face buried beneath his crossed arms. Rushing to his side, she dropped to the floor beside him. In a few minutes, they had to leave for their next seminar, but they also had a lot to pray about. Whatever they faced in the days ahead, she vowed they would do so on their knees, side by side. Like this.

Twenty-six

Season

By the time they reached the cabin after their fudge and coffee break, Max dropped on the bed and was snoring in thirty seconds. They shouldn't have risked sledding. But how could Season regret their experience on the mountain? They'd made new memories together that she would never forget. She sat beside him for a few minutes, watching him sleep, and praying for his healing.

They still hadn't talked openly like she'd hoped. During their snack time, she avoided probing for answers that might ruin their fragile bond. Perhaps he felt the same way.

Now he was sleeping, and she realized she needed to retrieve their lantern. She slipped out the door as quietly as possible, and hustled down the trail, so she could get back to the cabin before he woke up. As soon as she reached the lodge, she rushed up the stairs to the art room in the loft. She flipped on the light switch, and a warm glow spread across the room, revealing the canvases in various stages of completion. As she admired the paintings, she thought of how the married couples at the retreat were in different stages in their relationships too.

Some were starting over. Some required assistance. Others were celebrating their successes. She and Max were somewhere between needing to start over and needing a lot of help.

She strolled to her canvas and took a moment to ponder her artwork. In the painting, gray and white clouds banked across a darkened sky. Dirt rose and fell along the lower edge of the canvas. And the jar lay slightly askew with a glowing candle inside.

For a few minutes, she paused to consider the symbolism Summer had encouraged them to include. The gray clouds might represent storms in their marriage. Enough tempests had buffeted her and Max's relationship to blow them off course. Yet, they were still together. Not strong, but standing, despite the gales. How about the dirt? Maybe the soil represented the barren ground of their hearts. How they lost their way in the desert of life. How depressing. Except for there, amid storm clouds and bleakness of earth, a shining flame offered a hint of promise.

Love could light up a heart as brightly as a flame in the darkness, couldn't it? Like Jesus radiating love in the center of her brokenness. Like Max showing up here at Hart's Camp. Tears moistened her eyes. Silly for her to feel so sentimental. It was just a painting. Or was there more to it?

She scooped up her canning jar. "Time to make you glow again." Most of the candle had melted into a puddle of spent wax. Maybe she should replace it. She turned to leave, then glanced back at her painting. No Monet or Rembrandt. But that spark of fire in the middle of the painting spoke straight to some deep place within her, as if a flame had been ignited there also.

And yet, despite the awareness of new hope, whenever she thought of her and Max's last year together, a knot twisted beneath her ribs. More prayer was needed, apparently.

She went in search of the lighter downstairs. On the table in the main part of the lodge, she found a package of replacement candles and a butter knife. Using the silverware like a crowbar, she pried out chunks of old wax. Good thing someone had left a metal pot for the scrapings. Next, she lit the candle, tipped it sideways, and allowed melted wax to collect in a puddle at the bottom of the jar. Dropping the candle inside, she positioned it vertically. Now, if she could just get back to the cabin without the flame going out.

Two hours later, after texting the boys and reading her Bible, she changed into a pair of jeans and a thigh-length rust-colored sweater in preparation for the evening session. She was just putting in hoop earrings when she heard Max rustling in the bunk behind her.

She glanced at him and noticed his just-waking-up ruffled hair, his five o'clock shadow, and how his sideburns had gotten grayer in recent months. Kind of sexy looking, though. "Hey, sleepyhead." Part of her wanted to sit by him, stroke her fingers through his soft hair, and see if he was still the new Max, or if her grumpy husband had returned.

He groaned. "Sorry I slept so long. Thought I'd rest my eyes. Then, bam, I was out."

"Gets you every time." She inserted the other earring.

He flung his arm over his forehead as if blocking the light. "You're so beautiful."

Her gasp caught in her throat and made it difficult to swallow. The unfamiliar compliment buzzed in her ears. Apparently, he was still in a good mood. "Oh, uh, thanks." She fumbled to say something intelligent.

"Did I miss dinner?"

His change of subject confused her. "I thought you could use sleep more than food."

"Since when?" His befuddled expression made her laugh.

"Don't worry, Maggie will set out snacks after the meeting." She sat down on the foot of his bed. Time to get some stuff out in the open between them.

He lowered his hand to snag hers. She liked how he toyed with her fingers, twisting her wedding ring. Was he imagining their ceremony, twenty-two years ago when he slipped it on her finger, like she was?

"Would you mind if we talked before we go to the seminar?" Maybe she should have asked him how he was feeling first. "How are you doing?"

"I'm okay. Do we have time to talk?" He pushed himself to a sitting position and stuffed a couple of pillows behind his back. When he gripped his stomach, concern rushed through her.

"What is it?" Had he injured himself worse on the sledding hill?

He shook his head as if nothing were wrong.

"Show me, please?" She scooted to the side of the bed near his waist and tugged on his shirt. Enough with him acting stoic, she needed to see for herself what was wrong.

He glanced toward the darkened window. "Is it snowing?"

"No. The stars are out. A full moon. Beautiful night for a walk down to the lodge." But first, she needed to know how badly he was injured. "Show me what happened to your stomach, okay?"

"You are one stubborn woman."

"That makes two of us. Well, not the woman part." She hid a grin.

He guffawed, then groaned as he unbuttoned his shirt, and the fabric fell away. He pulled up his t-shirt, revealing a black and purple discoloration spanning from the middle of his torso to the right side of his ribs.

"Oh, Max." She couldn't believe he had such a huge bruise,

or that he'd gone sledding with the injury. "Why didn't you tell me it was so bad? I could have gotten ice or had you rest more." She felt terrible for being impatient with him sleeping so much.

"I'll be fine." He refastened the buttons. "And don't say I shouldn't have gone sledding. I wanted to do that with you." He stroked her cheek gently. "I'd do it again, now, if I could." His voice softened. "You and me under the stars sounds romantic."

"It does. But I'm sorry someone did such a terrible thing to you." Fury over the injustice ran through her veins.

"Sweet of you to worry. But it gets worse." He frowned.

"What could be worse than a concussion and a giant bruise?"

"Losing everything."

Everything? Did he mean *that* church the way he'd implied before? What about her? Their family? "You haven't lost everything. You still have me. And our sons."

He scooted over beside her, his feet touching the floor. "I'm glad to hear you say that, Seas." He lifted her chin and gazed into her eyes. "Do I still have you? Even with all my stupid decisions? After the discouraging days we spent in the RV?"

She swallowed hard. Despite the romantic moments they'd shared that day, the festering wound inside of her kept her from breathing freely. "We promised forever, didn't we?" She said the words, but she knew she hadn't been faithful to that ideal. Not when she'd wanted to leave him often enough.

"We did." He nodded. "I don't deserve such a wonderful woman like you. But I'm grateful for all the times you've done this."

"Done what?"

"Stood by me. Helped me out of the quicksand." He

rubbed his fingers over the back of her hand. "You supported me, even when I was a knucklehead."

"I tried. Failed sometimes." More than she wanted to admit.

"Still."

She looked up to find his eyes filled with water. Mesmerized, she couldn't look away from his tormented features. A tear trickled down his cheek, then another. "I'm so s-sorry." He shuddered and released her hand.

The air around them felt on fire with uncertainty. Like she was standing on the edge, holding her breath, waiting for something good to happen, fearing something equally bad might befall them instead.

"I don't know why I sank into such a trench of self-pity after I lost my job, my ministry." He rubbed his hands over his eyes. "I treated you badly. Ignored you. Threw in your face that you didn't want to be a pastor's wife, when I knew you'd always stood by me. To dull the pain, I lost myself in TV shows. And I stopped acting like your husband. I hated myself for that."

With each word he spoke, the hurting places in her spirit seemed to rip and tear, like Band-Aids being yanked off wounds. She wanted to sob to release the pain, but she wouldn't— couldn't—cry in front of him.

"I've barely prayed in the last two months, until today. Kept myself frozen so I wouldn't feel. I couldn't face what happened with the church. So I shut myself off. From you. And the boys." He leaned over, elbows on his knees. "Yet you stayed. Thank you for not leaving me."

She'd wanted to. Now, as she watched him fighting his own brokenness with a dull ache building up pressure in her chest, hot tears pooled in her eyes. But she barely blinked or moved. She didn't want to disturb Max's transparency or reveal her own level of unresolved misery.

"I've asked God to f-forgive me." He clasped her hand,

and she didn't pull away. "Now I'm asking you. Will you forgive me for hurting you?"

Forgiveness—a soul-wrenching word when raw emotions were at stake. Did she forgive him? She could say she did. But what if that wasn't true? He sincerely apologized and revealed his vulnerability and remorse, and she appreciated that. But within her chest, a war over resentments burned like poison.

His palms gently caressed her cheeks. "Can you forgive me, Seas?"

"I want to." Her answer didn't come easily. "I've carried this hurt for a long time." She massaged the upper part of her chest where it ached. "I want to let it go, but I'm not there yet." She wished she could tell him what he wanted to hear just to make him feel better.

He withdrew his hands and nodded. His eyes were wet, as were his cheeks. She'd never watched him cry before. He was a beautiful man when he was humble and repentant. His brown irises glistened like jewels. His scruffy cheeks made her want to run her palms over his rough skin. But that involved reaching out, and touching him, and becoming vulnerable herself. Right now, she felt too self-preserving, so she kept her hands in her lap.

"I love you." A slight smile creased his mouth.

Some of the tightness in her lungs eased. "I love you too, Max." That much was true. She'd loved him as her husband for twenty-two years. "I had fun sledding with you." She thought of something else. "And I like it when you call me Sea-girl." Although, admitting that felt odd. "How did you come up with the name?"

"All those times you wanted to escape to the sea. Seemed fitting." He sighed. "You used to call me something special too."

Husband. "Back when we were young and so in love." Before ice covered the bridge to her heart. Would that ever melt? Earlier today, she'd thought it might be happening. Now she wondered.

"I'm still in love with you." His lips brushed her cheek, but she didn't turn into the kiss.

Max's romancing on their sledding expedition had awakened something within her. But what would he be like when they returned to Darby? Would he be in love with her, then? Or would he go back to being in love with TV reruns? Maybe she should change the subject. "Why did you say you lost everything?"

"Because we're about to lose everything we own." So he hadn't been talking about the church.

"Why? We don't have much."

"Here's the thing ..." For the next twenty minutes, Max explained what had transpired in Darby—Clint's early morning visit and his revelations about Lee, Max's trip to the bank, his meal with Sandy at Annabelle's, Derek's text to meet him at the city gazebo, the rough behavior by Derek's so-called security, and as much as he could recall about the trashing of the RV. At the end of his explanation, she had a good idea of what he'd gone through in her absence.

"Oh, Max, I'm sorry all that happened to you." If she had been there, could she have done anything to help him?

"I just remembered something else." He touched his head. "A guy nearly strangled me." He sucked in a breath. "Maybe he's the one who bashed my head and threatened me."

"Threatened you with what?"

He scratched his forehead. "I'm not sure. But that's why I don't want you going back to Darby." He shuffled backward on the bed and leaned against the pillows. "When the conference ends, you should drive down to your mom's."

"I'm not running away from the only home we have left."

"So you like living in the RV now?" His voice deadpanned.

"Hardly." But it was their home. She stared into the

candle's flame that seemed stronger the darker the room got. "I have my job there. We need an income."

"We'll find employment elsewhere."

"You too?"

"I've applied for plenty of jobs."

"You have? Where?" She couldn't hide her surprise.

"Darby. Hamilton. Other places. And I will again. But first, we should decide, together, where we're going, then we can both apply for work." His eyes shone intensely.

Had he purposefully emphasized the word 'together?' "Does that mean you're ready to leave Darby?"

"Sure. The other day, I even thought about towing the RV to the Oregon Coast." He linked their fingers. "I thought you might like that."

"I'd love that!"

He leaned his head against hers. "I like sitting with you. We belong together, Seas."

Did they? What would it take for them to live the rest of their lives reconciled and in love with each other?

"Guess we should head down to the lodge. But there is one other thing." He dug into his pants pocket and withdrew a crumpled piece of paper. "Gladys left me a note. I found it after she passed. I'd like you to read it too."

She unfolded the note and skimmed the words written in the elderly woman's handwriting. *Whatever you must do to make things right with your wife, do that.* "How did she know we were having problems?" Had Max confided in her as Season had confided in Em?

"Beats me. But I haven't been able to get that last phrase out of my mind." He laid his arm over her shoulder. "Sweetheart, I vow I'll do everything I can to make things right between us. I know it'll take time. That's okay. But I will prove my love to you again."

His words made her want to weep. But that hardened feeling ingrained in her to not cry in front of him kept her from doing so. She stood and grabbed her peacoat, distracting herself by twisting the large buttons. "Thank you for sharing Gladys's note, and for talking with me. That means a lot."

He pushed off the bed and helped her put on her coat. "I want to be a better man for you."

"Thank you, Max."

Would he remember to be as kind and loving when they returned to Darby? And what would happen between them when they faced the extreme challenges he'd spoken of?

Twenty-seven

Max

Max listened as Ty and Winter took turns sharing ideas on marriage. His mind was thinking clearer this evening. The nap probably helped. As did his honest conversation with Season. It felt good to not be carrying a heavy load of guilt on his chest anymore. And it was nice of Josh and his wife to join them at their table, even though he and Season had arrived late.

For a few minutes, he got distracted, thinking back to when he'd asked Season to forgive him. When she said she wanted to but couldn't, that hurt. But he understood her need for time. What would it take for him to show her that he wasn't the self-absorbed passionless man he'd been? That he was determined to be a good husband for her?

Why had he gotten so distracted with everyone's lives in the church and community that he hadn't been aware of the gulf separating him from the one woman he should have treasured the most? Man, he had a massive amount of relationship mending to work on in the coming days. With Benny and Logan too. Perhaps, a good reason to visit Southern Idaho.

He tuned back in to Winter's voice. "Unforgiveness is deadly in our marriages. Tonight, since we've already discussed this topic for a few sessions, I think you're ready for a couple's exercise."

Groans reverberated around the room.

Couple's exercise? Was this the part he'd dreaded when he'd have to stand up and say something personal about his and Season's relationship? However, now that he already spilled his guts to Josh, repented before the Lord, and admitted his wrongs to his wife and asked her forgiveness, a public confession didn't sound like such a horrible idea.

"Okay, everyone, turn to your spouse." Winter moved her hand in a circular motion as if directing their seating. "Now, scoot your chairs around so you can see each other."

"Seriously?" Missy grumbled from the other side of the table.

Max repositioned his chair, as did Season.

"Now, men, take both of your wife's hands in yours." Winter strolled toward the right side of the room. "Oh, Ty-sweetie, I need you."

Ty leaped up and jogged to her, grinning. That got a few laughs.

Max clasped Season's cold hands. Why was she so chilly? From their walk down the trail? Or her internal reaction to what was going on between them? He massaged her fingers, trying to share his warmth. He tugged on the edge of her sweater, but she didn't give him the tiniest smile or glance.

He sighed. Reconciliation was harder than he'd thought.

"This is the tough part," Winter spoke to them while facing her own husband. "I want you to gaze into your spouse's eyes."

He heard Missy groan. Fred said something about getting a drink of water.

Season glanced at Max. Looked away. Closed her eyes. He still held her hands, waiting for her to get comfortable with him being this close to her. Finally, she blinked slowly, and her gaze melded with his. Her blue eyes swam in tears. Another punch to his stomach. Was she counting the ways he'd hurt her? Would most likely fail her again? Her clenched lips wobbled. Her hands trembled. Was she barely holding herself together? Stopping herself from crying? He remembered times in the past when he'd chided her for public emotional displays. Expected her to be as tough as him. And for what reason? So she'd bury her feelings? To appear in church as someone other than who she really was? Maybe, so she wouldn't hold him accountable for his imperfections? That made him want to kick himself in the backside.

But since he had repented, he knew God didn't want him consumed with shame and regret. He was forgiven. But now he had to do everything he could to help his wife recover from her hurts.

How could he reach her? After the way he'd treated her for the last months, he deserved her animosity. However, he wanted her to be free of every speck of anger and pain and bitterness—that he may have caused—that she held in her heart. And for her to experience forgiveness and love with him again. A rich married love for many years to come, if his prayers were answered. If reaching that place meant her bawling, yelling at him, or breaking down, right here, that's what he wanted for her. Whatever he could do to help her, that's what he was committed to doing.

"Keep gazing at each other," Winter coaxed them. "Talk to your spouse with your eyes and your heart."

He hoped Season could see all the love he had for her in his eyes. She was still gazing at him as if searching for the answers she needed. "I love you," he whispered. "So much."

Tears spilled over her eyelids and ran unchecked down her cheeks. She was shaking now. Like she was fighting a horrific battle to suppress her feelings.

"Oh, honey." He released one of her hands. As gently as he could, he brushed her cheek with his finger. "It's okay, go ahead and cry. Let it out. You've been through so much. I'm right here for you. I'll always be right here for you."

Her nod was brief.

He needed to apologize again. "Seas, I apologize for the ways I hurt you. From the depth of my heart, I really am sorry."

"I know." She closed her eyes. Covered her face with her hands. Shuddered.

"For those of you who feel this is true, I want you to tell your spouse you forgive them. Maybe they've wronged you. Maybe you've wronged them." The speaker seemed to be dealing with emotion too. "Whew. This is hard for me. Let the Lord lead you in whatever you need to say. But try to tell your spouse that you love and forgive her or him."

Hushed whispers filled the room.

Max shuffled his chair closer to Season's until their knees touched. He wrapped his arms around her shoulders and drew her to him. Then he leaned close to her ear so she could hear him. He wanted to make a vow to her like the one he'd said on their wedding day. "Season Prescott, from this day forward, I promise to love you like I promised I would twenty-two years ago. I'm yours if you'll have me. God is changing me, and I'm going to be the best husband I can be for you all the days of my life."

Her sudden, almost violent, sobs shook right through him. *Oh, honey.* Not pausing to second-guess if what he was doing would make things better, he drew her onto his lap and held her against his chest. He wrapped his arms around her, and she buried her face in his neck, weeping against him. "It's okay, sweetheart. I love you. We're going to be okay." Rocking her and wooing her with whispers of love, he held her while she cried in his arms. "You are an amazing wife and mother. You are precious to me. I couldn't live without you."

Then he did what used to come so naturally as a pastor, the thing he hadn't done much with his own wife—he prayed. With the sincerest words coming straight from his heart, he petitioned Heaven as if his life depended on it, because he was pretty sure it did.

* * * *

Season didn't know where the monsoon of tears was coming from. Bleeding from a crack in her spirit, perhaps? The sobs hurt as if they'd been buried under her ribs for years. Stagnant emotions came pouring out from a wellspring she could no longer suppress. The weird, but comforting, part was how Max held her so tenderly in his lap, offering his comfort. His arms around her were like a blanket of safety and love. He didn't seem to care that she was sobbing in public. Or that he had broken his rules of propriety by holding her close to him with people nearby. She leaned into his shoulder and kept begging God for His mercy and love to change her, and them. *Please take away the knot in my chest. Heal my heart. Help me forgive him.* She loved hearing Max pray over her too.

"Father, pour Your love into Season. Help her know she's loved and cared for by You, and me too. Guide us through the struggles in our marriage. Bless our future together. Give us hope. A sweeter love for each other."

Yes.

"Help me to be the husband she needs." He sniffed like he was crying too. "We're desperate for You, Lord. Change us for Your glory."

She remembered Summer's words from a couple of days ago. *Josh's and my marriage was transformed by the love of God.* Now she understood. The love of God was washing over her, right then, healing her, making her new, and yes, giving her hope in increasing waves.

"I love you, Sea-girl." Max's voice came softly. "You are my dream come true. My always and forever. Will you be mine?"

She sighed against him. Nodded. She really did love him, and might be falling in love with this sweeter, kinder, more loving Max.

"How about you and I escape to the Oregon Coast?" He leaned back and gazed at her. "I thought I'd ask you this time. Want to run away with me?"

"Yes, I'd like that." She rubbed the sleeve of her sweater across her face, sopping up moisture.

Then Max did something he never would have done in a public gathering in the past, other than on their wedding day. His lips touched hers so softly she barely felt his mouth against hers, him breathing into her, and her into him. She felt his heartbeat pounding against her palm on his chest. Her heart was surely melting into a puddle on the floor.

When they broke apart, she gazed into his warm dark eyes, and sighed, so relaxed and at peace.

She glanced around the room and saw other ladies in their husband's arms. Even Missy and Fred had their arms around each other. A few couples were on their knees praying. Some faced each other with clasped hands. It looked like plenty of tears were on men's and women's faces. Someone might have to send for a delivery truck of Kleenexes after this session.

She slid off Max's lap and scooted into her chair. She knew she needed to say some things to him also. She'd made her share of mistakes in this marriage. "I want to say, I'm sorry for everything I did to hurt you."

"No, Seas, it was all me."

"It's never just one person." She blanched as the truth

penetrated her thoughts. Hadn't she pretty much blamed him for everything that had gone wrong between them? "I'm sorry for yelling at you. For blaming you. For stubbornly coming to this conference without you. For thinking negative thoughts about you and our marriage."

He ran his hands over her arms. "I forgive you. Just think, if you hadn't come here, we wouldn't be sitting next to each other like this, sharing our hearts."

It would be easy for her to stop there, but she wanted to clear the debris from her heart. To start fresh with him. To love him as he deserved to be loved. "I have to confess ... I seriously thought of leaving you."

He looked sad, but not surprised. "I figured as much."

"Mentally, I had my suitcase packed. By harboring those plans, I was unfaithful to you."

"Thank you for telling me, but I understand. Really, I do." He kissed her cheek. "I'm thankful you're here with me now."

"I'm glad you're here too. Thank you for coming to Hart's Camp. For not giving up on us." She took a deep breath. "And I forgive you. You know, for the stuff you shared earlier." She was relieved to honestly say the words now and mean them.

His tender smile, his sparkling eyes, seemed a mix of humbleness and male bravado. "That means the world to me. Thank you."

Josh stood at the side of the room, his guitar strapped at his side. His honeyed tones poured over Season's spirit with words of praise and adoration to God. She joined in the lyrics as best she could. But mostly, she remained in her chair, pondering all that had happened between her and Max. God was transforming them. She could see it in her husband's face. In the gentle way he treated her tonight. She felt it in her own heart. She was breathing without the knot of bitterness strangling her like before. *Thank You, God.*

Max linked their fingers together and didn't let go until after the final "amen."

Would this amazing experience stay with them tomorrow, and the next day as they headed back to Darby?

Twenty-eight

Season

Thanks to clear blue skies, and Max being in the car with Season, the drive to Montana didn't take as long as the last time. He slept through half the journey, but when he was awake, Max kept the conversation lively as if he were trying to help them get to know each other again. He told her stories from his youth, some were new to her, others she'd heard before. He shared about books he'd read, and ones he'd like to read. Places he hoped to visit. Who knew he had a hankering to fish for halibut in Alaska? She enjoyed this Max, and she loved how close she was feeling toward him since two nights ago when they prayed together. *Thank You, God!*

Thinking about taking another break—she'd already stopped several times for gas or coffee—she took an off-ramp at Missoula in search of another coffee shop.

Max stretched and yawned. "Break time already?"

"Uh-huh." She was tired, but she couldn't complain or he'd offer to drive. His injuries seemed improved, but she didn't want him dozing off behind the steering wheel.

"How about that one?" He pointed to a sign displaying a coffee mug in the shape of a cowboy boot.

"Perfectly Montanan." She pulled into the parking lot. Barely waiting for the engine to stop, she jumped out of the Forrester and stretched.

"What is this, your fourth pit stop?" He seemed to be laughing at her.

"Maybe. But who's counting?"

"Me, I guess."

Chuckling, she strode inside the shop ahead of him. As soon as she entered the doorway, she stopped and admired the cowboy-themed artwork lining one wall. "Oh, cool." A stunning picture, that appeared to be an oil painting, portrayed a grizzled outlaw riding a Pinto across the wide-open prairie. Such detailed work! Every shadow and facial line magnified the strained countenance of the rider. She thought of her "clouds" painting wrapped in a blanket on the backseat that paled in comparison. But still, it was hers, and she felt a measure of pride in it.

Max stepped up behind her, his chin brushing her shoulder. "I could be your cowboy."

His newfound flirting surprised her every time. She turned slightly, met his gaze, and grinned. "I do like cowboys."

"I know." He feigned tipping his hat toward her.

Had they been alone, there might have been a simmering kiss like he'd already given her today.

"What can I get for you, little lady?" His lips brushed her ear. The ticklish sensation sent shivers up her neck.

"Well"—she decided to tease him—"your drawl might need some work." She elbowed him in the ribs.

He groaned and gripped his side.

"Oh, no!" She'd forgotten about his bruises. "Max, I'm so sorry."

"No worries." He cleared his throat and dropped his hands

to his side. "I guess I'll have to work on my cowboy brogue." He took her hand and led her to the counter. "Your regular?"

She nodded. Nice he remembered her favorite drink.

"Two double vanilla lattes with whipped cream." He winked at her, then paid the bill.

If he kept being so chivalrous, she'd have to come up with a dozen more excuses to stop between Missoula and Darby.

They found chairs close to the art display, but the narrow table between them was little more than a resting place for their clasped hands. Their knees bumped into each other's.

"Cozy." He rocked his eyebrows.

"I'll say. How are you feeling?" She still worried about him, especially now that she'd elbowed him in the ribs. Were they making the right decision in going back to a potentially volatile situation so soon?

"I'm getting better all the time." He touched the back of her hand. "I like us spending time together like this."

"Me too." She sighed, loving how his gaze danced in her direction.

The last day of the retreat had been an amazing time of reconnecting. Max attended all the sessions either with her, or when the groups split, he'd gone upstairs with the other husbands. The two of them had even pushed their bunks together to form a full-sized bed. She'd wanted to be closer to him and to fall asleep holding his hand.

When his cell phone buzzed, a frown puckered his eyebrows. "It's a 406 area code." He swiped the screen. "Max Prescott." After listening, he shook his head. "No, that's *not* happening. I said—"

"Who is it? Jayme?" She waved her hand in front of his face. "Max?"

"I will not be bullied." Volume increasing, he jabbed his index finger in the air as if articulating a point in a sermon.

"Fine. Do what you must do. But this is not over!" His thumb swept across the screen, ending the call. "The creep is back at it."

"Who was it? What did he say?"

The barista called Season's name, but she didn't move.

She tugged on Max's coat sleeve. "Tell me."

He stared at the wall of paintings as if he didn't hear her. "This is a mistake. We shouldn't go back to Darby. Let's turn around, and start over somewhere else, right now."

Anxiety sent prickles racing over her skin. If going back wasn't safe, maybe he was right. But they'd agreed to face the situation in Darby together. "Max, it'll be okay. We can do this."

He clenched his jaw. "What was I thinking, taking you back there? Acting as if I didn't already get beaten up?" He squeezed the bridge of his nose with his thumb and index finger.

"Was that Derek?" She clasped his other hand.

"No, he doesn't do his dirty work." He pulled his hand away and groaned. "Might have been the hooligan associated with Lee." The same one who'd caused his concussion?

"You've got to tell the police about Lee like we talked about with Ty and Josh."

"Probably." He just stared at her.

"Season? Your order is ready." The barista sounded impatient now.

She stood and hurried to the counter. "Thank you." Grabbing two heat resistant cuffs, she fitted them to the cups' middle section, then returned to the table. Max grabbed his to-go cup and took several sips. She did the same. Although, drinking caffeine on top of her current anxiety level might not have been the best idea.

"What if you drove back to Coeur d'Alene, and got a room?" He nodded in the westerly direction. "You could head to your mom's tomorrow. I'll catch the bus. Talk to the police in Darby. See Derek. Then meet up with you as soon as I can."

Leave him to face the belligerent father and the thugs by himself? "No thanks." She was his support system. She wouldn't forsake him now. "I have to go to work tomorrow and let Bess know that I'm quitting." She scooted her chair closer to his. "Remember, God is protecting us." The night she'd had her breakthrough, and then off and on yesterday, they'd talked about a lot of things, faced their past, and their demons. And after counseling with Ty, who had a business degree, and Josh, who'd been brave enough to confront Max in the first place, they'd agreed to go back to Darby and fix what they could. They were going to work through whatever banking issues they were responsible for, file complaints with the police, help Jayme if they could, get the truck fixed, and then leave Montana. They figured the process might take two to three weeks.

By the sick look on Max's face, he hadn't expected problems to escalate so quickly.

"Do you want to get a room here?" That made sense to her since Missoula was only a little over an hour north of Darby. "Tomorrow, we could head home early enough for me to work my shift."

He sipped his coffee, his focus obviously elsewhere.

"What did that guy say to you?"

"I won't repeat his foul words." He shook his head as if clearing his mind. "We can't stay in the RV tonight, that's for sure."

"Why not?" She touched his sleeve. "It's you and me now. We're not going back to the old Max and Season who don't communicate. I'm your wife." Her voice softened. "We're in this together." Hadn't she been worried he might revert to his old coping mechanism? Withdrawing into himself?

He was silent for several minutes. Then he shuddered.

"You're right. The guy says his 'boss' demands repayment. They'll confiscate our trailer as a down payment unless we come up with the cash tonight."

"Tonight?" Her relief that he was talking to her again was forgotten as panic seized her. "We don't have that kind of money."

"I know."

"I'm sorry, Max. The RV means a lot to you because it was your dad's, but what are we going to do?"

"It's not like I love it. If them taking possession of the trailer gets them off my back, they're welcome to it." His laugh sounded sarcastic. "Maybe they think it's worth something."

But she knew it meant something to him. "Where will we live? What about our stuff in the trailer?"

"I have no idea. That's why you should head to your mom's. Spend time with the boys." The defensive tone was back in his voice. "I can box up our belongings. Clint and Eloise are gone. I could probably stay at their place."

"No! That's the first place the brutes will look." No way would she leave him to that fate. "Before we reconciled, I would have jumped at the chance to get away from Darby. But I love you, Max. I want to stay with you. Let's head to the RV now and grab our belongings."

He covered his face. Groaned. Not the reaction she was hoping for.

God, please don't let us go backward. Give us wisdom. Lead us.

She remembered at the camp when Max held her in his arms and she'd sobbed against his chest. The way they'd rested together on the bed that night, talking through most of the hours. Promising each other a deeper level of commitment. And yesterday, how they'd clung to each other like newlyweds. His kisses and affection had been more romantic than ever. She'd fight for what they had now. "Max, we can do this. How about if we stay in a cheap motel for a few nights until we decide what to do?"

He stared at her. Then swallowed hard. "I'm sorry. I just don't want anything bad happening to you."

"Thank you, for that." She appreciated him honoring his promise to prioritize her in his life. "You really are my cowboy, you know."

"Cowboys keep their ladies safe." He drew her hand to his lips. But then his eyes clouded. "I also want to do God's will. If I rush out of town, is it right for me to leave Clint in the lurch? Or Jayme without a support system? I'd rather leave with—"

"Dignity?" She remembered the last time he'd told her that. Now, she understood him better. Her husband was an honorable guy who needed to do things right. "I understand."

"Thank you."

She stood and scooped up their cups. "We'd better get going. I'd rather arrive in Darby before dark." She dropped the paper products in the trash, wondering if he'd still argue about her going with him.

Finally, he stood. "Me too." He opened the door for her to exit first. Outside, they linked hands. She needed his touch. And it appeared he needed hers just as much.

* * * *

When they pulled into the parking space next to their RV, evening shadows covered the structure. Max wished for the security of full daylight, but that couldn't be helped. What if someone were in the trailer waiting for them? Apprehension nearly choked him.

"Stay behind me." He warned her as he stepped cautiously ahead of her.

She pointed at the door. "Look, it's not closed." She was right. The door stood ajar.

"I'm sure I shut it, even though the window is broken."

"Be careful." She clung to his jacket.

What could he use for protection? An old clay pot jutted out of a snow pile. He kicked it loose from the frozen ground. With the pottery in hand, he entered the RV, making sure Season was safely behind him.

"Peeuw. It stinks in here." She coughed.

He would have had the same reaction if he weren't on high alert. If someone lunged out of the bedroom, the intruder would get a clay-pot headache.

They stepped over broken dishes, clothes, and food spread out across the floor.

"Wait." Season sniffed. "I smell cigarettes."

He sniffed. Yep, someone had been smoking in here. He checked the back of the trailer. Not many places to hide. He looked in the shower. Empty. He sighed with relief, although he still felt wary. "Pack up everything you want as fast as you can. I'll stay with you while you grab your stuff." He picked up a couple of sweatshirts off the bed.

"Okay. Can you lift this?" She nudged the end of the bed.

He yanked up on the mattress, feeling the strain in his stomach muscles. He didn't flinch or show her how much his side still bothered him. They needed to leave quickly. This trailer wasn't worth another altercation.

She pulled two travel bags out of the storage space. Five minutes later, their suitcases were filled with books and pictures and clothes. He snagged a black garbage bag and tossed in bedding and towels.

She checked a few cupboards. "I'll replace the kitchen stuff."

"I know where you can get some amazing pans," he said, trying to lighten the ominous mood. "Remember that info-mercial I loved?" When she didn't laugh at his humor, he dropped the subject. "Let's get out of here."

"Gladly." Season scurried outside ahead of him.

He locked the door—might as well not make it easy for thieves—and they hustled to the Forrester. They tossed their belongings in the backseat, then he opened the passenger door for Season. "I'll drive."

Someone had declared war on them. Maybe the enemy of his soul had spurred on this fight. Maybe it originated with men's greed for power and money. One thing was for certain— he'd protect his wife, no matter the cost. And furthermore, God was in control of their future. Not Lee. Nor Derek. Nor the bank. They'd face their responsibilities the best they could. Help a few folks along the way. And then they were getting out of Darby.

Twenty-nine

Ty

On the drive back from Hart's Camp yesterday, Ty and Winter agreed to give the book and movie possibilities a few days' rest so they could wind down and relax after the conference. But seeing a stack of bills and junk mail Neil left on the table, Ty picked up a few envelopes as he drank his morning coffee. One addressed to Mr. and Mrs. Ty Williams piqued his curiosity.

He tore open the envelope, and his gaze zipped past the first two paragraphs to the sender's name. Mat Kaplan? The guy who contacted Neil about the rights to their story? He'd rather make that one a contribution for the trash can. Instead, with a sickening feeling in his gut, he scanned the letter.

I want to write a follow-up after my conversation with Mr. Neil Quinn, your correspondent, and encourage you to continue negotiations with DTM. Since your marriage and ministry are in the public eye, and we doubt malice or falsification are factors in the documents we possess, our legal team advises me that your concerns would fall under purview other than that of a private citizen.

Ty groaned. Just what he didn't want—to be in the public arena. And Mat doubted Randi's intent for malice? Ty didn't.

Winter shuffled into the kitchen in her slippers, looking cute with her hair wet from the shower. She had on her typical relaxing clothes of navy jogging pants and a hoodie. He hoped they could relax today.

"What are you reading so seriously?"

"You know that thing we're not talking about today?"

"Yeah." She dropped two pieces of wheat bread into the toaster. "Why?"

"We might have to discuss it, after all." He waved the business stationery in the air.

"What's going on?" She glanced in his direction as she poured hot water over a tea bag in a cup.

He wished they didn't have to get into this. "Mat Kaplan is asking us to reconsider negotiations with his firm." He read a portion of the letter out loud: "'The book is eighty percent edited. We're working on marketing to correlate with the primetime release of *Winter's Fall*.'"

"Oh, buhhhhrother. *Winter's Fall*? Seriously?"

"That's what it says. And since we're in the 'public eye,' our story is fair game." He let the paper freefall to the table.

"Oh, Ty, I'm sorry." She grabbed the letter and stared at it intently.

Leaning back against the counter, he sipped his coffee. They could still take DTM to court. But did they want more negative publicity by going to trial?

Someone knocked on the back door. Neil, most likely. His whistling alerted them he was coming down the hallway. "Everybody decent?"

Winter made a snorting sound and set the letter on the table. "We're always decent, no matter what Design Tech Media reports."

Ty shook his head. His wife was more lighthearted about the book thing than he was. Then again, she wasn't the one depicted as the antagonist in the first three chapters. In fact, she came across as angelic. And Randi, whose eyes the story was told through, wound up being the poor misunderstood assistant who gave her life's blood for the cause—figuratively, anyway. The book could be titled *A Husband's Demise*. Not that he'd be happy about that, either.

"Grab some coffee, Neil." Winter buttered her toast. "Need anything, Ty?"

"Nah." Maybe he'd head over to one of his and Kyle's mechanic shops. Working on rigs always helped him shovel off worries. And they could use the money for the mortgage payment. But weren't they supposed to be taking it easy? Why did Randi have to constantly upset their lives?

Neil poured black steaming liquid into a mug, then sat down at the table. He was unshaven. His hair stuck up like he'd strummed his fingers through the strands. Was he worried over decisions they still needed to make? Concerned how a media frenzy might ruin their team? Not that they were a high-profile group.

Winter slid into the seat next to Ty and across from Neil. "Heard anything from Deb?"

"Actually, yes." One of Neil's eyebrows arched. "Did she mention that she met someone?"

"Someone?" Winter grinned. "As in 'someone?'"

"Apparently."

"Cool." Ty figured it was about time.

"I knew this conference would be good for her." Winter laughed. "I'll call her and find out the details."

"What did Deb say?" Not that her business was automatically their business. But they were like a family. "Is she enjoying the conference?"

Neil shrugged. "She didn't say much. Just that she met a guy. Some fellow leading the conference."

"Tag Miles? Are you serious?" Winter's eyes widened like Deb had struck gold on the Klondike.

"Wait." Ty peered at his wife. "Who's Tag Miles, and why are you excited? Should I be worried?"

She cackled. "He's only the most eligible Christian bachelor in the Northwest."

"And you know this, how?"

"I read stuff. I've heard of Tag Miles speaking at conferences. I can't wait to meet him." She pointed at Neil. "Text Deb and tell her to bring him back here."

Ty snorted. "She just meets the guy, and you expect her to parade him over here?"

"Why not? This is the best news ever." She kept her hand over her mouth while she chewed. "Don't you think so, Neil?"

"I'm happy for her. But we should let things develop for her how she, and the Lord, want them to, without our interference." Good for Neil!

"I agree." Ty drank more of his coffee.

Winter groaned. "You two are no fun."

"Did you have a chance to read those chapters?" Neil was apparently ready for a subject change.

"I did." Ty stood and walked to the counter for a coffee refill. "Did you find out anything about the ending?"

Neil shuffled in his seat like he was uncomfortable with the question. "Mat said it's not a fairy-tale ending. Instead, it leaves the door open for the reader's interpretation."

Winter looked puzzled.

"What does that mean?" The one thing Ty had wanted was a positive ending.

Neil shrugged. "He's going to email me the rest of the manuscript. Then we'll see."

"I vote that we refuse the deal. Go to court, whatever." Ty trudged back to his chair.

Neil stroked his scruffy chin but didn't say anything as if in deep thought.

Once they got this book business out of the way, they could focus on doing what they loved. Winter speaking at some conferences, him working at TK Automotive, and them speaking at marriage conferences together when they were asked to do so. Someday, starting their own family. Did Winter ever think about having kids the way he did? The older he got, the more he wanted to have children. April and Chad were expecting soon. He'd have to give his Alaskan friend a call. Maybe Chad would have some pastoral advice for their situation.

"Winter?" Neil nodded toward her. "What's your opinion?"

She met Ty's gaze, and her green irises darkened like a forest on a rainy day. Uh-oh. Was she having second thoughts? Last night when they discussed the book, she didn't want anything to do with a media circus, same as him.

"I've been thinking it over." She gnawed on her lower lip.

She *was* changing her mind. He groaned. Would this turn into one of those situations where she was adamant they do things one way, and he chose the opposite side? He already knew how those votes typically ended. Neil would go along with her.

"I know we agreed not to discuss this for a couple of days." She made an apologetic grimace.

"Sorry." Neil coughed. "I didn't know."

Ty slid the sheet of stationery across the table. "This was in the mail stack. Mat doesn't think we stand a chance in court."

Neil stared at the paper. "Hmm."

Winter touched Ty's arm. "The thing is, this morning even before I read Mat's letter, I was revisiting the idea that God might be able to use DTM to reach more people than we could. I think we should try to work with Mat."

Why didn't she warn him privately that she was flip-flopping?

"What about our ministry itinerary? And focusing on"— he couldn't say 'making babies' in front of Neil—"other personal matters."

"We can still do all the scheduled retreats and conferences, right, Neil?" He could tell she wasn't seeing the bigger picture. "Nothing's going to change."

"I think it will." Ty faced Neil. "Tell her what could happen."

Neil swiveled his mug on the table. "If a book and a movie were successful, our lives and ministry could change significantly."

Like Randi wanted. But he didn't say so out loud.

"How?" Winter's eyes widened.

Neil shrugged. "TV and radio interviews. Travel. High expectations."

"That doesn't sound so bad." She smiled like everything was okay, while Ty's insides were on fire.

"For you, maybe."

"Why? What am I missing?" She laid her hand on his arm.

He'd rather not delve into personal issues in front of Neil. Although, the three of them, four if Deb were here, were the voting body of Passion's Prayer. They often had to confront uncomfortable topics. Sometimes private matters Ty didn't feel like discussing with them at all.

"A year ago, we had a similar discussion. Remember?" Thankfully, Neil took control of the conversation. "At that time, Ty didn't want to speak at marriage conferences."

That was the truth.

"I remember." Her voice came softly.

"Do you recall why?" Ty asked her.

She stared into her cup. "Because of our breakup. Because of all we'd been through." She drew in a long breath as if she were pondering that day at a rest stop in—Utah? "You didn't want to talk publicly about our divorce."

"I didn't want to relive that time. What I lost." Still didn't. Although, since then quite a few conference attendees had told him how much they appreciated his honesty when he shared about their past.

"All this time, sharing at retreats, have you resented telling your side of the story?" She blinked slowly as if she couldn't believe that of him.

"Certainly not." But that didn't mean he wanted some actor portraying him and making a mockery of their marriage vows, either.

"Then shouldn't we have a little faith and walk through the open door?" Her moist green eyes seemed to be urging him to be more understanding. And right there, he figured he'd lost the battle. Would he ever be free of his past? *God, help me.* Or was his pride, once again, rearing its ugly head?

"We want God's will for our lives, right?" Her gentle tone tugged on his spirit.

"Yes." That's all he trusted himself to say because what he wanted to do was grab his coat and head for the door. A walk might clear his mind.

"Good. Then, Neil, let's keep the dialogue open with DTM."

"Done."

Done? Ty groaned again. But just as defeat pressed down on him, another idea seeped into his thoughts. Inspiration from the Lord? Or comfort, maybe. "What if we scrapped Randi's point of view? Instead of catering to her poor-me tale, we tell our story, our way? What if we show Mat Kaplan the truth about us in its brokenness and redemption and hope? Like we do in our conferences."

Everyone was quiet for a minute. Then, as if a burst of ideas hit them, they all spoke at once.

"Wouldn't that take too long?"

"I could call Mat and see what he thinks."

"It's just an idea, but—"

They laughed. And the air felt more breathable.

"Winter's right. It might take us too long." Ty fingered the handle of his mug. "But it's a chance I'd rather take than having DTM publish Randi's"—he swayed his hand at the manuscript pages, not sure what to call it—"trash."

"Me too." Winter clasped his hand. He liked that she was agreeing with him.

Marriage was about compromise and finding a middle ground. Them writing about their journey, instead of Randi doing so, was a concession he could live with. "Neil, what do you think?"

Their co-leader shoved away from the table and stood. "It's worth a shot. I'll call Mat." He paused. "There's another angle. Randi's incarcerated in a mental lockdown. I wonder if that might be grounds for her contract to be reconsidered."

A rush of optimism sped through Ty. "You never know."

Neil jogged down the back hall and exited the house.

"Thanks for being open to my suggestion, Sas." Ty kissed her cheek.

"You're welcome." She smiled. "The whole thing will take a lot of work and time."

"I know."

And even if they wrote their version of their marital failings and reconciliation, did he want the whole world knowing the things he still struggled to share?

Thirty

Season

After her week at Hart's Camp, the uncertainty of staying in Darby the last two days, and not sleeping well, Season felt exhausted. It was difficult to stay focused on the job. Was Max okay? Was someone still after him? Was she safe? While checking in books that morning, she'd prayed for their safety. Later, as she alphabetized and shelved books on the best seller's display, she kept glancing over her shoulder, checking for anything suspicious. Was the man in the black jacket leaning against the roundwood beams staring at her? What about the guy at the computer wearing dark sunglasses? Who'd wear those in the middle of winter inside the library? Someone who didn't want to be recognized? Maybe she'd carry a large dictionary as a precautionary measure the next time she visited the lady's restroom.

For the next couple of hours, she stayed behind the circulation desk as much as possible. Better to be safe and stay in a central location.

When her phone vibrated, she jumped. Silly to be so tense, but how could she act normally when anyone could be Max's attacker? Or the one who might be after her? Gulp. The library had strict rules about employees not using their phones during work hours. But when Season turned in her notice, she'd explained to Bess about their situation, and that she might have to take a call. Now, pulling the cell out of her pocket, she glanced at the screen and saw her nickname for Max. *Husband.*

I filed a complaint against Lee.

Good. She tapped quickly. *What about Derek?*

I decided not to file one against him.

What? Why not?

I thought about it. Seems best for now.

That didn't make sense. Should she remind him that last night he said it was the right thing to do? Why did he change his mind?

I must face him myself.

Don't go near Derek alone.

She wished she could take a long break and call him. Or better yet, leave work and spend the afternoon with him.

I called Jayme, but she didn't answer.

Keep trying. If anyone had information, Derek's daughter seemed likely. Although, Season would have rather been present for that call.

Thought I'd walk over to the trailer.

Max, no.

What if the bad guys were at the RV? She already asked him not to go there by himself.

Just then, a teenager stepped up to the circulation desk with a tall stack of books.

She returned her attention to the screen. *I have to go! Stay safe.* She added a heart Emoji.

A rose appeared on her screen without words. So he wasn't agreeing to avoid trouble? She sighed. *Lord, please protect Max.*

* * * *

Max knew Season meant well by urging him to stay safe and to not go near Derek or the RV. But he had to face these issues before they could leave Darby.

That's why, an hour ago, he traipsed into the police station, planning to lodge complaints against Lee *and* Derek. Let the law take its course. His former councilmen deserved to sit in stark prison cells, contemplating how their misdeeds had hurt others.

When he pictured Lee stealing from widows and retirees in the congregation, Max's blood boiled. Then, Lee telling thugs—possibly the Barrister brothers—the church owed him money? How could he have done such a thing? And him leaving Clint and Max to pay off his debts? Unbelievable. Lee was far from the honorable man Max had thought him to be.

Then there was Derek spreading lies in the community, via Jayme, about Max breaking not only the Commandments but his covenant with his wife, all the while knowing the rumors were false. What was his motivation? To see Max's character destroyed? Well, that had pretty much happened. And why had he sent the security guy to beat him up?

But Max struggled with conflicting opinions and questions within himself. Was he justified in making Lee and Derek spend time in the slammer? They deserved it, right? But then, what about his creed as a pastor to do all he could to love his neighbor? To help, not harm others. Was bringing charges against men from his church the honorable thing to do? Did he want their public arrest plastered across the *Bitterroot Star* and the *Ravalli Republic* newspapers? Willa and Martha Clayton would certainly spread the tale like the plague. What kind of witness would that be to the community?

For him, the temptation wasn't seeing them thrown in jail—it was taking matters into his own hands. He'd like to find

Lee, grab him by the collar, and shake the truth out of him. But he'd probably fled the country as Clint said. However, Derek's bank was in Hamilton, not far at all. Max could drive there in his truck, and demand answers. Show Derek Clark that he wasn't some feeble man the banker could have beaten up and get away with it. He should have taken Derek to task long before now. But hadn't he always been intimidated by the businessman? Had held his wealth and prestige in the community in high esteem? Perhaps, now, he wouldn't have second thoughts about watching the cantankerous ex-councilmen squirm under fire.

But then, that still small voice whispered in his ear about loving and turning the other cheek. Thoughts he didn't wish to entertain.

A verse in Corinthians admonishing Christians not to take other believers to court pranced through his mind. He'd like to dig a grave and bury that one. Goodnight, these were modern times. People took other people to court all the time. But he'd been a pastor and knew his Bible. What about God's law of love? Didn't that supersede man's justice system? How did the rest of that verse go? *Why not rather be wronged? Why not rather be cheated?*

Ugh. Who wanted to be wronged? Wasn't it natural for him to want to defend himself? To demand justice? But was his desire for revenge right and loving?

His head still ached from the concussion. That's probably why he hadn't been thinking clearly. But if he still had doubts, and he did, shouldn't he investigate a few things himself?

Lee's case was different. He broke the law, and he'd have to face the consequences. Max had to stand up for the group he'd pastored, even if that congregation didn't exist anymore.

Derek had caused Max personal grief. He needed to have a duel-at-high-noon sort of meeting with that man and face those wrongs between the two of them. If that didn't work, Max might rethink his decision about filing a complaint against him too.

As he walked toward the motel, his mind leapfrogged to his next appointment with Rhonda Dennett at the bank. Could he convince the loan officer to remove his name from the document this time? He should try to make a good impression by dressing nicely. Last night, in all the rush, he hadn't grabbed his sport coat out of the trailer. Maybe he'd head that way now, despite Season's appeal for him not to, and grab it. Nothing would happen. Although, he wouldn't mind finding a big stick or a bat for protection, just in case.

He walked briskly down the center of town, past aging buildings. As he approached Annabelle's, he was tempted to cross to the other side. Hopefully, the Clayton sisters weren't coming or going from the restaurant. He didn't trust what he might say to those troublemakers.

Needing to think of something else, something nicer, he pictured Season, and how they'd been more loving toward each other lately. Last night, she'd acted so sweet, gazing into his eyes, holding his hand, leaning in to him as they walked. He'd been feeling more romantic too. Like he was twenty-something all over again. Strange how being on his knees, begging God for help, apologizing to his wife, then holding her in his arms while she cried and prayed, made him feel whole again. *Thank You, Lord.*

He paused in front of Merv's Hardware, a landmark building in Darby, and wondered if they had any bats in stock. Probably not in January. But still, he'd check.

"Why, if it isn't Pastor Prescott." Merv Richards, dressed in overalls and a cowboy hat greeted him at the door with a grin and a handshake.

"Nice to see you, Merv."

"Sorry to hear about your church." The business owner pulled a toothpick from his overall's front pocket and stuck it in his mouth.

"Thanks. I appreciate that." Max glanced around the old-fashioned store with its long, narrow aisles, trying to picture where a bat might be located. He'd been in the hardware store plenty of times, but not for sports equipment.

"What can I help you with?" Merv swayed his hand toward an endcap. "Need a shovel?"

"No. Would you have any bats?" Max mimed swinging a baseball bat.

"This time of year?"

Max shrugged. "Thought I'd check."

"Let me see, Peggy stocks sporting goods at the rear of the store." He twirled the toothpick.

"Thanks." Max strolled deeper into the store.

"Let me know if you need anything else. Got seeds in." Merv laughed as if he'd told a joke.

Seeds while there were still a couple of feet of snow? No thanks.

He reached the last aisle where a mismatched array of toys and sports equipment decorated the shelves. Two footballs. A soccer ball. A few ice skate boxes. A pile of ski goggles. And tucked in the far corner were two dusty bats. He lifted one. Could he hit another person with it? Not unless he was out of options. Or to protect his wife.

At the checkout, Merv eyed Max, then the bat, as if suspicious why he'd need such a—weapon? Max ignored his implied question, paid the price, then hustled out the door.

The police had warned him to stay clear of the RV. They said it was better for everyone involved if he laid low until the situation was resolved by local officials. But he wasn't snooping for trouble. He'd get in, grab his dress clothes, and get out.

As he approached the trailer park on the edge of town, he held the bat snug against his leg to make it less conspicuous. Didn't want any of the neighbors thinking he was a thug. However, when he reached Mrs. Brandt's single-wide, he clutched the bat's handle with both hands, primed to swing if he had to. Just let one of those brutes he previously encountered jump out at him, he'd be ready.

He paused a moment at the corner of Nellie's place, took a deep breath, and rushed into his rented parking space. The RV was gone!

Even though the guy had threatened to take it, Max was surprised, and angered, to find the lot empty of his trailer.

He stomped across frozen dirt where the snow hadn't reached beneath the trailer. He kicked the Styrofoam skirting he'd attached to the RV for winter insulation. How could they rob him of the little possessions he owned? He raised the bat and slammed it against a chunk of foam. *Take that.* They'd beaten him up, left him bloody and bruised, and thought nothing of it? He smashed another chunk. Pieces scattered like confetti. They'd stripped him of the only thing his dad had given him—other than the decrepit truck. He swung again. Then groaned as the impact jarred his ribs. Who was he kidding? Did he care about the RV? Thieves stealing from him was a personal affront. But if the creeps had to take something, better the trailer than harming Season or him, or Clint and Eloise.

Last night, they'd packed so fast. Had he gotten all his books out? What if they overlooked something in the benches? Photographs of the boys? His old sermon notebooks? He groaned.

Then he heard a siren's wail. Maybe two. What now? The sound increased. A fire truck and two police cars careened to a stop in front of him. Four men hopped out, two armed.

Bat in hand, Max gulped and faced them. Had someone seen him beating the Styrofoam and thought he was dangerous?

"What's going on here?" Jeff Sanders, a tough-looking officer, pointed at Max. "Who are you, first and last name?"

"Hey, Jeff." Max lifted his hand.

Jeff glanced at him again but didn't show any sign of recognition. Weird, since he'd attended Max's church for years.

"That's him! That's him!" Nellie squealed from where she now stood at the front of her mobile home. Still in her bathrobe, she squinted like she couldn't see a thing. "That's the man I saw beating the stuffing out of the place."

"Hello, Mrs. Brandt." Max waved at her, hoping she'd recognize him now.

"Who are you?" She clutched her robe with one hand.

"Stay back"—a younger policeman Max didn't recognize cautioned her. "For your own protection, go inside, ma'am."

She moved a couple of feet, then peered around as if trying to see better.

"State your name." Jeff Sanders glowered at Max.

"As you know, I'm Maxwell Prescott. I've lived in Darby for twenty years. Someone stole my RV." He swayed the bat toward the vacant lot. "I've rented this space for a couple of months."

"Max?" Nellie gasped. "I thought you were here earlier and pulled the trailer away."

"Nope. Someone else did." He pictured the probable duo—one tall, one short.

Nellie gasped. "How could such a thing happen in Darby?"

"Someone reported vandalism. Are you causing trouble?" Another officer, Rich Carmichael, who'd attended Max's church sporadically, scowled, hand near his hip. Near his gun? "What are you doing with the bat? Using it as a weapon?"

"Not really." Although, if given the chance, he might have.

"Put the weapon on the ground! I said—"

"I heard you." Max dropped the bat. He lifted his hands in surrender, even though they hadn't told him to do that yet. "Jeff and Rich, you both know I recently lost my pastorate. Your office has my report of a brutal attack I received here in my home last week. Since then, I've been out of town recuperating." He lowered his hand and swayed it toward the empty space. "I came back to this."

Neither Jeff nor Rich gave him the tiniest flicker of friendship or compassion.

Man, he was tired. Maybe he needed to head back to the motel and sleep. Or find some TV reruns to watch until Season got off work.

"I'll take your statement." The younger officer withdrew a small notepad from his pocket. "Maxwell Prescott, you said?"

"Yes."

"Occupation?"

"Was a pastor."

"Now?"

"Nothing." Saying that hurt. And "nothing" wasn't true. While he may have acted like a loser for weeks, he felt more like himself, now, than he had in years. Capable of making good decisions. Being a caring husband and dad. A better pastor, if God allowed him the chance in the future.

"I'm heading back to the station." The fireman returned to his truck and pulled away.

"Sorry for not recognizing you, Max." Nellie gave him a quick wave, then disappeared into her trailer.

The officer taking notes cleared his throat. "Make and model of the RV?"

Max answered his questions the best he could, then explained what he knew about the threat he'd received concerning the trailer's theft.

"What I don't understand"—the policeman stuffed the

notebook in his pocket—"is why you were smashing things with the bat."

"Frustration." He winced at the pain in his side. He glanced at Jeff and saw him shaking his head. Pity? That, he didn't want. "I was beaten up twice, so I wasn't coming here without protection."

"In the future, leave such matters to law enforcement." Rich took out what appeared to be a digital camera from his coat pocket and snapped several pictures.

Max stomped his feet a couple of times. Too cold to stand still for long.

"Stay out of trouble, if you can." Jeff's eyes held a strange glint. Had he heard of Jayme's rumors?

"We have all the information we need." The younger man nodded once. "If I were you, I'd keep the bat locked away until the batting cages open in the spring. Good day, Mr. Prescott."

"Yeah, sure."

The officers left, but Jeff kept his gaze on Max until they were out of sight.

Heaving a sigh, Max stacked the Styrofoam pieces in a pile and hoped they didn't blow away in the next storm. He'd have to come back to clean up the site or hire someone to do it. They needed their deposit back anyway.

Slowly he trudged to the motel, not letting go of his bat, no matter what the police said.

Now, he'd be facing the banker without the benefit of a sport coat or nice slacks. But if the loan officer refused to remove his name from the documents, or give them more time on the loan, what did it matter whether he was nicely dressed or not?

Thirty-one

Season

Season stared at the scrunched-up piece of paper her boss just handed her. "Where did this come from?"

"Someone left it on the circulation desk. It has your name on it." Bess hurried past her with an armload of books.

Season reluctantly smoothed out the torn paper. "Season Prescott" was written in large print. Had a child left her the note? That happened occasionally. She perused the library. Jonny and Becca Linderman, five-year-old twins, thumbed through books in the children's section. She doubted they'd write to her. Several locals sat at public computers. No reason to suspect any of them. The guy wearing sunglasses had left. Was anyone else in the aisles?

She unfolded the paper. "LEAVE TOWN" was written in block letters. A shiver raced up her arms.

Why was someone demanding that she and Max leave Darby? They weren't going anywhere until they chose to go. And she wouldn't allow this note to get to her either. But was it safe for her to remain at the library? Maybe she should ask to be excused from her shift. She checked the clock. Only one more hour remained until her lunch break, then she'd call Max. Maybe they could meet at Annabelle's. Or sit in the car and talk. She pulled out her cell to text him, but a patron asked her for a new library card. As she went through the motions of helping the woman, she wondered if someone might be watching her. Had the guy dressed in black left? Or was he in the biographies section where she didn't have a plain view from the desk?

Her cell phone vibrated. As soon as she finished her task, she glanced at the screen. *Husband.* Just seeing his contact name gave her comfort, but his text did not.

The RV is gone. Police came. We're officially homeless.

The thing he'd feared had happened. What would they do now? They were vagabonds—other than they still had their archaic motel room, where the owners insisted they keep the water running in all the faucets so the pipes didn't freeze. The temporary housing was too expensive to stay much longer, anyway.

With the trailer being taken, and now her getting this note, she'd like to talk to Max. She went straight for Bess's office and requested the rest of the day off. Fortunately, her boss was understanding.

When she opened the door to their motel room, Max leaped off the bed and gripped a bat in the air as if to threaten an intruder.

"Max! It's me."

"Oh, I'm sorry." He dropped the bat on the floor. "I didn't expect you so soon."

"I can see that. What's going on?" *Perry Mason* played loudly on the TV. The curtains were drawn, making the room darker. Was he resorting to his old ways? She fingered the piece of paper in her pocket.

"Sorry about the bat. I bought it at Merv's." Max tapped the remote, silencing the courtroom drama. Then he hugged her.

What had their world come to that her peaceable husband

would buy a bat as a weapon? He must be worried about another attack.

"I'm sorry about your dad's trailer." She was relieved to be here with him, standing in his arms. It would be tempting to forget the danger and uncertainties of the day and just hide in this motel room.

"Thanks. I thought you had to work until six."

"I did." She stepped away from him, removed her jacket, then dropped onto the end of the bed. "But I felt on edge all morning." She pulled the paper from her pocket. "Someone left this note for me at work. So after you told me about the RV, I had to get out of there."

He grabbed the wadded scrap and opened it. His eyes widened. "One of the thugs was at the library?"

"Two, possibly." Thinking of them secretly watching her, she shuddered.

Max sat down beside her and linked their fingers. "Tomorrow, I'll hang out at the library, all day if necessary."

"You don't have to do that." Although, that he wanted to protect her was sweet. She explained about the two guys who seemed suspicious.

He told her about the missing RV and how the local police had treated him.

"Why did you go back to the RV?"

"I forgot my sport coat. I have that appointment with the banker this afternoon." She noticed he had on a white shirt and black jeans that had seen better days.

"Would you mind if I went to the bank with you?" In the past, she never would have invited herself into one of his business meetings. Today, she wanted to stay as close to him as she could and support him.

"I don't mind." The worry lines on his face eased. "In fact, I'd like that. But the news could be bad."

"Still, I want to be with you." She kissed his cheek, then she stood and grabbed her makeup bag.

While she reapplied her lipstick in the alcove outside the bathroom, she sent up prayers for their safety, wisdom, and God's help.

* * * *

At the bank, they had to wait in the lobby for over an hour. Max alternated between sitting by Season and pacing. The receptionist kept apologizing and telling them Miss Dennett would see them shortly. Finally, when Max had convinced himself the manager was purposefully avoiding him, she rushed into the lobby on high heels.

"Mr. and Mrs. Prescott? Please, come into my office." Rhonda swayed her hand for them to precede her, looking calm and collected. Far from how Max felt. "Sorry for the delay. I was on a long-distance call. Have a seat." Miss Dennett walked to her chair.

He and Season settled into the guest chairs across from hers. Season clutched his hand like she was nervous.

"How can I help you?" The bank manager's pearly whites glistened in his direction. But the frown around her eyes contradicted her smile.

He drew in a long breath to assuage his irritation for having waited so long. "I'm here, again, to try to get my name removed from the documents involving Darby Community Church. As I told you the other day, I'm no longer the pastor."

"And as I told you, Mr. Prescott, your name is included as a trustee of the unincorporated church." She tapped her red painted nails on the desktop. "That makes you equally liable with the other three appointed members."

The weight of dread felt suffocating and intolerable. How could he fight these ridiculous legalities? "Seriously? I was fired two-and-a-half months ago." He heard his voice getting louder, but he didn't subdue it. "Surely, you can see that someone who's been removed from duty is no longer fiscally responsible."

Season squeezed his hand. A reminder for him to stay calm? *Okay.*

"I can see why you would think so." Rhonda spread out her hands. "However, I have no control over banking regulations. I'm simply following protocol. If there were any other ways to compensate for the bank's losses, we could investigate those things. As it is—" Something dinged on her computer. "Excuse me." She stared at the screen. Her fingers flew over the keys on her keyboard.

He leaned toward Season. "Coming here was a waste of time. Just like last time."

"Let's trust the Lord," she whispered in his ear. "We had to do this, right? How else could we know where we stand?"

He should have demanded that his church become incorporated. Not that Derek or Lee would have listened. Hadn't he tried to convince them to change their opinions multiple times?

Maybe he needed to pray again. *Lord, we'd really like to start over. Go to the coast. How can we do that if a financial disaster is falling—*

"I can't believe it." Miss Dennett chuckled. "The sun must be shining on you today, Mr. Prescott." The loan officer's facial features transformed with her smile. "I have good news for you."

He could use some good news.

"I've just received confirmation of a development with your church foreclosure."

His heart rate hammered up a notch. "What is it?"

Rhonda met his gaze. "The loan, in its entirety, has been purchased."

"What?" Both he and Season leaped to their feet.

"It's true. Our president, Mr. Dockerman, is finalizing the documents as we speak."

He struggled to process the banker's words. "The loan was purchased? Just now?"

"Yes." She laughed as if relieved to be free of the ordeal herself. "No more waiting for the results of the auction, after all."

"Oh, Max." Season squeezed his arm. "That's wonderful!"

Almost unbelievable. "How did this happen?" No more debt looming over his head? They could leave town. Breathe freely. He didn't know whether to shout "hallelujah" or demand clarification. "Who bought it?"

"Mr. Dockerman made the sale himself. At present, the buyer's name is private information." She wrote something on a sticky note. "Eventually, it will become public knowledge."

Season leaned toward him. "God answered our prayers, Max. Isn't that amazing?"

A weight the size of Mount Rushmore had tumbled off his shoulders and left him dazed. "Just so I understand, you sold the church building and the land, and there won't be any financial repercussions to the trustees?"

"Correct. No legal action will be required to recoup funds from you or the other members." She stood, signaling the end of their meeting. "Once escrow is finalized, you won't have to worry about the obligation in Darby ever again."

Just like that, it was over. He wanted to fall on his knees, and praise God.

Instead, he shook the banker's hand. "Thank you for your time, Miss Dennett." Hopefully, he'd never have the pleasure of her banking expertise again.

As soon as they were outside the bank, he pulled Season into his embrace. "We're free!" He did a little two-step with her on the sidewalk, both laughing. "Let's go celebrate. Eat ice cream. Buy steak dinners."

"I'm happy for you, and the others, Max." Her words were encouraging, but he could tell something was bothering her. "Wasn't that weird how the whole thing fell into place?"

"A miracle, right? As you said, God answered our prayers." An idea sprang to mind. "We could leave Darby tonight. I mean, what's holding us here now?"

"My job. We still have medical bills to pay." She stepped back and a shadow crossed her face. "There's the note left at the library. And your stolen trailer. With the garbage Derek's been pulling, do you think he's involved? And why was Miss Dennett so secretive?"

"I don't know. Maybe another church bought the property. Wouldn't that be great?" Why wasn't she as relieved as he was? "We could take off and—"

"What about Clint and Eloise's safety? And Derek's and Jayme's lies?" Why did she keep bringing up the things he wanted to forget?

"Come on." He took her hand and pulled her toward their car, still thinking of how they could celebrate on their limited finances. "I'm not responsible for any of those things. I'm not pastoring, remember?" He'd planned to see Derek tomorrow. But someone had sent his wife a suspicious note—that changed everything. He didn't want to risk her safety just to satisfy his need to know what had gone down in Darby over the last year. It was time for them to leave.

About three feet from the Forrester, Season came to a stop and crossed her arms. "I thought we came back to face those issues." She gave him one of her looks that said she knew him better than he knew himself. "Don't you still need to do what's right? Because even though you aren't pastoring a church, in here"—she brushed her fingertips against his chest—"you have a beautiful pastor's heart."

He swallowed back a rush of emotion.

"You care more about people than anyone I know. And I can see you're still troubled about some of your friends here."

That she knew him so well touched his heart. Still, he struggled. Should they stay or leave? He hadn't left before when he probably should have. And now, there were people he needed to face. But his wife's safety was foremost in his mind. "I guess I have a few things to do before we go. However, I want to protect you—which might mean us leaving sooner than we thought."

"Max, that's sweet and loving of you, but God is with us, right?" Her beautiful blue eyes glistened toward him. "When we've seen everyone we need to and finished our tasks, then we can leave the valley with clear consciences, and in freedom."

He pulled her into his arms. "I'm so lucky you're my wife." She leaned her cheek against his coat, his chin resting against her head, and he thanked God for their renewed love. When he noticed her shivering, he led her to the car. Once they were seated and he had the heater going, he faced her. "What do you say to us leaving in a few more days?"

"I'll tell Bess tomorrow." She held his hands, their gazes lost in each other's. "I really am falling in love with you, Max."

Her words shot a jolt through him. His wife was falling in love with him? "Oh, sweetheart, I'm in love with you too." For a few moments, his worries faded away as he pressed his lips against hers, enjoying kissing his wife—and he didn't even care if people walking past saw them. Maybe he was getting the hang of this romantic stuff, after all.

Thirty-two

Max

Max stood by the motel window to check on their car in the dark parking lot. A fresh layer of frost covered a dozen vehicles lined up in front of the single-level building. A car's headlights ricocheted off the trash bin and reflected shards of ice in its glow. If they were still living in the RV, their furnace would be going non-stop on such a freezing night that was typical for winter in the Bitterroot Valley. He shuddered, imagining it. Thankfully, the motel heater kept the room warm.

Season sat in a swivel chair reading from her Kindle, looking cozy with a throw blanket draped over her shoulders.

Something had been troubling him all evening, and he thought he'd share it with her instead of keeping his thoughts to himself. "I've been thinking of calling the boys."

She set the device in her lap and gazed at him. "Oh, yeah?"

"I know I haven't kept the lines of communication open with them." Hard to admit his failings, even to her. "There are things I need to say to them too. Apologies to be made." He was determined to be a better father now. Surely, it was never too late for that.

Her eyes sparkled. "They'll enjoy hearing from you. They need their dad—even when they're all grown up and may not realize it."

"Maybe I could meet with them. Go to a basketball game or something."

Her eyes widened.

"I know, they'll be shocked too."

"Pleased." She stood and stepped in front of him, linking their fingers together. "As am I, Max. You're a good man. A loving father."

Her words warmed his heart. He knew she was aware that he hadn't been as loving as he should have been for a while. But he was changing. He felt so tender toward his wife and his sons. He leaned his forehead against hers, enjoying their closeness. God had brought them so far in the last week, restoring their love and their friendship.

His cell vibrated on the table. "Sorry." He grabbed the device and checked the name. "It's Jayme."

"You should answer." She sat down and covered up with the blanket again. But he could see she was watching him instead of reading.

He tapped the display. "Hello?"

"Hey, Max, this is Jayme." She sounded upbeat. "I heard you were injured. Thought I'd check on you." So she wasn't returning his call from earlier?

"I'm better. Improving." Although, still suspicious of her.

"Cool. I'm relieved."

Neither of them spoke for a few moments.

"You there, Max?"

He wished she'd call him Mr. Prescott. "I'm here."

"I, um, shouldn't have told Season my father made me tell that story about you and me." She laughed in a high-pitched tone. "He'd never do that."

"What are you saying? That Derek didn't make you spread the lies?"

"No, he didn't."

"What game are you playing, Jayme?"

"What is it?" Season whispered.

He shook his head, couldn't speak for the acid burning up his throat.

"Max"—Jayme cooed his name—"don't you remember that night at church? You and me. Holding hands. That sweet moment we had?"

"Good grief! What are you talking about?" He stomped to the door and back, taking out his rage on the carpet. "We never had a 'moment.' And we certainly never held hands."

"What did she say?" Season stood, her eyes wide.

"I had to tell Daddy everything." Jayme's sugary tone made him sick.

"Everything what?" He should just hang up. But his years as a pastor had built up some tolerance in him. He'd wait and see where she was going with these ridiculous claims.

"About us being alone that night. You rubbing my shoulder, sitting close, being all understanding." She whispered "under-standing" like she might have said "sexy."

"For Pete's sake, I didn't rub your shoulder or sit close to you!" Outrage, unlike anything he'd ever experienced, spiked his adrenaline. He wanted to hurl the phone at the wall.

"Max?" Season touched his chest, bringing him back to his senses.

"You remember, don't you, Max? How one thing led to another?" Jayme's whispered words reminded him of someone setting a trap. Well, he wasn't falling for it.

"No, I don't remember, because none of what you said ever happened."

"Let me hear." Season got right next to his cheek, her ear pressed against the cell phone.

His heart thumped crazily. After this call, he might need a blood pressure test. "Are you talking about that time last year when you asked for prayer? 'Cause that's all that happened—prayer. No hand-holding. No touching." Why did things have to take another turn for the worst? Here he'd hoped to assist Jayme, get her connected with some compassionate people in the community. Now, another lie? "For the record, we were never alone." He'd made sure not to let that happen.

"Max, you forgot, that's all. You're such a tease."

"I am not!" A growl started somewhere in his gut and roared out his mouth. "In the future, refer to me as 'Mr. Prescott.' And if you so much as tell one more scandalous lie about me—"

Beep.

"She hung up on me." Max groaned and pressed redial, but she didn't answer. He dropped the cell phone on the bed so he wouldn't follow through with his temptation to throw it. "I didn't do any of the things she accused me of." He pressed both palms against his temples. "I could go to jail for her insinuations!"

Season wrapped her arms around him. "No, you can't. You didn't do anything wrong with her. We both know she's lying." She rubbed her hands over his back. "I trust you. You're honorable and caring. You would never do what she implied. We'll get through this. Now, tell me what she said. I couldn't hear everything."

He stepped out of her embrace, then paced from one wall to the other. Sometimes nothing could ease his anxiety like tromping back and forth across a room. With a cold wave of nausea hitting him, he relayed the young woman's accusations.

"She thinks you were being romantic with her?" Season dropped on the end of the bed, her blue eyes gazing up at him.

"She's delusional. And now she denies her dad put her up to the rumors."

"But she told me he did."

"I know. This reeks of Derek's masterminding. He's gunning to get rid of me. But why? He's already succeeded. I'm not the pastor. We're leaving town. We don't owe the building debt, so he should be thrilled." Panic raced up his neck. He would not sit idly by while a money-hungry scoundrel and his erratic daughter brought him to ruin. "We're getting out of here." He yanked open the closet door and grabbed his suitcase. He unzipped the top and tossed in clothes like he'd heard a tornado warning, and he had to run for his life.

"What are you doing?" Season jumped up.

He rushed into the bathroom to get his shaving gear. "We're leaving."

"Tonight? Max, be reasonable."

Reasonable? Right now, he didn't fathom the word. He yanked her suitcase out of the closet. "Hurry up and pack. We'll check out and go."

"You mean do exactly what Derek wants?" Why wasn't she packing? Didn't she see this was an emergency? "Basically obey him like he's the lord of the land?" She plopped down on the bed again, looking stubborn.

"Fine. I'll pack your stuff." He yanked open her drawer and grabbed her underthings and socks. He dumped the items in her case. He scooped up her shirts from the next drawer. Plopped them in a pile. "Come on, we have to get out of here."

"Think about what you're doing. Running. Acting guilty?" Her voice rose. "You haven't broken the law. You still haven't confronted Derek. You've got to talk to him. You must see this through, or it'll eat you up. Please, let's do this right, Max."

He grabbed her pants and sweaters, dropped them in the luggage. "I came back to make things right. But everything's turned out wrong. I lost the trailer. Someone's stalking you. Now, more lies? Everyone in town hates me. After twenty years here, this is what I get?"

She stepped in front of him. "You've served this community well. God sees that. Many people in the valley know that too." She snagged the clothes out of his hands and stuffed them back in the drawer. "What about the bank loan being paid? That was a blessing. What about you and me? We're doing pretty good, aren't we?"

A shuddering breath wrenched from his chest. Her gaze met his. She was right, again. What was he doing? Sneaking away in the night? Being manipulated by Derek and Jayme? Running scared?

"Jayme's probably being coerced. She was mad at her dad when she called me. Maybe now, he's bribed her with a car or something to get her to change her story." Season linked her fingers with his. "If you want to leave, I'll go with you. But I vote to stay until everything we need to do is finished."

He wrestled with indecision. Groaned. "Okay, yeah, me too." He sighed.

She wrapped her arms around his waist. The scent of her perfume took him to another time and place. He thought of the night back at Hart's Camp when she laid in his arms, and they shared their hearts until the wee hours of the morning. He wanted to breathe in deeply of his wife and forget Jayme's insinuations. But, how could he? He'd known ministers who'd gone to jail for supposed, inappropriate actions, even though they maintained their innocence. Ministries ruined. Families torn apart. Is that what would become of him? Because he got on Derek's bad side? Because he had compassion on an unwed pregnant woman? He finally understood why the "Sons of

Thunder" in the Bible wanted to call down fire from heaven. He could picture a few places he'd like to zap.

His cell vibrated and he was tempted to ignore it. Reluctantly, he picked up the phone. "Max Prescott."

"Hey, Max. This is Ty Williams."

"Ty?" Just hearing the younger man's voice gave him courage, like God was sending him help. He mouthed, "Ty Williams," to Season.

She smiled, then headed for the bathroom as if giving him privacy for the conversation.

"I didn't expect to hear from you again." He'd thought the camp leaders would continue their lives without thinking of him again. "But I'm glad you called."

Ty laughed. "I wanted to see how you and your bride are doing post-conference."

"We're okay." He sat down in the chair. "Better than before the retreat."

"Good," Ty said. "Working on the romancing?"

Max chuckled. Who talked about this kind of stuff? Yet, he appreciated the call from the conference leader, especially after the last one from Jayme. "I'm trying."

"Got to start somewhere." A pause. "And the legal battle?"

"A few strange twists." Max shared about the loan reversal, the RV theft, the cryptic note Season received, and the call from Jayme that left him ready to flee.

Ty seemed to be listening closely and asked questions. Then he shared about the unrest he and Winter were experiencing with someone writing a book about them, detailing their divorce and remarriage. Hard to imagine such an invasion of privacy. What if Derek or Lee reported enough sketchy details about him to write a slanted biography?

Ty promised to be in prayer about Max and Season's future. He asked if Max was still interested in pastoring. A question never far from his thoughts, he said he was praying about it.

Season exited the bathroom in her pajamas with a bathrobe tied over the top.

"Keep working on the topics we discussed at the camp." Ty cleared his throat. "You mentioned the young woman claims you were alone with her. If I were you, I'd get statements from others who were present at the church that night."

A glug of dread filled Max that he'd have to revisit the subject. "Yeah, okay. Thanks."

"Feel free to call if you ever need to talk." The call ended.

Season had her Kindle in hand and was already in bed. "That was cool of Ty to call."

"I know." The timely conversation made him feel better. Just then, he noticed something on the floor near the foot of the bed. Had he dropped it when he was loading up his wife's things? He leaned over and picked up a red silky garment.

"Uh, Max?" Season's face blushed crimson. She crawled rapidly across the bed, her hand lunging for the fabric. She ripped the cloth right out of his hands.

"What?" Then he realized what it was. *Ahhh.* "Nice." He couldn't let the moment pass without a little flirting. Why was his wife acting so embarrassed? "I see you chose my favorite color."

"Red is not your favorite color." She stuffed the nightwear in her drawer, then settled on the bed, not looking at him at all.

He sat down beside her and ran his fingers down her arm. "When did you get that, Seas?" Had she bought it today?

"Never mind, it's going in the trash tomorrow."

"Why?"

Her face was nearly as red as the nightgown. "I don't want to talk about it."

"Were you planning on wearing it tonight?"

"Of course not!" She hit him with one of the bed pillows.

He chuckled at her overreaction. "Then why did you buy it?" He gazed into her sea-blue eyes, asking her questions without saying the words.

She let out a long sigh. "Okay. On a whim, I bought the nightie before I left for Hart's Camp. Just in case you came with me—which you didn't. And perchance you had a miraculous dip in a magical love elixir, where you couldn't resist, well, you know, and I thought—"

"Yes?" He smiled, enjoying her discomfort over a topic he rather enjoyed.

Her lips responded with a slight smile he found irresistible. It took all his will power not to take advantage of the moment. They'd both been under such strain lately. And his injuries hadn't helped matters.

Yet here they were in a motel room.

She *had* bought that sexy, red thing.

And they were, after all, married.

Hoping she wasn't mad at him for prying about her purchase, he leaned toward her and his mouth found hers. Seemed he couldn't get enough of kissing her and holding her these days.

"Romance your wife," Ty had said. A lesson Max would do well to practice.

"For the record, I *was* doused in a love elixir." He rested his palms alongside her neck and jawbone. He brushed his thumbs across her pink cheeks as he stared into her alluring eyes drawing him closer. "You are my beautiful wife who I adore. I want to stay with you just like this, holding you."

"Forever?" Her whispered word struck a raw chord within him. Did she still doubt?

"Forever and ever"—he hurried to assure her—"you are mine. And I am yours."

She initiated the next round of kisses, and he was more than willing to follow her lead. Suddenly, she pulled back and tapped her finger against his chest. "I'm still not wearing that nightgown."

"Why?"

"Because"—she groaned as if she didn't want to tell him—"when I bought it, we were in a bad place. It represents a time in our marriage I don't want to think about anymore."

Her frown made him want to laugh. Chivalry kept his chuckle silenced. "Just promise not to throw it away, okay? Maybe someday it will represent something altogether different." He leaned close to her and kissed her cheek.

She gave him a look he couldn't quite interpret. Then she reached over and turned off the lights.

Thirty-three

Winter

Loud footsteps on the outside stairway alerted Winter that Neil was running from his apartment to their back door. Why the rush? Hopefully, he didn't slip on the ice.

She dropped the loose-leaf chapter she was reading. For two days, she and Ty had been pouring over the rest of the manuscript Mat Kaplan sent. Ty placed his laptop on the coffee table and stood as the back door slammed. Neil rumbled down the hallway and came to a stop in front of them. "You can change anything you want!"

"Really?"

"As in, everything?" Ty looked as surprised as she felt.

"DTM has taken full control of the project." Neil coughed like he was trying to catch his breath. "Contract negotiations broke down between them and Randi's intermediary. Apparently, they didn't appreciate being swindled into believing mistruths about the storyline either." Neil grinned with the biggest smile she'd ever seen on him.

"That's fantastic!" She jumped up and hugged Ty, then Neil. "God answered our prayers." As she'd read the manuscript, she could see for herself why Ty was so upset with Randi sabotaging his character and integrity.

"DTM will consider our version, as long as we don't take them to court or block the movie rights, should they proceed in that direction."

"Are they considering dropping the film?" Ty sounded hopeful.

"For now. While Christian films have received some lime-light, Mat thinks our version will lack the gritty appeal Randi's had." Neil dropped into a chair.

"That's for sure." Ty sat down on the couch. "Hers reads like a soap opera, and I'm the villain."

Neil tapped his shoes on the floor like he had excessive energy. "I've been on the phone for two hours. With Mat, then his artistic director, his financial manager, and then him again. How this all turned around is definitely a God thing!"

Winter laughed, sharing in his enthusiasm. *Thank You, Lord, for working things out for us.*

"So how can we write our story without sharing the details we don't want exposed?" Ty groaned, and Winter could see he still had some apprehension about the project.

She clasped his hand to show her support.

The serious, yet compassionate, look she'd come to expect from Neil crossed his face now. "I'd say, even if it hurts like your heart's on fire, keep the narrative honest. Be transparent. Tell the truth and give God the glory for mending your hearts and giving you a second chance in your marriage. We'll offer Mat Kaplan a true story he can't resist. Got coffee?" Neil jumped up. He surely didn't need caffeine.

"We have decaf." She chuckled.

"No, thanks." Neil worked in the kitchen, preparing the coffee. "And just so you know, Mat says anyone could write a biography of you based on the public record and what's online."

"Where would someone get the scoop on our lives?" Ty shook his head. "Other than the missing journal, where did Randi get her information?"

Neil returned to his chair. "From your conferences, no doubt. Anything you said during a seminar is probably public knowledge, whether through attendees' notes, handouts, or something on our website. Did Randi take notes? Or a recording?"

"Yes." When Winter had allowed her that probationary period to be her assistant again, she'd always been writing stuff down.

"I was the one who set up the website." Ty let out a sigh. "Put our testimonies in the bio too."

"Mat said we should check the Internet for what others have said about you." Neil glanced toward the kitchen as if checking the coffee maker.

"People could say anything." She met Ty's gaze.

"Exactly." He let go of her hand, then flipped through several pages. "Listen to this: 'Ty underhandedly manipulated events to gain a position on Passion's Prayer with the purpose of seducing the speaker, Winter Cowan.'" He roared. "That's her dirty opinion. Unless you wrote that in your journal?" His gaze snapped toward Winter's.

"No, I did not." She shuffled on the couch to look him fully in the eyes. "Ty, we all know you didn't do those things. Randi exaggerated. I'd never write that kind of stuff."

He sighed. "Just reading this garbage frustrates me."

She ran her hand over his arm. "Me too."

Neil stood and headed for the kitchen.

"Make that three cups, will you?" Ty called.

"Will do." A minute later, Neil was setting mugs on the table. "So, how would you guys like to proceed?"

The thought of doing a project like this excited Winter,

but she remained cautious for Ty's sake. "I think we should rely on the Lord to guide us. Then page by page, we can reconstruct what really happened." She glanced at Ty, wondering what he was thinking. "If we do it, we'll make sure it has a hopeful ending."

"Won't that take too long?" Ty drew in a long breath. "There's obviously a deadline."

"Neil?" She needed her co-leader's advice, but she also needed time alone to talk with her husband. "Will you call the marketing director and see how far the launch date can be pushed back?"

"Of course." He jumped up and jogged out the back door.

She gazed into Ty's eyes. "What do you think?"

He sat quietly for a minute. "That it will be hard to focus on this and still do everything else."

"I know." Even still, excitement surged through her. "But can you imagine our story in a book? Maybe in a movie? Doesn't that make you a little eager?"

"Not really." He put his arm over her shoulder, and she settled against him. "So you think lives will be changed by this book? More marriages restored?"

"God willing."

"And the publicity? Fans? How might the hoopla change us?"

"Not at all, I hope."

"I don't want anything to change between us, except for one area of our lives." He pulled her closer.

She gazed into his eyes. "Which is?" More alone time, she guessed.

He kissed her cheek. "Babies."

Oh. From past discussions, she knew he was serious. "We've been dealing with so much—the attack, our recovery, Randi's hearing, our first conference, and now Deb's possible romance."

"And her romance affects us how?"

"She's on our team and dating Tag Miles. Will she leave us to join his ministry?" Winter had already lost two team members—Jeremy, her nephew, and Randi. "What would we do without Deb?"

"Are you, perhaps, changing the subject on me?" He stroked some strands of her hair back.

"Maybe." She didn't have an answer about them having children other than waiting.

"When do you think you'll be ready for us to start a family?"

"I don't know, Ty. Not now, but soon?" She hated disappointing him. "How about if we take a few months to focus on the book and our ministry schedule, then we can talk about this again? I do want to have kids with you."

"Let's not wait too long, huh?"

"Agreed." She still hadn't resolved in her mind how children and traveling with the team would work. Others did it, surely, they could too. But back to their current problem. "Will you pray with me about making our story into something that will inspire hope in other marriages? I'm eager to do this project with you, if you're willing."

He kissed her cheek. "You and I can face anything together."

"I love you."

"Love you too, Sas." His words hovered near her ear. "More than ever."

Then, with his arm still around her, he led them in prayer, asking God to direct their writing and help them give Him glory in everything they did. Afterward, she prayed, thanking the Lord for new doors. And she asked Him to soon bless them with kids born of their renewed love.

A few minutes later, she picked up the chapter she'd dropped. Ty settled back with his laptop.

Then suddenly, he grabbed a pen and the title page off the coffee table. He scratched out *Winter's Fall*. "Let's start with a different name."

"I don't know what Mat will say, but I'm game." She grinned as an idea popped into her mind. "Let's each write down the first title we think of."

"Okay." His pen hovered over the page as if he already knew what he was going to write. "Go!"

They both scribbled on the sheet of paper.

"Done." Ty tapped his pen on the coffee table.

She crossed out her first choice and wrote a second idea. "Me too."

She read Ty's entry. "*Winter's Beauty?*" She laughed. "That's sweet, but—?"

"Let me read yours." He tugged on the paper. "*A Second Chance for a New Beginning.* Hmm. I actually like that."

They had been blessed with such a beautiful second chance, why shouldn't that be reflected in their book's title? Whatever they wrote, she hoped their words would be heartfelt, bring God glory, and touch couples' lives.

Thirty-four

Season

Earlier this morning, Season apologized to her boss for her not being able to work the full two weeks. Max wanted them to leave sooner. Bess seemed disappointed, but not surprised.

Now, Season had almost finished her task of returning checked-in books to the biography section. From that aisle, she lacked a clear view of the circulation desk, which made her nervous. All morning she'd felt like someone might be watching her. But that could have been her imagination. Still, just a couple more books to shelve, then she'd camp out behind the main desk until quitting time.

She visually followed the decimal numbers on the books' spines to locate where to put the Corrie Ten Boom biography. As she moved to the right, a stocky man bustled into the aisle beside her. She stepped back. He bumped into her. "Excuse me." She moved to the left. Only the guy—who she now realized wore black shoes, black slacks, a black leather jacket, and dark sunglasses—stepped right next to her. Too close. Her heart lurched. The biography crashed to the floor.

Belatedly, she realized she should have clung to the book for protection.

She veered one way. So did the guy. Was he purposefully keeping her hostage in the aisle?

"Excuse me," she said again, louder this time.

He stepped in front of her and laughed.

Panic diluted her usual clear thinking. How could she get out of this without making a scene? If she screamed, would that endanger the patrons in the library? Did the man have a concealed weapon? His sinister sneer made her think he might be violent. *Lord, help me!*

"What do you want?" Her voice came out shrill.

"Did you get my love note?" He leaned in and his breath smelled like rotten eggs.

"So it was you."

"Sure it was me." His lips curled. "Why aren't you and the preacher-man gone yet?"

"It's none of your business." She scooted backward.

He closed the gap and grabbed her arms. She pushed against him, but he yanked her against his body. "It's all my business, lady."

A mix of fear and rage fueled her. "Leave me alone." She gritted her teeth and tried to break free, but her arms were firmly in his grip. She sucked in a breath to yell for help, but one of his beefy hands slapped over her mouth. An awful taste made her want to spit.

Where was Max? Yesterday, he spent the day at the library, and nothing happened. Now, this?

She kicked her foot against the guy's shin.

"Stop." His lips touched her ear, which only notched up her fury.

She shoved against him, and he held her tighter. He was obviously stronger, but she'd keep wrestling. No way would she take his manhandling without a struggle. A few clients were in the building. If she could yell for Bess—

"You okay, Mrs. Prescott?"

She stilled. That voice sounded like a male teenager's.

"Need help?"

"Tell the kid you're fine," her captor whispered in her ear. "And that's all."

She nodded, faking acquiescence. When he released her mouth, she whirled around to find Ronnie Bledsoe, one of Benny's younger high school friends, standing four feet away. His face contorted like he couldn't believe what he was witnessing. What could she say without putting him in danger too? "I-I'm fine, Ronnie. Go back to whatever you were doing. This *gentleman* is just leaving." But then, summoning all her internal strength, she kicked her heel against the man, making solid contact with his knee. Hearing his groan, she yanked her hands free of his grip. He reached for her, but she grabbed the biggest book on the shelf and held it up to strike him. "Get away from me!" This time, she didn't care how loud she was.

He lunged toward her, but Ronnie charged forward, getting between them. "I'd do what the lady said, Mister." He rotated his cell phone in the air. "Cops are on their way."

The thug glared at the teenager, then her, as if stunned. Did he think he'd get away with his violent behavior? The guy jabbed his finger toward Season's face. "This ain't over. Remember what I said. Leave town!" He shoved past Ronnie, limping, and knocked over a chair in his haste to reach the front door.

Season hugged Ronnie. "Thank you. You were so brave."

"Who was that creep?"

"I don't know." She wiped her hand over her lips, wishing she could wash away the memory of the fiend's hand on her. "Did you really call the police?"

"Oh, yeah."

Just then, sirens sounded. Season and Ronnie rushed to the front windows in time to see a dark sedan speeding through the parking lot with two police cars in pursuit.

"Thank God," she whispered.

"Guess they'll want our statements." Robbie stood beside her like a guardian angel.

"They probably will." But all she wanted to do was get back to the motel room and stay with Max. Safe. Where no one could hurt them again. Thankfully, God had sent Ronnie just in time.

If the police captured the guy, would the threats against them end? Or did they still have to worry about the other thug who hurt Max before?

* * * *

Two days later, following Season's exit interview, she thanked Bess for giving her the chance to work at the library, and then she hugged her coworker, Janice, who'd told her about the marriage conference in the first place. Season wished her well on her second honeymoon in Hawaii, then she left the Darby library for the last time.

That morning, she and Max had packed the car with some of their belongings from the storage unit. The rest went to the secondhand store. They were starting over, the two of them, so they'd decided to only keep what they could fit into the Forrester.

And although it seemed as if the town where they'd served and loved so many had turned its back on them, she knew many wonderful people lived in Darby and Hamilton and the Bitterroot Valley. Her sons were raised here—fine young men whom she was immensely proud of—and it had been a good place to raise a family.

Max had told her he was going to visit a few people before they left this afternoon. After each of his meetings, he texted her.

Marsha Dickins said Derek visited her several times last year. He pressured her into attending Living Faith Center.

That was weird. So Derek had gone behind Max's back to sabotage the ministry? *Poor Max.* That must have been hard for him to hear.

Derek and Lee visited Jupe Johnson a lot. Said Pastor was squeezing the life out of them. They should go to Living Faith Center.

She whispered a prayer for her husband.

Martha Clayton has the meanest tongue in the valley. Told me it was none of my business who visited her. Says she knows the rumors are true and I deserve the town's contempt.

That riled Season. The Clayton sisters had caused more damage than they realized. Or maybe they did and didn't care. She'd have to keep praying for them.

Clint and Eloise still aren't home. The place looks deserted. When I called his cell, he said Derek urged him to leave the church many times. He doesn't remember the night I prayed with Jayme.

She sent him a text asking if he planned to contact Jayme.

Not without you present.

Good.

Talked to Harold Smith. He stood next to Clint that night. He recalls seeing me sitting on the pew—about two feet from Jayme. Talking and praying. Will help if it goes to court. He also had visits from Derek and Lee.

Would Max be relieved to know Derek plotted the church's demise? Or more disheartened by the depths of the man's deceit and mean spirit?

Lord, be with my husband. Help us leave Darby with clean hearts, forgiveness, and ready to embrace our future together.

After settling the motel bill, she said a few other goodbyes. She brought Nellie Brandt a bouquet of roses and thanked her for her help in getting Max to the ER the day he got injured.

"Even after Max cleaned the lot, those fancy cars kept trolling the joint. But I had my eyes on them." The elderly woman was a virtual spy. "They parked outside your old place"—the wrinkles beneath Nellie's eyes creased—"so I called the cops on them."

"You did?"

"Yep. They'll think twice before doing dirty work in my neighborhood again." Nellie harrumphed. "Police nabbed a tall, scary-looking fellow based on my say-so."

"Good job!"

So both ruffians had been caught. *Sweet relief.*

She hugged Nellie goodbye. Then, back in her car, she glanced at the lot where their RV used to sit. A fifth-wheel with several pullouts was parked there now. Life moved on, she knew, but she felt a bittersweet tug of emotion. Not that she'd miss life in the trailer. Goodness, no. However, a part of her felt sentimental over her and Max's experiences, here, that had brought them to their knees—and eventually, back to each other.

After she left the trailer court, she drove to the Lone Pine Cemetery. At Gladys Iris's gravestone, she dropped off a cluster of flowers. She had a few things to say to her, though Season doubted the older woman could hear her from heaven. But who knew for sure? She quietly expressed her appreciation for the note the woman left for Max. Writing those words had taken bravery and spunk. Season would always remember Gladys as a shining light in Darby.

Then, wanting to leave town with a clear conscience, Season stopped by to see her old friend, Liza, but she wasn't home. She was probably working. So Season decided whenever she got resettled, she'd write Liza a letter, thanking her for her friendship that had meant so much to her.

An hour later, she sat in a booth at Annabelle's waiting for

Max and sipping her second—or third?—cup of coffee. He'd texted her that he was running late. She didn't mind sitting here reminiscing, but she still hoped they could hit the road before dark.

Sandy topped off Season's coffee cup. "I wanted to say, I hope my little joke of laughing with Max that day didn't cause you grief."

"Not really." Season smiled at the waitress who had always been kind to her.

"I was just trying to help."

"I know. Thank you for your friendship with Max and me."

Sandy lifted the carafe as if saluting her, then rushed around serving more of the brew to the afternoon crowd.

The restaurant's sounds and smells took her back to dozens of times she'd sat in this restaurant with her sons, celebrating milestones, or meeting Liza for coffee. A few times, she and Max had sat across from each other. The good and the bad of life shared over hot coffee and burgers.

As she waited, she recalled the good-qualities list she'd made about Max at Hart's Camp. She dug her hand into her coat pocket. Sure enough, the scrap of paper was still there. She pulled it out and smoothed the wrinkles.

Honorable. Caring. Nice kisser. Loving eyes.

Had she only been able to think of four nice things about her husband? His whispered words of endearment from last night floated through her mind. She loved how he still called her "Sea-girl" and "my sweet." How their romance seemed to be getting better every day.

She grabbed a pen from her purse. Maybe she'd add a few more traits to the list. A couple of ideas came to mind. *Handsome. Kind. Wonderful listener. Adventure partner. Man of God. Romantic.* She smiled. Maybe when they reached the coast, she'd show him the list.

Max, hurry back to me.

Thirty-five

Max

As Max drove the rattletrap truck, which he still hoped to get rid of, to his next destination, he wished to forgo any more uncomfortable conversations. He'd had enough. Time for them to get on the road. He wanted to spend time with his wife, holding hands and walking the beaches of the Oregon Coast, even if it was the end of January. Last night, he'd called the boys and invited them to fly over and hang out with him and their mom. Hopefully, take in some dune buggy rides. Maybe rent fishing equipment. They hadn't fished together since the boys were ten and eleven, or so. Maybe they could walk on the beach and talk, reconnect like old times.

Thinking of reconnecting, he loved how many times, lately, he'd found his wife's gaze on him, as if she still found him attractive. And he felt more like the college-aged guy who was gaga over her. Maybe on the coast, they could sit together and kiss and talk to their heart's content. For years, he'd been so focused on not doing anything anyone would deem inappropriate—not even smooching with his wife in public—and yet the gossips, here, were condemning him for far worse. Now he was going to enjoy life with the woman he loved in the way they wanted, without any self-imposed rules. He sighed with the relief and wonder of their reconciled love.

It was time for him to prioritize his family. Love God. His wife. His kids. Then others. Simple formula. What more could he want? That is, if he lived through his next meeting.

The lawyer he visited this morning—the one whom he'd paid too much money for lousy advice—discouraged him from taking Derek to court. Hearsay wouldn't stand the heat of a trial, he said. Why stir up trouble in the community by forcing neighbors to testify against neighbors? The brute who'd grabbed Season in the library—that still drove him mad—had confessed to vandalism and bodily injury toward Max, but he hadn't ratted out on Derek Clark or the Mob boss or whoever his employer was.

It seemed Max would have to dig up his own answers. So he'd texted Derek to meet him at the community gazebo at three o'clock. Would the busy banker accommodate his request? Would Max finally get the answers he needed?

He parked the truck, trudged down the path to the wooden structure, and waited. What would he say when he faced his nemesis? Would Derek bring a different security guy this time, since his other one was in jail? A wealthy man like him could own as many bodyguards as he needed, right? But after all the problems Derek had caused, Max was determined to have a serious talk with him.

A few minutes later, a nearly silent Beemer pulled into the snow-cleared parking lot. Derek exited his fancy car alone.

Max would have to use extreme self-control to not punch the guy. Or grab him by the collar and shake him. At least, Max hadn't brought the bat. Although, he'd been tempted.

Turn the other cheek, whispered through his mind. *Live at peace with everyone.* How had Jesus been able to do that? When

He was beaten up by bad guys, did He ever, even for the slightest second, want to pummel someone? Had he ever wanted revenge like Max did now? Probably not. He groaned. *More grace, Lord.*

Derek strolled down the path toward him as if he had all day. His knee-length coat swayed in rhythm with his cowboy-boots' footsteps. His hands, covered in leather driving gloves, clenched and unclenched. His mouth spread in a mocking grin. "Well, *Pastor*, what do you want? Another council meeting?"

Hardly. "Let's talk." Max clenched his fists too but kept them at his sides. One hard punch to Derek's nose would soothe some of his feelings of injustice.

"Guess you heard." Derek stopped almost nose to nose with Max.

"Heard what? More of your daughter's lies?"

"Watch your tongue." Derek's eyes squinted a warning.

Make my day. "I've been to the lawyer's office concerning your slander." There, he'd get the truth out in the open.

Derek's mouth widened with a toothy smile. "You mean, Henry Tappin? Give him my regards. His wife works at my bank. Just had them over for dinner last week."

So Henry was in Derek's pocket too? No wonder he'd given such useless advice.

"I figured you planned this little chat after you caught wind of my purchase." Derek rubbed his gloved hands together. "The property is finally mine, as it always should have been."

What? A shudder rippled through Max. "You mean the church property?"

"What else?"

Of course, he'd considered Derek might have been the buyer. But hearing it was true hurt like burning embers to his spirit. "Why did you scheme and invent lies and go to such lengths to get my church?"

"Your church?" Derek spit. "Listen, Prescott, I attended that building before your voice changed in junior high. I've bided my time through twenty years of pathetic sermons and poor leadership. It was past time for you to leave."

"What's this about? Your need for control? Trying to own the whole valley?" Max took a step toward the other man, barely holding in his emotions. "Why do you hate me? Because I didn't give in to your demands? Was I just someone to squish under your thousand-dollar boots?"

"Doesn't matter. It's over." His glare intensified. "You're a zero compared to your predecessor."

"I had different strengths and weaknesses than Pastor Jonah."

"A plethora of weaknesses," Derek growled.

Max's fingers itched to slug the smirk off the man's face. But a humble approach would be less volatile. "We're all flawed and broken. Myself included."

"That's odd coming from the high and mighty Maxwell Prescott."

Derek's words punched him in the belly as hard as any fist could have. He had been prideful and self-righteous, at times. But since the conference, he knew he was a better man. "You and I were on opposite sides of most issues."

"Still are." Derek's chest puffed up. "I'm a wealthy banker. You're a loser."

Max clenched his teeth. Derek had insulted him. Lied about him. Spread rumors. Humility aside, a wave of anger hit him like a tsunami. He lunged forward and grabbed the lapels of Derek's coat. The other man's eyes widened. "I've had enough of your hateful schemes. Call off Jayme! This scandal hogwash is finished. You hear me?" His hands shook with his need to punch Derek and make him suffer.

"Or what?"

Max shoved him backward hard. Derek landed on his backside on the picnic table's bench, and he groaned and swore.

"Or I'll sue you, that's what." He wasn't under Derek's heel anymore. He could find another attorney. One who was honest. One who'd never heard of Derek Clark. Max jabbed his index finger toward his ex-councilman's face. "I have documented proof of your going from person to person convincing them to leave our fellowship."

"So what?" Derek's Adam's apple bobbed. "No law against visiting church folk."

Bile rose up Max's throat. But he couldn't focus on his temper. He needed to get to the truth. "You slandered me, hurt our friends, and your actions forced our building into default— for what? Financial gain? How can you live with yourself?"

"Quite well, thank you." Derek stood and faced Max with a dark glint in his eyes. "If you sue me, you'll lose, again. I'll win. I always do."

Max knew a day was coming when Derek wouldn't win unless he changed his ways. And their argument could go on forever. A snapshot of Season trembling in his arms after the thug's rough treatment of her in the library flashed through his mind. "How dare you send someone to harm my wife?" He gritted his teeth. "What did she ever do to you?"

Derek flinched. "That wasn't my fault. One of the boys took things too far. I may have strong-armed you to get you to leave town, but I'd never hurt Season."

At least there was that. "Did you know Lee was stealing from the church?"

"I knew he was in over his head in debt. He made stupid choices. Even I had to pay to keep the rats off my back."

So Derek had been forced to pay for Lee's crimes also? That seemed fitting.

"What are you going to do with the church?"

324

"Tear it down, of course."

A pain twisted in Max's gut.

"I'm building a resort. It's a prime location. Darby is growing." He swayed his hands toward the valley. "I've had blueprints in the works for two years."

Two years. While Max had been pouring out his heart, trying to build their congregation, Derek had been working equally hard to destroy it. And Lee too? The silent warfare had nearly cost Max his marriage and his family. And the building where he'd preached for twenty years would be obliterated as if it had never been? He should stay and fight. See Derek thrown in jail. But then those words crept into his thoughts again. *Why not rather be wronged? Why not rather be cheated?* Inwardly, he groaned. His wounded pride wrestled with his more recent scourge of humility. He regretted not filing charges against Derek. Maybe he could still—

Another picture came to mind. Season was waiting for him at Annabelle's. He and his bride were leaving and starting over together. His old congregation was already dispersed. No going back. "I'm leaving town today."

"Best news I've heard in a year."

The struggle to put Derek in his place still seethed, but there was something else to be said. "None of Lee's garbage was Clint's fault. Leave him and Eloise alone. Let them live their lives on the farm without harassment. Maybe even do what you can to help them."

"I don't have a beef against Clint." Derek straightened his coat and strode down the steps. "We're done here."

"Wait." Max couldn't let him go without trying to reach him. "God loves you, Derek. Right now, I'm having a hard time saying that, but it's t-true." His throat clogged. "He cared about you enough to send Jesus. And even through all this, I care about you and Jayme." Tough words to say. Tougher still to mean.

Derek spoke with his back toward Max. "Sixty-five years ago, my great-grandfather sold our family's land to the church for a pittance to repay an outstanding debt he owed."

Max hadn't known that bit of history.

"It was my inheritance. My land! Jayme's too."

"So this was about greed? Revenge? Possession of land?" Sadness and disbelief choked Max. "I feel sorry for you."

"Don't." Derek marched toward his shiny vehicle without looking back.

"I guess you won't be needing proof of a paternity test now!" Max yelled after him. "Not when it was all a lie."

Derek froze, clenched and unclenched his fists.

Max waited, tension rippling over him. Would the man come back and fight? If so, he was more than ready.

Derek's shoulders sank like all the air had left his lungs. "I guess not." He got in his car and sped out of the parking lot.

Max dropped onto the bench, disappointed by the news about the church, by his and Derek's lack of reconciliation, and by Lee's wrongdoing that had affected so many. He closed his eyes and thought about those lines from the Lord's Prayer. *Forgive us our debts, as we also have forgiven our debtors. And lead us not into temptation, but deliver us from the evil one.*

Help me forgive.

He glanced at his cell. He was late. And cold. He and Season should have left town by now, but he had one last visit. Then Darby, Montana, would be a chapter in his past.

His future was calling him westward, with a gorgeous, blue-eyed blond at his side.

Thirty-six

Season

Season contemplated Max's tardiness as she stared into her empty coffee cup. She'd taken up residency in the booth at Annabelle's for so long, she'd have to leave Sandy a double tip.

A knock on the window made her jump.

"Max!" Seeing his smiling, handsome face reminded her of the young guy she'd fallen in love with. She couldn't wait to hop in the car and head west with him. She dropped a twenty-dollar bill on the table and rushed for the door.

Outside, Max met her with a passionate kiss that made her toes curl—right there in front of the restaurant! Boy, had he changed. And she loved him for it.

"I was worried about you," she whispered against his cool cheek. She linked her hand in the crook of his arm and didn't mention how tired of waiting she'd become. "Are you ready to leave now?"

"I'm ready to go anywhere with you."

"That's what I was hoping to hear." With a spring in her step, she led him to their parked car. "Did you see everyone you needed to?"

"I didn't talk with Jayme."

"We'll keep praying for her."

"Yes, we will." He opened the passenger door and motioned for her to slide in. Apparently, he wanted to drive the first leg of the journey. He closed her door, ran around the car, and slid in behind the wheel. "I sold the truck to Merv."

"Hurray!" She cringed. "Oh, sorry. Do you feel bad about giving it up?"

"Not in the least. He said he'd fix it up for local deliveries. I also saw the lawyer, and a bunch of other people, including Derek." He started the car and drove north on Highway 93. "I'll tell you all about it as we cross the next three states." He said a quick prayer out loud for traveling safety.

"So we're really heading for the coast?"

"Yep." He took her hand and steered the car with his free hand. "Would you mind if we sing as we leave the valley? It's been a rough day, and I think singing praises to God would be a good conclusion to our two decades of service here."

"Absolutely. What shall we sing?"

"'The Doxology?'" In his deep baritone, he belted out the lyrics. In her quiet alto, she complemented his stronger voice as they left the area where they'd grown up as a couple, raised their sons, and had given so much of their hearts in ministry.

"'Praise God from whom all blessings flow; Praise him, all creatures here below; Praise him above, ye heavenly host: Praise Father, Son, and Holy Ghost.' Amen." They sang it through twice, then they held the final note like they used to do when they sang it at the close of a church service.

When she glanced at Max, tears were streaming down his cheeks, which made her eyes water too.

After a few sniffs, he cleared his throat. "I also saw Pastor Paul from Living Faith Center."

"You did?"

"I had to meet him before I left and apologize for my resentment. He didn't have a clue what I was talking about." He met her gaze for a second, then returned his attention to the road. "But I knew."

"Good for you, Max." She was so proud of him.

"I also warned him about Derek." He turned the windshield wipers on, brushing away snowflakes. "I didn't want something happening to his congregation like what happened to ours. Powerful men can manipulate too many things for their own good. I should have been wiser."

"You are now."

"You'll think this is funny." He chuckled. "I asked him what he thought about sin."

"No way. What did he say?"

"That it was bad." He guffawed, and she laughed too. "Derek had told me Pastor Paul didn't ever preach on sin. That he only spoke on happy topics. A lot of bunk." He snorted. "That's what I get for listening to gossip."

She patted his arm and decided to change the subject. "By the time we get to Seaside, it'll be the middle of the night."

"Sorry we're running so late, but I had to do all that stuff before I could leave the past behind."

"I know. That's okay." She was just glad they were on their way now.

He drank from the water bottle she'd left in the console.

His cell made a chirping sound. "Can you get that?" He passed his phone to her.

"It says 'Ty.'" She swiped the screen. "Hello, Ty. This is Season. Sorry, but Max is driving."

"Hey, Season. What's going on?"

"We just left Darby. I'm sure Max wants to tell you everything. Shall I have him call you later?"

"Sure." He paused. "Why don't you tell him I have news."

"I could put you on speakerphone."

"That would be awesome."

She turned to Max. "He wants to tell you something." She tapped the speaker icon. "Okay, Ty. Max can hear you now."

"Hey, Max! I was talking to my buddy, Chad Gray, who pastors a church in Ketchikan, Alaska."

"I remember you mentioning him." Max slowed down the car, probably to focus on the call.

"Here's the thing, he's a ministry workaholic."

"I can relate."

So could Season.

A semitruck zoomed past in the opposite lane, splattering them with slush. Max increased the windshield wiper speed.

"Chad and April are expecting their first baby in a few weeks." Ty continued sharing in a light tone. "He'd like to lay low for a couple of months and be there for his wife and newborn."

Season glanced at Max, saw his mouth form an "O."

"Problem is he doesn't have an assistant to cover for him."

"Oh, yeah?" Max met her gaze briefly.

Alaska, huh? She remembered their conversation when Max told her he'd like to go halibut fishing there.

"We were wondering if you might be available."

She and Max both gasped.

Static came across the speaker. "Short notice, I know, but they'd pay your way. Winter's mom has a house there, and she'd love for you to stay with her. We already asked. She's a nice lady with a sense of humor. Used to be a missionary in the Philippines with her husband."

"Ty, this is amazing timing," Max spoke over the sound of the car engine and the wipers. "We just left Darby for good."

"Heading east or west?"

"The Oregon Coast." Season let out a cheer. They were finally going to see the ocean.

"Nice! How long are you staying?"

"We don't have plans." Max chuckled. "We're stepping out in faith."

"That's cool! Why don't you two talk this over? April's concerned Chad will get wrapped up in church activities and forget their little one, and her. Not that he would. He's a great guy." Ty snickered. "Winter's jabbing my arm telling me not to pressure you. Pray about it, then get back with me, okay?"

"Will do. And thanks. That you thought of us means a lot."

"Good night. Drive safe." The call ended.

Max drove a few miles without saying a word.

Season didn't know if she should intrude on his thoughts. Was he considering going to Alaska? If she remembered correctly, Ketchikan was on an island. First City? She'd have to Google it and find out more information. She couldn't stay quiet any longer. "Going to Alaska would be quite the adventure, huh?" She nudged his arm.

"I'll say." At the next gas station, he turned off the road and veered the car toward the parking area. As soon as he shut off the engine, he clasped her hands. "What do you think?" His eyes were bright, and he was grinning like a kid on Christmas morning.

"What do *you* think is the question?" Although she figured she knew his answer.

"Alaska is far from the boys. You might not like that." Nice of him to consider her feelings.

"Phones work there, right?" She could handle being away from her sons for a while if they could text and call. And it might be an amazing place for her and Max to dream new dreams together. "Sounds like an open door, like we prayed about earlier."

"I know." His hands were trembling. "Let's ask God what we should do, huh?" She loved that he was praying with her more. He bowed his head and thanked the Lord for Ty's call, and he prayed for God's will to be done. Then Max thanked Him for how wonderful it felt for someone to want him in ministry again.

Oh, Max. His words touched a deep place in her heart. Tears pooled in her eyes. But now wasn't a time for sadness. This was a triumphant moment in their lives. They'd left Darby. A new opportunity was shining before them. "I'm ready for a road trip with you, husband." Even if that meant traveling to Alaska.

"My heart turns to mush whenever I hear you call me that." He grinned.

"I guess I'd better say it more often then." She leaned toward him until her lips brushed the corner of his mouth. "Husband."

"My sweet." He met her lips fully, lingering close as if he didn't want to stop kissing her. Finally, he sighed and started the engine again. "Shall we press on and walk the beach at dawn?"

"Sounds amazing. I hear they have great beaches in Alaska too."

"Might be a perfect place for us." He stroked her cheek. "Anywhere with you by my side is the best place in the world."

A few weeks ago, she wondered if she could ever love him again. Now, there were no second thoughts. "I'm so in love with you, Max."

"And I'm in love with you." He winked at her, then put the car in reverse. Suddenly, he braked. "What about our lantern? You didn't throw it away, did you?"

"Never." She nodded toward the back seat piled high with their belongings. "It's safe. And I think the flame of our love burns brighter now than ever. I feel so close to you." She smoothed her fingers over his arm as he drove back onto the road.

"I feel that way too. You are in my heart, and I can't live without you." He glanced at her, then faced the road. "Every once in a while, could you still ask me if we can escape somewhere?"

"Okay." Maybe she should ask him right now. "Max?"

"Hmm?"

"Shall we escape to our love shack?"

"You bet!"

"How about a faraway place?"

"Like—?" He wore a huge smile.

"Alaska?"

"You really want to go?" He sounded so hopeful.

"I do."

"I do too."

They reached for each other's hand and held on tightly. Just like they promised each other they'd do for the rest of their lives.

Epilogue

Winter

Five months later

Downtown Spokane was bursting at the seams with athletes and spectators from all over the world since it was the weekend of the Spokane Hoopfest, the biggest three-on-three outdoor basketball tournament on the Earth. To Winter, the sun seemed to be blazing especially warm this June day.

Ty had parked in a crowded lot several blocks away, and the two of them had made their way down the bustling sidewalks to where streets were cordoned off, and multiple half-courts were set up per block. Bodies were packed together on the sidewalks like the proverbial "can of sardines," with barely a trail to walk through, as parents and friends cheered on teams.

Winter clasped her husband's hand tightly, hoping they wouldn't lose each other as they made their way through the multitude, sometimes through a narrow parting of people. Observers and participants moved through the crowds like a long train en route to other locations—basketball games, or booths selling food and trinkets and henna tattoos, or as she'd heard one person say, to report their game scores to the official Master Scoreboard in Riverfront Park.

Today was a day off for her and Ty. She'd asked him what he'd like to do, and this was the event he chose. But she had something else in mind other than watching basketball. She had news.

For most of the last five months, they'd been preoccupied with writing their book, creating a workbook and PowerPoint presentation for the summer conferences, and sticking to their ministry schedule. *A Second Chance for a New Beginning* was set to release in one week. Mat Kaplan stayed true to his word, allowing them a full rewrite. She and Ty were pleased with the outcome. A movie was still being discussed. Time would tell if a story about a married couple breaking up, then falling in love again, would be worthy of television airtime.

They'd made two quick weekend trips to Bend, Oregon, to visit Randi. Small steps of progress were made. On their second visit, Randi didn't scream at Ty to get out. The first time, he stood by the door, arms crossed throughout her outburst. Two wonderful things came from those trips. She and Ty talked a lot about their dreams and plans. And on their second visit, Randi let Winter pray for her.

Today, she wanted to enjoy holding Ty's hand and eating ice cream. Boy, she'd thought a lot about dessert lately! But first, where could they talk privately during all this chaos? What did the local reporter say on the radio? Over two hundred thousand people were downtown this weekend? Crazy. And yet, so cool.

The air was ripe with the smell of sunscreen and popcorn. The public water fountain near the entrance to the park was a magnetic draw for children and adults alike. She was tempted to run through the water spraying into the air, to cool off, herself. The sound system throbbing out "Surfin' USA" made her want to dance with Ty and shout out her news.

"Where shall we go?" He pointed at a row of outdoor merchant tents. "Hungry?"

"Yes, but could we find a quiet spot to talk first?" She hoped he wouldn't think she had something troubling to discuss, as was often the case when she said she wanted to talk. "Near the river, maybe?" She tugged on his hand, couldn't hide the smile spreading across her face. "Come on." She walked faster but maneuvering through the crowd was difficult.

They followed the paved trail past the giant Red Wagon at the children's play area. Kids and adults were climbing the ladder, gazing down from the twelve-foot-high wagon bed, or sliding down the handle-like slide. A fun and memorable day for all, it seemed.

She and Ty would never forget this day, she was sure.

They strolled beneath a viaduct and followed the wide path paralleling the river until they finally left the congestion behind.

"How's this?" Ty drew her toward the water's edge where a planter containing a mass of purple and pink petunias created a natural barrier between them and the current. Beyond that, mama and papa ducks swam in the water with their young in a line.

"It's perfect." She watched the ducklings and smiled. She couldn't wait another second. "Ty"—she faced him, their hands clasped—"we're going to have a baby!" She grinned so wide her cheeks hurt.

He drew in a sharp breath. "You mean it?" A huge smile crossed his lips as well.

"Uh-huh" was drowned out as she kissed him with all the happiness of finally getting to tell him what he'd waited so long to hear.

He held her close, and she loved being in her husband's arms, sharing this moment with him.

"Oh, Sas," he whispered. "Thank you." Then he laughed. "I can't believe it!"

"I know."

"When did you find out?" His eyes glowed like shiny fudge.

"I've suspected for two weeks. I took the test this morning." Happy tears flooded her eyes. "And it was positive!"

He held her to his chest again. "When will the baby be born?"

"The end of January. Not long after our second anniversary." She stepped back. "So what do you think?"

"That I'm the happiest man alive!" He cupped her cheeks with his hands, gazing into her eyes.

That he was so excited, like she'd known he would be, made her giddy. "Thank you for being with me, Ty. If we hadn't gotten back together—"

His mouth pressed against hers, stopping her from finishing her what-if. "We are together, forever, you and me—"

"And the baby!" They both said at the same time. Then laughed.

He held her hand and they strolled farther down the path. "Are you still worried about how raising kids on the road will affect them, and our team?" Nice of him to mention that, since they'd talked about it several times in the last months.

"We'll figure it out as we go like we always do."

"I'm glad we finished the book project. Now, you'll be able to rest more." Was he already fretting over her pregnancy?

"Ty, I'll hardly be resting." She chuckled over the idea. "In fact, I think we should squeeze in a trip to Ketchikan."

"Really?" His smile widened.

"I'd love to tell Mom about the baby in person. And I'd be thrilled to see April and Chad's little guy, Marcus Delaney Gray."

"That would be amazing! I'll text Neil about changing our schedule." He swung their hands between them as they walked. "I'm eager to see Max and Season again. Chad said they've been a huge blessing to them and their church. He might not want to let them leave."

"Mom loves them too." Winter leaned her head against his shoulder. "You were right about us. Things will change." She stroked her hand down her flat tummy.

"Yes, but for all the right reasons." He pulled her into his arms again. Not for a big kiss, although she would have liked that. Instead, he held her tenderly, and she heard him softly praying. "Father, I thank you for this gift, this precious child. Protect the little one. Thank You for bringing Sas and me back together and making us into a family."

"Amen." She breathed in the air around her that seemed charged with excitement and somewhere—she was sure of it—ice cream! "Come on." She grabbed Ty's hand and tugged him in the direction of the booths. "It's celebration time!"

She heard him laughing as he followed her. She and Ty were going to be parents! A new season was coming. One filled with joy, love, and hope. A baby. And lots of second chances.

If you enjoyed *Season's Flame*, or mostly enjoyed it, please leave a review wherever you purchased this book. They say reviews are the lifeblood for authors, and I would consider it a personal favor if you wrote one. Even one line is great. Thank you! ~Mary

If you'd like to be one of the first to hear about Mary's new releases and upcoming projects, sign up for her newsletter!

As a thank you gift, you can receive two pdfs: "To Winter, With Love—Romantic Letters Between Ty and Winter," that takes place between *Winter's Past* and *April's Storm*, and "Rekindle Your Romance! 50+ Date Night Ideas for Married Couples."

www.maryehanks.com/FREE.html

Have you read the Restored series? Check out the first book:

Ocean of Regret.

A prodigal wife is heading home, but facing her husband, her father, and the past will take every ounce of courage she has.

A huge *thank you* to …

Paula McGrew ~ for bravely being the first person to read my work. I appreciate your critique and thoughts so much. You are such an encouraging lady! I'm blessed that our paths crossed a few years ago.

Michelle Storm ~ for helping me with all five books in this series! I appreciate your candor and insight. You often find those things I've been blind to. Thank you for taking your time to help me again.

Kathy Vancil, Melissa Hammerstrom, Brice Quinn, and Jenn Schulker ~ for reading through this story and finding the parts that needed fine-tuning, telling me what you liked about it, and for making Season's Flame a more heartwarming tale. Your ideas and suggestions, and your encouragement, are such a blessing to me. You are amazing!

Jason Hanks ~ for reading this story and cheering me on. I'll always remember that day at the restaurant when we plotted some of the things that could happen to Max. I hope you enjoyed this pastoral tale.

Suzanne Williams ~ for another beautiful cover. I appreciate all the special touches you add. Thanks for letting me participate in the process. I love how it turned out!

Annette Irby ~ for working with me on all five books in this series. You always help me dig deeper into the characters and push me to find the hero's heart. Thank you for that.

Readers ~ for cheering me on, encouraging me when I need it, and for being willing to write those reviews. You are a blessing to me!

Books by Mary Hanks

Second Chance Series

Winter's Past

April's Storm

Summer's Dream

Autumn's Break

Season's Flame

Restored Series

Ocean of Regret

Sea of Rescue

Bay of Refuge

Tide of Resolve (July 2020)

Marriage Encouragement

Thoughts of You (A Marriage Journal)

Youth Theater Adventures

Stage Wars

Stage Woes (2020)

maryehanks.com

About Mary E. Hanks

Mary's favorite stories are inspirational tales about marriage reconciliation. She and Jason have been married for 40+ years. They've been buffeted by their share of storms—kind of like the couples in her stories—but by God's grace they have stayed together. Whenever she can, Mary likes to include her love for romance, chocolate, second chances, and ocean settings in her books.

For many years, Mary worked in Christian education. She still loves Youth Theater and has written and directed over twenty full-stage productions. Her love of theater inspired her to write the Youth Theater Adventures for readers age 10-14, beginning with Stage Wars.

Besides writing, Mary likes to read, do artsy stuff, go on adventures with Jason, and meet her four adult kids for coffee or breakfast.

Connect with Mary by signing up for her newsletter on her website—www.maryehanks.com.

"Like" her Facebook Author page:

www.facebook.com/MaryEHanksAuthor

You can email Mary at maryhanks@maryehanks.com

www.maryehanks